Down... Set... Hut!!!
The Untold Story of College Football

Matthew William Nighswonger

Copyright © 2015 Matthew William Nighswonger
All rights reserved.
Cover Design © 2015 Pantin Roland Ali
Cover Photo © 2015 istockphoto.com
All rights reserved.

No part of this book may be reproduced in any written, electronic, recording,
or photocopied form without written permission from the author.
The only exception is in the form of brief quotations embedded in articles or reviews.

The characters and events in this book are fictitious. Any similarities to living persons, living or dead, is purely coincidental and not intended by the author.

Copyright © 2015 Matthew William Nighswonger
All rights reserved.
Printed and published by BGT Publishing
ISBN-13: 9780996356527

Leaders

The bright sun of the early afternoon pierced Charlie's already woozy head as he walked out of his dim apartment. Last night he had consumed too many beers and was paying the price today. The pain from his headache was soon abated by the excitement he felt as he hopped in his truck to go to the team meeting. Today there were more important things than a silly little headache. Today was the day. Charlie was going to find out if his dream would be realized. He had been anticipating this day since he was a young boy. His enthusiasm was difficult to contain.

Charlie showed up early to the meeting. He was always early to the meetings, but today he was earlier than usual. In fact, every player was early for everything football related. Football happened to be the only thing they were ever punctual for. Each and every one of them was afraid of being late because it meant a verbal thrashing and extra running. There was already enough running and all one's energy needed to be saved for practice. Not enough energy in practice might mean a poor performance, which could lead to losing one's spot on the depth chart. The coaches never cared what time your watch or clock said, so it was better to be early and avoid any chance of punishment.

Charlie came extra early today because he was a little nervous and didn't want to talk to anyone. Fortunately, the door to the meeting room was already unlocked. He walked in and took a seat in the front row. Sitting down in the silent empty room he started to think. *If I sit in the front it might seem like I am expecting something. Almost as if I am expecting to be captain. I don't want to seem too eager or excited about this,* he almost said out loud.

Standing up and looking at the room from the front he was trying to scope out the best place to sit that wouldn't give away everything he was thinking and feeling at the moment. He decided on the middle of the third row. That way he would be at the front, which he thought showed how interested and focused he was about football, and fewer people could casually sit by him. If any of the guys wanted to sit by him they would have to shuffle in to be near him.

Taking his seat at his now strategically located spot, Charlie began to hear the voices of the other early arrivers in the corridor. A group of the guys were gathering, waiting for a large enough contingency to come into the room, thereby avoiding having to sit alone. To keep himself from analyzing everything he had done in the current off season to see if it added up to captain material, he tried listening to the conversations in the hall. He was able to pick out a few voices and some of what was being talked about. Most of it was just bull shit about how much somebody drank, how hung over another guy was, or who got with who last night.

Once enough bodies had arrived, players started filing in the room. They noticed that Charlie had been in the room alone since they had arrived, but it didn't surprise any of them. A few of the guys gave him some smart ass remarks wondering how long he had been there.

The meeting was a late start, 3:00 PM. Coach Jackson had enough experience and he knew that any earlier on the day after the spring game and half the team would still be exuding alcoholic fumes. Despite the late start, there were still plenty of guys stumbling in to the meeting, looking like they had just rolled out of bed still in last night's clothes. Last night had been a good party night and Charlie had partaken, but he woke up at a decent hour, took a shower, had something to eat, and tried to make sure he felt good for this meeting. Today was very important to him, his dream would be fulfilled or remain just that, a dream.

Players continued to file in. Charlie had a few small conversations and plenty of hellos. He kept things light, not getting into any deep conversations. As if planned and coordinated, the assistant coaches entered the meeting room after all the players, followed by the head coach, Coach Jackson. He didn't enter until everyone was seated, including the players and coaches. It was a little bit of a show, but always had the effect of putting a hush over the entire room. As he approached the front, the room grew quieter. By the time he was standing behind the podium the room was silent.

Coach Jackson started talking about the spring game the previous day, the entire spring training, things that needed improvement, and what was expected of the players between now and "fall" camp, a misnomer because camp started in the sweltering August heat. Everyone listened because he was well liked and respected by his players.

This coming season was going to be Coach Jackson's ninth season. He had taken over the team during a rebuilding time. The Puma had always been a prestigious program, but like the rest of the college football world, had some occasional down seasons. He had rebuilt the program quickly winning back to back conference championships in his fourth and fifth years as head coach. This had ensured him a contract extension and better recruits. The last few years they had been on the verge of contending for a championship but were not able to win the close games. This kept them in the middle of the conference standings for the last three seasons, each of Charlie's seasons. The last three seasons the team had been one game away from a winning record and losing wasn't okay for the Puma program. Being what things are in sports and how expectations remain high, Coach Jackson was feeling pressure from both the administration and the boosters for a conference championship. Pressure was felt by all the coaches and players as he was making more and more demands on everyone.

Coach Jackson had a tall, athletic frame, with a body that displayed hints of his former playing days. His eyes were perpetually bloodshot and fierce. Allowing his coordinators to do their job, he was a good delegator. He conducted meetings every day and had to be kept informed about each week's game plan, so he was very involved with the team. Often times he would sit down with the defensive coaches and come up with the game plan together. He liked letting his coaches do their job, but always wanted to know everything that happened. He was completely in charge of the direction of the team, making all the final decisions and ensuring that the team policies and rules fit with his personal philosophy.

One of the reasons the guys liked him so much was because he wasn't a loud, yelling type of coach. He wouldn't get in players' faces and chastise them in front of the rest of the team. He had an intense, quiet behavior, but everyone knew when he was pissed off. His message of hard work and full effort was continuously preached. To play for him each player had to buy into this philosophy. The way he coached and prepared was a good example of the hard work and dedication he expected of all the players and coaches. Leading by example helped to inspire his players. His love for football was easily apparent and the amount of time he devoted to the game was amazing. To say he was a workaholic was an understatement. He did maintain a marriage, but nobody seemed to know how he gave any energy to his relationship after giving so much to football every day.

Charlie was starting to get anxious as Coach Jackson took a deep breath, paused looking around the room, and checked his yellow legal pad for any missed notes. Charlie's heart started to race. He knew the moment he had been waiting for was coming very soon. He felt like this would be a defining moment in his life. *Had he achieved his goal? Had he done everything he could have to receive such an honor?* Charlie thought to himself. It was time to find out. Anything else would be a disappointment. He felt like all his work, sweat, and effort had been to this one end.

"Okay, gentlemen. Now to the most important part of this meeting," Coach Jackson bellowed. He had paced the front of the room during the meeting and was now in front of the podium. "Time to announce this year's team captains as chosen by you, the guys who will lead you to a conference championship. They have both worked very hard and are deserving of this post. I couldn't have chosen a better pair myself. For defense your team captain is Junior Atwood."

Junior stood up in response to the applause now being given. The clapping lingered for a minute before Junior took his seat again. Charlie's heart was now at a full gallop. He wondered if it was loud enough for the people sitting near him to hear. He was clenching his now sweaty hands into fists. This announcement couldn't come fast enough. As the clapping began to die down, Coach Jackson announced "and your offensive captain is Charlie Peterson."

As the room started filling with applause, Charlie slowly stood up acknowledging the clapping. He felt like a weight had been lifted from his shoulders that almost made it physically easier to stand. The joy he felt was overwhelming. It was enough to allow him to break into a big grin standing in front of his peers and remain standing longer than he thought was humble. He waved his hand a few times, looking around the room, and sat down before he thought people might think he was reveling in the moment.

He wanted to scream out with joy, he wanted to start skipping around the room. He was bursting at the seams with excitement and had a longing to share this feeling with someone. Under the present circumstances, he didn't feel like it was the right place to freely display his emotions.

"That's about it for today. I need to see those two gentlemen for a moment. Everyone else enjoy the week off before we get back to training. Remember close games are won and lost in the off season. Championships are built in the time away from the field." Coach Jackson paused, as if to display his seriousness about this point. "All right, you are free to go." Coach Jackson watched from the front as the players walked up the rows to the exits in back. Some of the players made their way to the front to congratulate Charlie and Junior on their most recent honor.

Charlie received congrats and high fives from all the players around him. He even received bro hugs from a few of the guys that were close friends, like Johnny. The assistant coaches ritualistically waited for all the players to exit before they left the room. With the room emptying out, Charlie and Junior made their way to the front. Upon reaching the front, they smiled at each other, extended their hands, and gave each other a bro hug. Good jobs and congrats were also exchanged during the short embrace.

Realizing what a fine choice had been made, Coach Jackson let a rare smile show its presence on his stoic, measured face. With still a hint of a grin, Coach Jackson offered them his praise before moving on to business. "Just a few short things to say today before we sit down to a proper meeting. You two know what a big honor this is and how important this is to the team. I am very excited to have captains from the offensive and defensive lines, the foundation of any good team. I expect a lot from you two. You need to be leaders on and off the field. This is something you have been doing, just continue the good work. There are a few things I would like to talk about in depth, so I want to have a meeting Wednesday at 4:00. I'll see you then. Congrats again and Wednesday at 4:00, okay?"

"Okay," they responded in unison, shook his hand once more and were on their way out of the room. Charlie felt like he was walking with an extra spring in his step and chatted lightly with Junior on their way to the parking lot. With a grin broadly stretched across his face, Charlie hurried home in anticipation of sharing the news with his parents and girlfriend. The joy and excitement he was feeling had to be shared with someone, he couldn't hold out any longer.

No Time

As Blake finished tallying up the stats from the spring game, he looked at the clock. It was already past 6:00 PM. *Shit,* he thought. He was supposed to be home already. His in-laws would be there, bringing back the baby, and dinner would be starting soon. *Oh well, they know I'm at football and how important it is. I'll be there when I can,* he justified to himself. He counted up the last numbers and went by Coach Jackson's office to make sure they were finished for the night.

Peeking his head around the corner, Blake casually asked, hoping it would be short, "We done for the night, Coach?"

"Oh, hey, Coach Jones. Yeah we are. I'd like to talk to you about a few things before you go, though," he answered, only looking up to see who it was.

"Okay, but can we make it quick? I'm supposed to be home soon." Blake reluctantly sat down across the desk from Coach Jackson. "So what's on your mind?"

"We will see. I want to hear about some of your ideas and how you are going to put your philosophy into play, Blake. I'm not in a hurry. This is important, you know that, and your commitment is one of the reasons I extended this new position to you."

Blake would do just about anything to show that he deserved this job. He had been offered the defensive coordinator position last night at Coach Jackson's house during the BBQ. Coach Jackson had taken him aside to a quiet study filled with football memorabilia and offered the job to him. Nobody thought the job would be given out last night, but anticipating the offer, Blake jumped at the chance and graciously accepted. It was a huge promotion coming at a time his growing family needed it. More money and responsibility also meant more time and commitment. He and April had just had their first child six months ago and had moved into a bigger house. The mortgage was high and there had been talk of April having to get a job in order to afford the new home. Now there wouldn't be any worrying about money and April would be able to stay home with Conner.

Blake was the third coordinator in four years. Coach Jackson was a defensive coach and always managed to keep the games close, so he didn't put up with a porous defense. Coach Jackson wasn't patient with defensive coordinators that gave up too many points. Now he had to show he deserved it and would be the right person for the job. Blake was willing to do a few extra things in his attempt to show that Coach Jackson had made the right decision and that he could be successful with more responsibility. It was another step on the coaching ladder, where head coach was the dreamed of top rung.

After going through things in depth, the time had flown by. Blake had gotten lost in his explanation of how and what he wanted the defense to look like. It was a high for him. He knew this is where he should be. With only a few pauses, the meeting continued for three hours. Suddenly Blake looked up and realized he had to get going. He had to get home before his whole family was in bed. He excused himself and told Coach Jackson he would be back in the morning to finish talking about things and putting the playbook together.

By the time Blake arrived home, most of the lights were off. He looked at his watch while closing the front door behind him. It was already 9:30. *Oh shit, I'm three hours late.* The table was already cleared, so he checked the oven to see if a plate had been saved for him. Affectionately wrapped in tin foil was a plate with extra portions of all his favorite dishes. Popping it in the microwave, he walked downstairs to say hello to his in laws who would be staying in the extra bedroom.

Expectations

In an effort to show how appreciative and worthy he was of the honor of being a team captain, Charlie got to the football office 15 minutes early for the meeting with Coach Jackson and the new team captains, Junior and himself. The door to Coach Jackson's office was closed. His secretary, La Dean, told Charlie to sit down, that Coach Jackson would be with him soon and was expecting the meeting to start promptly at 4:00. He sat down in the cushioned chair. It was comfortable enough for a waiting room chair, but nobody would want to sit in it for too long.

La Dean chatted with him, only taking her eyes off her typing when asking him a question. The way she looked at him over her glasses perched on the brim of her nose gave her a grandmother-like quality. Her warm, caring eyes peeking out made Charlie, along with most of the guys, comfortable any time they came into the office. She greeted each player with a smile and somehow knew everyone's name, which helped the players feel welcome.

La Dean was always behind her desk, so only a few of the guys realized how short she was when not sitting on her slightly elevated chair. She was married and never had kids, which was part of the reason she was so motherly to all of the guys. She had always longed for children, but for one reason or another, it never worked out. Her personal presentation was conservative. She never wore anything flashy, always looking business like even when everyone else was casual.

She closely followed the team, but seemed to take more of an interest in personal performance rather than wins and losses. Her lack of concern about the team record helped her always stay positive and pleasant to be around no matter how the current season might be shaping up. Her smile was the only one that had a permanent presence in and around the football complex.

Charlie sat there politely engaging in small talk and listening to La Dean answer the phone and type for ten minutes before Junior showed up. They shook hands, Junior said hi to La Dean and joined him on one of the chairs along the wall. Charlie felt a stab of embarrassment run through him. He was, in fact, hoping that Junior might be late or that Coach Jackson would finish his meeting before Junior arrived so that Charlie would be seen as the first one there. He felt that would have shown how much he cared and how serious this new position of leadership was to him. It had almost been his whole life's work to get to this point of being a team captain of a college football team.

Now that he was a captain, Charlie wanted to be the BEST captain, he wanted to be THE team leader. He didn't want to push anyone out of the way, but as far as he was concerned two captains were too many. He was going to pull the team together. He wanted all the responsibility along with all the positive and negative consequences that came hand in hand with this responsibility. He wouldn't ever tell anyone this, nor did he like to consciously acknowledge these thoughts.

Charlie and Junior talked for a few minutes but didn't get far before Coach Jackson pulled open the door, following his visitor out of the office. As the two gentlemen approached Charlie and Junior they stopped in mid stride. "Hi guys, I would like to introduce you to someone important. This is Wayne Snyder." Coach Jackson introduced him as if he were a dignitary.

Hearing the reverence in Coach Jackson's voice, Charlie and Junior stood up to greet him and shake hands. Wayne shook their hands one at a time very deliberately, grasping with both of his hands, as if to show who was more important and who was in charge. He had a firm grip that didn't match his body size. It was an attempt to show that he did belong in the rough and tough world of football, even though his body hadn't been given the natural gifts required to play the sport.

"Hello, gentlemen," Wayne said, eyeing them up and down. He looked at Coach Jackson as if to show his approval. "I hear you two are this year's team captains. This is quite an honor. Coach Jackson tells me there aren't two more deserving guys on the team. I have seen you two the past couple of years and am excited to see the conclusion of two great careers here with the Puma. You know we have a long, proud history and we have been in the process of regaining that glory. This season we are looking for a good showing. I'm sure you two will do everything you can to help us realize this goal. It was nice to meet you and I'm sure I will be seeing more of you."

This was the first chance Charlie and Junior had to respond to anything Wayne had said. "Nice to meet you, too," they said one after the other as he again shook their hands with more force than necessary.

He turned to go while saying good bye to Coach Jackson. La Dean surprisingly got out of her chair and rose to shake his hand. "Nice to see you again Wayne. Stop by anytime."

"Thanks, La Dean." He walked out of the office and towards the door with a sense of purpose, like he had somewhere to be. His clothes were top of the line and had been freshly pressed. His designer leather shoes looked like they were polished on a regular basis. The way he dressed and carried himself gave the impression that he was always on his way to, or coming from, the country club.

Charlie didn't know it at the time, but Wayne was the head of the booster club. Relationships between college football coaches and booster clubs are always precarious. Coaches need money that boosters raise to keep their programs going and some boosters thought that big money donations came with influence and privilege that coaches never wanted to abdicate. With the increasing pressure to win this season, the relationship was tipping towards the precipice of being overly strained. Coach Jackson needed their help, but was growing tired of the unrealistic demands being put on him and his staff. He knew Wayne was only a "friend" as long as the Puma were a solid program.

Coach Jackson didn't take his eyes off of Wayne until he was out of sight. Charlie couldn't tell if he had malice or respect in his eyes. Once Wayne was out of sight, Coach Jackson turned and acknowledged Charlie and Junior. "Thanks for being on time. I shouldn't expect anything less from you guys though, right?" He turned towards the now open door to his office with a half grin and a more relaxed posture that had been absent when Wayne was in the office. "Well, shall we?" he nodded towards his office. "Hold my calls La Dean, please."

He motioned to the two chairs in front of his desk. Coach

Jackson, with a sense of purpose and full control over the surroundings, walked to the other side of the desk to his posh chair. The high backed executive looking chair added an air of regalness to the room. Any person who happened to sit in this chair would seem to be displaying a sense of superiority, expecting everyone to know who was in charge. It seemed to be raised slightly, forcing the speakers to physically look up. This feeling was increased by the fact that right now it was Coach Jackson, their head coach, sitting across the desk in his throne-like chair.

"Well gentlemen," Coach Jackson shuffled through a small stack on his desk, rearranging it to have something specific on the top. "I'm glad you got to meet Wayne. He is a big supporter of this program. No doubt you will see him around plenty or he will see you around." He paused as if they were supposed to understand what was being said without any more explanation. "I want to talk to you guys about being captains. First off, how do you feel about this honor?"

They looked at each other. Feeling like Junior's hesitation was an invitation to go first, Charlie spoke up. "I am very excited about it. It is something I feel proud and privileged to be able to be a part of. I know a lot of responsibilities come with this role, but I am prepared for that. It is something I am going to take very seriously and put all of my energy and efforts into doing the best job I can." He knew there wasn't a correct answer, but if there was, this surely would have landed him an A. He didn't say this just to please anyone. It really was how he felt. He wondered for a moment if he had gone too light because he knew all of his energy and effort would be put towards being The Best captain. But he refrained from saying all of his thoughts. He was worried that full disclosure might put him and Junior into a confrontation and competition, which he didn't want.

After a short silence, Junior spoke up. "Yeah, I feel the same way about everything Coach. I am very excited and will do everything asked of me and more."

Coach Jackson looked at both of them, giving them an approving, satisfied glance before crossing something off the paper that had been moved to the top of the stack. "Great! That is what I was hoping to hear and what I have come to expect from you two. You are seniors in this program, the leaders of the team, and the ones who are going to steer the team. Coaches can only take a program so far, most of the shaping and leading of the team has to be done by the players. Since you two have been chosen by your peers as the ones to lead this year, it is in your hands. On that note, I want to ask you both what some of your plans are to help guide the team towards a championship season."

    There was a pause. Charlie looked down at his hands in his lap and since he had already been thinking about some ideas, he answered without looking at Junior this time. "I think we need more player meetings. A players' only meeting the night before each game, allowing anyone to speak about the upcoming game, is a good idea. I also think we need to have goals for the season and some of them need to be decided upon by just the players without the coaches being around. I realize these meetings need to be arranged and guided by someone. With the help of Junior, I think we could do that." He unclenched his now sweating hands and shrugged his shoulders as if to show that he wasn't completely sure of himself and his ideas. He didn't want to appear overconfident in this setting.

    Coach Jackson nodded, jotting something down on the note pad. "Those are both very good ideas. I like them a lot." He looked Charlie in the eyes and gave him an approving nod before moving his eyes to Junior. "What kind of things are you thinking about right now, Junior?"

    "Hhhhhhhhmmmm, I like what Charlie said and I agree. That is something I would help to plan and carry out. I think that would help bring us closer together as a team. On top of that, I don't really have any ideas at the moment. I will continue to give my full effort all the time and be a leader on and off the field." He looked around the room to signal that he was finished.

    I'm glad I had already been thinking about this. I think that shows how serious I am about being a captain and how good I will be in that role, Charlie thought to himself during a brief pause.

    Coach Jackson crossed something else off of his note pad. "That is all great. I expect you both to follow through with that. I will remind you of it from time to time and ask how things are going. I also have a few other suggestions." He looked at his notes. "Summer is coming up. That is an important time of the off season. Under the rules, there can't be very much contact between players and coaches during the summer. Not many things can be mandatory. But, it is a time when teams can come together or teams can drift apart. There's a lot of free time and a lot of chances to plan events that can bring the group together. Now, it doesn't need to be anything big. It can just be playing cards with some of the guys or having a BBQ. I'm not condoning any illegal behavior, but have fun together, become friends. Friends share a stronger bond on the field and are less likely to give up on each other. These events and activities need to include everyone. It doesn't help the team to just have the same group of friends hanging out together. I am going to have La Dean print out a list with everyone's phone number so that you can reach everyone. If you ever need help arranging a place to get together come and talk to me. I can't give you any money, but I can give you ideas and speak to some people if I need to do that. Is that something I can count on you two to do?"

"Of course," Charlie blurted out.

"Yeah," Junior said calmly.

"Okay, good," Coach Jackson leaned over his desk to look at his note pad and then leaned back again into his chair, releasing a deep breath. He crossed his legs, uncrossed them, folded his arms across his chest, and looked down at the floor, betraying the nervousness he was really feeling.

Looking back up and regaining a measure of composure, he started again. "This is a big year for everyone here. There are a lot of expectations for us this year. The expectations start right from the top and trickle down to the bottom. Coaches, captains, players, and walk-ons are all going to have more expected of them this year. We have had a few rebuilding years and now are on the verge of being back at the top. Now is the time to show what all this hard work and effort have gone towards. Everyone is feeling the pressure this year. I am going to demand more from each and every member of the Puma family this year. I am going to put pressure on people and see if they can step up and perform. If they can't, then we will have to find a replacement.

From a players' standpoint, this starts with you guys. I expect a lot from you and am going to be very demanding of both of you. I don't think you have anything to worry about. As long as you keep doing what you have been doing everything will be fine. I just want you to know what is coming. I am going to push each player to his limit and beyond. There is not a lot of room for mistakes this year. Each and every game is vital. I know you two are on board, I just need you to help me pull everyone else along. I can't do it without good captains and I couldn't have picked two better guys myself."

He took another deep breath, looked them both in the eyes and gave a half grin. "That's all I need you for today, guys. Thanks for coming in." He extended his hand over the desk, shaking both of their hands.

After showing themselves out of Coach Jackson's office, La Dean handed Charlie and Junior the phone list of the players without anything being said, as if she knew what had gone on in the meeting. They gave her a smile and a "thanks" as they left and she returned to her work. During the slow walk to their cars, Charlie and Junior talked about a few things, boring classes, what girls they thought were hot, avoiding what had just been dropped on them. Something that would grow and become so big it would come to define Charlie's life. A huge responsibility had been given to them and Charlie, for one, was excited for everything that came with that. He wouldn't want it any other way.

Meaning

It was finals week, the week without classes or practice for students to prepare for and take their finals. Charlie needed to take some time off from studying. He stepped outside to get on his bike and cycle over to Johnny's house. The weather was abnormally warm for the middle of May. The approach of summer could be felt in the hot air. The heat was always welcomed at the beginning of summer, but by the end of the season the cool fall air was a nice relief. Feeling the sun on his skin, Charlie jumped on his bike. It was only a ten minute ride and the early summer warmth made the journey more strenuous than normal.

He arrived at Johnny's house with a thin layer of perspiration already showing its presence. Johnny's house looked like a typical college living space. It was a four-plex and Johnny was in the top right corner of the building. The yard was given the least amount of maintenance possible, just enough to keep the lawn from dying. Once a week the landlord would come over and mow the lawn, usually leaving a few un-mowed strips of grass, and pick up the beer cans that seemed to collect over the weekend. The railing up the short concrete steps was as unstable as the stock market during a recession. Loosely bolted in place, it could easily be pulled off with the slightest effort. On the small patio there was a big garbage bag full of a week's worth of smell and mess. It was good Johnny had put it outside, otherwise Charlie might not want to be inside. No one could reasonably predict when the bag might actually make it to the bigger can to be carried away by the garbage pick-up. Johnny didn't excel at these seemingly small duties, although it was only another 20 yards to the big green garbage can.

Johnny was the kind of guy who never locked his door and, if it was locked, he would probably never answer it. Charlie didn't know if it was laziness or if Johnny really didn't give a shit. Inside the place continued to look like somewhere a typical male college student might live. There was a stack of dirty dishes in the sink. They almost seemed to beg for soap and water. Clothes and towels were lying around in their own chosen destination with no care given to order or aesthetics. Empty bottles and cans of beer, Gatorade, water, and almost any other drinkable substance, littered the floor, even making an appearance in the bathroom.

It was not a big place by any means, but it had plenty of room for one person and the limited amount of things a single college male might want in his house. It wasn't clean, by anyone's standard, which was okay. It felt comfortable and Charlie always enjoyed coming over, as long as he didn't have to live there. Upon entering, his thoughts were interrupted by Bob Marley jamming throughout the small apartment.

"Hello, anyone here!?" Charlie belted out to try and announce his presence. He didn't want to walk in on any self-satisfying activities, which had happened on previous unannounced visits.

Turning the corner, Charlie saw Johnny sprawled out, fully clothed (this time), with his hand down his pants staring at the silent TV screen watching baseball, almost unaware or unconcerned about who it might be. Upon seeing Charlie's face, he yelled back, "Hey…, what up dude?" at least acknowledging his presence.

"Nothing. Mind if I turn this down so I don't have to yell?" Charlie asked, trying not to strain his voice.

"Yeah, it's over there," Johnny hollered back pointing to the source of the Rasta vibes.

With the volume down to a conversational level, Charlie made himself at home, falling limply into the lazy boy. "It is already hot out there and it is only May! This seems like the place to be." The apartment had the AC blasting, all the shades drawn, and was almost chilly compared to the outside temperature. "What are you doing?" Charlie asked, trying to pull Johnny into a conversation.

"Watching baseball. I'm supposed to call this girl named Jenny later. Just fucking chilling, dude, trying to stay cool. I hope this isn't an indication of how hot it will get this summer. How about you?" he answered, taking his eyes away from the screen for only a moment.

"Oh, about the same," Charlie said, pausing to watch the next pitch be a called strike, which the batter didn't agree with. Johnny didn't particularly seem to want to chat, but Charlie wasn't letting him off the hook that easily. "I don't know how you can watch this all day. I have a hard time watching a whole game, unless I am at the game," Charlie commented, now trying to drag Johnny into at least some kind of a conversation.

"Well, nothing else to do. I only have one more test and that isn't until tomorrow. I don't feel like doing anything. Plus, lots of people say that football is boring to watch. There's a lot of strategy in baseball. It's like any sport, the more you know about it, the more fun it is to watch," Johnny countered back.

"Yeah, I guess," Charlie replied feeling like it might be difficult to take Johnny away from his baseball game and into a conversation.

"No, no guessing. That's how it is, jerk off," Johnny snapped back sarcastically, throwing the nearest empty Gatorade bottle at him.

Blocking the bottle, Charlie thought, *well, he's finally showing some life. Good, maybe I can get him to talk.* He decided to give in. "All right asshole. You're right, again!" Charlie lobbed the bottle back at Johnny, hoping to keep him engaged in the conversation. After suffering a direct hit, Johnny looked back towards Charlie, surprised at the retaliation. They smiled and shook their heads at each other. "Football has a lot of strategy and we understand it because we have been playing it for so long."

"Yep, exactly," Johnny chimed in.

"It's still hard for me to believe this is going to be our senior year. It has all gone by way too fast," Charlie lamented.

"I know, dude." Johnny shook his head at this thought. "It's hard to imagine this being the end." Johnny sat up to change his position on the couch and alternate the hand that was resting on his crotch.

"Do you want this to be the end? I mean are you ready to call this the end? That is kind of a scary thought. I'm not sure I am ready to say that yet," Charlie said with complete sincerity.

"I don't want this to be the end. It is hard to picture life without football. I have been doing it for so long. I'm not sure what else I would do. I just don't know how realistic it is to think I will be able to play much longer," Johnny replied honestly.

"I know what you mean. Football has been our life. It is almost all we have known and done for the past few years. It's not like we have been taught much else. Do we have any other skills?"

Johnny pondered this for a moment before answering. "Well, our coaches always try to preach that football is preparation for life. I'm not sure what they really mean. They never give us an example." He paused, trying to sum up his thoughts about this. "We are always on time. I guess that is one thing. Well, let me take that back. We are always on time for football, not much else."

Charlie nodded, "mmmmmhhhhmmmm."

"I mean, most guys can't ever be relied on to be on time to class. We are all on time for football because otherwise we will get our asses kicked and yelled at and have to do extra running after practice."

"Exactly," Charlie jumped in, not knowing if Johnny had finished his thought. "That is what I am talking about. Have we really been taught any life skills the past four to five years since we have been here? I mean, what is a concrete example we can give for something we have learned about life in the last five years because of football?"

"Hmmmmm. Well, I guess I can be truthful with you. You're not one of my parents. You can't get mad at me. Even if you did I would just kick your ass, so I don't care."

"Yeah, right. Anyway, is there something, anything?"

"Just a sec, let me think." Johnny was trying to think of a candid answer. His hand seemed to move while he was thinking, as if the added stimulation might get things going. "I sure have learned how to drink. We do plenty of drinking. I can drink more beer than I used to be able to drink. That has to be a skill somewhere in the world, right?" he asked cracking a smile.

"Yeah, that sure is a skill, dumb ass. I am just not sure if that is something that I want to put on my resume or mention in a job interview," Charlie said, stating the obvious.

"Well, who said anything about a job? It is hard to even think about a job. I am getting a degree in history and what the hell am I going to do with that?" Johnny asked, not expecting an answer. "For me, all I can imagine is either trying to pursue playing football longer or coaching. Like we said earlier, football has been our lives for a long time. I don't really know anything else. Sure, now I know some history, but I just picked that subject because I had to decide on a major to be eligible for football. I guess I can teach, but I would do that just to be able to coach. My focus would be on football and coaching, not teaching. I mean, what other areas of our life have we even been able to give any focus to? All we do is practice football, play football, get ready to play football, and recover from football. If we ever have time or energy after that we might get some loving or, more likely, get drunk."

"Well, exactly. That is what I am talking about. We don't know anything else."

"That is a good point. There has to be something else we have been taught from football that we can use in life." Johnny sat for a moment to think and Charlie didn't interrupt, he would let him take another swing. "The coaches always say academics come first, but that is a load of shit."

"Hell, yeah," Charlie reiterated. "If you really did need some time to get a project done or catch up on some homework you better just plan on getting a bad grade. Or if you did take the time, then plan on not starting in the next game. If you asked for time off for school, the coaches would probably laugh at you and wonder if you were serious."

"Yep, academics come first, as long as they don't interfere with practice or games. I mean the only time they really care is when someone isn't eligible and then I guess it matters. But we all know that if you are a star there are strings that can be pulled." Johnny was really trying to think of something else to add that he had been taught which might prove useful. "Hmmmm, we have learned that winning and producing results are all that really matters. I mean losing isn't acceptable in athletics, it is more like a job now. If we don't produce then we are benched and if coach doesn't win then he is fired. I'm not sure if that is a good thing or a bad thing. Maybe just teaching us how life will be for us when we are done."

"Maybe football has taught us how to trust people and count on them," Charlie said, trying to add something positive. "Football is a total team sport and each player must do his job to the best of his ability on each play or the play is fucked and nothing will get accomplished. There are eleven of us out there and we all have to trust that each one will do his job. I think that is part of the reason players become such good friends. We have to rely on each other, so we learn to trust each other and become friends. Part of becoming such good friends is also from everything we go through together. We bleed, sweat, and cry together for many years. It creates a strong bond."

"Yeah, I agree. I also think it has taught us not to give up and good mental toughness. One of the few things I remember from all the speeches is, 'It is not what happens to you, it is how you react.' I think that is good. In any game every player screws up and you have to be willing to come back the next play and try again. If we were to dwell on the negatives and mistakes, then we would just fuck up again and again. I think that is true in life, too. There will be bad things that happen in our lives. If we go into a shell and get all depressed, our life will just stay on a negative path and we will lose out on chances to be happy and live a good life." Johnny stopped to try and remember his other point. "Oh and we sure have had to use a lot of mental toughness. I mean by the end of the third quarter in a close game the team that is going to win is the team that won't give up and will just keep playing hard. I mean we are tired for so much of the game and we have to be able to keep going, just block it out and give it all on the next play. I think that can help us in life."

"Oh, for sure. I have just been thinking about this lately and wanted to talk about it. So there are some things that football has taught us about life. It just probably isn't as much as our coaches claim and it for sure isn't the only way a person can learn these types of things. I am sure there are plenty of other ways to learn the same lessons. We are so focused on football and may, or may not, be losing out in other areas of life," Charlie stated, matter of factly.

"Is that bad?" Johnny asked.

"It doesn't have to be good or bad. It is just how it is. We have had good careers and enjoyed our experience tremendously, so I guess for what we are concerned about right now it is good." Charlie paused, deciding to steer the conversation in a different direction, "It is hard to think of life without football. It is almost scary. For me, as probably with many athletes, my sport is how I define myself," Charlie thought aloud, wondering how much of himself he wanted to reveal.

He decided to let it all out. "I think of myself as a football player first. That is where a lot of my self-esteem and self-worth come from. You know how it is. How hard we are on ourselves. It really is just a game, but when we have a bad one, we get totally depressed and down. We think it means we are a bad person or even that we let the team down. If we tried our hardest, it shouldn't really matter, but it does. The amount of time, energy, and pressure that is involved in playing the game makes it more than just a game. It becomes all-consuming and all involving. We are football players but are we anything else? It is going to be difficult. I am not ready to hang up my pads and call it a career in a few short months. I know I am not going to get drafted to play in the N.F.L. or anything. That is fine, I can try for some of the smaller leagues and see where that takes me. In a few years, who knows where I might be?"

"Yeah, we don't have to be done yet. Like Tyson, the defensive end from last year's team. He is still playing and he wasn't any superstar. He is playing in some European league. There are quite a few opportunities out there now-a-days. We could go play in Europe or in one of the smaller leagues here in the states. We just need a start and then to make the most of the opportunity. I know that we could both make it somewhere," Johnny stated optimistically.

"We just have to stay in shape and hope for a chance. That is the problem, though. We have to be disciplined. Nobody will be telling us that we have to work out, it will just have to be on our own initiative to go," Charlie confessed.

"Yeah, staying in shape is a pain in the ass. It will be hard to keep going to the gym and working hard enough to stay in football shape. That is why coaching sounds like a good option." Johnny looked at Charlie, trying to give some alternatives. "Think about not being sore every fucking day. Think about doing the kind of lifts we want to do. That would be sweet. The soreness isn't just from working out, it is from the games and practices also. I just don't know how much longer my body can stay together. In the off season we are sore every fucking day from workouts. We have to work our asses off in order to stay competitive and that means being sore the next day. Then during the season there are days that we feel like we are 80 years old. You know how it is, those Sundays after a game, how hard it is to get out of bed. Every single inch of your body seems to hurt. We have talked about it before, it feels like you could just die right then and there. It takes a full effort just to roll out of bed. During the season most of us, including you and I, have to take 1,000 milligrams of Advil several times a day just to get through practice and we are only in college. It isn't hard to understand why so many professional athletes get addicted to pain pills. There are days we sometimes wish for a full-body transplant. Bodies aren't meant to go through what we put ours through. Each year of football probably puts on an extra seven years to our body. It is almost like dog years. Imagine how we are going to feel when we are 40. We are only 22 right now and we already feel this way. Are we even going to be able to walk when we are 50? At some point we do have to think about our future, even if it does mean giving up our dream. I know that it is hard and I am not sure I want to deal with it yet."

"Well, like you said, it is a dream," Charlie paused, trying to imagine football being over. He wasn't comfortable with this thought. "I love it, though. It is a part of me, I am part of football. That is why I am willing to go through all the pain and the long hard hours. I haven't discovered anything else that compares to the high I get from playing football. It might be a lack of looking because of laser focus, but I love the game. The friends I have made and the places it has taken me are incredible. I don't know who or where I would be if it weren't for football. I might be sore a lot and I might have more pains than a normal 40 year old when I get there. But, so far it has all been worth it. I wouldn't trade in a day of it. Deciding to give it up without giving it my all to try and keep playing is something I am not willing to do. I feel like I would regret it for the rest of my life. I might be a beaten down old man, but at least I will know that I chased my dream as far as I could. For me it would be more difficult to live life with regret than with body aches. At least that is what I believe right now."

"That is for sure," agreed Johnny. "We heal fast now and our bodies are young. When we are old we might look back and wonder what the hell we were thinking. But hey, we are having fun now, so let's enjoy it. We still have one more season before we even have to start worrying about it. Let's have a great season and try to improve our prospects for moving on. It is our last shot as college players," Johnny reflected. "Enough talk of retirement, we are too young to be thinking about that. Wanna go get a six pack and something to eat?"

"Yeah, let's go," said Charlie, and with that they hopped up and walked back out into the early summer day. It was beginning to cool down with the sun ending its long day of showing off its ability to dispense large quantities of abundant, unrestrained energy.

Tired and half drunk, Charlie lay in bed trying to fall asleep. With his mind racing a million miles a minute this was proving to be difficult. His mind had wandered back to the earlier conversation with Johnny. He knew there was a whole season left to play before he had to worry about anything, but that wasn't helping. He liked to know what to plan on and what was going to happen. An unknown and uncertain future scared him, he had to have a plan.

He was a football player and had been since he could remember. Trying to think back to life without football was straining his memory bank. Since early adolescence, that is how he had thought of himself. It wasn't as if that was the only thing he did, or all that he was, only that football was and had been the most important thing in life for as long as he remembered. It was how he defined himself.

There were other areas of his life that were important and strangely enough, to the outside world, he steadfastly did not want to be thought of as only a football player. He just felt like football was the area of his life that he was best at and where he had won awards, gained acceptance, notoriety, and self-confidence. For whatever reason, he was good at football. His first year of football he stepped into an established team and quickly became one of the better players. In high school he was always the leader, even as a younger classman. In college he had always been counted on by his coach and teammates to set the tempo and level for the offensive linemen, as a group.

As a shy, self-conscious, unsure adolescent, a group of friends had accepted and even loved him. He had received more praise and awards in football than all other areas combined in his young life. People he met seemed to think that being a football player made him instantly cool. He was living the dream and felt like the reason for life's good blessings was his talent and dedication to football.

Lying there with these thoughts running through his head, he couldn't imagine where he would be without football. Picturing life without football made him feel like a lost child searching for his identity. Tears began to form and he was glad to be alone tonight, in his own apartment. This wasn't something he wanted to share with everyone. Warm, salty tears began to flow down his cheeks and soak into the pillow.

Feeling emotional and wanting to express his thoughts, he got out of bed. In the past when he didn't want to talk, but needed to let his emotions out, writing had helped. So he found a pen and some paper. He wanted to put down his thoughts about how much football meant to him.

> To me football is more than a game.
> It represents who I am,
> It is a part of me, but not all of me.
> It shows if you are a winner,
> It shows if you are a loser.
> It shows if you are a quitter,
> It shows if you are a person with heart.
> It shows if you are selfish.
> It shows if you are a complainer.
> You can be a different person on the field.
> Problems don't matter for a while.
> It is about a dream.
> It is about coming together with 80 other guys.
> These guys become more than just teammates,
> They are almost like brothers.
> This game is my passion,
> I have given it my heart and soul.

Upon finishing, he reread his spontaneously inspired poem and thought it described his feelings accurately. Putting his thoughts on paper made them feel more real. He felt much better and was glad he hadn't just held everything in. It had been cathartic for him. A smile began to show across his still-damp cheeks, as he began to think of the upcoming season and all the potential of his senior year and being team captain.

Realizing that worrying about the future wouldn't accomplish anything, he tried to think about the approaching season and what he wanted to achieve this year. He wrote down some goals for the summer.

-Be THE team leader!!!
-Stay positive
-Have fun
-Get bigger, stronger, and faster
-Show everyone how dedicated I am to my role as team captain

With his focus more on the present, some of Charlie's uneasiness began to slip away. He knew that by taking care of this season and doing his best, the future would take care of itself. Checking his alarm clock once more, he slipped back in bed and drifted to sleep thinking of the crisp autumn air and kicking ass again in what would be his most important season ever.

Planning

    The next morning through the haze of waking up, Charlie remembered everything he had committed himself to the previous night. Instead of feeling overwhelmed about what he would need to do to fulfill these goals, he felt energized. Now that he knew where he wanted to go, he could begin to think about how to get there.

    He knew reaching these goals would not be easy, so to help accomplish them he came up with a game plan. He thought the best way to help lead the team towards accomplishing all their goals was to incorporate everything Coach Jackson was preaching. He wholeheartedly bought into the philosophy and style of Coach Jackson's methods. He knew that if he, as a leader, followed Coach Jackson's ideas then the rest of the team would come along. He also knew that he could help bring the team closer together and create opportunities for everyone to become friends. He decided to focus on how to accomplish this team building. He knew it had to come from the captains and he wanted to be THE captain.

    The only things that might be different from Charlie's previous behavior would be his attempt to befriend everyone and the planning of events that would bring the guys together in social settings, creating an opportunity for them to bond. For Charlie it came down to the old idea of leading by example. He would take all of Coach Jackson's suggestions, plus some of his own ideas, and put them into practice.

    One of the first things he wanted to do was make sure he knew everyone on the team by name. There weren't many guys that he didn't know, but in the few meetings and weight lifting sessions during the summer he would approach those guys and talk to them, trying to remember their names. Around campus he would also be friendlier to anyone from the team that he might run into and if he wasn't busy he would chat for a while, getting to know more of the guys.

    During the summer, he would also arrange some get togethers for everyone who was still around. When this wasn't possible, he would hang out with a different group of guys, not just his normal group of friends. He would invite everyone out and try to bring groups together that didn't always hang out with each other. At times it would just be small gatherings for a night of cards or a day at the local water park, but it would have the intended effect of bringing the team closer together.

Charlie would have to do most of the planning and calling, after all it would be him that knew everyone on the team. Junior would help with the organizing and putting together the events. When they wanted to have a BBQ they could speak with Coach Jackson about getting some cheap food for everyone. A couple of bucks from each guy would be enough to provide plenty of food for a bunch of hungry football players. Charlie knew these events would be a success and help the team to grow closer during the off season. He knew that these types of gatherings were what Coach Jackson had in mind when he had talked to Charlie and Junior during their meeting the previous day.

Charlie didn't mind doing most of the leg work and being the one who was really in charge. This was the way he wanted it. This was just the beginning. During the off season he would set the stage for him to become THE LEADER during the season. He knew that recognition and praise for all this work would come during the season. He would keep working just as hard, if not harder, to be worthy of being recognized as THE LEADER of the Puma this season. It was a task he wanted to pursue. He had no way of knowing how all-consuming and demanding this task would be for him to accomplish.

From now until the end of the season there would be more surprises than Charlie, Blake, April, or any member of the Puma team could have guessed. There were going to be ups and downs, challenges and setbacks. All of them felt like they were prepared to handle whatever might be waiting, but it would prove to be more difficult than any of them had ever imagined.

Offseason
May-August 2000

Free Time

It was now summer for Charlie and the rest of the Puma team. Although summer didn't officially start for another few weeks on the calendar, school was over and that was when summer started for the team. After spring ball and the announcement of team captains, the last few weeks of school had flown by. Charlie had a difficult time staying focused on the task of studying for and passing his finals. Many other things had been on his mind.

His dream of being a team captain had been realized. Now came the reality and responsibility that went along with this position of leadership. Prior to becoming a captain, Charlie hadn't completely realized how much went into being a successful leader. This team was his to lead now. He had been spending most of his time determining how best to guide the team towards achieving all of its goals. To him this seemed a lot more important than receiving an A or a B in a few classes.

The feeling of freedom that goes along with finishing that last final and being done with school until September is hard to describe. It is one that brings back carefree childhood memories, like all that is important for a few months is play. It is a great time of year. There is a lot of time for relaxing, wasting time between the few responsibilities of summer and finding things to do to keep from being bored. It was great to have down time after another school year of being busy every day. There would be lots of beer, lots of BBQs, lots of movies, and lots of chilling. Summer was always great!

Yet this sublime feeling wasn't as strong as it was in one's youth because of the need to find a summer job and the voluntary, really mandatory attendance of summer workouts four times a week. Also with summer came one of the mysteries of life, the contradictory feelings of not wanting the summer to end but at the same time looking forward to the end of it so one can start something new, begin achieving again, begin working hard again.

Charlie already had a job for the summer. A job wasn't a requirement, it just provided spending money. It also allowed him to save some money for the school year when the cash flow was limited by the small stipends and the inability to have any kind of a part time job. These summer jobs were never the greatest, but they fulfilled their intended purpose. In his days of college jobs, Charlie had worked at a variety of places; a pizza shop, as a telemarketer, and in landscaping. Landscaping had required way too much work and had actually taken away from his energy for training. So, for his senior year, Charlie had made sure his job would not take away from his ability to prepare for the season. He didn't care if it was going to be boring, as long as he could make some money and have all his energy to put towards being in the best shape of his life for the most important year of football ever. He got a job at a hardware store.

His job description wasn't complicated. He would be doing a complete inventory of the small hardware store and entering all the data into the computer. He was hoping that with some luck he might be allowed to take one of the few tractors that were for sale in the back lot for a test drive.

The owner of the shop was a short stubby man who was a member of the booster club. He had, himself, once been a player, but Charlie doubted he was as good as he had related through his stories during their initial visit. Coach Jackson had recommended Charlie for the job. It wasn't a free ride, though. Charlie and Coach Jackson had talked about doing everything by the rules. Coach Jackson told Charlie he wouldn't send anyone else because he knew that Charlie wouldn't accept any special favors which might be offered by a member of the booster club. Charlie had gone to an interview, like any other prospective employee, and was given the standard entry wage. If he hadn't done this he could be subject to punishment by the NCAA for using his position as a college amateur athlete to get special treatment.

It was the first Monday after school had been let out for summer. Workouts didn't start until the next week, so Charlie decided he might as well get started at his job. Today was going to be his first day. He was really happy about the shift he had been given. Working from 3:00 pm to 8:00 pm meant that he didn't need to be there early and would be off with plenty of time to catch up with his buddies after work. Today he was leaving early for work so that he could stop by his girlfriend Mary's place to see her one more time before she went home for the summer. He would help her pack a few things into the car and say an intimate goodbye.

They had known each other for over three years and had been together for the last two years. There had always been a mutual attraction, but it wasn't until a party a couple of springs ago that either of them had acted upon their feelings. They began dating after that night and soon decided to date each other exclusively. But the subject of anything more serious was avoided. A future together and even the word "love" were not things they talked about.

One of the reasons their relationship had worked out was because neither one of them was too demanding of the other's time. They were both very driven, Charlie with football and Mary with her business studies. They allowed each other to have their own priorities and spent time together when they could. They would see each other a few times a week, but it wasn't a situation where they felt obligated to spend every night together. It worked well for both of them.

Mary went home every summer because in her home town she could work for her dad's business firm. She was intent on working in a big brokerage after school and hoped that her experience of working every summer, combined with her excellent academic record, would help her land a job with a big-name firm after graduation. She would visit him regularly throughout the summer and he might even make a trip to her home during the summer months. Charlie would miss her, but was also glad he would be able to fully commit himself to training and bringing the team together this summer. Glancing at the clock he noticed it was time to leave if he was going to say goodbye and still get to work on time. Descending the small flight of stairs from his apartment to the parking lot, Charlie smiled with the thought of the coming months. The smell of summer was in the air and the rising mercury of the early afternoon could be felt as he got into his truck.

Defense

Now that it was summer Blake would be around the house more. He did have some duties and responsibilities with football, but his presence at home with the family would be much more frequent. April now felt like she might have her husband and partner back again for a time. The longest stretch of togetherness was always the summer. She cherished the long hot summer days and balmy nights. This was when they could connect again as a couple and friends.

Since Blake had taken a job as a college football coach their summers had been precious. Even when the season was over he was very busy while school was in session. There was training, recruiting, spring ball, and players to look after. Just keeping all of his guys eligible and on track was a stressful job. June and half of July was the only time they had together, when plans wouldn't be contingent on late meetings, a new game plan, or team troubles. This summer meant even more to April because of Blake's new job, which would mean more of a commitment during the season. Plus, now with a baby, there were more demands and less time.

Things were going great so far this summer. April and Blake had spent a lot of time together and with their baby. There hadn't been any problems, but April had a sense of anxiety that she couldn't let go. These feelings stemmed from the fact that whenever she tried to bring up worries about the season and their relationship suffering because of football Blake became defensive and non-communicative.

He would tell her that they could make it. It might be hard for a few months, but they always had times like this to rekindle the spark. They loved each other and that was what mattered. He liked to remind her that she knew this was his dream before they got married and asked her to please be supportive. Lines about him trying his best for the family and that things weren't going to change were second nature. He would not have a discussion about it and because of the predictable reaction April hesitated to bring it up. Counseling had been mentioned, but met with stiff resistance from Blake who thought their relationship was strong enough and didn't need the help of any outside party. He told her to look at the other football couples around them and notice just how strong their relationships were.

She realized these were warning signs, things that were going to make the road ahead difficult. She even acknowledged silently to herself that before the vows had been said the red flags had been apparent to her.

When one is young and in love warning signs and red flags don't really matter. The power and majesty of love is most important. It wasn't that she thought he would change once they were married. It was more that she just thought things would work themselves out, that the problems wouldn't be so bad once they were committed to making the relationship last for a lifetime.

And perhaps this was true. Maybe after some time, several years or so, these details wouldn't bother her. It wasn't as if there was an absence of love between them. During certain times of the year it was just an absence of Blake. This absence gave them even less time to deal with the issues of their relationship. She didn't know if that was good or bad. No relationship was perfect and she didn't expect hers to be an exception. She just wanted stronger lines of communication and a consistent dose of Blake throughout the year.

Sitting on the porch, watching Blake play with Conner, April's mind continued to wonder. The feeling of warmth and love that she felt seeing the interaction of her husband and son triggered other tender memories of their past together. She thought back to their courtship. Blake was the man of her dreams. He had a tall athletic body from playing football that looked as if it had been chiseled from granite. In the years since, his body had lost some of its muscle, but she liked it even better now. She had loved watching him play. Before meeting him she wasn't too much of a football fan. Her first few games she wasn't even sure what was going on half the time. It seemed like crazy guys running around trying to hurt each other. Her watching of the games only consisted of finding his number and watching to make sure he didn't get killed.

Dating a football player she got to know many of the guys on the team. There were plenty of boring, dumb guys. Most of them seemed like they had received a few too many hits to the head. These same guys were also the type who thought that they were too cool and could get any girl they wanted. They were just out for a piece of ass, nothing more. She was glad that Blake wasn't one of those guys. He went to class, even read books, and could carry on a conversation about something more than just football or last weekend's party. Not that she didn't like the football players, she just wanted more than that.

    Blake was a special person. He was not only a sexy, athletic young man, he was smart and respectful. April had heard the horror stories about how football players treat women, yet Blake had treated her like a princess throughout their entire time together. He talked with an open heart and let her into places few men are willing to talk about. Any subject was okay, even why football was so important to him. They would spend late nights just chatting about their lives, their dreams, their fears, and sometimes nothing. He was a complete gentleman to her. Even after they had been dating for months and were comfortable with each other, he continued to open doors for her and tell her how nice she looked. It was everything she wanted in a man.

    They had been dating for over a year when graduation came around for both of them. This threw the decision about their future together right into the open. They both loved each other and wanted to stay together. During the past year they hadn't lived together, but that didn't seem like an issue. Their caring for each other and desire to stay together seemed to outweigh all else. Against the wishes of their parents, they decided to get married. Blake had been offered a Graduate Assistant position at a university in the neighboring state.

    He would receive a full ride scholarship for his Master's Degree, including room and board. In exchange for his scholarship Blake would work as an assistant coach for the football team. There was no pay other than the scholarship. They would be able to live for free on campus and would receive a meal card, but the rest of their expenses would need to be covered by April getting a job.

    This didn't bother April. She had graduated with high honors from the school's highly reputable business college, and she knew it wouldn't be a problem for her to find a job. At first, the coaching job didn't seem like much to April and she wasn't sure why he would take a job that would demand so many hours for no pay. But after hearing Blake explain that this was the way into a college coaching career and that it was his dream, she was fully on board with their decision to try it out.

Love was in the air and they wanted to help each other accomplish their dreams. At the same time, they made a commitment to keep their relationship the number one priority. Before getting married they read relationship books and wanted to ensure they had discussed everything and that their relationship was something that would last. They both wanted to have kids and a house full of love and happiness. Raising a family and having a strong relationship together were their goals.

Personally, April dreamed of nothing more than being with Blake forever, being his soul mate, growing together, and having his children. Her work life came second to all that. In college she had discovered that the things she needed to know and understand in order to be successful in the business world came naturally to her. It wasn't something she had needed to put an effort into. Work was just work for her, a way to earn money. She cared more about Blake than she had cared about anyone previously in her life. Throughout the years it had been hard to imagine her life without him.

Blake shared these same goals and thoughts with the addition of one other very important thing in his life, football. His lifelong dream was to be involved with football until he retired. Once he finished playing football after his senior year, he realized his continued involvement would not be as a player, so he moved his focus to coaching.

April knew football was important to him, at times it even scared her. Watching him play she wondered why he would put his body through such torture. Every time they were together he was complaining of some body part being sore. After a game he needed a whole day to feel normal again. Yet, he still went back, each and every day, and gave the game his heart and soul. Just by watching him play she could tell how much it meant to him. He wasn't the biggest or the best player, but he tried the hardest and never gave up. After a loss he was devastated, acting as if his few personal mistakes had been the reason for the outcome. Yet, April could never have predicted just how big of a role football would have in his life.

However, when they were together, she felt as if she was the only thing on earth that mattered. He told her how much he loved her, loved being with her, and how he wanted to be with her forever. His parents were still together, but only seemed to be hanging on for appearance sake. They didn't show any outward affection towards each other and barely communicated. It wasn't a good relationship to have as a model. April's fears about this were dissipated because Blake always told her that his fear was that his relationship would end up like that and that he was willing to do anything to make sure that didn't happen.

So, after graduation, a humble wedding, and a job offer, they packed up their things and headed off to a new town together. They didn't have any money, just a strong love for each other. It would be a challenge, one they wanted to share together, on the adventure of life.

This had happened about six years ago. April didn't know how those years had slipped by so fast. Looking back on those years was like looking at scattered puzzle pieces, she could only see bits and pieces of that time, like fragments of their past. Even putting them together didn't quite make an entire picture. She guessed that the past never did make a full picture, but there were times when she wished that she could see the whole picture again.

Blake's first two years of being a Graduate Assistant had flown by. Being a newbie at her accounting firm meant April was busy just trying to keep up with the demands of a new job. Many nights she worked as late as Blake did those first two years of their marriage. After his G.A. position was finished, the team offered Blake a full time position as outside linebacker coach.

Once Blake had finished his advanced degree, April decided it was time for her to get hers out of the way. She knew that it would take an M.B.A. to move up in the company and to secure a higher salary. The next year and a half was consumed with work and school. She barely had time to think. A few months after she finished school, they were pregnant. April worked right up until the baby was born.

Because life had been so busy the first five and a half years of their relationship, April had not really had time to notice how much time Blake spent with football. She was as busy as Blake was a lot of the time. If they had any spare time, they had spent it together. Now, as April was home with the baby, she had a lot of spare time and too much time to think. She was beginning to dislike football because it kept Blake away from her. She was starting to wonder if their relationship really was Blake's number one priority.

She pushed these negative thoughts away and smiled as her attention came back to the present. She heard Conner giggling as Blake was tickling him on top of the blue baby blanket out in their yard. The smell of freshly cut grass and the late evening light reminded her it was summer and that meant more time with Blake. This rejuvenated her. She took one more sip of her strawberry margarita and sauntered over to join her family.

Summer. Torture.

Summer time brought with it loose shoulders, long days, and time to recharge one's battery. Summer had always been a good time for Charlie. When he was young his family would take vacations to the beach. His father and grandfather would take him fishing, sometimes they would go camping overnight. Charlie loved those times, he loved the smell of the campfire. He would get home and his clothes would still smell like the campfire. His mom would make him take off his clothes right away and put them in the washer. He would take off his shirt last so that he could get one last whiff of the campfire before his clothes smelled like Tide again.

Charlie's love for summer continued unabated through his college life. He didn't have the whole summer to lounge around because of football workouts. But, between workouts and an easy summer job, there was still plenty of time for relaxing. It was strange staying around his college town during the summer. Like Mary, a lot of the students went home for the summer. The campus was kind of like a ghost town. This made it easy for Charlie to focus on football, though. Instead of the crowded walkways and the noisy student union, it felt deserted. The basic services were available, but the hustle and bustle of a college campus was conspicuously absent.

Charlie kind of liked this, though. It meant no struggle for parking and he almost felt like he owned the place. With no one around to argue, maybe he did. It also made him feel like he was truly dedicated to football. Charlie braved the empty college bars, celibacy, and the lack of college coeds by staying in town and working out with the team and Jim, the conditioning coach. Summer was the time to get bigger and stronger for the coming year. There were no distractions with school or his girlfriend. He could manage for a few months because his focus was clearly on preparing for his most important season yet, his senior year in college football. He also felt that since he was a team captain that it was his implicit duty to be part of the summer "voluntary" team workouts. But, these workouts meant sleeping in during the summer was a thing of childhood's past.

The red glow of the clock read 8:29....

....8:30. "Beep...beep...beep...beep." Charlie slowly opened his eyes and checked the clock to make sure he wasn't missing out on any extra minutes of sleep. Every one counted, especially when Jim's workout was what awaited him. Charlie stretched out his arm and shut the alarm off.

He had his quick routine that he got right into. He grabbed one piece of bread and a glass of water. Orange juice stuck in his throat keeping him thirsty during the whole workout. While eating his piece of bread, Charlie watched the morning news. Although this was a small breakfast, he had experimented with more food in the past. This just left him feeling like he was on the verge of vomiting during the intense workout. The key was to have a little bit of food in one's stomach, but not too much, or one was liable to throw up. If he wanted to eat more, he would have to wake up earlier, which was out of the question.

At 8:35 he was in the bathroom ridding himself of any waste in his system. If a guy wasn't fully emptied before these workouts body fluids might not only come out of one's mouth. Charlie had witnessed it happen. After a short toilet break, he swiped some deodorant on, brushed his teeth, and slipped on his workout clothes. By 8:45 he was out of the door for the short five minute drive up to the football facilities and the weight room. Charlie's session didn't begin until 9:00, but everyone arrived early to guarantee tardiness was avoided. Even half a minute late to Jim's workout meant extra running at the end of what was already a grueling workout. Plus, Jim's clock was about five minutes fast, so 10 minutes early wasn't much leeway.

Arriving early also meant that one could see the previous group finishing the workout. This was good and bad because the more guys that were sprawled out on the ground at the end of the workout the more likely one was to get psyched out about the upcoming workout. On the other hand, it did show that the session would end and that people did indeed live through the experience.

Many of the guys hated Jim. It wasn't that he was a bad person, it was because this was who made them work hard all year round. He pushed them to work even harder than they thought possible. This is part of what Charlie liked about him, the work ethic he demanded of the guys and the fact that he held everyone to the same standard.

Jim liked Charlie, too. This was something of an anomaly because Jim wasn't someone who displayed how he felt or thought very often. Charlie's teammates liked to give him a hard time about this, not so subtly hinting that he was a sycophant. This didn't bother Charlie because he knew why Jim, along with the other coaches, liked him. It was simple. He worked hard, didn't complain, stayed out of trouble, and did what was asked of him.

Jim was an intense guy. He rarely smiled during workouts or games. His brown eyes had a constant intensity to them that made Charlie think of a drill sergeant. Getting ready for football was serious to him, it was no laughing matter. At the same time, he preferred to just be called Jim, Coach was not necessary. He was a short, buff man, and many of the guys wondered if he had ever played football. Despite this, he had respect among the team because he worked hard and one could tell he genuinely cared about each player's individual success in addition to the success of the team. Plus, the consequences for not following his directions were enough to enforce obedience on the most unruly of players.

Because of his many years of being directly involved with strength and conditioning, his body was solid and athletic. To go with his smaller stature he had a little bit of a small man's syndrome. He was short, he knew it, and he didn't care. He was the boss of the weight room and made sure everyone knew it. He took everything personally about what happened in the weight room. If a guy fucked up he never hesitated to let him and everyone else know. At times it almost seemed like a show, designed to make his point and embarrass whoever he was yelling at just a little more. He knew that being berated by a short little guy added to the embarrassment and he seemed to revel in this fact, as if it somehow made up for his vertically challenged genes. This had never happened to Charlie because he had never given Jim a reason to chastise him. So, Charlie lacked a motive for hatred towards Jim that some of the other guys had.

Jim's workouts were legendary. He liked to kick ass as often as possible. It was impossible not to be sore after a week's worth of workouts with Jim. Each day was a punishing challenge, both mentally and physically. Charlie didn't know which were worse, winter or summer workouts. Winter workouts meant two times a day with Jim, once at 6:00 am for an hour of running and then in the afternoon for two hours of weight lifting. Summer workouts were just one brutal three hour session of weight lifting and running.

Once every training cycle, about 10 weeks, Jim liked to add some extra pain. This particular form of torment he called "Agony". It involved mostly legs, but one's whole body would be sore for three days afterword. Their legs would be so worn out that they could barely even walk the next day. One set of Agony was enough leg work for a week, but Jim had them do five sets.

Each set was comprised of 20 squats at 50% of the person's squat max. This was followed by lunges down the length of the room. Next were side lunges with five body squats every five yards. And finally, 12 box step ups on each leg. In between each set there was only a 10 minute rest, so there was barely enough time to catch one's breath. After one set, every players' legs were burning. After two sets, everyone was ready to collapse. It took every ounce of mental and physical strength to get through sets three and four. The fifth set was when one began to feel like he was genuinely being tortured. Many of the guys would collapse trying to finish the exercises. Some of the guys would throw up. It didn't matter, they had to finish. Sometimes somebody would even faint. Everyone was staggering at the end of the workout and nobody had anything left in their tank, either mentally or physically.

Jim's creativity was apparent in many of his workouts. He would have the players try a number of different exercises, all in an effort to increase their size, strength, and speed. At times they would run while dragging tires, holding weights, or through the sand. They lifted huge fifty pound chains or tractor tires on top of rubber exercise balls. Some of the players would make fun of these experimental exercises, wondering what the hell they were doing and why they had to be the guinea pigs. It all paid off though. The team was one of the strongest and fastest in the conference. Charlie's speed, size, and strength had all increased substantially since he began training under Jim. This was the most important thing a conditioning coach could do.

Fortunately today was just a normal day. No "Agony," but as always it would be an arduous workout. Jim's workouts began with abdominal strengthening, lower back exercises, and stretching. Jim put a lot of emphasis on the mid-section. This would be the first of three sets of ab and lower back exercises for today's workout. It was only a warm-up for the rest of the workout but Charlie along with most of the players was already sweating.

Next came power cleans, Jim's favorite. Each day they would do some sort of Olympic explosive lift. Tomorrow would probably be squats and snatches, the next day bench and clean and jerk, and the last day of the week would be deadlifts. This core lift, today's power clean, took up half the workout. They had 14 sets to complete. The players struggled to complete the last rep or two of each set. This part of the workout was exhausting. Charlie was dripping sweat by the end of the core lift and it was still only the beginning of the workout.

During the next hour the entire body was worked, muscle group by muscle group, until each area was burned out. Many of the lifts were designed specifically for football, focusing on power and explosion. Charlie's entire body was aching and tired at the end of the two hour lifting portion of the workout.

At exactly two hours into the session, the players were marched out together for their speed training and conditioning. They completed exercises designed specifically to improve speed and running technique. After this it was conditioning, gut check time.

Jim's goal in conditioning each day seemed to be to push everyone to the point of absolute exhaustion and then go one step farther. Missing even a couple of workouts meant falling behind and possibly not being able to even finish the prescribed activities because each day the exhaustion point was raised.

Because of the intensity of the workouts and the precision in which they occurred, one was reminded of a military training camp. The shouting that went along with the drills completed the feeling of a military setting. But, unlike the military, the players could escape after a few hours, only having to return the next day for another dose.

Making it through one of these workouts was an accomplishment. A whole summer seemed impossible. Not giving up and continuing to give a full effort required as much mental strength as physical strength. Jim expected and demanded a full effort on each repetition of each exercise and drill. Any less than this was met with yelling and another required repetition. Guys not fully committed to football and to getting stronger didn't last through many workouts. As a result, they weren't on the team for long.

Today's conditioning involved gassers, so named because after each exercise one felt like he didn't have any gas left. But there was always more than one set, just to ensure that nobody had any gas left by the end. Each gasser involved sprinting the width of the field three times. This had to be done in a certain amount of time. The guys were split into three groups; receivers, quarterbacks, and defensive secondary were one group. The second group was running backs, tight ends, and linebackers. The last group was offensive and defensive linemen. All the guys from each group had to finish within the time allotted or the repetition did not count. This meant that the guys got on each other to finish because they did not want to do more. It was an effective form of peer pressure.

Today they had to do eight gassers. Charlie breezed through the first five, but he was beginning to wear out by the sixth one. This made him nervous because he knew that if he was having trouble, then the other linemen who weren't as mentally tough as he was would probably not make the last two. Just as Charlie feared, some of the guys did not make their time for the last two reps. Now, the whole group had to do two more reps. This upset everyone and a barrage of cuss words were thrown at the guys coming in after the allotted time. Everyone was dead tired at this point, nobody seemed like they could handle more. Somehow they willed themselves through two more. Charlie knew not everyone made it. Jim let it slide since he had more conditioning planned.

This was the time that Jim loved. It was time to push the guys beyond their limit. Now they had to complete plyometrics, three sets of eight box jumps. This part was especially hard and one had to mentally concentrate because if he did not get enough of a jump, then he would fall down and this meant more energy wasted. So guys took their time and made sure they completed the exercise as required. Finally, it seemed like it was over. But Jim had a surprise today; tire flips. Somehow Jim had acquired a dozen huge tractor tires. These tires had to weigh at least two hundred pounds each. The smaller guys were allowed to work in pairs to flip the tires, but the big guys had to work alone. Jim made them flip the tires across the width of the field and back again. As each guy flipped the tire the last time to make it across the sideline, he practically passed out. A few of the guys had to lie on the field because they couldn't move anymore. Everyone was trembling from exhaustion, just like the end of all of Jim's workouts. This regimen would be repeated four days a week for 10 weeks. After going through this kind of training, the players were ready for war, brutal hand to hand combat where the goal was to annihilate the guy across from one's self. A season of college football.

At around noon, Charlie dragged himself to the locker room, drenched in sweat and totally drained. He finally left Jim and the workout behind. Now he could take a deep breath and relax, he had a few hours to kill, the beauty of summer. Since Mary was not around, he usually spent his free time between workouts and his lame summer job with the guys. They all had easy summer jobs and time to kill, as well.

While taking his time in the shower, Charlie wondered what he was going to do today. He had been hanging out with teammates a lot lately. Today he didn't feel like doing what he should do or what was expected of him. Instead he was going to do what he wanted to do. He decided to go where he went when he didn't want to be alone, but wanted to relax. Somewhere he could chill out, be himself, and talk if he wanted to talk. He was going to go to Johnny's house. It was the perfect place to spend a leisurely afternoon before going to work. As he let the water rinse the soap off of his tired and sore body he smiled, he was glad to be doing something for himself.

Paradise Lost

    Sitting in a lounge chair next to the pool, April was letting the sun warm her body. Blake was in the pool, relaxing in the cool water. It was the first time they had been able to spend more than a night together since having Conner. Their life had been hectic enough with just football, but now with a child there were even more demands. Now that Conner was a little older they could leave him with her parents.

    They went to a posh, secluded mountain resort to get away from everything and connect again. In April's mind, it could not have come at a better time. Their relationship was suffering from lack of effort and lack of attention. April was hoping this week could mend and strengthen the bond between them. After a couple of nights she was already feeling better.

    Feeling happy to have some time with her husband, April smiled. She took off her sunglasses, leaned forward in her lounge chair to find Blake and flash him a smile. She wanted to share her warm feelings even if it was nonverbally. She saw him staring off into the distance with only his head above water. It only took a moment of looking before Blake turned his head to meet her gaze. Their eyes locked and they saw in each other's eyes what had brought them together and had been missing lately. They smiled broadly at each other, not wanting to break away. Finally, Blake dove under the water, heading for the stairs so he could get out and join his lovely wife.

    As Blake was underwater, April caught a swift, determined movement out of the corner of her eye. She turned to see the well-dressed front desk manager walking directly towards her. The feeling of love and peace quickly left her. She was nervous about why he would be coming to talk to her. As he approached, Blake broke the surface near the stairs so was able to hear the news.

    Looking directly at April, the overdressed manager excused the interruption and delivered the message. "There is a Mr. Jackson on the phone asking for Blake Smith. He says it is urgent. I am sorry to bother you, but he wouldn't give up until I found you."

April dropped her head and with it all the positive feelings crashed to the ground like a crystal glass scattering in every direction. "Okay, thank you," Blake replied, emerging from the pool.

The manager turned to face Blake, "Okay sir. Just come to the front desk after you have dried off. He is still on the phone waiting for you." He set off for the lobby as Blake reached for his towel.

Blake avoided April's eyes as he began drying off. He didn't need to look at her to feel the bitterness coming towards him. April finally broke the silence. "Please don't answer it. This is our vacation. You have been promising me this for months now."

Pausing for a moment, knowing anything he said would not be what she wanted to hear, he bent down and kissed her on the forehead. "I have to take it, babe. He is my boss and this is my job."

He slipped on his shirt and avoided her narrowed, pleading look. Before turning towards the lobby, he shot her a forced smile that was only returned with a look husbands don't like to see.

"Hey Coach, what's up?" Blake answered the phone with concern. He knew Coach Jackson wouldn't bother him unless it was important. He also knew his wife expected his full attention this entire week.

"Hi Blake," Coach Jackson answered with excitement. Once Blake's tone had registered, he changed to a more business-like manner. "Sorry to bother you. I know you are on vacation, but boy am I glad that I finally found you. I have some great news. We have a chance to land a top prospect. He had scholarship offers from all of the big names, but they backed off when he didn't pass his SAT. Now that he has achieved a high enough score, none of the other schools have a scholarship available. I had been saving a scholarship for one of the walk-on kids this fall, but that can wait. I know he's interested because his coach, an old friend, personally called me and asked if we had any scholarships open. If we show him a good time and all that we have to offer, I know we can get him."

There was an uncomfortable pause. The bait was laid out, Blake knew there was no good option. He couldn't just tell Coach Jackson to butt out of his vacation, this was part of his new responsibility. And he knew that April expected a week together for time to reconnect. There was no other choice, he took the line hard and went full force, "Who is he?"

Coach Jackson knew Blake was on board. The long pause and forceful question was all that he needed to hear. He slowed down and spoke with conviction, "His name is Trevor Price. He plays linebacker and will have an immediate impact. He'll fill in that hole of yours at strong side linebacker."

This last part started to get Blake excited. He badly needed a guy for that spot and none of the returners were proving to be a decent fill in. It had been a weak spot all spring and Blake lost sleep at night thinking of going through the season with his current players. "When are you bringing him in?" he asked, trying to hide his now increasing excitement. When he picked up the phone, his thoughts had been on his vacation and spending more time with his wife. Now he was in football mode. The peaceful mountain surroundings were the furthest thing from his mind.

"He'll be here at noon tomorrow. I'm going to pick him up myself and I want you to be there with me. You would be his position coach and he needs to feel comfortable with you. You also need to see if he will fit in with our program. We are one of only three schools in the running to get him. He wants a scholarship and a chance to start his freshman year. We can offer him both. This is very important. If we don't do it now we will have missed our chance. I know you're on vacation, but I need you here." Coach Jackson paused, he had hooked him well and now just needed to reel him in. "So, can I count on you to be here? You're the defensive coordinator." He emphasized this last part.

His wife flashed through his mind, but was quickly submerged by thoughts of football. The decision seemed to have already been made. He hesitated for only a moment. "Yeah, I'll be there. See you at noon tomorrow." Blake hung up the phone. Stepping away from the polished wood of the front desk, he felt a sense of excitement. This was soon replaced by the realization that he had to break the news to April.

Walking towards April, the hot summer sun gleaming off of her freshly oiled legs, Blake admired her body. She had already regained her sexy, attractive body from the pregnancy nine months earlier. Slightly browning in the high altitude rays, her curves were even more tempting. For a minute he realized how nice it would be to just enjoy each other the rest of the week. Prior to this get away, he couldn't remember the last time they had even enjoyed each other's company for a complete weekend. And now after just three days, they were going to have to shorten this outing. Approaching April he wore a genuine smile this time, but knew her reaction would not be the same.

Blake sat down as casually as possible in the lounge chair next to April. He purposefully sat beside her to avoid receiving her negative reaction head on.

BOOM!!! The slamming of the door and the shaking of the hotel room walls jolted Blake upright from pulling his clothes out of the drawers. He cautiously turned towards the door to see April standing with her hands on her hips, a scowl on her face, and flushed cheeks.

As Blake made eye contact, April tried to keep herself from exploding. To avoid unleashing a tirade, she took a couple of shallow breaths. "This is bullshit!!! You can't leave! I won't let you leave!"

"Keep it down, there are other people in this hotel. There is no need to freak out. Plus, you don't get to tell me what I can or can't do. I'm an adult. I get to decide what I do."

"Okay!!! Then please don't go," she said through clenched teeth. "You promised me this week. I need it. We need it." Her eyes fell to the floor, as if admitting defeat. "Why do you have to go?!" she asked, mustering one last pleading attempt at changing his mind.

"Stop the screaming. There is no need to raise your voice. You need to calm down."

"I don't NEED to do anything!!! The time for calm, rational conversation ended when you walked away from the pool while I was still talking."

"It was more like a lecture."

"I don't care!" Her voice was still loud, but not a scream. "This was our week together, not just your week. It shouldn't have just been your decision on what was going to happen. This is a relationship. There are two people. Input needs to come from both of us. It's not fair that you just get to make the decision."

"There wasn't anything to be decided or discussed. It's my job. I need to be there, so that's that." He continued packing his bag.

"That's all you do now, is your job. You keep telling me as soon as this month is over, we will have more time together. That's all I have heard for the past four years. Now it's worse with this job promotion. I keep thinking you will get more free time, but each year it is less and less. I'm tired of it. When is there going to be any time for me or the family? This is the first chance we have had to get away and be together since we had the baby. We have been planning it for six months. It is what has kept me going through all the hard times. I need you, I need us. This is the only time we have for just the two of us before the season starts and then you are as good as gone." She collapsed onto the king size plush bed under the weight of these last words. "This is hard Blake, harder than I thought it would be."

"I know, honey. We need this job, though. We just got the house. The mortgage payments are not cheap and now we have a child to support. If I'm going to keep this job, I have to make some sacrifices. It will all be worth it in the long run, dear. Plus, we have never been this financially stable." He paused on this last statement thinking it added up to a concise, convincing argument. He looked over at her lying on the bed staring at the ceiling in a trance-like gaze. "If you come home with me tonight, we will still have a few more nights before your parents bring Conner back."

"Well, what else am I going to do? Stay here by myself?"

"All right then, let's get ready to go. I'm going to hop in the shower. While I'm in there, why don't you hurry and pack and then join me in the shower?" He kissed her on the forehead as gently as possible, trying not to revive her anger. Her eyes didn't move while he stood over her.

"I don't want to take a shower." She avoided making eye contact. She didn't want him to think she was okay with the decision to leave.

"Oh, quit being such a boob. Tomorrow I want you to come to dinner at Coach Jackson's house. All the other wives will be there. You will get to hang out with them."

"You know I don't care about that. I don't even like those events. They aren't my type of people. All they do is bitch and moan and talk about their latest shopping spree. I'd rather not."

"You sure are negative towards those ladies. They are so nice to you, just try to be a little more open minded." Blake turned on the water to the shower. "You need to pack up. It's a long drive and I want to get some sleep tonight so that I feel good tomorrow."

As they pulled out of the mountain resort, the air was beginning to cool down with the drop in evening temperature. April sat looking out the window. She didn't want to talk to Blake and she wanted to enjoy the last of the beautiful mountain vistas. The crisp mountain air coming through the window gave her goose bumps. She was still in her shorts and tank top, enough just to cover her swimsuit. The pleasant smell of fresh mountain air mixing with the tanning oil still on her body was enough to soothe her nerves for a moment. She leaned back in the seat and curled her legs up next to her body, turning away from Blake. Feeling the fresh air over her body, she took in the pleasing aroma with a deep breath and let gravity take over her eyelids. There weren't very many clouds in the sky, but she knew a personal storm was coming. She was worried that this tempest would be one that she would have to battle by herself. As she drifted off to sleep, she saw images of old wooden ships being battered by fierce, menacing waves.

Forever Parties

    Charlie didn't really know what he was going to do with the recruit tonight because it was summer and there weren't as many people in town as usual. Since Charlie knew all the guys and would be able to show the recruit a good time Coach Jackson had asked him to be the chaperon for the night. The bars and clubs were eerily silent during the summer months. The only college-age kids around were athletes who stuck around to stay in shape and some of the people from the small town that supported the university. But, he was happy to be getting a free meal and possibly a little extra cash. Dinner was going to be a private BBQ at Coach Jackson's house. To Charlie, this gesture of having the dinner at his own home, demonstrated just how badly Coach Jackson wanted the recruit. Players were usually taken to a nice restaurant with no concern for the price. This was a very personal touch added to try and lure the recruit.

    Because most recruits have other schools that are also offering them scholarships, the purpose of a recruiting trip is to wow the guy so that he will choose your school. Elaborate measures are taken to accomplish this. Recruiting trips may or may not paint an accurate picture of what is in store, but the underlying goal is to show the guy a good time.

    Each player on the team knew what went into making a decision. A young 18 to 20 year old would not want to go to a school for the next five years of what might be the most enjoyable years of his life if it had no party scene or girls to offer. The program, of course, would have to sell its coaches, its facilities, and its academics. But how many seniors in high school or junior college transfers really care about those mundane specifics? The average guy cared most about knowing that their choice of college would be one where they had a good chance of getting laid often, drinking a lot of beer, and having fun. The coaches, facilities, and academics were fairly similar across the board. Only rarely did one school reach above and beyond the other choices.

    Charlie had hosted recruits before. This just meant he was in charge of the recruit for the night, trying to show him a good time, getting him back to his hotel, and making sure he didn't get in too much trouble. Showing a recruit a good time usually meant getting him drunk, introducing him to the team, and getting some girls to flirt or advance a little further with him.

Some of the events were bigger than others. Many times it was just a normal house party where everyone would get shit faced, in particular the recruits, and as many girls as possible were invited. Once everyone had enough drinks to loosen up, each host would parade his recruit around the party introducing him to the players and any girl they passed. If the host knew the girl and she was drunk enough, he might try to talk her into some flirting or at least some innocent chit-chat. Occasionally, one of the team groupies might be talked into sleeping with one of the recruits. If this happened, the guy almost always ended up signing a commitment to become a Puma.

Recruits, whether in high school or junior college, weren't old enough to get into bars. There were always a few bars that would let the guy in without an ID, but this was sketchy so bars were usually avoided with the recruits. Since options of going out were limited, elaborate parties were planned for big recruiting weekends. There were times when recruits for more than one sport, like basketball, women's soccer, and track and field, all came in at the same time. These weekends produced huge parties that would last well into the morning and keep everyone entertained. Guys from each team would get together and arrange them and made sure there was plenty of booze. They might even rent a dance hall and have one of the guys act as the DJ. Whatever it was, it was always a happening scene.

Strippers had even been arranged a few times. These were usually just girls from around the university who were looking for an easy way to make some money, wanted to try it, or wanted to be part of the "in" crowd with the team. It was never a lot of money and there were even girls who would do it for free if they thought there was a chance that they would get laid by one of the guys they liked on the team. With a room full of drunk guys and a naked girl the situation could easily grow sleazy. Guys would end up touching and grabbing anywhere they wanted. The strange thing to Charlie was that the girl seemed to enjoy it. He also realized later on that she just might have been too scared to protest the unwanted interest. Fortunately, the times when Charlie had been around and the girl wanted things to stop the guys would back off and let her leave. Since he had been with the Puma there had been no reports of rape, or at least not any reported from the events he knew about.

Coaches always try to act like this kind of behavior doesn't happen on their team, but it happens on all teams. They don't ask questions because they don't want to know the answers. They don't even make demands, the only piece of advice given to a host is, "be careful." As long as nobody is arrested or ends up in the hospital, everything is fine. Many of the coaches would even make jokes about the parties to Charlie. At dinner they would tell him and the recruits to drink plenty of water in order to be hydrated for the upcoming big night out. The coaches' policy matched the armed forces at the time, "don't ask, don't tell."

After all, what else should coaches expect when they send a host out with $40.00 of NCAA approved money for a night of entertainment without any requirements or stipulations about what goes on for the evening or with the money? $40.00 a night for one person can't buy much more than booze and some snacks. Hosts would organize these parties and buy alcohol in large quantities in order to get the most out of the small amount of money they had been given. Hosts didn't tell the recruits how much money they were given for the night and recruits didn't realize that a certain amount had been given to the host for their night of enjoyment. Hosts tried to get by without spending all of the $40.00. Being able to pocket even $5.00 meant an extra night out at McDonald's.

Since it was summer and it was last minute there weren't any plans for a big party. He wasn't even sure of who was around this weekend. Getting drunk and playing cards with some of the guys didn't sound bad to Charlie. Hopefully this guy was okay with that. But, he didn't know much about this recruit. Right now he couldn't even remember his name. Oh well, a quiet night meant he might be able to keep some of the $40.00 for the night's entertainment.

Charlie pushed the knob, pulled open the heavy creaky door, and climbed into his truck. *I should get some WD-40* he thought to himself and realized he had been saying this for the past couple of months. He drove an old 70s Chevy truck. The kind that was built to last. When this thing got in an accident, the other car was the only one with any damage. It puttered along and went through gas almost as fast as he could fill it up. The inside leather upholstery was worn with seams running along the width of the car. The cracked leather mixed with stale sweat gave the cab a mildew smell that felt comfortable and reminded him of working with his father and grandfather when he was young. It had been his grandfather's truck and when he passed away, it had been handed down to Charlie. He drove it for a year in high school and took it with him to college.

Charlie pulled out onto the almost-deserted road and headed for the recruiting dinner at Coach Jackson's house. As he rolled along in his cozy truck, Charlie smiled, thinking back to his recruiting trip.

The drive from Charlie's home town to his college town was only about four hours, three and a half in a fast car. He had thought that one of the coaches would pick him up and drive him up for the trip, but the head coach had insisted on him flying. With security and wait time at the airport, the trip had taken almost the same amount of time as driving. But Charlie easily acquiesced when Coach Jackson insisted.

Charlie had flown up after school on a Friday afternoon and came back on Sunday afternoon. In between, the trip was kind of a blurry haze of first class treatment. The dinners were at the nicest restaurants in town with appetizers, soft drinks (alcohol would come later), and dessert ordered with each meal. He was full the entire weekend. They had breakfast, lunch, dinner, and snacks in between. He usually only ate that much food during the holidays. He met all of the coaches, the support staff, checked out all the football facilities, and toured the campus. What stuck out most to Charlie were the parties at night.

He was an eighteen year old high school senior and had been to plenty of parties, but the college parties were in another league. It was a busy recruiting weekend, so the team had organized a special party. After dinner on Friday night, Charlie and the other recruits were chauffeured by their hosts. They went over to a house where a few of the guys from the team lived. As soon as they arrived, they sat down at the kitchen table and had beers lined up in front of them.

Charlie's host, Deron, a stout, solid built middle linebacker, opened the fridge and pulled out a bottle of Jagermeister. Deron, along with three other team members lived there. "This will help get you guys loosened up and get the party started. Chad and the other guys have gone to get the kegs. They will be back soon. When they get back we will tap the kegs and the rest of the party should be here in a couple of hours." Deron lined the counter with as many shot glasses as he could find. "You guys need to learn how to drink if you are going to play college football. No pussies allowed on this team." Charlie and the other guys looked at each other sheepishly and shrugged their shoulders. They weren't going to say no. They all came on this trip knowing they would party and expecting to get wasted.

One of the recruits at the opposite end of the table piped up, "Sounds good, let's get it on."

Deron smiled and passed out the grungy looking shot glasses filled with brown fiery liquid. "That's what I like to hear, but you still ain't shit. We will see if you can handle this college scene." He raised his glass. "Here's to a wild night. Bottoms up, boys." They all raised their glasses and followed Deron's lead in downing the alcohol.

That was the beginning of an inebriation fest. After a shot, Charlie and the other recruits began to loosen up. They had a couple more shots and a few beers playing a beer drinking dice game. All of this was before the kegs showed up. A large part of the football team arrived with the kegs and all the recruits did the introduction rounds. As soon as the kegs were tapped, Charlie and the recruits were roped into doing keg stands.

Charlie volunteered to go first. He was already feeling tipsy and on top of the world, nothing could phase him at this point. A couple of the lineman grabbed his feet and lifted him upside down and over the top of the keg. He sucked as much beer as his stomach could hold and as it began to flow back the opposite way Charlie kicked to be let down. He woozily stood up and felt his head spin and the beer almost come back up, but he held it down and let out a big burp. Some of the players shouted encouragement and the others close to him gave him high fives. Before he even had his bearings, the next recruit made his way up to the keg, moving Charlie out of the way so that he could be the next to show these college guys that he wasn't out of his league.

Deron grabbed Charlie and took him out of the garage and back into the house. He handed him a plastic cup full of keg beer, put his arm around him, and congratulated him, "Good job big man, maybe you're not such a puss after all," and punched him jokingly in the arm.

Charlie bumped with his shoulder and shot back, "I can handle this shit all night long."

"All right dude, just don't get sick or I will be in shit tomorrow with the coaches."

"I am totally fine," Charlie retorted, but knew that he had to slow down or it would be an ugly night.

"Good, follow me. I want you to meet some people." Deron led him into the house where the party had begun. The previously empty house was now full of people. They had to squirm through the crowd. Deron took Charlie over to a group of young college co-eds. Charlie couldn't help but check out all of them and he tried not to stare too long. Deron introduced Charlie to the first one as his girlfriend, Amanda. Amanda was with her other friends who she introduced to Charlie. After they had been introduced, he asked the girls to look after Charlie and introduce him around. He had to look after some of the other recruits and would be back soon.

Charlie chatted with the group of beautiful college babes for a while. He was glad the movies hadn't lied about college women. Amanda later took him around and introduced him to a seemingly endless supply of hot girls. Deron seemed to appear on cue with a fresh beer every time Charlie's was gone. As Charlie continued to drink, he got more and more friendly. He was talking shit and laughing it up with the other recruits and football players and trying to flirt with the college girls. Just the thought of flirting with a college girl made him smile inside. The parties and the girls back home wouldn't seem the same after this weekend.

Charlie had no idea what time it was, but sometime in the early morning, the party began to thin out. He was talking to some girl that Amanda had introduced him to whose name he couldn't remember. He was looking at her mouth and couldn't quite make out the words, it seemed like a gargled line of noise. Realizing that the time for acting cool had long since passed, he knew that if he didn't sit down soon he might do something to embarrass himself. He began to look for an escape route. Behind her in the now empty TV room Charlie noticed the couch.

"Sssskuss me, I ha to si daun." He stepped around her and headed for the couch. When he reached it he spun around and plopped down. The couch felt more comfortable than he had imagined. He looked around and noticed he was the only one in the room. The only thing he could hear was noise from a conversation in the kitchen. Even the garage was quiet now. He closed his eyes for a moment and felt the earth spinning underneath him. *Holy shit, I am fucking wasted*, he thought to himself. He relaxed and drifted into a dreamless sleep.

The next morning he woke up face down on the bed in his hotel room. His raging headache and stretched bladder forced him up and into the bathroom. He emptied his bladder and chugged a few glasses of water from the facet. He looked at the clock and was thankful it was only seven o'clock. He wasn't being picked up until nine thirty. He needed more rest. As he crashed on the bed again, he tried to remember how he got back to the room.

He vaguely remembered Deron waking him up and getting him out to the car. He was in and out of sleep on the drive to the hotel and had stumbled back to his room. He just hoped that he hadn't said or done anything stupid on the drive. Oh well, he thought, I am sure the other recruits were just as bad as I was. He remembered seeing one of them throwing up during the party. *At least I wasn't a puss like that idiot,* he thought to himself before he drifted off again.

The next night of the recruiting trip was even more unexpected than the first. Deron picked Charlie up after dinner and took him to an apartment where one of the players lived. "We will have something a little bit different for you tonight," Deron blurted out as they walked into the apartment building.

They walked up a short flight of stairs and down a dimly light hall with carpet that needed to be steam cleaned. Deron stopped at the end of the hallway and knocked on the door. A muffled, "Come in," could be heard from the other side of the door. He flung open the door and Charlie followed him in. The apartment looked like a typical college bachelor pad. The living room was decorated with posters thumb tacked to the wall and the two couches faced the TV, which had a video game console hooked up to the front.

They made their way through the square living room and into the kitchen. There were four guys sitting around a circular table and one girl. Deron introduced him to everyone, pulled out two more chairs, and they squeezed around the table. Although Charlie still had a headache, he wasn't going to turn down any alcohol.

Some of the guys asked Charlie the usual questions about his trip so far. While they were making small talk, Deron slipped into the kitchen and made a whiskey and Coke for himself and Charlie. Charlie kept up the chit chat with Shane, the guy next to him, until Deron got back. The first drink almost burned his throat. It was so strong that he couldn't ignore it. He choked down the swallow and blurted out a cough. The table laughed and Deron patted him on the back commenting, "Don't worry, man. You will get used to college life soon."

After Charlie forced down the first drink, his hangover had been cured and he felt comfortable. They played cards for a while, talking shit, and hanging out. Charlie tried not to stare at the girl across from him. She was the only girl and she was gorgeous. She had big round eyes with lashes that looked fake. Her smile lightened up the table every time she laughed. Her facial structure looked like it had been chiseled by an artist. She wore a halter top that showed off her toned upper body and had the slightest bit of perfume that completed the seduction. She dressed to be noticed, hoping for turned heads and double takes.

After a half dozen hands, the player sitting next to the girl, whose name he later learned was Tierra, whispered something to her. She gave him a seductive look and said out loud, "You are going to have to feed me a few more drinks and will have to hook Rachel up with some booze to loosen her up, too. I will go get her, though. Have drinks ready for both of us and we will get this party started soon." In no hurry, she walked around the table and out of the kitchen. Charlie had to make an effort not to stare at her. A moment later the door opened and shut right away.

He didn't know it at the time, but Charlie would learn later on that she had just gone down the hall to her apartment to change and get her roommate. She was one of those girls who liked to hang around the football team. She wasn't ever really someone's girlfriend, but she was always around. There were a few of these girls and if someone was looking for an easy score, these were the girls that came to mind.

Charlie never fully understood why these girls were so interested in the team but he guessed it was because they liked the attention. Most of them weren't very cute, but this girl was an exception. That is why her actions were even more of an enigma to Charlie. She could get attention from any group she decided to be with, but for some reason she chose the football team. He would see her around the next year when he came to school. He would smile unabashedly and make small talk with her. In spite of her reputation and actions, Charlie still felt intimidated by her beauty. He felt like she was in another league, she certainly didn't belong in the groupie crowd.

Deron turned and flashed a knowing smile at Charlie. The party continued like nothing had changed. About half an hour later, Charlie heard the door to the apartment open again. Tierra walked into the kitchen with someone following her. She introduced the other girl as Rachel. The entire kitchen checked them both out from top to bottom. Nobody could hide their lustful eyes. They had both applied fresh make up, were wearing red stilettos, and long coats. Everyone crowded together a little more, making room for the two knockouts to sit at the table. Charlie was awestruck. The reality of the situation hit him. His heart started beating and he began to feel a yearning in his loins.

He sat back down with a grin and a newfound sense of excitement for the night.

They all had a couple more drinks. The card game died down somewhat. A couple of the guys kept playing, while most of the table broke off into small conversations. Mostly guys were just trying to hit on the two ladies who were obviously there for more than just drinks. Charlie stuck to the game, not feeling comfortable enough to chit chat with anyone at the table. Each time Charlie looked up from his cards, he stared at Tierra, her shiny red lipstick and graceful features made her impossible to ignore.

After Tierra finished her second drink, she looked at Rachel and winked. Rachel smiled back and nodded. Tierra again whispered to the guy sitting next to her. Charlie tried to remember the guy's name. It had been the guy who lived at the apartment, but Charlie had lost the name somewhere in the web of memories and names stored in his head. Tierra pulled away from the guy's ear wearing a secretive grin and excused Rachel and herself from the table.

As soon as the bathroom door down the hall closed, the rest of the guys got up from the table as if on cue. It seemed like they all had known what was in store for the night, but didn't want to let Charlie in on the secret. As the rest of the guys got up, Charlie hesitated. Deron patted him on the shoulder, "Just grab your chair bro and follow me." Charlie did as he was told.

As they walked into the living room, the couches were being pushed against the walls. Four others besides Deron and Charlie lined their chairs up against the wall across from and next to the couches. Shane turned off the lights, except for the small table lamp in the corner. Someone else turned on some dance music. Charlie just looked around in stunned silence. He still couldn't believe where he was and what he was seeing.

Half way through the first song, the girls made their appearance. They walked confidently and forcefully to the center of the room. They were only wearing their stilettos with lingerie that matched. Charlie's mouth dropped open, this seemed too good to be real. He felt like he was in a movie. He looked over at Deron who was smiling from ear to ear. Charlie took a big swig from his drink and got comfortable.

     The two girls started gyrating with each other in the middle of the room to the beat of the music. "Hell yeah," someone shouted out. The light was dim and all that could be seen were shadows and figures. Charlie couldn't make out anyone's face, even the girls' faces were hard to discern. "You two are fucking HOT!!!" "Shit yeah, show us your stuff." Cat calls came from all over the room. The girls turned towards different areas of the room and grooved to the music rubbing themselves up and down for added effect.

  Into the third or fourth song, it was hard to keep track with the distraction of these beautiful half naked girls in front of him and the booze running through his bloodstream, things got even more hot and heavy. All of a sudden Tierra started giving a lap dance to one of the guys. Charlie gawked at this scene, feeling excited, and half wishing she was doing it to him instead.

  With startling quickness, Charlie's head was jerked forward. Rachel was standing in front of him holding his chin. "Hey high school man, you think you can handle this?" Charlie sat staring at her dumbstruck. Before he could say anything, she was on his lap.

  From the side Deron blurted out, "There you go Charlie, live it up man." He stuck out his hand for a high five. Charlie slapped his waiting hand to the dismay of Rachel, who shot Deron a scowl.

  She got over it quickly and began gyrating her hips on Charlie's lap. Charlie didn't know what to do, so he just sat there looking at all the skin in front of him and tried not to drool. Back home he had had a couple of girlfriends, but none of them compared to these two girls. Their bodies were lean with curves in all the right places, tits and ass that no high school girl could match.

  Suddenly Rachel leaned into Charlie and began whispering in his ear, "I saw you staring at us from the instant we walked in. Do you like what you see?" Charlie just nodded his head, feeling a little dumb and in over his head. She grabbed his right hand and placed it on her boob and started moving it around. "You can touch me if you want." Charlie couldn't hold back the inevitable any more, his blood made a full charge to his midsection. Rachel felt his reaction and began to rub harder on his lap. She looked down at him and grinned, "I knew you would." She placed his other hand on her ass and the rhythm of her hips sped up. The harder he got, the faster she rubbed. He began to let his hands wander a little bit. He rubbed her ass and massaged her nipples. Just as Charlie felt like he might explode, she stood up slowly. "Don't worry big boy, I'm not going far," she said as she moved over to Deron.

Deron welcomed her in and didn't need an invitation to begin feeling her body. The girls made the rounds, giving each guy a lap dance. Charlie had been keeping his eyes on Tierra and could hardly wait for his turn. She plopped right down on Charlie and immediately grabbed his hand. She placed it on the front of her damp panties. Charlie couldn't contain his excitement. His shorts stretched from his bulge. Tierra felt this and kept moving his hand farther and farther. Charlie could feel her swollen lips and thought she would stop, but she kept going. She pushed her panties aside and guided his hand inside her. Charlie couldn't believe what was happening, but didn't want it to stop. She began moving up and down on his finger. She pressed her chest forward into Charlie's face and writhed in pleasure. She let out a moan and pulled herself away from Charlie almost as quickly as she had arrived.

She walked directly over to the guy she had been whispering to at the table. He didn't hesitate in removing her bra. Charlie watched it fall to the floor. When he looked back up, the guy's face was buried in Tierra's chest. His other hand was moving around in her crotch. Charlie looked around the room to find Rachel. In the far corner of the room, she was now giving more than a lap dance to a couple of the guys. Tierra got up and lead the way to the bedroom with the guy whom she was already getting physical with. A crowd was now forming around Rachel.

Charlie began to feel a little uncomfortable and was glad when Deron tapped him on the shoulder and said, "I think this is the time when we should take off." They snuck out the door and drove back to Charlie's hotel in silence.

It was late, Charlie was half drunk, the weekend had been more than he had expected, and he was glad to be calling it a night. As they pulled up to the hotel entrance, Deron asked him if he wanted any snacks or a few beers to take up to the room.

"I'm okay for food, but I might take a couple of beers," Charlie answered.

Deron reached in the back and handed him a half empty case of beer, "This should be enough. I hope you had a good time and I hope to see you back here in the fall, Charlie. This is a great place to play football. The coaching staff is top notch and, as you saw, it is a fantastic place to enjoy your college years."

"Well, it sure was more than expected in that department. This weekend was more wild and crazy than the other trips I went on. I had a great time. Thanks a lot for everything you did this weekend. Playing for the Puma is at the top of my list." Charlie shook Deron's hand and they gave each other a bro hug. "Well, if I am back here in the fall I will have to kick your butt."

"We will have to see about that," Deron said with confidence. "Now have a good sleep and keep us at the top of your list."

Charlie hopped out of the car and made his way to his room. The Puma was at the top of his list after everything he had experienced that weekend. The party scene was just the icing on the cake. Two weeks after his visit to the Puma, Charlie signed a letter of intent to attend school and play football there.

As Charlie turned onto Coach Jackson's street, his mind came back to the present. Looking back on that night of his recruiting trip, Charlie felt lucky nothing bad had happened. During his time at school he had been to a couple more parties like that. Every couple of years there seemed to be another story of a college athlete being accused of rape or sexual harassment. That ruined the players involved and the team. Charlie felt grateful that fate had never steered the Puma team or its members in that direction.

Charlie pulled to a stop a couple of houses down from Coach Jackson's. There were no spots any closer to the house. He realized that the other cars belonged to the entire coaching staff and that they must be really serious about landing this guy if all of them were here just for him.

Gotta Go

"Well, hello." Peggy answered the door with what April thought was fake enthusiasm. "Nice to see you, come on in," the chirpiness of her voice was annoying, but was a welcome relief from the unspoken tension that had been going on between April and Blake while waiting for Peggy to answer the door. April was mad because Blake had dragged her to a dinner being given in honor of the very reason their vacation had ended prematurely. Blake was mad because of April's choice of clothing.

In retaliation for the abrupt end of their vacation, April decided to wear something which showed off her reacquired sexy body. She wore a mini skirt and a tank top that revealed the light tan she had been able to absorb during their short excursion. April knew it was too casual and risqué for the occasion and that was precisely why she wore it. From the time Blake had picked her up at home, unwisely voicing his displeasure, until Peggy had opened the door, no words had been exchanged or looks acknowledged.

"Come in, come in. Blake you know where the guys are." Peggy pointed towards the staircase. "April, join us in the kitchen." Blake and April finally made eye contact as Blake descended the stairs. One had the look of happiness, warmth, and anticipation, while the other contained disappointment and a longing to be somewhere else. Sensing the apprehension, Peggy slipped her arm through April's and guided her towards the kitchen.

During the short walk to the kitchen, Peggy stopped a couple of times to show April new pieces of furniture or decorations. Each time the item seemed like something that could be bought at any home décor shop, but became trendy and cool because it was a brand name sold in a fancy store. Nearing the kitchen, April heard the voices growing louder. To April, it sounded like a bunch of stray cats trying to get attention from each other. The loudest voice would control the floor for the moment. April's sense of dread about the next few hours jumped a notch before turning the corner to the scene that awaited her.

April was greeted by the women, most of whom were sitting around the rectangular table. A few sat at the bar directly behind the table. "Hi April, how nice of you to make it. I know you had to change your plans. That sure was nice of you." April couldn't really tell who, or how many of the ladies, were speaking to her. It seemed to come in unison, shortly followed by a round of nods. A few of the women hugged her and offered compliments on how nice she looked. "You look so nice. One could hardly tell you just had a baby, except for the hips, of course. Those never come back the way they were." Followed by another round of nods, "Ain't that the truth. Before I started having kids…" April's mind trailed away from the conversation. She walked to the rear of the table and took a seat at the only available space.

    Her attention faded in and out of the conversation going on at the table. She looked around at the faces and activity. Peggy and a couple of other women were busy preparing the dishes that would go with dinner. The others chit chatted while occasionally grabbing a vegetable from the platter on the table. April didn't know these ladies very well. They weren't her type of crowd.

    The conversations consisted of talking about the most recent big purchase, how much they loved not having their husbands around all the time, and criticizing someone who wasn't there. April wondered what would be said about her outfit once she wasn't around. It surprised April that no one seemed to mind being practically alone during a large part of the year. It wasn't something she liked and none of these women would talk about the subject with her. They would only tell her how important it was for a wife to support her husband and that they must endure this sacrifice to be a good wife. It drove April crazy.

    April had had a friend that she really liked among the coach's wives. Her name was Kathy. They shared a lot of things in common and allowed each other to vent, sharing their feelings about the other wives and being away from their husbands. The one lady she liked and enjoyed spending time with was not around this year because her husband, Clark, got another job offer, which they accepted. The new coaching job had taken them halfway across the country. Now, for April, these gatherings were just mundane events that she had to endure.

Once the side dishes were finished, Peggy and a select few quietly marched the completed dishes downstairs. This seemed to happen at precise intervals throughout the night. Peggy ran a tight show and there was not any deviating from her plan.

It might have been because of the way she was dressed, but April was not summoned for any of these missions to the basement. Her feelings were not hurt by this lack of inclusion.

When the women sat down to eat, Peggy sat at the head of table. The other end actually had to be shared between two women. She directed the flow and direction of the conversation from her position. Occasionally a party of women would check on the men or take more food and drinks to the dinner going on in the basement.

Throughout the night no mingling took place between the sexes. The men had their area and the women theirs. If something was needed, a runner was sent from one of the groups.

Finally, as the food and daylight disappeared, Coach Jackson ascended the stairs with two young men. April noticed because she hoped it signaled the end of tonight's festivities. He walked the gentlemen into the kitchen to introduce them to the wives. They both seemed very nice. One April recognized as a player she had seen around for a few years, the other she assumed was the recruit. His name slipped out of her mind almost as fast as it had gone in. After saying a quick hello, Coach Jackson showed the two to the door. After saying goodbye Coach Jackson seemed to loiter a bit before finally closing the door.

Sensing her chance, April made her way around the table and into the living room in order to catch Coach Jackson before he went downstairs again. As she did this, she received cold, confused, shocked stares from the women at the table. It was as if she were violating some unwritten rule, a wife shouldn't interrupt the men in the middle of their important dealings. As Coach Jackson made his way for the stairway, April, as bold as possible, called out, "Uh…Grant."

He quickly turned and upon seeing it was April he didn't even try to hide his shock. "Oh!? Yes, what is it Mrs. Jones?"

"I need to speak with Blake. Will you ask him to come up, please?"

"Sure, I will." He looked at her like he was hoping for a reason. April didn't give into his prying body language. She just looked him in the eyes and didn't offer any more details. After a moment of silence, "I'll send him right up," he let her know as he began making his way down the first stair.

April didn't want to receive any more menacing looks from the women, so she waited in the quiet of the living room. After a few moments, Blake showed up with a harried look on his face. "Is everything okay? Jim said this was important."

"Oh, everything is fine. He just wants it to be important in order to let you leave for a minute. It's nothing just that I want to go."

"Now!?"

"Yeah, now!"

"Calm down, calm down. There is no reason to get excited. Why don't you relax with the ladies for a little bit. I have a few things we need to talk over with everyone before we can go."

April took a deep breath and tried to remain calm. She had to keep her voice low, she knew everything she said would be gossip for the next few weeks. "This wasn't my choice to come. I want to go home now. I don't think anymore needs to be said right now." April gave him a powerful, determined look that finished her thought.

"Okay…okay. Here are the keys, you go ahead. I will get one of the guys to drop me off when we are done." Blake handed her the keys.

April looked at him with bewilderment. "You're joking, right?"

"No, I have to stay for a while," Blake answered, straight faced.

April shook her head and turned away. "See you at home," she said with her back turned.

"Okay, see you. I love you," Blake said to her back before returning to the basement.

April made her way back to the kitchen and standing next to Peggy's chair excused herself. "Well, I am going to go now. Thanks for the nice evening. See you all later," she said avoiding eye contact.

Peggy moved to stand up. "Oh, no, no." April blocked her from moving away from the table. "I will show myself out. Good night ladies and thanks again." April turned and without hesitating walked to the front door and out to their car. She drove home by herself in the fast approaching darkness of twilight.

Recruit

    Upon arriving at Coach Jackson's house, Charlie was cordially welcomed at the door by Mrs. Jackson. She was a tall, pretty woman, the type that was never seen without make up and fashionable clothes on. Charlie couldn't remember her first name, so he always stuck to Mrs. Jackson. This seemed to be fine by her, she liked to be in the background, living her own life, doing her own thing, but supported (at least financially) by her husband. They seemed to have a fine relationship, but nobody really knew because there were never any public displays of affection between the two.

    They lived by themselves and hadn't ever had kids. Charlie and the rest of the team had no idea how hard they had tried earlier in their marriage to become pregnant, without success. It was something Coach Jackson kept hidden in his bag of dark secrets. She was loyal and so was he, but to Charlie the whole thing seemed like more of a business relationship than a personal relationship.

    The house was far too big for two people and was as much a status symbol as anything else. The inside of the house was exquisitely decorated with everything in its designated spot. Charlie knew Coach and Mrs. Jackson didn't get to see each other a lot. Coach Jackson was always at the football office and Mrs. Jackson didn't work, so he wondered if keeping the house clean and tidy was what she did with most of her time.

    After the obligatory pleasantries, Charlie was shown to the top of the stairs that descended to the plush basement. He remembered that he needed to ask about the recruit's name. "Mrs. Jackson, I forgot the recruit's name. Do you know his name?"

    "Of course I do," she replied with too much courtesy. "His name is Trevor." She gave him a wide smile.

    While standing at the top of the stairs during this brief exchange, Charlie saw the group of chattering wives tucked away around the table in the kitchen. It seemed that most of the wives were here tonight. Like Mrs. Jackson, he had met them all, but could not remember their first names. Plus, he didn't talk to them enough or see them for more than a moment or two at functions like this. He gave a quick wave and hello to the group of women before descending the stairs. One of the strange things Charlie had noticed at these gatherings was the separation of the sexes. It didn't matter what event it was, the guys (coaches) were in one group and the gals (wives) were in another group. Interaction and mingling was done only on a perfunctory level. It was as if the guys thought that football was too much for the gals, or vice versa. Charlie had been here a few times and knew where to find the guys in the basement, so he felt comfortable walking through the house by himself.

When he got to the TV room, Charlie was warmly greeted by the coaches. They all said hello and he was lead to the recruit by the first coach who shook his hand, Coach Lider.

"Hey Charlie." Coach Lider put his hand on his lower back to guide him towards the big lounge chair that was the center of everyone's attention. The lounge chair was in the best spot to view the basketball game on the big screen TV. There was a cooler next to the chair filled with a variety of drinks and a small table above the cooler with bowls of different snacks. Fold out chairs were pulled close to Trevor and a couple of sofas almost framed the chair as if it were the head of a table. "Let me introduce you to Trevor."

Coach Jackson saw Charlie approaching and offered his chair to Charlie. He situated the chair a little bit closer to Trevor. "Hi Charlie, go ahead and sit here," he said while shaking Charlie's hand and making room for Charlie to sit down. Coach Jackson was anxious to let Charlie sit next to Trevor. He had talked to Trevor for long enough, it was time for one of his peers to pick up the conversation.

Before sitting down, Charlie introduced himself to Trevor, extending his hand. "Hi, I'm Charlie."

"Hey, I'm Trevor. Nice to meet you." He stood up politely for a moment before sitting back down and grabbing his opened Coke can again.

Charlie made small talk, asking plenty of questions and got to know the basics about Trevor. This lasted about ten minutes before they were interrupted by another of the coaches who asked Charlie if he could sit next to Trevor. Charlie gave up his spot, wandered around the room saying hello to the rest of the coaches, and looked for something to drink. With a handful of snacks and an unopened pop, Charlie took a seat on one of the sofas next to some of the coaches and checked out what was going on with the game. He was kind of paying attention to the NBA playoffs, but he didn't care who won.

At what seemed like predetermined intervals, the coaches took turns sitting next to Trevor, introducing themselves to him. As the coaches were winding down their personal introductions to Trevor, the wives brought down a parade of salads and entrees. They set them on the long fold out table that had been set up for the night at the back of the room. They were very unobtrusive, barely noticed, and hardly acknowledged.

On cue, Coach Jenkins, the graduate assistant relegated to the lower duties, walked in with two plates stacked full of thick, steaming, juicy steaks. He set them down on the table with the other enticing food dishes. It was quite a spread; green salad, pasta salad, baked beans, fruit salad, baked potatoes, creamy casseroles, rolls, and of course steaks. Charlie felt a grumble in his stomach and drool start to form in his mouth. Everyone sat down and started filling their plates. Coach Jackson and Charlie were on each side of Trevor. Coach Jackson made sure that Trevor got to choose the steak he wanted before passing the plate down the line.

The dinner passed in relative quiet, except for the noise coming from the basketball game. *It was funny how food seemed to make people quiet,* Charlie pondered. As stomachs filled, the room grew even more mellow and relaxed with everyone leaning back into their chair. It was a feast. The plates that each of them had were more like platters. Charlie could barely finish the first plate. Despite egging on from the coaches, Trevor also stuck to just one plate. The first coaches to finish began clearing the plates and kept an eye on Trevor, who when he was finished had his plate immediately cleared.

After dinner the atmosphere was much more casual. The coaches were mingling, even allowing Trevor to be by himself for moment. Without all the formality, Charlie felt more comfortable approaching Trevor and chatting with him. They stayed until the end of the game, forcing some dessert down despite their bloated stomachs.

During the evening while off to the side and out of sight, Charlie had been given the money for the night and signed a legal form saying the money was for entertaining the recruit only. After getting the go ahead from Coach Jackson, Charlie asked Trevor if he was ready to go.

This caused a melee. Charlie received a casual group good bye, while each coach personally came up to say good bye and shake Trevor's hand. Coach Jackson escorted the two up the stairs and to the front door, stopping for a brief hello to the wives. Trevor and Charlie both thanked the women for the dinner and told them how tasty it was. At the front door, Coach Jackson bid them farewell. "See you in the hotel lobby at 9:00 tomorrow morning, Trevor?"

"Yeah, I'll be there. I will have to call the front desk for a wakeup call so that I don't sleep in, though."

"Okay, don't have too much fun tonight. We have a lot to go over and a lot for you to see tomorrow. Charlie….have a good time tonight and be safe. Thanks for coming. See you guys later." Coach Jackson's silhouetted figure remained in front of the open door until Charlie and Trevor had driven down the street and out of sight.

Since Charlie found out about the recruit last night, the options for entertainment were limited. Most of the football guys were back in town for summer training after being given two weeks to go home and visit. Summer training wasn't mandatory under NCAA rules, but it was HIGHLY recommended. Since a good chunk of the team was back, Charlie knew that he could call some of the guys and they would come over to Johnny's house and make tonight at least somewhat entertaining. Charlie was also trying to come up with a scheme so that he might not have to spend very much of the money he had been allocated for the night. Anything left over from the night, he got to keep. Since they had already eaten, he wouldn't have to spend any money on food. Maybe a few snacks after they were drunk, but that was it.

He had spoken to Johnny before dinner and told him that he would be stopping by with the recruit. On the way over, they stopped and bought some beer. Charlie had just turned 22, but

Trevor, being just out of high school, wasn't drinking age which meant that the bar scene would be a stretch. Luckily Trevor didn't seem to mind just hanging out tonight. He was full, tired, and wanted to relax after being bombarded by the coaches all evening. It had been even more stressful than normal tonight because he was the only recruit.

The night was spent hanging out at Johnny's grungy apartment. After a few beers had gone down and their stomachs loosened up, they moved from the small TV room into the kitchen where they could play cards and drinking games. There was no chance of a full-on party on this night, but Charlie called the guys who were in town while Johnny and Trevor chatted.

Some of them came over and hung out for the night, while some others just stopped by to say hello. Seeing some girls seemed like a necessity, so Charlie and Johnny called the girls they knew who were still in town for the summer and asked them to come over with friends, if possible. They even promised free booze if they came over. Trevor probably wasn't going to get any action tonight, but as long as some hot girls showed up for at least an appearance, he would know that there would be plenty of chances if he were to make this his university.

Enough people showed up that Trevor and everyone else could mingle about the now cramped apartment. By the time the beer was gone, Trevor was ready to go to his hotel room and crash. Charlie had tried to take it easy on the beer, but was still not in the best shape to be driving. He dropped Trevor off and made it back home safely. As he plopped into bed he looked at his clock, it was two o'clock. The night had turned out surprisingly well. Trevor was a cool guy, one Charlie liked and would love to have on the team. It seemed like Trevor had had a fun time. Most importantly, he had gotten drunk and met some cute girls.

Charlie had talked to Trevor as much as he could that night, a lot considering they had just met that evening. He had tried to do his best sales job of college life there and of the Puma team itself. Apparently, it was enough because, less than a week later, Trevor signed with the Puma.

Young Love

It was the time of year when air conditioners had to be running for a comfortable sleep, when cups full of iced tea had condensation on them after only a few minutes. It was the time of year to be outside by the lake or in the mountains and the only sensible place to cook was the porch with the barbeque.

On this hot summer afternoon April felt elated with Blake around. She stared at him while he was working on the computer. Conner was taking a nap and the house was quiet. These past few weeks it had been a regular occurrence to have some free time and for Blake to be home for more than just a couple of hours in the evening. This made April feel okay about everything. Watching him work, she lost herself in the moment, feeling a connection again.

Blake and April had been together since they were in college. When they were dating and in their first years of marriage, it seemed like they would be together forever. It was what April had dreamed of since she was a little girl. She could even remember the first time they met. Her mind drifted back to that memory.

On a warm day in March, with the first signs of spring starting to show itself, April had decided to eat outside. She liked to eat her lunch on campus and try to get some studying in while she was eating. On this day she was alone because her friends had decided to go back and catch a nap between classes after the big party the previous night.

April was sitting right outside the exit to the outdoor patio and could clearly see anyone who might walk in and buy their lunch at the main cafeteria. As if on cue, she looked up at the same time a guy she had a crush on walked into the cafeteria. She did not know his name, but had seen him around campus and always tried to attract his attention. They had smiled and said hello to each other, but never had a chance to officially meet. Acknowledging the warm weather, he was wearing a short sleeve, sky blue golf shirt with a pair of khaki cargo pants. Watching him walk through the cafeteria, stopping at different stations to construct his lunch, April's eyes revealed her interest. She knew he thought she was cute, he always smiled when he saw her and got that little sparkle in his eye. She really thought he was a good looking young stud. As he got to the cashier with April still eyeing him, she began to hope that he would decide to sit outside today. Trying to send telepathic messages she repeated, *It is a beautiful day. You want to come eat outside. When you come outside you will notice me and ask to join me for lunch*, until he began to approach the door.

Oh shit, she thought, *it worked, it worked! Okay be cool. Act like you haven't been staring at him. Just look up as he is about to walk by, and say a casual hello. Make sure to give him your best smile and maybe fling your hair a little.*

As Blake opened the door and made his way outside, April was looking at her books, trying to pretend she was studying something very important. Scanning the small patio, Blake found a group of empty tables near the back of the patio. Walking deliberately, he headed for the back when he noticed a cute brunette directly in his path, intently studying. He hoped it was this girl he had seen around campus and wanted to talk to, but hadn't had the opportunity yet. He didn't know her name, so he felt weird just saying, "hey you," and starting up a conversation. So as he walked by the table he slowed down, hoping she would look up at him.

Just as he was approaching her table, April looked up with the sexiest smile she could muster. Immediately making eye contact, each of their faces broke into a full grin. Acting as casual and calm as possible, April said, "Hello", trying to sound interested and show that she was alone at this big table.

Blake reminded himself to remain calm and cool before saying, "Hi," and scanning the patio, as if he were looking for somebody. Bringing his eyes back to her he made up the first thing that came to his mind. "Well, my friends aren't here. I was supposed to meet them. I see that you are alone, do you mind if I join you?"

With her heart racing, April's first thought was, *Oh, yeah! It worked! Yes, please join me. Just kiss me right here. This stuff is boring. I want you to sit down right now. I have been waiting for this moment.* Regaining her composure, she tried not to display her complete desire for him and replied back,

"Sure, that would be fine. Let me just move some of this stuff out of the way."

Moving her books and binders out of the way, Blake sat down at the opposite side of the table. He tried to start out being a little bit of a charmer. "I have seen you around a few times and have been wanting to say hello to you, but I haven't had a chance. I was just hoping you would be available when we finally met. My name is Blake, what's yours?"

Turning red from the obvious pick up line, April extended her hand, "My name is April. I have been wanting to meet you, too. I was hoping it would be sooner rather than later."

Their lunch lasted for well over an hour, with the two of them talking like they were old friends. They seemed to have a lot in common and many of the same interests. Exchanging phone numbers, they both knew they wanted to stay in contact. It only took two more days before their first official date and everything moved steadily from that point on.

Reveling in this sweet memory, April forgot about all the hard things that had been happening lately. Being completely wrapped up in these feelings of love, she moved towards Blake at the computer terminal. He was surprised when she reached out to touch him. He looked up and saw a burning, passionate look in her eyes. Before he even had time to save his work, April's lips were next to his, moving back and forth, pulsating with desire. Feeling the spontaneity of the moment, Blake let his work go and reciprocated her advances. Soon they were intertwined with each other's bodies, connecting in a way that seemed to be happening with less frequency over the past few years.

Quandary

    After his workout, Charlie made the short walk over to the coaches' office. He had been asked to come over and talk to the secretary about a chance to make some extra money. Although he had taken a quick shower, he was still sweating. It had been a typical summer workout and his body still hadn't had time to completely cool down. He felt the tension and aching of the week's workouts. It was Friday, which means party time. This past week had been the peak of the summer workouts. It would now start slowing down in preparation for the approaching season. He and his teammates had been pushing their bodies to the limit, lifting more and running harder than they had thought possible. Getting through each day was an accomplishment.

    It's possible that the workouts weren't any harder than the previous year's, but they sure seemed like it. Maybe Charlie and the other players had just mentally blocked out their experience from the previous summer. They probably had to do this, one didn't want to remember the torture endured or it would be tougher to come back and do it again. By blocking out the memories of last summer, they didn't allow their minds to become too overloaded with pain and suffering, almost like a defense mechanism. This made it seem like this summer's workouts were the penultimate in torture, when in reality, each year the punishment dished out by Jim was probably the same, it was that the methods and techniques varied.

    With purposeful steps, Charlie made his way to the office. The summer air was beginning to grow hot in the early afternoon, but the gentle breeze made the day feel almost perfect. Upon entering, he was immediately greeted by La Dean's warm, genuine smile. La Dean was approaching retirement, in her early 60s. She was a grandmother-like presence for the team, which was badly needed for the testosterone filled program. Her caring and concern for all the players and coaches was easily felt. She had the short curly hairstyle that seemed standard on women from her generation. She dressed conservatively, even in the hot summer months. She had on dress pants today.

"Oh, hi Charlie," she greeted him.

"Hi, La Dean." She liked to be on a first name basis with all the guys.

"How was the workout?" Nobody ever knew if she really liked football, or knew a lot about it. But since she was the head football secretary, she always knew what was going on with the team, more so than most of the coaches.

"All right. I'm glad it's Friday. They sure have been kicking our a…, I mean butts this week." It didn't seem natural to swear in front of La Dean. She seemed pleased that he spared her ears from vulgarity. "If we aren't successful this year, it won't be for a lack of training. But I think all of this will pay off during the season. That's why we do it and put so much effort into it."

"Yeah, you guys sure are working hard. I am excited to see it pay off this season." She tried to sound understanding. "Well, anyway, I won't keep you waiting around. I have a job for tomorrow that I thought you might be interested in. There's a gentleman who needs some work done out at his cabin. He says it is just basic yard work, but he would like two guys from the team. He will pay you and since you will be out there for some time, he will feed you lunch and dinner, too." She paused to allow Charlie a moment. "Is this something you might be interested in?" she asked, looking at him inquisitively and with an air suggesting it wasn't something he should turn down.

Charlie scratched his head, acting as if he needed to give it consideration and to make it seem like he was really thinking. "Yeah, that sounds all right. As long as it's not too early," he said, trying to sound firm and determined.

"No, not too early, and you'll get $15.00 an hour. You don't have to be there until ten. It will take about an hour, so you will have to leave by nine. Is there someone who will go with you that you want to ask, or should I call one of the other guys?"

"Oh, no, no, that's fine." Charlie didn't want to spend his Saturday working with someone who he didn't really like. "I'll ask Johnny. I'm pretty sure he'll go. He doesn't have anything to do. If I can't find anyone, then I'll let you know and you can call someone else."

"Sounds great." Opening up a lower drawer, she bent down under her desk and pulled out a hand drawn map. "Here's how to get to his place. It shouldn't be too hard to find if you've been out to the lake. Do you know how to get out there?"

"Yeah, I've been there before."

"Okay, well let me write down his number in case you get lost and need some directions." She flipped through the big address book on her desk, found the name, and jotted it down. Handing it over to him she said, "His name is Ron, I can't remember his wife's name. They are both very nice. Try to be on time, okay?"

With a grin and a hint of defensiveness, Charlie said, "I know, I know. Thanks La Dean." He moved towards the door. "See you later. Always nice to see you," he added, with a cheesy grin.

Just as Charlie was leaving, La Dean said in a serious, ominous tone looking straight into his eyes, "Have a nice weekend, but DON'T take anything you shouldn't, Charlie," and moved her eyes back to the computer screen to being typing again, as if that was all she was going to say on that subject.

In a quiet voice, more to himself than anyone, Charlie said, "Okay," as he left the office. He thought the last statement from La Dean was a little weird. She was not the type to make demands, offer stern warnings, or be anything other than light hearted. This last comment had been made without any hint of a joke. Charlie let the thought escape his mind by the time he got to his truck.

Just as he was getting to his truck, Johnny was leaving the locker room after showering. "Hey dude, got this job I'm going to do tomorrow. Easy yard work. We will get paid $15.00 an hour and get free food for lunch and dinner. The only bad thing is we need to leave at nine tomorrow morning. I need another person, wanna go?"

"Tomorrow? That is Saturday," Johnny said as if Charlie were insulting him.

"I know, but what the hell else do you have to do?"

"Sleep in!" Johnny replied back with a straight face.

"All right dude. I'm not gonna argue with you. I know you need some extra money and it will be easy cash. If you don't want to do it, I'll ask someone else." Trying to seem confident in his decisiveness, Charlie continued walking towards his truck.

Without moving or turning to face him, Johnny stood still for a moment, weighing his options. He shouted over his shoulder with a half-smile, "All right, I'll go. But you have to fucking drive. Pick me up at my house at nine. You get to see my bright and early Saturday morning face." Without waiting for acknowledgment, Johnny started opening his car door and hesitated before getting in. "Call me later tonight, asshole." He gave him the one finger salute.

Charlie returned the hand gesture. "Okay, dickhead. No need to get grumpy already. It's not Saturday morning yet." Charlie hopped into his truck, feeling his tired legs as he engaged the clutch and turned the key. Johnny blindly waved as he drove by Charlie on his way out of the parking lot. Charlie started his truck and drove home without any concern for time.

With the morning summer air already warming up, Charlie pulled up to Johnny's apartment. The yard looked unusually clean and groomed. Charlie thought that the landlord must have recently paid a visit and done some work around the small complex. He knew it was a little early to be honking on a Saturday morning, but he was lazy and had to wake up before noon on his Saturday, so he did it anyway.

In a couple of minutes, Johnny was in the passenger's seat and they were on their way. Without needing words, Charlie looked at Johnny and saw just how hard this waking up business was. His clothes seemed to be pulled out of a pile without any regard for what was clean or what matched. His disheveled hair, going every direction, was soon covered by a hat. He obviously hadn't taken a shower, but fortunately Charlie could smell toothpaste and wouldn't have to smell his breath all day long. They drove on in silence, exchanging only the basic formalities and using only the minimal number of words necessary for any questions asked and answered.

After a little more than an hour, with rocks crunching under their tires, they pulled into the gravel driveway of the cabin. As they pulled to a stop, a distinguished gentleman was walking forward to greet them. He was a tall man who looked unusually firm and toned for his age. Neatly trimmed grey hair added to his appearance. His personal care and grooming combined with how he carried himself gave off the appearance of wealth. His plain white t-shirt and shorts made them think he would be helping with the work. He approached Charlie first, extending his hand, "Hi, I'm Ron. You must be Charlie." His hand shake was more firm than necessary, his eyes seemed playful and care free.

"Hi, nice to meet you."

Before Charlie had even finished, he walked over to Johnny, once again extending his hand, "Hi and you must be Johnny. Nice to meet you both."

"Yeah, you too," Johnny replied, trying to sound fully alert. He had been dozing off and on during the drive.

"Follow me, there's something I want to get started on before it gets too warm out here." Ron had already turned around and was leading the way. He wasn't moving fast, just with deliberation, not wanting to waste a step. His demeanor and presence had an air of relaxed confidence.

Johnny and Charlie looked at each other a little dumbfounded and began to follow him. As they passed the front entrance, Ron said, "Oh, there is my wife, her name is Allison. You'll be seeing more of her in a little bit," without stopping or slowing down. Charlie and Johnny waved to the cute little face looking up from the sink and peering out the small window.

Ron led them down the small slope of a grassy hill, which ran the length of the cabin. The home had the look of one that belongs in the mountains, it seemed to naturally fit with the surrounding landscape. Its colors were by no means a camouflage, but it seemed to blend in with the grass and countless trees that surrounded it. It was a one story home with space under the house made into a makeshift basement on the slope end of the house.

From this point one looked out on the small bay of the lake less than 50 yards away. The light blue of the lake stretched for miles. Clear of trees from the home to the lake, the yard folded out into dark green grass dotted with flower beds and shrubbery that had been planted with care. Looking out towards the water, mountains towered into the sky at the far end of the lake. More cabins circled the quiet, peaceful bay. Each cabin was laid out equidistant from the other, allowing plenty of privacy.

They each had their own wooden docks built out into the water. Some had simple fishing boats tied up, others had fancy, expensive boats. The boat in front of Ron's cabin was one of the latter. Walking out into this display of nature, Charlie paused for a moment noticing the pristine beauty in front of him. This peaceful reflection was soon interrupted by Johnny clearing his throat, ensuring Charlie was close behind him.

In front of them, in stark contrast to the natural surroundings, lay a dirt pile with two shovels propped up and a wheelbarrow; obviously their job. Ron explained that they needed to use the dirt to add some distance to the hastily made boat ramp next to the dock. "One of these years I will be smart and get the ramp made into concrete. Maybe next summer I can have you two up again and have it done right." Walking off, leaving them without any more instruction, he called, "I'll be back to check on you in a little bit. If you need anything just come up and ask Allison." He plodded up the slope without saying anything else.

"We better get paid fucking good for this," Johnny said looking at Charlie with a worried look on his face. "Shoveling dirt on a Saturday isn't my idea of fun."

They weren't left alone for more than an hour before Ron was back to check on them. He came with a tray full of drinks, a folding chair, and wearing a new set of clothes. He approached them from the direction of the house. "So, how's it going boys?" he said, looking away from them while he settled into his folding chair.

With the utmost respect, Charlie answered, "Doing great, sir. Got almost half of the pile done already." Johnny nodded his head and gave a silent grin in response.

"I can see that. You boys sure do work hard. Here, have a drink. Take a break for a minute." Ron extended the drinks towards them while remaining in his chair. "I surely thought it would take longer than that. I guess I forgot who was doing it. Two strong, in shape football players."

Breaking his silence, Johnny chimed in, "Yeah, we know how to work hard." He pushed his shovel into the remaining dirt and sat down next to it. He was covered in dirt. "This sure is a nice place you have. A nice little house and beautiful surroundings. I'm sure you enjoy coming up here."

Nodding his head in agreement and observing the nature around him, Ron's eyes showed a proud sense of achievement. "Thanks…it is a great place. It has taken a lot of work to get it in its present state." Looking out towards the mountains beyond the lake, Ron remained silent for a moment, as if absorbing his reward. Charlie and Johnny looked at each other with a confused look. This guy was getting a little emotional on them. They barely knew him, meeting him for the first time an hour ago. They were also thinking they didn't need a break yet, they were just getting in a groove and had barely broken a sweat. *Oh well*, thought Charlie, *we aren't at football and don't have to be working our asses off the whole time.*

Suddenly Ron spoke up, shattering the silence, "Well, I'm going to get going. I have a few more things to do before the afternoon. I'll leave you the rest of the lemonade." He set the tray down with the full pitcher on top of it and headed back up the hill with the folding chair in tow.

"Thanks Ron, we appreciate it," Charlie shouted after him. Johnny raised his glass in his appreciation.

"Don't work too hard," Ron shouted back at them. "Lunch won't be ready for another hour. Take your time."

Feeling relieved that they didn't need to work hard and fast, having done enough of that during the week, they began to realize this work day wouldn't be too bad. They shot a cheesy grin at each other and finished their lemonades in one swift chug. Charlie walked over to the tray and began refilling his glass. "I told you this wouldn't be bad."

"Yeah, yeah," Johnny held his glass up towards Charlie, "Just give me some more damn lemonade." Johnny couldn't keep his grin hidden. "All right, you were right. As always you are the bomb." Johnny settled onto his patch of dirt. "Let's just chill for a minute."

As Charlie and Johnny were clearing the dirt to grass level, Ron arrived again, with his air of confidence surrounding him. Sauntering down the gentle slope, he couldn't hide his surprise. "Wow, you two sure are hard workers." His eyes didn't leave the spot where the dirt had formerly been.

"Yeah, it really wasn't that bad," Charlie said with a smile. Charlie continued looking at Ron, waiting for the next course of action to become clear. Now gazing at the extended make shift ramp, Ron seemed to be pondering his next move, betraying his sense of feeling unprepared for this situation. Johnny glared at Charlie to prod him towards doing something to end the awkward silence. Feeling comfortable and wanting to see Johnny suffer, Charlie remained silent.

Realizing he had been in a daze, Ron jolted back to the scene in front of him. "Well, that was good timing," he said, acting as if nothing had been amiss. "You are just finishing up and lunch is ready. Follow me and you can get washed up and then we'll eat." As he finished this last sentence, he was already on his way towards the house. Charlie and Johnny let their shovels fall where they were and quickly caught up.

As Charlie was approaching the house, he wondered if Ron was in the beginning stages of dementia. He had seen it happen with his own grandfather and that's what it had been like in the beginning. It had been frustrating for the family to watch his grandpa go down that agonizing slow one way path of memory loss. His grandfather died before it could develop into severe dementia. Although they were sad for the loss of their loved one. Charlie couldn't help thinking that maybe it was best his grandfather had died before he had to suffer from a full blown memory meltdown. He also hoped Ron didn't descend too far into forgetfulness.

After taking their shoes off and taking turns washing their hands, Charlie and Johnny made their way to the table. It was only a vacation home, but it had more amenities than most people's full time homes. The table was oak, stained dark auburn, which was made more vivid by the almost gleaming white contrast of the dining room carpet. The table had service for four spaced evenly apart. It was big enough to have seated eight comfortably. Various dishes filled the middle of the table.

Steam was coming out of the many pots. It reminded Charlie of a feast his family might have when the extended family came over for a holiday. It was enough food for twenty people.

On his way to the table, Charlie looked around the house, taking in the scene. It was nicely decorated and felt like a place where one could sit down and get comfortable. Obviously, a lot was done to make the house look inviting and well decorated. The furniture was all top of the line and seemed to be bought to impress as much as for comfort or practicality. In Charlie's opinion, there were also a few too many ornate knickknacks that were prominently displayed.

Allison anxiously waited on them like a woman who missed having children around to mother. She smelled of perfumed elegance. She always made sure they had enough from each of the dishes laid out on the table. When someone would ask for something, she would scurry to find it and return with a smile and the requested item. Throughout most of the meal she kept the conversation going and asked most of the questions. None of them were thought provoking questions, just polite small talk. Ron would add a comment here and there, but for the most part, he was content to stick to eating and letting Allison entertain the guests.

Every one of the dishes were incredible. It was the work of someone who enjoyed cooking for people and did it on a regular basis. The roast was tender, the mashed potatoes and gravy melted in their mouths. Sweet potatoes, stuffing, baked beans, and macaroni salad were all too good to say "no." Even the steamed vegetables had more flavor than normal. After two plates full of food and barely putting a dent in all the prepared food, Charlie and Johnny had to call it quits. Their stomachs might burst if they had any more to eat. Allison began clearing the table, refusing all offers of help, insisting they all remain seated. Pushing their chairs farther from the table to make room for their bloated stomachs, the three men leaned back and relaxed. Each time Allison came back to clear the table, Charlie and Johnny dished out compliments on the great food and the generous hospitality. The rest of the time the gentlemen were silent, allowing their full energy to be devoted to digesting their grand meal.

After a while Ron spoke up. "Well, to be honest, that is all the work I had planned. I expected it to take most of the day, not just over two hours. I hope you'll stay for a while, though." Looking at both of them with sincerity, he added, "We have dinner planned still and some entertainment for you, as well."

Charlie and Johnny looked at each other, nodded, turned their heads back to Ron, and nodded again. "We're in no hurry, Ron," Charlie replied.

"Good, I have a few more things to get ready on the boat. We can be out on the lake in two hours, which is what we will need after a meal like that. In the meantime, you guys can cruise around on the four wheelers." With more effort than normal, Ron got up. "Come on, let me show you how they work and you can screw around for a while." He stretched the elastic on his designer shorts to ensure they would still fit as he led them through the door again. Sluggishly they followed, giving Allison one more, "Thank you," on their way through the kitchen and outside.

Ron showed them to the shed where there were two four wheelers. They were both brand new and top of the line models. Ron found the keys and two helmets without even looking. Handing the helmets to them, he paused for a moment, sizing them up with a little suspicion. "I'm sure you know how to use these. Just be careful, don't get lost, and be back in a couple of hours. Behind the house, away from the lake, are some good trails. Just stick to those today." He looked them both squarely in the eyes, nodded his approval, and turned to go. It wasn't until Ron had reached his truck that Charlie and Johnny made their next move.

Without a word, Charlie and Johnny moved towards the four wheelers. With big grins they looked at each other and almost at the same time said, "Cool!!!"

For a couple of hours they explored the foothills of the mountains with a childlike enthusiasm. They zipped through untouched fields and splashed through the occasional mud patches. They found their way back to the house, thinking that their fun and playing were done for the day. When they dismounted the four wheelers, they noticed the flashy new boat tied to the dock behind the cabin. They scanned the boat and saw Ron lounging in the bow with a beer in one hand. Once their eyes met his, he waved them over and shouted, "Come on!" Without further hesitation, they walked over and hopped into the boat.

"After some hard work and on a warm afternoon I thought it was a good time to head out on the lake." Ron started the boat before they had time to say anything. He guided the boat out of the small bay into the open water before hitting the throttle. The temperature of the clear afternoon was beginning to rise. Johnny removed his shirt, shoes, and socks to soak in the afternoon rays. Charlie caught these motions out of the corner of his eye and followed his lead. Their tan-lined bodies were now only covered with dirty work shorts and splotches of mud from the ride through the mountains. With the rising strength of the afternoon heat, the clouds had disappeared and the high mountain air was clean and hot. Ron skimmed across the water with no particular destination in mind. Charlie looked back at the rapidly disappearing shore, feeling the air rush past his now naked torso. It had a clean, refreshing smell to it and helped cool down his warming body.

After making it appear like they might just fly to the other side of the lake, Ron laid off the throttle and came to a stop. Before turning around to face the boys, he stripped off his shirt revealing a tanned, grey haired body that many men 20 years his junior would be envious of. Without saying a word, he reached for a latch in the middle of the floor and pulled out a pair of skis and a long rope. "Anyone up for some water skiing?" he asked, looking at them with a glint of excitement and happiness in his eyes.

Charlie and Johnny looked at each other noncommittally for a moment. "I would love to give it a whirl," Charlie said, springing to his feet with excitement.

"All right!!! That's my boy!" Ron said, reaching for a life jacket stuffed into a side compartment.

"It's been a while. So it might take a couple tries for me to get up," Charlie said as he slipped into the life jacket.

Johnny hopped up to grab the skis while Ron tied the rope without an extra thought. Johnny stood behind Charlie on the stern of the boat, waiting for him to jump in so that he could hand him the skis. Charlie pulled the last of the life vest straps tight and jumped in.

The water was a refreshing change of temperature. The perfect relief from the summer afternoon heat. Johnny plopped the skis in a little too far away from Charlie just to piss him off and to make him swim after them. Once Charlie had corralled the skis, he slipped them on and flipped Johnny the bird.

After a few adjustments, Charlie was ready and made his way towards the rope. He held it up to let them know he had found it and Ron nudged the boat forward to get rid of the slack. Charlie watched the boat as the distance grew and began to wonder what Johnny and Ron were talking about. He saw Ron talking and was curious because in the few minutes that it took to pull out the slack Ron had said more to Johnny than he had said all day.

Getting himself in position and being gently pulled by the boat, Charlie gave the thumbs up sign. Ron hit the throttle, giving Charlie the boat's full power. The boat forcefully pulled Charlie and he flexed his knees in a strong bent position, the water flowing around his whole body. Pulling him faster and faster, Charlie knew it was time to get up or be jerked forward by the boat into a face plant. Charlie pushed against the water with all of his leg strength and was suddenly on top of the water.

He smiled, realizing he had gotten up on the first try and adjusted his grip to make sure it wouldn't be a short trip. Feeling the water splashing on his back and neck, Charlie leaned back against the rope and felt the breeze flow across him. He began to glide back and forth with graceful motion.

Staying on the calm water, Charlie allowed his gaze to drift to the mountains passing along his field of vision. He felt at peace for a moment, absorbing the natural beauty around him and flying on top of the water. This feeling of peace gave him a sense of being high and increased self-confidence.

Feeling a little too confident, Charlie leaned back into the wake thinking he could jump it and land safely on the other side. Charlie was jolted back to reality with a slap of sharp pain from slamming into the water after he failed miserably on his attempted jump. He landed awkwardly and crashed sideways rolling violently on top of the water for a moment.

Charlie treaded water and shook his head to regain his bearings. Once his senses were clear again, he was surprised to see how far the boat had pulled away from him. His brow furrowed when he realized the boat wasn't stopping. Soon it was a speck in the distance. When it was about to disappear from his field of vision it finally came to a halt. The boat just seemed to bob up and down without moving again.

After a couple of minutes, Charlie began to get nervous. He didn't know what to do. He kept looking at the boat, expecting it to turn around and come back for him. He could feel himself getting anxious. S*tay calm man, everything is going to be okay. They will be back for you soon. Panicking will only make it worse.* He tried to keep himself calm.

He saw the skis floating away from him and decided that swimming to get them would keep his mind off of his current dire straits. Without any grace he paddled himself over to the skis that seemed farther than he anticipated. Holding onto the skis allowed him to float a little higher in the water and to ease some of his increasing fatigue. He looked around to find the boat, it was still floating on the horizon. *What the fuck are they doing? Why aren't they coming back to get me? I'm getting tired. I have a headache from that fall and it is starting to get cold in this stupid MOTHER FUCKING LAKE!!* "Hey, you idiots, get back here! What the fuck are you doing!!!?" he yelled out, hoping to relieve some of his worry.

He felt his breathing coming in shorter gasps and his heart rate pick up. He knew that he had to calm down. He looked back towards the boat and didn't even know if it was still out on the horizon. He knew he had to save his energy, but at the same time he got even more nervous.

He laid his arms on the skis and leaned backwards, letting the lifejacket float his body up to the surface and gazed up at the deep blue sky. *Just lay like this for a little bit to rest and relax. Get some of your energy back and then reevaluate the situation in a few minutes.* He looked up, watching the clouds tumble across the sky, trying to forget about the desperate situation he was in.

Finally, after what seemed like 30 minutes to Charlie, he heard a boat. He kicked his feet back down and looked towards the sound. He waved one of his arms as high as he could. He saw that they noticed and were coming towards him.

When they finally pulled to a stop next to him, Charlie started to yell. "What the hell have….," but stopped at seeing Johnny's face.

Johnny just shook his head, as if to tell Charlie not to say anything else, or ask about anything. "Sorry man, we had some technical difficulties back there. I will explain it all later." Johnny smiled and nodded at Charlie as if to tell him everything would be okay.

Despite his anger and desire to know what the fuck had gone on out there, Charlie let it go. He knew Johnny would fill him in later, and swam towards the now idling boat. He passed the skis to Johnny and pulled himself onto the boat.

Ron hollered back, "Sorry about that Charlie that was my mistake. Johnny helped me out and everything will be fine. I hope you're okay."

"Yeah, yeah. I'm okay. I'm just glad you're back. I was getting a little cold and worried." Johnny reached into the boat and handed him a towel. Charlie mouthed to him, 'everything okay?' Johnny nodded back and did not seem worried, so Charlie let it go for the time being.

Charlie stood on the stern for a few moments letting his anger and confusion slip away. Nobody bothered him, they seemed to know he needed some quiet. As he was standing there letting the last of the water drip off, Ron got up and produced a big cooler from one of the compartments. By the time Charlie was inside the boat, Ron had cracked open a beer and was already sipping it. It was early, but Charlie and Johnny were never ones to turn down a beer, especially a free one.

Seeing the desire in their eyes, Ron acknowledged their wanting. "I know you guys want some of these and I want to share…but, if you are going to be driving home later, I don't want to give you any. If you got in trouble, Coach Jackson would have my ass. You are both welcome to spend the night. As you saw, we have plenty of room. Then we can all drink our fair share and you can have a good breakfast before leaving. This boat could also use a wash tomorrow after playing around with it today, which you would be paid for. How does that sound?" The thought of free beer and more good food quickly dissipated any of Charlie's lingering negative emotions.

Charlie looked at Johnny. Johnny just shrugged his shoulders. He was a little weirded out by Ron's behavior, but not enough to say no. Charlie knew that if Johnny really had a problem with it he would speak up. Plus, Charlie wanted to stay anyway. It sounded fun to him. Since Johnny didn't offer any resistance, Charlie spoke up for the two of them. "Yeah, that would be great. We don't have anything to get back to tonight. Plus, a little extra money and another great meal are too much to pass up. That okay Johnny?"

"Sounds good to me, dude," Johnny said, already moving for the beer cooler.

For the next twenty minutes they just let the boat sit in the water, bouncing up and down, moving side to side with the movement of the water while drinking their cheap American beer. Soaking up the sun and the scene, they relaxed and each finished two beers in the warming temperature of the afternoon sun. They chatted a little about football, the mountains, and fishing. Nothing too serious or deep. During the next couple of hours, they enjoyed the lake and the surrounding beauty while catching a buzz. Occasionally, one of the two younger guys hopped out for water skiing.

As the afternoon passed they stopped next to a small island, close enough to tie the boat up and get off for a short hike. The five minute climb to the top of the small pinnacle was an easy one, but the view would have been worth an extraordinary effort.

It was a place that Charlie would love to come back to alone to spend some time writing, as it inspired creativeness. Or perhaps return with a lady friend and enjoy each other amongst all the natural surrounding beauty.

It offered a panorama of the lake with mountain peaks dominating the skyline on all sides. The nearest shorelines were dotted with quaint little homes that could have been drawn by an artist. A lone tree was at the top, offering relief and protection from the sun. It seemed to be too perfect a placement to be a random act of nature. In the distance, bare mountains rising above the trees offered an inviting chance of exploration to any adventurous soul.

They enjoyed the scenic spot in silence until each of them had finished another beer. Ron stood up and broke the silence. "I think it's time to get back." On the way back Charlie dozed off, his eyes heavy from a buzz, fatigue, and the sun.

They returned to the newly improved landing dock as the day was turning into evening and the temperature was beginning to fall. It was a great time to be leaving the water and returning to dry land. They took a few extra minutes loading the boat back onto the trailer.

As Ron pulled the boat up to the garage the boys walked towards the house and Charlie motioned to Johnny to slow down. "Hey dude, so what the fuck really happened out there?" He looked at him with total sincerity.

"I don't really know man. After you fell down, I looked back at him and yelled that you had fallen. He didn't stop, so I walked up to him and told him you had fallen, but he only looked at me with far away eyes, like he didn't know who I was, or what was going on, and he kept going. I yelled at him, but he still wouldn't stop. Finally, I had to reach over and pull down the throttle myself. He gave a little resistance at first, but then let me stop the boat." Johnny looked at Charlie shaking his head.

"Holy shit. That's crazy. I'm glad you were in there. It must be dementia. My grandpa had that and would sometimes blank out like that. He seemed to be doing a little bit of that this morning when we were working.

"Yeah, probably something like that. I had to sit there and explain to him what was going on. I just chatted with him for a while and then all of a sudden, he was back to normal. He looked behind us for you and began making his way towards you. It was really weird man, I was glad once you were back in the boat." Johnny pursed his lips with worry. Charlie shook his head and before they could talk more about it Ron was walking up to them from the garage to show them into the house.

Walking into the home, they were greeted with smells that foreshadowed a great feast. Their stomachs were just barely making room from the earlier chow down. Allison graciously offered them fresh towels and a chance to clean up in the bathroom, an opportunity both Johnny and Charlie took. By the time Charlie got out of the bathroom, dinner was on the table and he helped to bring out the last of the dishes.

Once again they were treated to a taste bud sensation. Charlie felt like it was the holiday season. He didn't eat this well, on this regular of a basis, except during the holidays. It was an early treat for Charlie. Only now he wasn't sure how his mother's cooking would compare to Allison's.

After dinner and offers to help clean up, which were refused, the boys went outside and got the fire pit ready to use with Ron. Once the sun went down, the fire was going strong, keeping everyone warm enough that it felt great to be outside. They chatted like they had known each other for more than just a day and enjoyed each other's company. Johnny and Charlie both drank a few too many beers and ate a few too many s'mores. The two single beds in the extra room were more than comfortable after a day spent doing more playing than working.

In the morning, breakfast was another delightful meal. With a touch of a hangover and full stomachs, Charlie and Johnny cleaned the boat with more than the usual sluggishness. It took a little over an hour. They finished before the sun was beginning to heat up the day. They both wanted to get home and had received much more hospitality than they expected. Luckily, Ron didn't make it an issue when they came back in the house after finishing the boat. "Well, is there anything else we can get for you before you take off?" he asked upon their entrance, almost reading their minds.

"Oh, no, not at all. We have had a great time. Thanks for everything, it was very kind of you." Charlie spoke for both of them.

"Sit down for a minute and let me get some money for you." Ron folded his newspaper carefully and walked into the bedroom. Johnny and Charlie sat down on the couch, not getting comfortable. They heard Allison in the kitchen rustling around doing something.

"Thanks so much, Allison, for everything," Charlie volunteered.

"Yeah, thanks. Everything was so delicious. I don't get to eat like that very often," Johnny echoed.

"Oh, are you two leaving? Well you are not getting away that easy." Allison wandered out in her apron with a big smile. She was walking towards the couch, and as she kept getting closer, they could tell she was aiming for a hug. Johnny and Charlie got up and embraced her warmly. "If you ever need a good meal or just want to stop by, feel free. You don't need to come here just to work."

"Thanks a lot, we would love to come again."

"Please do, boys. Oh, here is Ron with the money." She moved out of the way, seeing Ron coming from the bedroom.

"Well, guys. You only worked for two hours yesterday, but it was an afternoon's worth of work and then an hour again today. I think this will cover it." Ron extended a large wad of green bills to each of them. It sure looked like more than they were expecting and, not wanting to count it, they both just stuffed it into their pockets. Ron gave them a handshake and also invited them to come back again, giving Charlie his phone number in the city and out here at the cabin then showed them to the door.

Johnny and Charlie got in the car, not checking to see if they had left anything behind since they had come only expecting to spend a day. Allison and Ron stood at the porch waving until their car was out of sight.

"Well, that sure was worth it," Charlie stated, getting comfortable in the driver's seat.

"Yeah, this sure is a wad of cash." Johnny pulled out the roll of bills. "I wonder how much it is."

"I don't know, count it." Charlie thought to himself they would be lucky to get 50 bucks or more.

"Holly shit, dude. This is a lot of money. When he handed this to me I thought it would all be small bills. It is not, there are fifties and hundreds in here."

"Wow!!! Well, how much is it?"

"Just a minute, hold your horses." Johnny flipped through the last of the bills with his eyes lighting up at the total they had received. Taking a breath and turning to Charlie, he haltingly said, "He paid us fifteen hundred dollars! Holy shit!"

"Fucking A… That is a lot of money. I didn't expect that much. Are you sure it is that much?"

"Yeah, I am sure. I know. This seems like too much to pay us for a couple hours of work. The food and hospitality would have been enough by itself."

Charlie took his eyes off the road to look at Johnny who he could tell was staring at him looking for an answer. Charlie gave him a cold, worried look before returning his attention to the road. His mind began to race. *What if this is some sort of infraction? What if we both get suspended for this? We would feel terrible and our teammates would be so upset. I have heard of stories from my friends at bigger schools where the stars get some cash or special deals from the local merchants, but this doesn't seem like that. We did do some work, he just over paid us. How is this any different from regular guys who happened to get paid a little extra? Would college students who were not athletes be expected to give this money back?...No way! It might be a little questionable, but it is not like we got something for nothing.* Then he remembered what La Dean had said to him. "Now I know why La Dean warned me about not taking something we shouldn't." Charlie turned to look at Johnny.

"Oh, she said that?" Johnny's tone grew ominous, he started to worry. Losing his senior year was the worst thing he could imagine. He didn't feel like they had done anything wrong, but he did realize that this kind of treatment and generous pay was coming only because Ron was a former Puma player and now they were current players. It wasn't for any other reason. "I wonder if this is a violation or something. It is not like he just gave it to us."

"Yeah, we did do some work, but not that much. I sure do need the money, though." Charlie's excitement was waning fast.

The fear of losing out on their senior year or being the cause of their team receiving NCAA sanctions was driving their minds to imagine every possible negative scenario. It was too much to handle and not something they could live with. They were wondering what they could do or what options were available to them. They knew that if they brought it up to any of the coaches, then most of the money would have to be returned, something they didn't want. If they just kept it to themselves and word got out, something may or may not happen.

"Do you think we should tell anyone, ask Coach Jackson what we should do?" Charlie offered one possible option, trying to stay calm and suppress the conflict going on within him.

"Oh, I don't know, dude," Johnny wheezed out his answer not even trying to hide how hard this dilemma was for him. "I mean it might be special treatment, but it is not like anyone besides you and I need to know about it. He did pay us a lot of money, but his wife probably doesn't even know how much he paid us. There is no record or no receipt. We are the only ones who have to know. I know I can keep a secret." Johnny put both hands in the air as if trying to make a point. He took a deep breath and let Charlie think about it for a while. This is what he wanted to do and hoped it would be what Charlie would want to do.

Charlie didn't take his eyes off the road, but his grip on the steering wheel tightened up. He seemed to ponder what Johnny said a little too long, Johnny thought. So he spoke up again. "I really don't think there is anything to worry about Charlie. You know how much this means to me. I would not risk our senior year for anything in the world. But no one is going to know about it."

What about risking it all for just this stupid fifteen hundred dollars? Charlie thought to himself. Then he realized that no one else had to know. Nobody would probably even ask. "Well, maybe we can just keep it to ourselves. If we don't tell anyone, then there is nothing to worry about. It is not like it is a regular occurrence. We just need to make sure it does not happen again. Let's keep it to ourselves. If anyone asks, we will just tell them it went well. I don't think anyone will ask how much we got paid. If they do, we will tell them fifteen an hour. How does that sound?"

"Yeah, that sounds like a plan. Don't worry, as long as we don't say anything, nobody is going to ask." They drove the rest of the way home in silence. It wasn't something they ever talked about to each other again. They would end up talking about it to others that they had hoped to avoid.

Connections

Charlie looked at the clock. *5:35* PM, *oh shit! I better hurry and get in the shower.* Mary was supposed to be to his house in less than half an hour. She was leaving work early and coming to spend the weekend at his place. Her parents were on a vacation, so she was free to escape her hometown for the weekend and be with Charlie. It wasn't as if her parents didn't like Charlie. They just wanted to act like their daughter wasn't busy sleeping with some guy that she may or may not marry. Of course, they knew that she was sleeping with Charlie, but their cognitive dissonance lessened when they asked her not to have him sleep in the same room with her when he visited their house and by not giving her their blessing to visit him during the weekends while she was staying with them in the summer. When she was away at college, they had no control over what she did. But while she was living at home, they tried to act like they still had an influence over how she lived her life.

He had also left work early today to come home and clean up his little one bedroom apartment. He wasn't a great cleaner, but he wanted his place to look nice when she came over and for the toilet to be free of any leftover discharge. He had vacuumed, wiped down everything, and was just finishing the bathroom. He took off his sweaty clothes. He didn't have AC in his apartment and in the middle of the summer, even with fans running constantly, he had to either sit still so he wouldn't sweat or move around and sweat. He hopped in the shower, even shaving for Mary's arrival. By 5:55 he was out of the shower, done with his minimal grooming, and into some fresh clothes. He grabbed a beer, turned on some summer tunes, and sat down on the couch.

A little after six, Mary tapped lightly on the door. Charlie tried not to get to the door too fast. He was excited to see her, but he didn't want her to know how excited. He opened the door and was met by her big grin and beautiful eyes. They gave each other an awkward hug and kiss, not wanting to seem like a married couple reuniting, but one that did express their longing for each other.

Charlie carried her bag into his room and welcomed her. She had been here many times and walked around comfortably.

"I'm going to go to the bathroom. I didn't stop on the whole three hour ride. I wanted to get here as soon as possible."

"Okay, you know where it is." Charlie put her bag down, walked past the bathroom, and into the kitchen to get himself another beer and one for Mary.

"Wow, somebody did some cleaning. I hope it wasn't all on my behalf," Mary said sarcastically, with a gleam in her eye. She walked into the TV room saw the beer and sat down next to Charlie. "This is just what I need. I don't get to drink much at home. No sex and no beer makes for a long summer."

"It sure does. It has been almost a month. My pornos are getting a little bit too familiar." Charlie laughed and took another swig.

"I'm glad I'm here," she replied. She took another long drink from her beer, leaned back into the used couch, and gave him that look that let him know he could take her anytime.

"Me too. I've had fun, but not as much fun as when you are around." Charlie poured the rest of the beer down his throat and set it down, knowing what was coming soon. He leaned back into the couch and relaxed, wanting to make Mary work for it a little more.

She looked at him as if he had done something wrong, took one more swallow of beer, and then made her move. They were both naked in seconds. Within minutes they were panting on top of each other, both satisfied and smiling.
"Ohhhhhhhhhhhh!!! I needed that," Mary belted out, unabashed.

"That was great. It's going to be a fun weekend." Charlie winked at her.

"Don't think you're getting off that easy. I expect some romance, too. You better be taking me out to dinner or something." She glared at him.

"Don't worry your pretty little smile off. Let's get dressed and go out to dinner. I have a reservation for us. Even you will think this place is romantic." Charlie stood up and grabbed her underwear. "You call these things panties? Somebody wanted to get laid. I hope to see these again later tonight." He teased her a little more, shaking them and making her reach up to snatch them away.

"Well, if you play your cards right, and especially if you are taking me to a restaurant that really does require reservations. That is quite a step up." She reached around to hook on her bra, in that crazy, flexible way that women seem able to do so naturally. Charlie always thought to himself that he would have to dislocate one of his shoulders to do that with a bra.

After dinner, Charlie led Mary back to his car. The sun was beginning to approach the western horizon and the air was still warm. It was one of those summer nights that was too nice to do anything indoors. Charlie opened the door for Mary and walked around back to the driver's side. "Well, that was very nice, Charlie. A real reservation and three courses. Wow!!! You earned yourself brownie points. It's a beautiful evening. What do you want to do?"

Charlie smiled, "I have an idea." He thought to himself, *she better have liked the dinner. That was a week's worth of pay from my boring summer job. It's a good thing Ron paid us so much or this would have broken the bank. Oh well, like she said, I'll be getting some favors this weekend.*

Charlie always kept a blanket and a cooler in his truck. He had learned long ago that if he had the supplies, the party could be anywhere. He drove down the road to a convenience store. "I'll be right back." He smiled at her and dashed into the store. He bought a 12 pack of good beer, some snacks, and ice. He filled the cooler up and was back in the driver's seat. "I have somewhere I want to take you."

"Cool, I can't wait." She gave him a content look and then gazed towards the west to see the changing colors.

After a few minutes, Charlie pulled off onto a dirt road. It led to an isolated spot on top of a small butte that overlooked the town and the setting sun. There was still plenty of light left in the evening sky. "How did you find this?" Mary asked.

"There are many benefits to staying in town over the summer. Sometimes the local guys show me the good make out spots," he replied with confidence.

"With that cooler and blanket, it looks like you're planning on more than a make out session," she said with a grin.

"Just hoping," he smirked back at her.

"I better be the only one you do this with, Mister." She playfully punched him in the arm, but looked at him with eyes that needed assurance.

"Of course, babe." He leaned over and kissed her.

Her eyes once again looked content. Charlie turned the old truck off and got out. He looked around the area for a comfortable spot. He found what looked like the softest spot, went to the back of the truck to grab the blanket and cooler, and set up their spot looking into the mixed colors of the western sky.

Mary slipped off her sandals, plopped down on her cute behind, and pulled Charlie by the arm, imploring him to sit down right next to her. "This is fun. This is exactly what I was hoping for. I really didn't expect this much romance tonight, especially after you already got laid." She snuggled her head into his neck.

Charlie reached for the cooler to grab a couple of beers, while trying not to pull away from her embrace. He opened a beer, handed it to Mary, opened his beer, and took a sip without breaking away from her. They sat quietly for a while watching the bright colors disappear behind the horizon and the darkness take its hold on the evening sky. As the last of the reds, violets, and blues colored the twilight sky, Charlie broke the silence. "I'm glad you're here. You get my mind off of football."

"I thought you needed to give extra focus to football this year," Mary replied confused.

"I do," he paused, "but it is good to get my mind off of it for a while." Mary pulled away enough to look into his eyes, imploring him to say more. She knew getting him to talk wasn't easy and that it had to come from him wanting to talk, not her prodding him. He looked down at her eyes. He felt safe. He broke their embrace and laid back onto the blanket looking up into the night sky. "I haven't been this nervous about a football season since I started high school. I am a little bit scared."

"What do you mean, scared?"

"I'm nervous. I feel a lot of pressure. I feel like I might not be up to the challenge of being team captain. I want to be the best and I also don't want to screw things up. I feel like the weight of the season and the team are on me."

"Why do you feel like that? You can't be responsible for everyone," Mary chimed in.

"I know that, but I still feel like the team will follow the direction that I lead it. It's strange to be a team captain, I don't feel any different. I know that I am a leader, though. It seems like all it takes to be one is the desire and willingness to step up, makes decisions, and some confidence. I am not the best guy on the team, I am not the loudest, I am not the coolest, but for some reason I am the one everyone looks up to. I never thought that people would follow me. I never thought that people would do what I say, especially my peers. It's like everyone is just waiting for someone to say and do something and then they will know what to say and do. I guess I am that person. I guess I wanted that because I voted for myself for team captain. I'm not sure I voted for myself because I think I am the best person to be telling my teammates what to say, how to act, and what to do. It's just because I felt like I am the person who cares the most about this team. I didn't feel like anyone else was as devoted to the team, as focused on winning, and who works as hard. That's why I voted for myself. That's why I think I should be a captain.

"But, I don't always want to be a captain because that means I have responsibility. Whether I want to admit it or not. I am the one who has to set a good example. I have to set the direction of the team at the peer level. That is a lot to worry about, sometimes it gives me stress and makes me nervous. I know that I am not the sole person who will determine the success or failure of the team, but my leadership can make the team one notch better or one notch worse. I hope that I am ready for that. I hope that I can do the right things to bring the level of the team up one notch rather than take it down one notch. That's why I am nervous and that's why I am sometimes scared."

"You will do fine. You care A LOT! I think that is the most important ingredient. The guys love you and so do the coaches. They will follow your lead and your lead is always good and always positive, so try not to worry." Mary tried to sound reassuring. She had never heard him say he was nervous or scared before.

"I hope so, I really hope so. Whatever happens with our success or failure this year as a team, I will feel responsible for the outcome. I know it isn't all me, but a large portion is. It's a lot of pressure and I enjoy letting go of it when I am around you."

"I'm glad I can help," she perked up. "You're great and I'm glad I can come to you and escape my academic stress during the year. My parents don't hesitate to let me know I better have a good job after I graduate. They keep telling me they aren't paying all of this money just to have me working a job that only pays the bills. It's also great to come here during the summer and get out of my parents' house and away from my internship. I like the college life and it's fun to have someone to share it with."

"Yeah, it's nice." Charlie sat up, chugged the rest of his beer and opened another one.

Mary didn't want to let Charlie's temporary loquaciousness pass without getting more from him, so she decided to prod some more, something she usually avoided with Charlie. She wanted to be close to him, but she was nervous about getting too close. She knew that might mean feelings that last longer than college. She didn't know if she was ready for that. "Tell me about the other time you were this nervous, when you started high school football?"

"Mmmmmm…, it's kind of a long story," Charlie replied hesitantly.

"Oh, come on. I want to hear about it."

Charlie looked over at her and furrowed his brow. He was met with a big smile and a nod that seemed to be prodding him along. As he continued to stall, Mary leaned over and kissed him on the cheek. His brow line relaxed and he smiled back at her. "Okay, okay, here goes. My first year of high school was a little tumultuous for me."

Charlie began telling her about his first day of high school football as he reminisced about this vivid memory.

Charlie went to a different high school than he had been anticipating because his family had bought a new home and moved across town the summer before he began high school. He now lived too far away to get to his first choice of high school without having a car. This was especially hard for Charlie because that meant a new football team. All the guys he had been playing with on his middle school team for the last few years, the friendships he had made, the starting position on that team with that group of guys, and his reputation with that program were all things he would be leaving behind. These weren't the only challenges Charlie would face going to a new school with new people, but the challenges relating to football were the first ones Charlie thought about and cared about. At this point, football was already his priority and where he had begun to gain his sense of self and acceptance among peers.

    The first day of practice for this new high school was a flashbulb memory for Charlie. He almost re-experienced the day as he talked to Mary. It was an intimidating day. Lucky for Charlie, his dad went along to help him out. He took Charlie to the new school about an hour early so that they could meet the coaches and introduce themselves before practice started. The coaches seemed to be excited by Charlie's size and many players were needed for the younger teams, so they welcomed him to the team and said he would be part of the sophomore team if he made it through two-a-days. Taking this as a challenge, Charlie welcomed it as a chance to prove to himself and everyone else that he could do it. The coaches gave him and his dad directions to the meeting room and told Charlie to wait there until the rest of the players arrived and the meeting began.

    In the unfamiliar surroundings of this new school, Charlie and his dad walked through the halls to the basement to find the room. This was not without its challenges. The halls in the basement seemed more like a maze with bare white walls and dull red tiles on the floor that dimly reflected the glaring fluorescent lights. The ceiling of the basement was left open, with uncovered pipes, heat vents, and cords in full view. They passed the locker rooms as they hunted for the room. It smelled like a dungeon long forgotten by cleaning agents. Stale sweat overpowered the air and made one immediately aware that this was the athletic area of the building.

Looking for the designated room, Charlie and his father quietly searched the musty halls. At last they stumbled upon a hall that had doors with room numbers. The second door proved to be the room they were looking for. They entered the room with caution, almost expecting a rat or cockroaches to scurry away as they opened the door, and instead found it empty. The front wall was full of chalkboards, over forty desks filled the room in five nice straight rows with extra folding chairs stacked near the back. The only sign of academia was the bulky steal teacher's desk in the back corner with a small stack of random textbooks.

Charlie's dad patted him on the back. He told him that the meeting would start in about half an hour and to sit down and relax. Sensing that Charlie was nervous, his dad gave him a big hug, told him to try and stay calm, and reminded him that if he was just himself and gave his best effort, then he would do fine. He recommended that Charlie sit in the front row to show his eagerness and told him to remember that he could do this. Then his dad left, telling him he would be back to pick him up after practice, but that he had to go back to work now.

Now on his own, the first thing Charlie did was to change seats. He didn't want to be in the front row. This was his first day, he was just trying to fit in and he wasn't interested in starting any trends. He moved to the middle against the wall. This made him feel like he could hide a little bit. Thinking about the approaching meeting, Charlie got nervous. He didn't know any of the players who would be coming to this meeting and he had to start over on a new team to prove himself as a solid player.

Daydreaming about the end of the summer, Charlie kept his gaze out the window in the back of the room. About fifteen minutes later, the first of many waves of young men began to arrive. There were about ten guys in this group, who all seemed to be friends. Now Charlie's nerves really began to rise. His heart started racing, he felt like a scared little boy. His meager efforts to avoid being nervous failed miserably. He couldn't even look at the guys coming into the room. He thought they all looked so different and big. He was intimidated. He hoped that these weren't the guys he would have to go against in practice.

As the room kept filling with players, Charlie kept his head down, or faced the wall, avoiding eye contact with anyone. He knew that he looked silly, he felt like a shy timid boy, but he didn't want the other guys to see the fear showing in his eyes. As time went on, Charlie grew more and more anxious for the meeting to start. Finally, as the room was crowded with bodies and the last guys to arrive had to stand in the back, the coaches walked in and told everyone to be quiet and listen. The meeting carried on for about twenty minutes, most of it being about improving from last year and what needed to be done this year. Charlie didn't listen to most of it, he just tried to keep himself calm and constantly reminded himself that he was as good as anyone else there.

The room began to heat up from all the bodies. Beads of sweat began to run down the sides of Charlie's face. As he reached up to wipe them off, he could see a dark ring growing under his armpit. Charlie looked around, some of the other guys looked hot, but none seemed to have pit stains already showing. Charlie's nerves were making him sweat even more than the heat. He began to get even more nervous as outward physical signs showed the level of his discomfort. Just as it seemed that he couldn't take it anymore, the team was finally dismissed to go outside and put their cleats on for practice. This was good for Charlie. He didn't have to sit there, feeling uncomfortable, with a bunch of strangers surrounding him. Now he could get out there and communicate with everyone just by his actions. He didn't have to talk to anyone, just run around and hustle.

In the early evening of the August heat, his sweating continued and he seemed to be half soaked after the warm-up lap, but the exercise actually calmed him down. He was glad they didn't have to wear pads. They were just doing technique drills and conditioning to ensure that everyone was in good enough shape for the upcoming two-a-days. Some of the guys even threw up and struggled to finish practice.

Charlie didn't have much social contact with any of the players this first day. Eventually, he was befriended by a gregarious, popular guy. He was the same age as Charlie, but knew most of the guys from the sophomore team, the junior varsity team, and the varsity team. Charlie would later learn this was because his older brother was the star running back on the varsity team and this guy would end up being the star running back on the sophomore team that year.

During a water break, Charlie got his drink and began to make his way back to the field. Guys were still standing around, getting their last few moments of rest, before the whistle was blown again when somebody walked up next to him. Out of nervousness, Charlie began to move aside to allow him to pass. He stopped right next to Charlie with some friends closely following him. Although his friends didn't pay any attention, this young guy looked Charlie in the eyes, smiled, and asked him what was up. After Charlie answered back, he introduced himself as Nate and asked Charlie his name. Nate told him it was nice to meet him and that he would see him back on the field.

Charlie watched him trot back onto the field and join another group of players from the young team. This common, friendly gesture helped Charlie feel more comfortable and was the beginning of what would be Charlie's closest friendship during his high school years.

As the team lay down to stretch out at the end of practice, Charlie felt a sense of accomplishment. He had just completed his first high school football practice. His body was drenched with sweat and he was exhausted, but he still had a smile on his face. As the first stars of the evening began to twinkle above, Charlie felt alive and that this was where he was supposed to be. He only had one friend, but he was starting to feel comfortable. Under the darkening sky, laying on his back with the feeling of grass against his head and neck and the smell of dirt mixing with the sweat of full effort, Charlie had an overwhelming sense of inner peacefulness. He didn't know it at the time, but this was the beginning of a great high school career for him, one that would lead him to a college football scholarship. His high school days would be a success on and off the field, his shyness would fade away, and his self-confidence would grow, mostly from his success and acceptance in football. His career would grow exponentially from this humble beginning.

Charlie again looked up at the twinkling stars as he finished telling Mary his story. This time the sky was fully dark. "Eight years later, I almost feel like that insecure 14 year old again. I'm not sure I'm up for the challenges ahead and I'm not sure what is going to happen. I hide my doubts with an exaggerated sense of self confidence. I feel like a fake sometimes." He paused.

Mary waited for a moment, she wanted to make sure that Charlie was done sharing his inner thoughts and feelings. She didn't want to stop something that happened so rarely. After an extended silence, she spoke up, "I would try not to worry too much. Look at how great your high school experience turned out. This year will turn out great, too. The one thing I do know is that you're not a fake. You may seem a little over confident at times, but that is part of your charm." She tried to reassure him by rubbing his arm.

"I hope so." Charlie was tired of talking about this. He sat back up and popped open another beer. He got a new one out for Mary. He downed his entire beer in two long chugs and opened another one. He took one more swallow from his new beer and then reached over and put his hand under Mary's shirt, feeling for the bra strap. She leaned into him and relaxed as they explored each other's mouths. Under the stars, they fooled around and drank beer until the darkness started to fade from the east side of the horizon.

Dog Days of Summer

By the end of July, summer begins to have its own contradictions. All the excitement and anticipation about the extended vacation begin to wear off. The killing of time and searching for things to do become more like chores than novelties. While the break is always nice, there comes a time when getting back to tasks and taking action again is needed. Preparation and hard work need to lead to something. Summer had reached this point for Charlie. As much as he loved it, Charlie was now looking forward to the end of the summer and the beginning of the season. It was time to put all of this training into action and he couldn't wait.

Charlie had stepped up his training and dedication to football this summer, giving everything towards being 110% ready, being in the best shape of his life, and being the team leader. Each and every workout he had left completely exhausted. He was bigger, faster, and stronger than he had ever been in his life. He was already watching game film on this season's first opponent and on himself, seeing what areas he could improve in. Workouts four times a week were enough to get anyone in shape. On off days, Charlie would ride his bike to get all the extra exercise he could handle. Some days it was just around the neighborhood, while other times he would go for a full ride.

Embracing his role as captain and buying into Coach Jackson's idea of bringing the team together as friends, Charlie had organized get-togethers, outings, and parties this summer. Twice, springing the up-front cost by himself. He had been able to afford it after working for Ron. Johnny and Charlie had thrown a party and bought the keg themselves. Although unsaid, they almost felt obligated to do it. Charlie had organized a couple of other parties with the help of a willing host. He knew, after all, the best bonding for football players often took place while drunk.

All of the guys that were in town for the summer came to these parties. They were a success. A few times he had gotten some of the guys together for swimming or camping. He tried to mix the groups up a little bit, not having the same guys always hanging with each other. Many times throughout the summer he had arranged nights out on the town, or just drinking at somebody's house. There were more teammates hanging out together and more often than Charlie could remember since his time with the team.

Charlie felt like he had more than fulfilled his duties and obligations as team captain this summer. It was a week until max day, where the players would show off their strength gains by lifting as much as possible in each of the core lifts. Two-a-days were about two weeks away. He wanted to do some things for himself between now and then. Of course he would be the leader at the training sessions, but for his free time in these last two weeks, Charlie wanted to do more for himself.

He decided that he would go visit Mary in her hometown this weekend. Even though this meant he would have to sleep in a separate room, it would still be fun to be with her and get to know her family more. They would sneak off for some fun time, though. The sneaking around added to the thrill of getting laid. The last weekend before two-a-days he wanted to go home for a short visit, as well. His parents would be glad to see him before the season. His mom always spoiled him when he came home, so he knew he would come back for camp with some extra calories to burn. He almost felt like the guys wouldn't know what to do without him over the next two weekends, but they would have to make do.

Charlie was looking forward to these next two weekends, being able to relax, be himself, and not be in charge. Most of all, he was looking forward to starting the season. It was time to get back in the saddle, it was time to assume his position as leader of the team, and it was time to move the team towards all of its goals.

Duties

As Blake walked from his car to the entrance of the football complex the smell of grass beginning to brown from the heat of the summer filled his nostrils. It was the end of July, which meant that football camps would be starting across the nation soon. The summer sun had been beating down on the grass for months now and the sprinklers were having a hard time winning the battle against the heat for green grass. As soon as he opened the door, he was met with a cool breeze of air escaping the office building. He walked into the football offices and saw that Coach Jackson was already in the big conference room waiting for him.

"Hey Coach." Blake notified him of his arrival.

"Hi Coach Jones," Coach Jackson replied, without looking up from his papers. "I've been looking through your revised playbook and I like what I see. After you made those changes that I recommended, I feel very confident in what you have here." He finally made eye contact with Blake.

"Thanks, I have spent a lot of time on it. I hope that the season goes well. It's not going to be from lack of effort if it doesn't."

"I certainly hope not." Coach Jackson gave him a hard look. "This is a big year. If we don't have a good year, I think we might all be out of here. The boosters are all over my ass this year, Blake. Everyone wants to pretend that the boosters don't decide who stays and who goes, but we all know that they have a very big influence." He paused and closed the folder containing Blake's playbook. "You've already given me your full commitment and I am going to hold you to that this season. We're going to have a lot of late nights and long weekends this year. With your new position comes new and expanded responsibilities. You are the one accountable for the defense, not anyone else. You have to have the plan first, then we give it out to the other coaches."

"Yeah, I am totally prepared for that. The team has my full commitment." Blake felt like he was being treated like a kid who needed to be reminded of what he had taken on when he accepted this job.

"Well, I hope your family is ready for all of this, too. It can be hard on a family if they don't know what to expect." Coach Jackson looked at him with sincerity.

"I hope so, too. I have let my wife know about the duties that go along with this new job title. I also like to remind her of the significant increase in compensation. She knows what's going on and she is fine with everything," Blake said with more confidence than he really had about his wife's feelings towards his new job.

"Great, that is good to hear. Let me know if you or your family need anything. Also, tell your wife she is always welcome to call Peggy to chat or to get together at any time." Coach Jackson paused while Blake nodded his head. "Anyway, I wanted to meet with each coach to chat one last time before we start this thing. Your playbook is great. Go ahead and have La Dean make enough copies to give to the players when they report for camp and for each of your coaches. Give them to your coaches tomorrow at max day. I want all of the coaches there for max day. I think it is important that we be there for support and to see the players' summer progress. We can't do any coaching, we are just there as spectators. After max day you have three days off. All of the coaches need to report on Monday at 6:00 AM. I want to get used to the early days we will be having soon. We will go over our schedule for camp and you will meet with your defensive staff to go over your expectations and plans. Then the players report the next morning. I'll see you tomorrow in the weight room at 8:00 AM." Coach Jackson stood up to shake his hand.

"Sounds good, see you then," Blake replied.

"Go and spend some time with your family this weekend. I promise not to bug you." Coach Jackson smiled. "Well, let me take that back, I promise not to bother you unless something important comes up."

"Oh, no worries. I know you wouldn't call unless it was something big. Like this summer. We landed that kid and it will pay off for us immediately." As Blake began leaving the office, he said, "It will be nice to be with the family this weekend."

"Have a good evening, Blake. Tell your wife hello for me," Coach Jackson said as he turned to tidy up his desk and get ready to leave.

Blake sauntered back to his car. He felt the afternoon summer heat as soon as he left the air conditioned building. Despite the sudden uncomfortable change in temperature, he did not pick up his pace. He thought to himself, *this is going to be a tough year. I knew I was going to be busy, but I didn't know there would be this much pressure. I think I'm ready for it. I just hope April can handle everything. I'm living my dream, though, and I hope she understands that. I know that I won't be around as much as she wants me to be, but this is what I love. This doesn't feel like a job. It feels like I am getting paid to do my hobby. I hope I'm being a good husband, but I know that this is what I'm meant to be doing.*

He got to his car and unlocked the door. He sat down and took a deep breath before starting the car. His mind kept drifting back to April. *She's not going to like this at all, I already know that. Oh well, there isn't much more that I can do. I'll have to plan something nice for her this weekend.*

Exertion

  This was it, the last chance for Charlie to show the team he was the leader before the season started. After maxes today, the team had a few days off before reporting to two-a-days. Charlie wanted to cement his role among the team even before action began. He had accomplished all his summer goals up to this point, but this last one would be a stretch. Charlie had set this goal because it was attainable and would be a team record. He wanted to hang clean 405 pounds. He would get his picture on the prestigious record wall. This would be one more thing for his teammates to rally behind with him. It was another chance to step up and show that he wanted the pressure, one more chance to prove his teammates had made a wise decision in choosing him as captain. It was an opportunity he wasn't going to let slip by.

  His sympathetic nervous system had already kicked in, giving him energy as he popped out of bed a half an hour early. He didn't want to be rushing anything today, everything would be meticulous and determined.

  Normally Charlie didn't like eating anything before going to workouts, today would be an exception. He had never been into supplements. They were expensive, unproven, and some bordered on illegal. The farthest Charlie had ever gone was protein and weight gain shakes. This morning he was willing to try something new. To reach today's goal he was going to need all of his strength, plus a little more. Today he was going to have an energy drink. It was a little risky because he had never tried it, but no rules were being broken and today's workout was only maxes and a light run. Throwing up wouldn't be a problem, which is what usually happened to Charlie if he ate breakfast before a tough summer training session. Because the workout would be short, he felt okay trying something new and putting more into his system than normal.

  He downed the thick, grainy shake trying to do so fast enough to avoid his taste buds. With half his glass empty he plopped down and turned on the TV. He found a station showing sports highlights and tried concentrating on the scores instead of his drink. Looking at the time, Charlie realized he needed to finish it now, so that it wouldn't be sitting in his stomach during warm ups. He gulped the rest of the energy drink in one swift movement. "Fuck! This shit better help. Now I remember why I avoid this stuff," he said to his empty apartment. He usually tried this kind of thing once a year, after the memory of the last drink had faded.

    Charlie finished the rest of his morning routine and headed up to the weight room. He got there 20 minutes early, even beating Jim, an extreme rarity. There was not an earlier group today because the whole team came together for one morning session during maxes. Charlie was glad the session was during his normal workout time. His circadian rhythm would not be out of whack, his body was used to exerting itself at this time of day.

    While waiting for Jim to show up, Charlie got out of his truck. He was already feeling a nervous excitement and didn't want to be cooped up. Wandering around the practice field, Charlie took in the fresh morning air, his feet slightly sunken into the ground that was still soft from being watered during the night. It was the end of July. The temperature was already beginning to rise in the morning hours. Pacing back and forth, Charlie tried to stay focused on today's purpose. Thoughts of his family, Mary, the approaching season, school, and if he had been working hard enough swirled through his head during these few quiet minutes. Charlie didn't let his mind wander far before returning his concentration to the task at hand.

    Jim sped into the parking lot and stopped directly in front of the weight room entrance. Getting out of his car Jim looked at Charlie without an ounce of surprise on his face, "Ready to go, huh?"

    "I sure am," Charlie replied, walking towards the entrance with Jim.

    "Well, start getting focused. There's no reason you can't do it today." Jim opened the door for Charlie and disappeared around the corner to turn on the lights. By the time the lights were fully illuminated, there was a steady stream of teammates showing up. Charlie was glad because now he didn't have to be alone with his thoughts.

Charlie bullshitted around with some of the guys for a few minutes before Jim brought them together to start warm ups. Today's warm ups were light, designed just to get the body going, not the normal workout before the workout. Joking also stopped when Jim began the session because on Jim's max days everything was business. The room turned steamy and stuffy fast with the large group working out all together.

After warm ups, with a light sweat, the players broke up into groups of three or four. The guys partnered up with others of similar strength. As they dispersed to their stations, Jim turned on some pulse-quickening music. He didn't usually play it loud, but max day was a day when formalities went out the window. The intensity and focus of the day could already be felt. Testosterone was in an over abundant supply. The building teemed with pent up energy.

During all of this, the coaching staff quietly filed in along the back wall of the weight room. They still weren't allowed to coach, the summer wasn't over. They were just observing today. Jim was the only one giving direct instructions to the players. A few of the coaches would make eye contact and nod at some of their position players. When the players came by they would greet them. A few of them mingled to say hi to their guys. But, most of them just stood stoically, trying to be as inconspicuous as possible. Coach Jackson even pulled out a folder and began taking notes. He continued writing in his notebook until a player was ready to max out. Only then would he look up from his notebook and watch the exertion take place before returning his eyes to his notebook.

Once the mood had been set and a few of the players were ready to try for their max, the music was turned down to a level where Jim's commands and encouragement could be heard. Charlie and the bigger guys were only beginning their slow climb to the heavy weights, while some of the smaller guys were already going for their goal. Each time a player went for his max, the team gathered around to offer support. The crowd was smaller and less enthusiastic at the beginning because of the lower weights involved and most of the guys were still concentrating on their own goal. Nobody wanted to cheer too loud, spending his energy on someone else's attempt. Charlie always stood at the rear of the group, focusing more on his concerns than what was happening in front of him.

As the weights started getting heavier, the cheering started getting louder. The energy continued to grow, and Charlie's heart began pounding. He had planned it almost perfectly. As the smaller, lighter players began finishing, the big guys would be the last to go. Charlie would be one of the last ones, which meant everyone could give him their full attention and support. This raised his energy and enthusiasm one more notch. He began to pump himself up, mentally getting ready for the heavy weight.

Getting pumped up for a lift involved any number of things, most of them were superstitions. What worked for a guy one time, tended to be what he did every subsequent time. One of the strangest rituals was promising one's self he will get laid by the girl of his choice if he completes the exercise. The promise of sex, however false it might be, was a strong motivator for any man. However, this tended to distract Charlie. Today he chose to focus on visualizing a positive result.

Now every time Charlie did a repetition, he strapped his belt on tight, visualized good technique, and approached the exercise with tenacity. He kept the vision of getting the team record for power cleans in front of him. This was the most difficult lift that required the best technique, but a lot could be made up for in this lift with pure effort. Effort is what Charlie was so good at and was why he had gone after this particular record.

As more and more maxes were attempted, the crowd around the big guys grew bigger and bigger. Charlie was now up to weights that were requiring a full mental and physical effort. He was already receiving encouragement from the crowd. He only had two more sets before he went for it. Jim allowed a rep max of up to three repetitions and since Charlie was going for a new record of 405 pounds, he had to do 375 pounds three times. As his moment grew nearer, Charlie's determination grew visible and his pulse more rapid, his system was now in overdrive.

He approached the bar with 330 pounds, focused for a moment, and snapped it up. *Easy!* he told himself as he dropped the bar. Loosening his belt, Charlie felt good. That was the easiest 330 pounds had ever been. He was going to do one more set at 355 pounds before the big one. Guys were already patting him on the back as he rested between sets. Everyone knew Charlie was going for the record today.

After a few minutes of rest, Charlie pulled the belt tight again, almost forcing the air out of his stomach. He chalked up his hands, adjusted the wraps, and snapped the weight up to a handful of cheers. *I'm just getting started,* Charlie thought to himself. This time, Charlie took his belt and wraps all the way off. He told his partners to put on the weight. Jim looked across the room at Charlie with a questioning look. Charlie shook his head and responded, "Not yet, give me a few minutes."

Charlie pushed through the crowd to get to the water fountain. After slurping a few gulps, he noticed the coaches along the back wall. A few of them nodded to him, sending him encouragement. Even Coach Jackson had closed his notebook and seemed interested in what was going on. He turned to go back to his station, but paused for a moment before entering the crowd. He took a deep breath, closed his eyes, and focused on his goal one more time. He even stayed back when a teammate did his max. Charlie heard the cheers and yells, knowing it would be for him soon.

He visualized the whole exercise in his head. He saw himself do it with perfect technique three times. He had done 375 once before, but had struggled on that day two weeks ago. Today that seemed like a distant memory. The only thing he saw was the lift being completed. *Easy weight, easy weight. Ain't no thing. NOTHING. You got this, no problem,* Charlie repeated to himself.

Charlie chalked up his hands before breaking through the crowd again. He made his way in front of his station and grabbed the belt and wraps lying in front of it. He gave Jim a nod. This was all that was needed. Jim could see the determination on Charlie's face and knew it was time.

Jim called the players in. They gathered in front of Charlie's station. Charlie pulled the belt as tight as it would go. He could barely exhale with it this tight. The noise and excitement began to grow behind him. The crowd was circling around him, gathering only a few feet away from him. "Come on, Charlie!" "You got it!" "Come on, man!" "You can do it!" "This is easy, go for it!"

Before his attention could shift to the comments being made, Charlie approached the bar. The talking around him drowned to a dull, indistinguishable roar and his pulse shot up. He adjusted the wraps, gave himself one last look of confidence in the mirror, stiffened his body, and without thought, exploded with every ounce of energy in his body. The first repetition he had up and was standing easier than he had thought. *Oh, this is easy!*

Charlie let the bar down slowly and exploded again. This time he got it up, but was stuck for a moment straightening his legs and back.

"Come on!!! You got it!!! Push it!!!" Charlie heard the yells behind him. He finished the lift straining with everything he had. As he stood erect with the weight, he paused for a fraction of a second to gather the last of his strength and energy for one last repetition. The noise behind him was deafening.

This time he lowered the bar a little faster and exploded up again. He jerked the bar as high as he could. Snapping under it, he felt the strain on his knees and back. It felt as if he might pop in half. He blocked everything out, summoned every fiber of strength in his body, and stood upright with the weight.

Charlie opened his eyes and regained his senses. His face was bright red and his teammates were closing in on him, hooting and hollering. In a triumphant act of accomplishment, he threw the weight down and turned to join them in celebration.

Charlie collided with his nearest teammates and Jim. He began yelling and jumping up and down with the guys. The group converged around Charlie celebrating in an act of comradery over a great accomplishment by one of their teammates. The celebrating continued at a deafening level for several minutes.

Charlie was on top of the world. *Hell yeah!!! I did it! I did it!!!* He allowed himself some praise. *This is what it is all about, bringing the team together and accomplishing goals. This is only the beginning.*

The celebration began to die down and the guys started giving Charlie high fives, bro hugs, and even hugs. Each guy took a turn coming by and congratulating him. Some of the coaches crossed the room and took a moment to acknowledge the feat. Coach Havili approached him from the side, gave him a big bro hug, and told him, "Great job! You are the man. I am so excited for this year. That almost inspired me to lift again." He smiled and patted Charlie on the shoulder before turning and leaving with the other coaches. Coach Jackson nodded at Charlie and mouthed the words, 'Good job,' as he held the door for the last coach to leave the weight room and then let himself out the door.

As the adrenaline began to wear off, Charlie could already feel his knees and back tightening up. He took off his belt, threw the wraps across the room, and almost collapsed on the weight bench at his station. He felt satisfyingly exhausted. He let his mind think about his other goals and the goals of the team for this upcoming season. He let his mind drift and daydream about leading the team to their dreamed-of heights. Charlie would cling to today's moment of success throughout the tumultuous times of the upcoming season. This moment of personal glory and team celebration, this moment of things going right when one works toward a goal and accomplishes it, this moment of peace, purpose, and fulfillment, would stick with Charlie through the upcoming season.

Couple's Retreat

Blake rolled over with his eyes still heavy. The clock read 6:17. *Oh cool, perfect timing.* He knew, from his wife telling him, not personal experience, that Conner wasn't usually up for about 45 minutes. He snuck out of bed and took a quiet shower in their guest bedroom. He didn't want to wake up April. He had a romantic surprise for her, one that he knew he needed to do before the long demanding season that was looming ahead for them. He showered and started some coffee before waking up April.

He sat down gently on her side of the bed and started to rub her arm. She moved a little, trying to fight the return to reality. Her eyelids began to rise methodically. She looked up at him with a confused look. "Good morning," came out barely noticeable. Then she looked at the clock, 6:51. "Why are you up so early?" she asked as she closed her eyes again.

Blake grinned, more to himself since April had already closed her eyes again. "I've got a surprise for you. I want to do something nice for you before I get back into being busy again on Monday. We are going away for the weekend. We are meeting your parents, they are going to take Conner for two nights. It will be just you and me, and I promise we won't be leaving early."

April's eyes perked open with excitement. Then she remembered their last 'getaway'. "I don't even want to get all eager to spend the weekend and just be disappointed again when you have to leave early. If that's going to happen again, let's just stay here and have a quiet weekend at home." She looked at him intently.

"I know, I know, don't worry. I promise it will just be you and me this weekend and that I won't be leaving early." He knew this wasn't a promise he had total control over. He just hoped that he wouldn't be getting called away by Coach Jackson. He felt more trepidation than confidence in making the promise.

"Okay, fine, you better not go back on your promise, though. Forgiveness won't come so easy this time." Her eyes were fully open and she was geared up to get out of bed.

"Don't get up so fast. I'm going to get Conner up in a few minutes. I will get all of my stuff ready and then get him up. You take your time, lay around for a few minutes, and then get up when you are ready. I'll even make us some breakfast. We are meeting your parents half way at about noon, so we don't need to leave for a couple of hours."

"When are you going to take a shower?" April asked with suspicion.

"I already have. I got up early so that you could have some extra rest," Blake said, pleased with himself. He bent down and kissed her on the cheek as he left their room.

"Wow," April smiled and stretched out on the bed. "Trying to get all the brownie points that you can before the season, huh?"

Blake hesitated before answering, "Just have a nice relaxing morning. It is going to be a fun weekend."

After meeting her parents and dropping off Conner, they arrived at their hotel around three in the afternoon. Blake had brought her to a romantic resort hotel overlooking the river. Their room was half way up the modern glass hotel tower and had a great view of the river. The windows looked to the west and promised a great view for the sunset. It was a nice room with all of the amenities. After looking around, April gave Blake a hug and said, "Thank you. I'm glad we get to spend some time together before the craziness of the season starts. This is a nice surprise." She looked in his eyes with sincere gratitude and kissed him. It wasn't a deep passionate kiss, it was more of a comfortable kiss. She wasn't ready to let her guard down yet. She had been devastated the last time she had been anticipating a long weekend alone with him. She didn't want to let high expectations of this weekend ruin it for her again.

As April broke away from their embrace, Blake acknowledged her gratitude. "You're welcome. I'm glad we were able to do this." He looked around the room and was happy about the big screen TV with the recliner positioned for a good view. "What do you want to do?"

"It's so quiet, let's just lie down and relax for a little bit. I'm tired and could use some r and r." She smiled at him as she was already lying down in the oversized bed.

"Okay, sounds good. Do you mind if I turn on the TV?" Blake asked with the remote in his hand as he was moving towards the recliner.

"No, just keep it down, please." Her eyes were already closed.

"Okay, sounds good." Blake turned on the TV and let himself relax. Before he had even found ESPN he heard his wife's rhythmic breathing and knew she was already asleep. Within a few minutes of listening to 'expert' sports analysis he drifted off to sleep, as well.

April didn't let herself totally loosen up until Saturday evening. She had been guarding herself against Blake being called and having to leave again. As Saturday evening came upon them, she knew that he wasn't going to be called away. This made her feel comfortable and able to fully relax with Blake for the first time during their little getaway. She knew that this feeling wouldn't last. On Sunday when they got home, he would be in the study going over his football stuff, doing last minutes changes and preparations. Then on Monday he had to report to camp, and that meant he would hardly be around the house for the rest of the summer and all of the fall. It wasn't just her that missed him during this time, it was Conner, too. Blake didn't get to see a lot of Conner and his little changes that seem to happen so fast in a little baby.

As she was getting ready for this last evening together, she walked over to Blake and kissed him passionately. Blake reciprocated and they made out in the bathroom. Blake pulled away for a moment. "I'm so glad we got to relax and unwind this weekend. I know that things will get busy for a while." He felt like he should talk to her about the season while she was in a good mood and happy with him. "I know that it can be hard during the season…"

April kissed him again, "I don't want to talk about it right now. I am enjoying this time too much. I don't want to go to that place. Just kiss me." She moved her body closer and began moving her hips against his, the sexual energy began to build between the two of them.

Blake picked her up and walked her to the bed. They had passionate sex for the first time all summer. April let all of her worries out of her mind and Blake gorged himself on her sensual desires.

Afterwards, they laid together on the bed, still intertwined with each other's bodies. They didn't want to let each other go, they hadn't connected like that physically for a long time. Blake began to think about dinner as his mind drifted and his touch loosened. April didn't want to let go, she seemed to be holding on tighter than ever. She knew that once they went out they would come back and fall asleep and that meant her time with Blake was over for the season. It would be her and Conner for most of the fall. She didn't want that time to come yet. She held on desperately, not wanting to talk or move. It was as if as long as they laid there, the real world didn't have to exist. This fantasy didn't last though.

Blake started sliding away from her and sitting up, not knowing how much April just wanted him to stay there. "Well, should we go get something to eat? I'm starving."

"Sure," April replied through a fake smile, knowing deep in her heart things would only get worse.

Section II

"Whether you think you can
or you think you can't,
you are probably right."
– Henry Ford

Football Camp
August 2000

Two-a-Days

After all the workouts, testing, meetings, and speeches were finished real practice was finally ready to begin. It had been a long time coming. All the hard work and sweat was in preparation for the season beginning. Getting dressed in the locker room, there was a buzz. The players were all excited. The endless hours of build up to the season created a sense of anticipation that would explode on the field with the first hitting drills. All of one's pent up energy could finally be released again, this time onto someone else.

Being the first practice, it took a little longer to get dressed. All the pads had to be tightened, the helmet had to be adjusted, and the cleats laced up. The first day was always a little uncomfortable, but everyone had to ignore all the added pains because starting positions were already on the line. The intensity of the first day was palpable.

It was an early August morning and the temperature was already rising. By the time Charlie got all his pads on and trotted out to the practice field, he was sweating. The familiar feeling of his cleats sinking into the hard ground of the field gave him a sense of comfort. After a few minutes of banal chatting, the team snapped into action as Coach Jackson blew his whistle.

The rookies looked a little confused, not understanding what was expected, but quickly followed the veterans as the group made its way around the far end of the practice field for the warm up run. The hooting and hollering had already begun. The excitement echoed off the surrounding buildings. Even the coaches got into the act, letting out what sounded like ancient tribal war cries. Players pranced around the goalpost, allowing the excitement to take hold.

As the group made its way back to Coach Jackson, Charlie and Junior took their places at the front and the stretch lines were formed. Jim led them through their stretch routine, which after a few days would become so automatic nobody needed to think about what was coming next. Today would take longer than normal, since this was new to many of the guys.

After the warm ups, Coach Jackson surprised everyone by calling the team together. All of the players sprinted over to Coach Jackson, eagerly awaiting their next assignment. With eyes full of excitement and energy, he yelled out that this year's season was no joke and was going to start out intense. At the top of his lungs he hollered, "Right away we are going to find out who is going to step up and be a champion. I love the energy and excitement we started out with this morning and I want to tap into that." With spit flying and veins in his forehead bulging he bellowed, "We are starting out with the gauntlet!!!" He pointed with his whole body to the north east corner of the field where the drill had been set up by some of the other coaches.

The players charged towards the designated area, yelling and screaming the entire distance. The gauntlet was a drill with four players on offense and four players on defense. Three offensive linemen would line up against three defensive linemen with a running back on the offensive side and a linebacker on the defensive side. The drill was just a pure hitting drill, where everyone bashed into each other as hard and intensely as possible. The players were confined to a space ten yards long by five yards wide. The offense wanted the running back to cover the ten yards within four tries and the defense wanted to stop the running back from covering the ten yards. The goal of this drill was plain and simple, see how hard people would hit. Its added purpose was getting the whole team quickly excited.

Charlie was part of the first group on offense. He didn't even care who was on the other side or who was running the ball behind him. This was the perfect way to begin. He looked his partners in the eyes and let them know he expected full effort and wanted to win this drill. The running back told them where he wanted to run and the three sprinted up to the start line. With the entire team crowding around the ten yard by five yard area, it almost looked like a tunnel. With the noise coming from his teammates, he couldn't hear anything.

The offensive linemen got set in their stances. Charlie stared at his opponent across from him in the eyes with a sense of purpose and intensity to let him know what was coming. As the coach's cadence broke through the noise, "Down, set, hut!" Charlie exploded into his opponent's chest. He could feel the momentum carrying him forward, relentlessly pumping his legs, while extending his arms. In an instant, he felt the drill converge on him as the running back tried to break through the mass of bodies. Everything collapsed around Charlie as he fell forward. The entire team was shouting, one side yelling, "Hell yeah!" the other side, "Stop him!"

  Charlie pushed off his opponent and saw that the ball had gone as far as he had moved his man, almost five yards. He pumped his fist, jogging back to the makeshift huddle. "Great job," he let his partners and running back know, "one more like that." After the running back let them know his intentions, Charlie and his line mates were back up to the line of scrimmage, this time with only five yards to go.

  Again the noise grew deafening. Through the noise, Charlie heard the cadence, this time quicker to try and catch the defense off guard. "Down, set!" The offense plowed forward again, this time with more ease. Charlie drove his man to the ground and while falling, saw his running back cross the ten yard mark. This provided him with an extra boost and he hopped back up almost as soon as hitting the ground. He and the entire offensive side of the team mobbed the running back. "That's how it is done!" Charlie yelled out.

  Now it was Charlie's turn to watch and try to add some motivation to his offensive teammates. He could smile during the rest of the drill knowing he had done his part and shown the team how determined he would be this year. The next attempts were foiled by the defense with the same kind of intensity the offense had previously used.

  After a few more attempts, Coach Jackson blew his whistle, signifying the end of the drill. He brought the team around him again and let them know what he thought. "That was awesome! I was hoping for that kind of reaction. I could not have asked for anything better. That is how to start out a season. If that drill is any kind of an indication, I think there are good things in store for this season. Great job, keep it up. Now off to your position coaches." Without hesitation, the players all broke up into groups, following their position coaches to their patch of grass for the next set of drills.

Because it was the first day of practice, a lot of time was spent within each position group going over technique and assignments. After four years, this was all second nature to Charlie, so he was the one who was called upon when a demonstration was needed. The rest of this first practice was laid back compared to how it began, which was okay with Charlie since he had a raging headache. Every year on the first day of practice, he got a smashing headache no matter what. It was just part of the getting back to the game of football. As the sun began to approach its midpoint for the day, practice was wrapping up.

The excitement and energy were still apparent as the first session of the first day of two-a-days ended. It wasn't until the players began dressing for the next practice, only five hours later, that the excitement began to abate.

As they were getting ready for the second practice of the first day they began to realize that the long haul had just begun. They were still tired and sore from the first practice. Headaches from the first hitting drill were still pounding, shoulder pads and cleats were still wet with sweat. The weight of all the equipment they were forced to wear seemed to drag them down rather than embolden them. It was going to be a challenge. Mental toughness and a good attitude were already necessary to keep spirits high and to strive through football camp.

To get through the ordeal, many of the players would count down the days and practices. Half a day and one practice were already under their belts, only eleven and a half days and twenty practices left. Saturdays were only half days, thankfully, and Sundays were a day off. It seemed like an eternity, but knowing that something was behind them made it easier to see the light at the end of the tunnel.

The second practice began at 4:00 in the afternoon. It was the hottest time of the day and even before the warm up lap, sweat was making its presence known on each and every player. The practices didn't get any easier. A lot of kinks and miscues had to be worked out in the short two weeks of camp before the team began its full focus on the first opponent.

Two-a-days was to find out who was going to be a team contributor and who was going to be a team supporter. The contributors would be on the depth chart and the supporters would be on the practice squad, imitating each week's opponent. Being on the practice squad meant the first and second stringers would beat up on you since you wouldn't be playing in the game. The competition for the depth chart was intense and brought out each player's tenacity.

During two-a-days there were more fights going on at practice than any other time of year. In the heat of the summer, exhaustion always on the horizon and starting spots on the line, tempers easily flared. At least every other day during camp, a fight had to be broken up. Fights were unnecessary and unwanted, but they did help to bump up the intensity. It always seemed a little silly to Charlie to be punching someone who was wearing padding over most of his body.

The other reason for two-a-days was to get in game shape. Each athlete came to camp in the best shape of his life, yet wasn't quite ready for the rigors of the season. In addition to the superb physical condition required to persevere through an entire season, players needed to acclimate themselves to the beating their bodies would take.

Two-a-days helped the players' bodies get used to the innumerable collisions they would take part in throughout the season. The collisions meant new and different parts of the body would be sore. During the first week of camp, every inch of a player's body would be sore. Headaches lasted the entire two weeks and didn't stop until camp was over. It was a long season and if players weren't accustomed to the brutality of the sport then they were more likely to get injured. Getting one's body used to this kind of punishment is hell. Because of this, football camp was often referred to as "Hell Week" or in many cases, "Hell Weeks."

For the next two weeks Charlie and the entire Puma team ate, slept, and drank football. It was literally their life for this time. The players even stayed together. The team was bunked up at the campus dorms. This made it so that nobody could have any excuses for being late or missing practice. The dorms were adjacent to the practice fields and the cafeteria was in the basement of the dorms. The players only brought their clothes and a few personal things to have at the dorms. During the week they would either be at the dorms or football. On Saturday evening and Sunday, the players had free time and could sleep wherever the pleased, but had to report back on Sunday evening for the team meeting.

The dorms were in a tall, eight story building. The outside was grey concrete and could have passed for any other building on campus. Inside, the rooms were barely big enough for two single beds. At the foot of each bed was a small desk. While the football team was staying there, the desk wouldn't see many books, but some of the guys would bring a small TV to put in that space so they could unwind in their limited spare time. The white washed walls throughout the building brought a feeling of sterility to the place. On each floor, in the center of the building, was a common bathroom for the guys to share. This year the team was bunking on the top three floors of the building.

Not only could the coaches keep a close eye on the players this way, but it was also a way for the players to bond and really become a team. There was a lot of joking and laughing to try and take their minds off of the strenuous task at hand. It was a good idea because when camp began, there were always a lot of new faces and it took time to become teammates. By the end of camp, there were fewer fights on the practice field because the guys had gotten to know each other and didn't want to be fighting someone who was now a friend.

Reality

Summer was a dream for April. She got to have her husband back and her family was whole. It was a time for the three of them to connect and create a bond that would help them through the long season. Blake was able to spend a lot of time with the family and she felt like a real couple during the summer. It wasn't just brief encounters between practices and games, but quality time spent together. Summer wasn't completely free, there were summer camps for high school kids and last minute recruiting. But even during those times, Blake had time for her and Conner before and after work. To April, each season seemed to get longer and longer. So each year two-a-days was a shock for her.

She barely saw Blake during two-a-days. He would leave the house by 7:00 in the morning, stay at the football complex during lunch for meetings and wouldn't return home until 11:00 or midnight. By that time, after being in the sun all day and all the talking at meetings, he would say a word or two before falling fast asleep and wake up eight hours later to repeat the whole marathon again. It was two weeks of only football for Blake and two weeks of loneliness for April. Neither of them liked it, but they knew that it would come every year.

This year was going to be a little easier because it was her first summer with a constant playmate, Conner. He was now eight months old and she wanted to start teaching him how to swim. There was a local pool a few blocks down the street that she could walk to every day. Each morning at 9:00 there was a special lesson for parents and their young babies.

On Blake's first day of two-a-days, April took Conner to the mall and they went shopping for bathing suits. They picked out two cute swimsuits each and were ready to begin the swimming program the next morning.

April kept her mornings busy with swimming and her afternoons doing odds and ends around the home while Conner was napping. But, it was in the evenings that she longed for Blake. She missed cuddling with his large muscular body, his big arms wrapped around her when he would come home. Talking to Conner was important and helped create a mother-son bond, but she sorely wanted someone to have a real conversation with. Her parents were a few hours away and the friends they had made in town just weren't her cup of tea. Despite her knowledge that this would happen every year and her attempt at being prepared for it, she still dreaded it and counted down the days until it was over just as eagerly as any of the players or coaches.

Hell Weeks

"Wake up call!!!" Bang, Bang, Bang!!! "Wake up call!!!" Bang, Bang, Bang!!!

Charlie opened his eyes and through the haze the clock read 6:32. It was the morning wake up call.

"Wake up call!!!" Bang, Bang, Bang!!! "Wake up call!!!" carried on down the hall. The graduate assistant coach, the low guy on the totem pole who had to do the early morning grunt work, was in charge of today's wakeup call and continued pounding on the doors and shouting to make sure all of the guys were awake.

Charlie rolled onto his back and was sore already. It was only the morning of the second day of two-a-days. *This is going to be a long camp,* he admitted to himself. This wasn't a comment he would ever make out loud. He was a team captain and had to be a leader. Complaining wasn't a way to lead the team. He had to be mentally tough and, at the very least, feign a good attitude.

He laid in bed for a few more minutes before acquiescing to the day ahead of him. As he slowly got up, he said hello to his roommate, Anthony. Anthony was still refusing to give into the early morning hour and had not opened his eyes.

Charlie didn't care what Anthony was going to do, he needed to get some food in him to make it through practice and he had to do it early enough or he risked throwing it up at practice. He put on a pair of lounge shorts, grabbed his toothbrush, and walked to the dorm bathroom.

When he returned to drop off his toothbrush on the way down to breakfast he encouraged Anthony to get going. He didn't waste too much time, though. He had to stay on schedule.

During camp, the players would eat all of their meals in the cafeteria. The food was mediocre, but the main thing was there were unlimited quantities. One good thing about two-a-days, possibly the only thing, was the fact that one could eat anything and everything and still lose weight. It was nearly impossible to put in more calories than one would burn off during a day of two exhausting practices.

After his breakfast, Charlie sauntered over to the football complex. He got taped and was in the locker room before the big rush of players arrived. By doing this, he could get mentally ready for practice. He popped a few headache pills and began focusing. It was a bad idea to look at the whole of two-a-days as one task as it became overwhelming. Getting through one practice was achievable, surviving twenty more practices seemed next to impossible. One at a time was the pragmatic thing to do. It was the way to not only survive, but to excel in each and every practice. He also knew that a good mental outlook was vital. So he decided that there was nowhere he would rather be and that he would outwardly portray this and eventually begin to believe it. So while Charlie got his gear on, he began to smile. He realized a long time ago that a smile can go a long way towards establishing one's attitude.

At 9:00 AM sharp practice was called to a start. It went by according to plan. There were technique drills, hitting drills, position drills, and team drills. All of the drills were completed with extra enthusiasm since starting jobs were yet to be determined at many positions. By the end of practice, Charlie's headache was in full force. Having a headache made concentrating that much more difficult. But it happened every year and each player knew it was something he would have to fight through. It helped knowing the other guys were experiencing the same discomfort.

At 11:00 the first practice ended. By the time Charlie got undressed and lingered in a cold shower it was 11:30 and time for lunch. Practice was full speed all the time, so when he was away from the field Charlie, like many other guys, was very relaxed and slow moving. Every ounce of energy had to be saved for practice.

After a leisurely lunch, the players had their only free time of the day. From 12:30 to 2:30 they would watch TV, play video games, or take a nap. In an effort to be more gregarious, Charlie would wander the dorm for the first half hour trying to get to know more of the new guys on the team. He thought as the leader of the team he needed to be on a personal basis with all of the guys. Finally, as the noise died down throughout the dorm, Charlie devoted the next hour to rest and laid down to take a nap.

Charlie wanted to ensure he was on time for his offensive line position meeting at 2:30, so at 2:00 his alarm sounded. During the forty-five minute meeting the group went over film of the morning's practice. The coach would point out correct technique and miscues throughout the session. At 3:15 the players were dismissed and were ready for the next practice by 3:45. Nobody wanted to be late, even less so during two-a-days. If a guy was late, he would have to run extra after practice. Running extra during two-a-days was a disaster. This extra work would make it next to impossible to give a full effort during practice. To ensure there was no chance of tardiness, all of the guys made sure to be ten or fifteen minutes early.

As Charlie slipped on his helmet, he went into captain mode. He blocked out his fatigue and smiled broadly. If he had a positive attitude about each and every practice, this would rub off onto his teammates. A team full of positive attitudes would go a long way towards creating a championship season. As the leader, Charlie knew he would have to start the trend and encourage the guys to follow his lead. He kept repeating the phrase, "There is no place I would rather be," over and over in his head. After enough repetitions, he would believe it. It wasn't very difficult to convince himself of this today, but each practice and each day it was harder and harder to bring an energetic, upbeat attitude to the field. As he jogged out onto the field, he slapped Cedric on the behind and yelled out to the guys around, "Hell yeah, boys! Such a beautiful day for another practice."

Cedric replied by shoving him and saying, "Yeah, yeah, fuck off. I am going to kick your ass in one on ones today. So don't mess with me."

"Ohhhh, did somebody miss his nap?" Anthony helped Charlie out from the edge of the group.

"Hey, fuck all you guys. This shit is getting old already. Only our fourth practice and I am tired as fuck. I hope this heat dies down. Yeah, I am ornery, but I am just going to take it out on you asshole offensive lineman. A bunch of fat, lazy asses anyway."

Now he had the attention of everyone around him. "Oh, shit Cedric, look at your fat ass. You barely even finished the conditioning test, so I wouldn't be talking if I were you. With all your shit talking you better watch it today. We fat asses are gonna knock you down and then lay on you if you don't watch it," Anthony shot back, joining the shit talking.

"The o-line ain't knocking anybody down. We kicked your ass this morning and are going to do it again this afternoon. We will see who is laying on who at the end of the afternoon." Now Junior was adding to the fire.

Charlie loved it. The dull, humdrum of just another practice was broken. The intensity was back into the mix. He couldn't help but chime in, "Man, o-line is always kicking your ass. Look at you guys, you are all tired and beat up. We are all smiling and energized," Charlie lied.

"All right, we will see," Junior retorted, as Coach Jackson came out of the building, blowing his whistle, sending the players off on their warm up jog.

As the group began coalescing, Charlie had to keep things going and hollered, "O-line!!! Whose house??? O-line!!! Whose house??? O-line!!!" After a few chants by himself, his fellow offensive lineman joined him in chanting. He didn't know if it energized him and his o-line buddies or if it motivated the d-line for that practice. Nevertheless, that afternoon's practice was as intense as the first practice of camp.

Finally removing his pads for the last time that day at about 6:15, Charlie plodded into the showers and anchored himself under a spray of cold water. It was so damn hot outside that he was still sweating. As the water washed away the sweat, dirt, and blood, Charlie's body finally began to cool down.

The players moved like a herd of cattle from the locker room to the cafeteria. Dinner was from 6:30-7:30. This was the best meal of the day because nobody had to worry about how much they ate. There was no chance of throwing it up, practice was done for the day. It was time to pig out. Charlie made sure to get dessert on his first go around. He had learned from his previous camps that if he waited until he was done with his main course, all of the good desserts were gone. If after his first time there were still good desserts left, then he would have another one, but this way he assured himself of at least one good dessert.

At 8:00 PM Charlie was back at the stadium in the guest locker room for his second position meeting of the day. This was the offensive line's designated meeting spot and would be their meeting room throughout the season. In fact, it had been that way since Charlie was with the Puma. At this meeting they spent a little bit of time going over film of the afternoon practice before moving on to the new plays that would be used in practice the next day.

By 8:45 they were dismissed and wandered down the hall for the team meeting that began at 9:00. At the beginning of the team meeting, each player got a sack with a snack, as if they needed more food. The coaches liked to keep the players fed because weight loss during two-a-days was a serious concern. The players had worked so hard to bulk up with muscle mass that the coaches didn't want all of the work to disappear in a matter of two weeks. Keeping the players fed, almost forcing food down their throats, helped eliminate unwanted weight loss. Even with the four meals a day, most of the guys would lose a few pounds.

At the team meeting Coach Jackson had his chance to get up in front of the team and give his perspective on the day's activities. He ranted and raved about what had yet to be accomplished. He pointed out a few of the positive things that had happened, but admonished them all that the team was far from reaching its potential.

After Coach Jackson gave his speeches and told them what was expected of them the next day, it was time for some inspiration. They watched a video featuring players from the NFL Each player would talk about the qualities it takes to be successful; hard work, determination, and a belief in one's self. It went on to examine the elements that were necessary for a team to be champions; a bond with each other, believing in one another, and giving your best on each play.

At 9:45, with every person completely exhausted, the team was dismissed for the night. Charlie chatted with a few of the guys on the short walk to the dorms. He went straight to his room, brushed his teeth, and collapsed in his bed. The coaches would be around at 10:30 to ensure that all of the lights were out, but Charlie would be asleep before they walked through the halls.

This is how two-a-days continued for two weeks. Charlie and his Puma teammates woke up, ate, went to football, ate, took a nap, went to football, ate, went to football, and then slept through the night. They had Saturday afternoon until dinner time on Sunday off, and then they began the next week.

In a foggy haze filled with headaches, cramps, and exhaustion, Charlie and his teammates survived two-a-days. He had taken it one practice at a time and one day at a time. In adhering to the role of team leader, Charlie had brought a positive attitude and high energy to each practice. By the end of camp, the team had rallied around Charlie as the leader and looked to him whenever guidance was needed. His persistence and determination had paid off. Then, finally the light at the end of the tunnel had come. It was the last night of camp. Tomorrow's scrimmage would mark the official end of camp.

On the way out of the last meeting of the night, Charlie was stopped by his position coach, Coach Havili. "Hey Charlie. Great job today. I have something to request."

"Okay, Coach, go ahead," Charlie responded, a little surprised.

"Tomorrow after the scrimmage, before the team is dismissed from camp, Coach Jackson wants you and Junior to get up in front of the team and give a speech. Can you do that?" he asked, matter of factly.

Before Charlie had time to even think about what was being requested of him, he enthusiastically responded, "Yeah, sure. That'll be fine."

"All right, see you tomorrow. Get some sleep."

"Okay, good night coach." All of the players were half way across the field, on their way to the dorms, by the time Charlie left the complex. He became anxious about his task tomorrow. He felt maladroit at speaking in front of everyone. But, he knew that this was a great chance to make an impression on his teammates and coaches. This task and opportunity kept him awake longer that he wanted that night, as he lay in bed, pondering what he would say the next day.

Staring into the darkness of the dorm room, he began to ponder how he had become a leader and why he had been so eagerly accepted as a leader. His mind began to wander, running back to something his high school coach had once said about leaders. He could still remember the speech, his coach had even written down the name of the speech on the chalkboard at the front of the room. His mind drifted back to that moment.

The team was crammed in a small classroom in the corner of the school near the locker room. It was also the last night of two-a-days. His high school team had a tradition of having a slumber party on this last night of camp to help the team complete their bond and learn to rely on each other. It was a night Charlie always enjoyed while in high school. The room smelled of stale sweat, most of the guys still hadn't taken showers. Plus, it was summer so the air conditioning wasn't running in the building. His coach's face was red from sunburn. He had titled the speech 'What is a Leader?'

He had a lot of quotes and stories of things people had done, but what stuck in Charlie's mind was what he said at the end of the speech. As his coach had continued talking, sweat started beading up on his forehead. Spit had begun to fly as he became passionate about the subject. Then he took a deep breath, waited to ensure he had everyone's complete attention, and calmly told them, "A leader is someone who WANTS to make the decision. It is someone who relishes being counted on in crunch time and who wants to be counted on. It is someone who doesn't need to be asked to do something and when he is asked to do something he does more than what was asked of him. It is also someone who doesn't shy away from responsibility, but rather someone who seeks out responsibility."

Charlie had taken this speech and advice to heart. He already knew at that point in time that he wanted to be a leader. He had taken all this in, digested it, and tried to live his life like that.

Drifting back to his white washed dorm room with snores coming from his roommate, Charlie realized he had done all of this. He knew now, in this moment, that was why his peers had embraced him as a leader. All it had taken was the courage to stand up, to say something, to be singled out. It didn't really matter what he had said, it was the fact that he had been brave enough to say something at all. It was as if they were looking for someone to follow, someone strong enough to go for it all, who would risk everything and be vulnerable in front of everyone. People want someone to follow, they don't want to make all the decisions. Charlie was that person. He had a dream and a vision, saw that the opportunity was there, and had accomplished his goal. He began to feel confident and comfortable in his new role for the first time. He finally grasped the fact that he had done all that he could to be in this position and deserved to be a captain. He understood that whatever he said tomorrow, the guys would listen and respect what he was saying. He knew that they were looking for someone to lead them and that, at this point in time, he was the one to do it.

Challenge

It was Saturday afternoon, camp was over, the scrimmage had gone well, the team was beginning to blend and mesh together. The only thing left was the final meeting. Everyone felt better, from the coaches, to the trainers, to the players. Making it through two-a-days was an accomplishment not to be taken lightly. It was something one survived, both players and coaches. The coaches didn't have to do the physical part of it, but their entire lives had been football for the past two weeks. From 7:00 AM to 11:00 PM the only thing they had done was football. It was a relief to the entire Puma staff to be done with this year's football camp.

The meeting started out with a few comments from Coach Jackson about the scrimmage. "There are some things we did well, but in other areas we need obvious improvement. We have come a long way, but that means we need to work harder. The minute we get complacent we will start to regress, which is not something we can afford at this point. Our first game is only two weeks from tonight. We will give you everything you need to be ready, what you do with that is up to you. We can't be the ones out there making plays, you have to make the plays." It all seemed like things Charlie had heard a thousand times, plus he was having a hard time concentrating. He would be giving his speech immediately following Coach Jackson. "Well, that is enough about the scrimmage. I want to talk about the upcoming season. But before I do, I have two special guests who are going to speak to you today. They are your team captains, as selected by you. They are both not only excellent players, but also great people. Give them your full attention. Now, first please give a hand to Charlie Peterson."

Charlie made his way to the front of the room. The applause died down as he reached the middle of the room. He looked out towards the team. He didn't really see individual faces, just a big mass of people. Although it was only a little over 100 people, including the coaches, it seemed like a large crowd to Charlie. This was the first time he had spoken in front of this many people and he was nervous about it. He smiled for a moment, fidgeted with his hands, and began before any more nerves could take a hold of him. He started with the only thing that came to his mind, "Well guys, we made it. We are done with two-a-days. Now, that is something to be happy about."

Some of the guys responded with cheers and laughs, which relaxed him and allowed him to remember what he wanted to talk about. "This is a big year, guys. I am a senior and this season is extremely important to me. I want to go out on a high note. I want to end my college career on top. It is not just enough to have a winning record, I want to be the best. I am going to be the best player I can this year and I want this team to be the best it can be. It has been four years since this team has won a conference championship. It has been four years since this team has been in the postseason. There have been some close calls, but close isn't good enough this year. That means that I, along with the rest of the seniors, haven't had a conference championship or a post season. We came in right after a championship, but didn't do enough to keep the good times riding high. I expect all of that to change this year and I am going to do everything in my power to make it change."

"To me it is simple. Why can't this be our year? I will tell you why. There is no reason at all. It can be our year just as easily as it can be someone else's year. The only reason why it won't be our year is because of two things. Either we don't believe in our hearts that it is our year or we don't give our full effort. If we believe in ourselves and give 110% effort every play and every practice, then there is no reason why we can't win every game."

"Think about it for a minute. Is there anyone who has worked harder than we have this off season? No! Is there anyone who is faster or stronger than we are? No! Is there anyone who practices harder than we do during the week? No! Is there anyone who has better coaches or better preparation than we do? No! So, then why can't we win every game? Like I said, only two reasons. Either we don't believe in ourselves or we don't give full effort. Those are the only two reasons, plain and simple. There is nothing more, no excuses, and no complaining. If we don't win, we know that it was our problem and our fault. We can't blame anyone or anything else. It is up to us, and us alone, whether we win or lose." He paused for a moment to collect his thoughts.

"So, I am going to challenge myself. I am going to challenge myself to believe in not only myself, but in each and every one of you. I am going to believe that Anthony will get that block. I am going to believe that Johnny will make that throw. I am going to believe that Junior will make that tackle. Then, by believing in each and every player on the team, I will inevitably believe in the team as a whole. If I believe in the team and that each player will do his job, then I will know in my heart that we can win every single game."

"On top of this, if I believe in everyone on the team and everyone on the team believes in me, then I won't want to let anyone down. And the only way to not let my teammates down is to give 110% effort every time I step on that field. If I am not prepared to give my full effort, then I won't step on the field because I will know that I would be betraying my teammates belief and trust in me. Trust is not an easy thing to regain, once it is lost. I am also going to challenge myself to play as hard as I possibly can, each and every play. If I do that, and I know that everyone else is doing that, there is nothing that can stop us."

"But, I am not only going to challenge myself. I am going to challenge each and every one of you. I challenge all of you to believe in yourself and your teammates. I also challenge you to give 110% at all times. I wouldn't issue this challenge if I wasn't willing to step up to the plate myself. Just think about it over the weekend. This is serious. We have to visualize ourselves as winners and believe that it will happen, or it can't be achieved." Charlie paused, wondering how far he should take this line of thought.

He looked around and saw that the players were engaged in his speech, he saw that even the coaches had put down their notebooks and were listening. He felt emboldened by this and went for the gusto. "While you are away from football for a couple days, think about what I said. Think about whether it is something that you can do. Can you commit to giving your best effort and, most importantly, commit to believing in yourself and our team? If not, then don't come back. This season is too important. If you aren't all in, then we can't have you on the team. I like and respect everyone here, but the only way we can move forward is with everyone on the same page and working towards the same goal."

He noticed that some of the players and coaches were surprised at what he was saying, but he knew the look on most people's faces was respect, not surprise. He then wrapped it up. "I believe. And I look forward to seeing everyone back here Tuesday to begin our quest for the conference championship." Charlie gave a little nod and quickly made his way back to his seat. *If that isn't the players taking control and stepping up to take responsibility for the direction of the team, then I don't know what is*, Charlie almost thought out loud.

Coach Jackson was back in front by the time Charlie had taken his seat. "Great speech, Charlie. I appreciated everything you said. You summed it up great. I want to be the first to accept your challenge. I promise to give 110% and to believe in this team and myself. Thanks, Charlie. Now, I agree with what Charlie said and I expect to see everyone back here on Tuesday. I don't think we have anyone who is going to quit that easily, right?" He scanned the room to make sure he was receiving affirmative nods from the entire team. "Now, let me welcome your defensive captain, Junior Atwood."

Junior got up and gave a speech about how well he thought the team would do and how much he loved the game of football. The speech was short and sweet, without much that the players would remember afterwards.

Coach Jackson again took the floor and called the team together for the last time during this camp. "I know everyone is anxious to get going. This has been a long camp and we all want to get out of here. That is fine, we will be done shortly. But, this is very important. I need you all to listen and to give me your full attention. So I want you to stand up and stretch, or shake, or whatever you need to do in order to concentrate for ten more minutes." He stopped and gave the team a moment to stand up and stretch before continuing.

"I need to reiterate that this is an important season. It has been four years since we have won a conference championship or been to the postseason. That is way too long. That is not acceptable any more. This year anything less than a conference championship is a let down. We have too much invested and too much talent not to finish at the top. Now to accomplish this, I am going to demand and expect more from every one of you this year. From the starters, to the backups, to the walk-ons. Everyone needs to step his level of play up a notch. If you can't do this, then I will find someone who can. If you can't do this, then you will be watching the games from the sidelines. I need the best people out on the field at every moment. If the backups can't step up enough to be on special teams, then I will have to use the starters for special teams. This isn't a threat or a warning, it is just an announcement that this is how it is going to be this year. We are not going to settle for anything less than the top. If you have been giving your best, give me more. However strong or fast you are now, I need you to be stronger and faster. However much time you put into studying film, I need you to put in more time. And I am not going to let up. You will have to give me better than your best effort in every practice, in every game, and on every play. If you aren't capable of that, then we will find someone who is. Expectations are high this year from the top to the bottom. The only reason we won't fulfill those expectations is if we become complacent. So the entire coaching staff and I will be on your ass to make sure that you don't become complacent."

"Camp this year was great. The intensity level and competitiveness was superb. I will expect that kind of energy every day at practice. It was hard, and I know we pushed you. But you are going to be pushed like that every day. Practice is going to be harder than the game, that way when you are in the game, it will be easier. Plus, we are going to continue to do conditioning. We are in good shape now, we will be in great shape for the entire season. So that means we will be running at the end of every practice. You know that is coming, so I don't want any complaining. We have tomorrow and Monday off, but that doesn't mean you can't be in here on Monday looking at tape. We had all of two-a-days filmed so that you can watch yourself and learn from your mistakes. It is also not too early to be watching film on State, our first opponent. When we are back on Tuesday, it is all business. We will be back into full practice mode. I expect you to all be recovered and ready to give this team everything you have. Tuesday will not be a light day, we will be stepping up the tempo. Be prepared!!!" With a look of determination he glanced around the room, seeming to catch everyone's eye. He then looked down at his notes to make sure he had covered everything.

"School starts on Monday. Your responsibilities don't start and stop with the football field. You are here to get an education. I expect you to all be at class and to maintain your eligibility. You have been given notes by your position coach. It lets the professor know that you will be gone from class a few times and asks for their cooperation in letting you make up missed work. It also lets them know that you WILL do all of the work that you miss. Make sure to live up to your part of the bargain. I want you to give the note to each of your professors and talk to them about it on the first day of class. Don't wait, do it the first chance you have." Coach Jackson put down his notebook and smiled from ear to ear. "Well boys, you have done it. Just be careful tonight and don't do anything stupid. That is it. Now, get the hell out of here and don't even think about football until Monday. Great job, see you later!"

With that, they all headed for the exit. Even the coaches left without first going back to their offices. They all loved football, but were sick and tired of it right now. The only thing on most of the guys' minds was beer, women, and relaxation. Charlie couldn't wait to see Mary, who had just gotten back into town earlier today, and to taste that first sip of cold beer.

Relief

Knock, knock, knock!!!

"Come in." The soft feminine voice could barely be heard through the door.

Charlie swung the door open to the beige carpeted living room. The apartment was spotless and smelled like the floors had just been cleaned. The walls were decorated with a couple of nature pictures and doilies topped by candles were in every corner. It was well lit and had a warm, comfortable feeling. The two plush brown sofas that faced the TV were always inviting. From the adjoining kitchen, Mary sprang up from one of the wooden chairs that surrounded the tan colored table. "Hey, Charlie," she enthusiastically let out as she bounded towards him.

"Hi Mary," Charlie replied back as they embraced in a passionate hug. Their lips met and they stayed frozen in time for a moment.

As they let go of each other, Johnny tried to quietly sneak into the kitchen. Mary greeted him with a friendly hug. "Hey Johnny. How are ya?"

"Good, thanks," Johnny smiled and continued towards the table where Mary's roommate Rebekah was sitting. He plopped a case of Keystone on the table. "What's up, Rebekah."

"Not too much. Just back for school." Rebekah looked back to the living room. "Hey, Charlie."

"Hi Rebekah." Charlie and Mary made their way slowly towards the kitchen table. They had stars in their eyes as they gazed at each other. "It is great to see you again. I am glad you are back in town. I haven't talked to you much the past two weeks. How was the end of your summer?"

"Oh, it was fine. I finished up my internship. They threw me a nice going away party, so I guess they liked me. Spent plenty of time with the fam. The same old stuff, you know." Mary filled him in on what had happened with her while he was in two-a-days.

Mary was tall with sandy blond hair. Her smile was amazing and she had a nice body. Today her hair was pulled back and it highlighted the incredible bone structure of her face.

She was very attractive and Charlie always looked at her with passion. She was a serious student and had never thought she would date a football player. She had always heard such bad things about them. She had tried to avoid too much drama, because school was very important to her. She was studying business and would be graduating this spring at the top of her class. She wanted to get done with school and get out in the real world so she could begin making a name for herself. Because of her goal oriented attitude, they made a good couple. They really loved and cared for each other, but also needed a lot of time to pursue their own goals. They trusted each other and were able to allow each other space in reaching for what they individually wanted. "It is awesome to see you. I'm glad we get to spend some time together before school starts up," she said, genuinely, as they joined the other two at the kitchen table.

"Mary and I were waiting for you two before we started drinking. If you had been much longer, I don't know if we could have held out," Rebekah impatiently blurted out. "So, what do you say? Should we get to partying?" She was a cute girl. She was shorter than Mary and a little bit stout with a cute face. Her long, silky black hair was a turn on for many guys. But her feisty spirit seemed to keep any serious courters away.

"Well, I'm not waiting any longer," Johnny answered back, as he broke into the beer. Before another word was said, Johnny had the can to his mouth. After a long guzzle, Johnny let out a big, "Ahhhhhhhhh. Now that is what I am talking about. That hits the spot after the crazy ass, stupid, long two-a-days. Nothing like a cold beer to help forget the living hell we just went through."

Charlie reached across the table and grabbed one for himself. "Cheers to that, buddy. Let's get drunk!" They clinked their cans together and downed half of their beer.

The girls were already up and fixing their own drinks. They didn't really like beer. The four of them sat around in the evening hours chatting about the summer, the crappy jobs they had during the summer, and the strange feelings they had in regards to this being their last year in college.

At 9:00, with a good buzz, they decided it was time to go to the party. Johnny claimed he was okay to drive the dozen blocks to the party, so the four of them piled into his pick-up. It was a silver mid 80's Nissan truck. The interior was maroon and the floor barely had an inch that wasn't covered with garbage. They all knew four people in a pick-up with a driver who is tipsy wasn't a good idea, but being young and stupid freed them from any rational thought processes.

After a jerky ten minute ride down back streets, they arrived at the party. It was a plain, one story house. The grass had more brown patches than green patches and the exterior looked about five years overdue for a new paint job. The inside was decorated with lots of hand-me-down couches and posters of bikini clad models. It was a typical male college pad, comfortable and with all the essentials, but perpetually messy. Junior and a few other football players lived there. There were people flowing out of the house into the front yard already. Some of the people had cups of beer from the keg that was in the basement and many others were carrying around jugs full of their own concoctions. Tonight everyone would be getting drunk.

The four walked to the front gate together before Johnny took off for the basement, he was in need of more beer. Rebekah spotted some friends and headed that direction. Charlie and Mary walked inside together, still holding hands. After saying hello to a few of the football guys, Mary decided to hang with her friends for a while. They kissed each other goodbye and Charlie began doing his rounds of the party.

Football camp is a great way for a football team to bond on the field. A party where all the teammates get drunk is a great way for a team to bond off the field. Charlie made his way to the kitchen and began looking through the cupboards. After finding a pitcher, he headed to the basement. He didn't want to come back to the keg every 15 minutes, so he got the biggest container he could find. Once it was full he began to make his rounds. He wanted to at least say hi to all the guys on the team. He talked with everyone, making a concerted effort to remember all their names. He would sit down from time to time with a group of the guys and talk some shit, or check out the girls that walked by them.

By midnight the house was packed and people were overflowing from every door in the house. From all of the body heat, it was hot and humid in the house. Charlie was wasted and beginning to feel tired. He finagled his way outside and found a deck chair tipped over on the lawn. He righted the chair and carefully made his way into the comfortable seat. He wanted a moment by himself and a minute to get some fresh air. The summer breeze felt good running against the sweat that was on his skin. He tilted his head back and looked up through the leaves to the scattered stars dotting the infinite blackness above. Moving his head back down to the scene at the party, things began to spin. His eyes went wide for a moment before he came back to reality and felt better.

As his vision came back into focus, he could see Mary standing at the far side of the yard with her back to him. She was wearing a Levi skirt and a red sleeveless blouse. The moonlight gently reflected off of her smooth shoulders. Her brown, tanned skin looked so inviting. The breeze blew her pulled back hair enough to expose her neck. Her beauty brought a smile to Charlie's face.

He gingerly stood up and made sure he had his balance before making his way across the yard. As he approached her, he grabbed her gently around the waist and bent down to her ear. "You look amazing. Can I take you home with me?" he whispered into her ear.

Mary's group of friends who she had been talking with gave her a suspicious glance, and then said hello to Charlie. "Hi ladies, how are you? Sorry to interrupt, but I need to take Mary away."

"Well, everyone, see you later," Mary said, before turning towards Charlie. "Of course you can take me home, but first give me a kiss." They leaned into each other and began making out. They didn't want to stop until people started cheering and clapping. They turned red for a moment and gave a wave to the facetious crowd.

"I guess we should go." Charlie stated the obvious, as he pulled back from her lips.

"Yeah, where should we go?" Mary asked.

"Let's go to my place, it is only a few minutes away." They stumbled the couple blocks to Charlie's apartment holding each other tightly the entire way.

Once inside they were all over each other. All night they had barely been able to contain their passion for each other. They made love until they passed out. They slept most of the next day, trying to get out of their alcohol induced haze. They spent the day and night together again at Mary's place.

It wasn't until they had to go to class on Monday morning that they left each other's side. It was the longest amount of time they would have to spend together until the season was over. So they tried to make it last and savored each minute. It was great to be young and in love. Charlie had no idea that he would be the one to jeopardize this by going against all of his values. He couldn't know that he was heading towards a breakdown that would lead him to rebel against someone he cared for so much and to almost abandon all he had worked to be.

Supportive Wife

Blake and April were on their way to Shooters, the local bar where the coaches went on the weekends. It was a slightly fancy, alumni-owned bar on the outskirts of town. This was the chosen destination for the coaches because they knew the chance of running into any of the players was slim. The drinks were too expensive for college kids on a tight budget. It had real wooden tables and servers who paid attention to each of the customers. Big screens were on every wall with smaller TVs filling in the gaps. Most of the TVs had different sporting events with the big screens reserved for the big games of the night. Puma memorabilia adorned the remaining space on the walls. Signed pictures or jerseys from former Puma players who had made it to the NFL, NBA, MLB, or any other professional league were also proudly displayed.

April had given up arguing about attending all of these coaches' parties. She knew that it was a losing battle, and she was tired of fighting. Although they had barely seen each other over the past two weeks, the get together of the coaches and their partners had become the first priority.

Arriving at the bar, Blake pulled open the heavy wooden door to the main entrance. They were instantly greeted by the smell of liquor and cigarettes. The place was just one big open room with the kitchen and the bar off to one side. In the far corner, a couple wearing tight jeans was studying the jukebox as some classic rock gently hummed from the machine. April was wearing an off white sleeveless summer dress that went down to her knees and showed off her tan well. While Blake had been completely consumed with football for the past two weeks, she had taken Conner to the pool every day. It was something fun to do and kept her busy during that solitary time.

Their group was in the middle of the room spread out across four different tables that had been pushed together. They were waved over by Coach Jackson who had spotted them upon entering. Despite April's acquiescence about coming tonight, she flashed a broad smile as they approached the crowded table.

Coach Jackson directed them towards two open chairs next to him. He pulled out the one directly adjacent to him for

April to sit in. She wasn't thrilled with the thought of spending the evening next to Coach Jackson, who became more gregarious with each drink, but she gracefully accepted his offer.

After April and Blake exchanged greetings with everyone, Coach Jackson requested the table's attention. He stood up to ensure that he could be heard and seen by all of his guests. "Now that we have everyone here, I would like to first say thank you to all of the ladies. I know I took your partners from you, almost entirely, for two weeks, and I am grateful for your understanding and willingness to allow them to be so dedicated during our camp. I also want to thank my staff who have worked their asses off the past two weeks. This is an important year and we started out on the right foot. I am expecting big things and I think we did a lot to move in that direction. After all of your hard work and the ladies' patience, I would like to treat everyone tonight. Drinks and food are on me. Order up, have fun, and forget about football for a while." He nodded his head and sat down to a chorus of "thank yous".

Beer and cocktails began to be consumed in earnest. The coaches and their partners were just as eager to forget what they had been through recently. Blake poured a beer for April from the frothy pitcher and offered his mug for a cheers. They clanked their mugs together, gave each other a kiss, and let the cold beer run down their throats. People chitchatted aimlessly as food and beverages came and went faster than April could keep track of.

April talked a little bit with the women across from her, but mostly listened to their complaining and whining. Donna, Coach Miller's wife, wore too much make up and dressed in clothes that were nicer than April could afford. This summer, her problem had been trying to get the new puppy to stop peeing in the house. She didn't like cleaning and thought the shoe selection at the mall was abysmal. Peggy, Coach Jackson's wife, had had too many plastic surgeries. Her face looked like she had been stuck in a wind tunnel all summer. She complained about the fried food and the lack of wine selection at the bar. Her biggest worry was when to close the swimming pool for the year.

Jenny, Coach Kaifer's girlfriend, was on one of the new fad diets. She said that all of the previous diets had just been a scam, but that this new one was fool proof. She asked for tips on how to be a good, supportive partner to a football coach. April didn't feel like she had anything in common with these women. She didn't really want to be there, so she kept putting down the beers to dull the boredom. Whenever she got really bored, she would tug on Blake and make him talk to her for a while.

Throughout the night, she had a few light conversations with Coach Jackson, but nothing more than small talk. Then, as the night was nearing the end, Coach Jackson turned to her and asked if he could talk to her. "Of course, Grant. What is it?" she replied in a friendly, alcohol induced state.

"Well, I want to talk to you about Blake," he said, lowering his voice and leaning towards her to avoid having their conversation heard by the entire table.

"Okay, I love talking about Blake. Plus, you have seen more of him lately than I have." Her true thoughts were hard to hide after so many beers.

"Blake is doing a great job in his new position. He has really stepped up and taken charge. I want you to know how much I appreciate all his work."

"Well, thank you," April replied without much emotion. *It's as if he is giving me a pep talk*, she thought to herself. *I don't need a stupid pep talk. I just need more of my husband.*

"You're welcome." He paused and looked around the room, like he didn't want anyone to hear what he had to say next. "But I know that behind every great man is a great woman. I know that you are also giving a lot. You are sacrificing and giving Blake the support he needs to be a great coach. So, I need to thank you for that."

April's face grew sour. She didn't like what Grant was saying to her and she felt like it was manipulative. *As if I am responsible for Blake's success or not. As if all good wives just sit back and let their husbands dedicate their lives to this sport. Marriages don't need as much attention as a game, right*? She wanted to say all of these things, but bit her tongue. "I really am not doing much. I am glad Blake is pursuing his dream. I just wish he had a little more time to spend at home."

"Well, hang in there. Just keep up the good work. Blake has a bright future." He nodded to her and winked as if this had been their own little secret.

April's eyes narrowed and she became defensive. "Oh, I will hang in there, Grant. Thanks," she snapped back sarcastically, as Coach Jackson rose to leave with his wife.

April was glad he was leaving. She turned to find that Blake had congregated towards the end of the table with the rest of the coaches. She looked at him with serious eyes, full of determination. She was ready to go home. She was feeling the effects of all the beer she had drunk and was tired of socializing with the people here.

After seeing the look in her eye, Blake knew it was time to go. He excused himself and got up to meet April as she made her way towards him. He gave her a hug and rhetorically asked, "Ready to go?"

"Yeah, it is time to go." April turned to the table, smiled, and waved good bye to everyone. "Good night everyone. Thanks for a fun evening," she lied.

"See you guys on Monday. Ladies, it is always a pleasure." They turned and made their way outside. On the drive home, they avoided talking about the party. Instead they talked about Conner who was spending the night with April's parents. They arrived home and silently walked to their room before passing out.

FOOTBALL SEASON
AUGUST – NOVEMBER 2000

School

It was a late August Monday morning. The alarm clock wailed out at 8:00 AM. Charlie fumbled to shut it off, and then he smiled. He kissed Mary good morning and told her goodbye. He clumsily put his clothes on and went out to his truck. He drove back to his house to get ready for classes.

It was the first day of school. Although school was starting early this year, it also meant that two-a-days were finished. Even Charlie, a devout, enthusiastic football player, was glad when football camp was finished. It was great to get back into college life, which included football, classes, girls, and drinking.

He showered, shaved, and put on some new clothes. He enjoyed looking nice on the first day of class. He wanted the teachers to know that he was serious and, even though he had a girlfriend, it didn't mean that he couldn't flirt.

Leaving early, he parked his truck and took the long way to class. He had time to kill and wanted to take the scenic route in order to see some of the old faces from around campus and catch up with people from last year. As he strolled around the quad, he wore a big grin. Brown patches of scorched grass showed the damages of the long, hot summer. It was already getting warm in the morning hour. The bushes had been trimmed and the leaves on the trees were a dark green. The gardeners had made an effort to have the grounds look good for the first day. Charlie breathed in the smell of fresh cut grass and was glad to be back, he enjoyed school. It was a challenge of a different nature. His professors often underestimated him and tried to pigeonhole him into a simple category, dumb football player. He loved surprising them, and often times could tell they begrudgingly gave him his good marks. It was a new year full of unlimited possibilities.

Seeing a group of football guys, he took a detour, veering left. He exchanged greetings with all of them and settled into the crowd. Some of the guys started bitching about having to go to classes. Charlie reminded them that it was a hell of a lot better than two-a-days, which was met with a, "hell, yeah," from the entire gathering. They chatted for a few minutes, saying hello to the cute girls as they walked by, before they separated to go to class.

Charlie was the first to excuse himself. "Well, guys, I gotta go. Anyone going to History of Medieval Europe?"

They all looked at each other before Anthony responded. "Why the hell do you take those kinds of classes, dude? You actually have to read books and do papers. Plus, who needs history? All of that stuff happened so long ago. It doesn't matter anymore. Come to bowling with me and drop that lame class, man." The group nodded their heads in approval of Anthony's statement.

"Hey, it's interesting. I love it. History is the stuff of life. You need it to understand today's world. History isn't just a study of the past, it is a study of human behavior, human interaction. You guys will never know what you are missing. And anyway, football will be over some day. I want to be a teacher when it is over, but hopefully that isn't for a while. Well, I am going. See you guys." Charlie waved over his shoulder.

"Okay teacher, can I have an A, please? I promise to do whatever you say. I'll even stay after school if you want me to," Anthony teased him. The guys responded with laughs and joined in, "Come on Mr. Peterson. Please give me an A."

Charlie turned around and with a sarcastic tone said, "None of you guys are getting A's from me. You'll actually have to read a book. So, that eliminates most of you. Now go to class, it is time to go." They all looked at the clock tower, said a few goodbyes, and went their own ways. Charlie looked at Anthony again and told him, "Especially you. You have a lot to make up for, young man." Anthony gave him the bird, smiled, and they both laughed before turning around and going to class.

Down, Set, Hut

Preconceptions

    The first day of school was going well. Charlie liked his classes and there were a few girls in each class who he could flirt with when the lectures got boring. Since he had a girlfriend that was all it would be, but nice scenery always makes everything better. The professors had been understanding about his forthcoming absences on Fridays when the team was traveling for their road games. Then it all changed with his third and final class of the day.

    Charlie had to walk across the quad to the human sciences building for his Health and Society Awareness class. He was excited because he ran into T.J. and Bart from the team who had the same class. They were all seniors taking their last required general education class. It wasn't their first choice of classes, but it worked with their schedules, and was just a 100 level class, so they all thought it would be a breeze.

    They rolled into the class and took up real estate near the back of the classroom. Charlie usually sat closer to the front, but since he had some friends in class, he decided to sit near them. It was a large classroom with about 100 desks. There was a podium at the front with a large white board behind it, over which a screen had been pulled down. The rows of desks rose up from the podium, creating an amphitheater effect. The room's furnishings were sparse, with nothing to distinguish it from any other lecture hall. About half the seats were full, which created islands of students sitting near their friends.

    Precisely at 11:30, the professor walked into the classroom. The eerie silence which accompanied his brisk, formal entrance portended the struggles which lay ahead in this class. He was a tall, lanky man. The skin on his face was brown and taut, looking like he had spent too much time in the sun over the summer. He walked with an air of importance, like the world answered to him and him only. As he approached the front, he scanned the classroom and locked his eyes on Charlie and his friends. His gaze narrowed and his brow furrowed, like he was preparing for battle. He didn't break eye contact until the players looked away. They looked at each other with confused looks, not knowing why this guy was staring them down.

He took his spot behind the podium, neatly placed his file down, and cleared his throat. The remaining chatters stopped. "I am Dr. Donovan. This is Health and Society Awareness 142. If that is not the class you signed up for, then you are in the wrong room. Check your schedule and proceed to the correct lecture hall." Charlie, T.J, and Bart all turned to each other with an uncertain look.

"Now, first thing, I need each of you to sign this paper with the exact name you are registered under." He placed a yellow legal pad on the desk of the only student in the front row. "Pass it around and will the last person bring it up to me, please?" He then walked back to the podium and grabbed a stack of papers. "This is the course syllabus. We will spend most of today's class going over this. Take one and pass it back." He returned to the front and turned on the overhead which portrayed a copy of the syllabus onto the screen. He waited quietly for a few minutes to ensure that each student received a copy.

"To begin with, I want to tell you a little about the class title. We will be focusing on personal health and how society influences each individual's health, as well as how each individual's personal health can have an impact on the overall health of society." He paused for a moment. "Before we get more into the class material, I want to talk about the rules and procedures of the class. If you will look at Roman numeral one, you will see the title, Class Rules and Procedures." As he began to go over the rules, he stared at Charlie and his friends again with what seemed like malice in his eyes. "I do not accept late work. I do not accept make up work. Many times we do work in class. If you aren't here, then you won't get the points. Classroom discussion is a part of your final mark. If you aren't here in class to take part in the discussions, then your overall grade will suffer. Cheating and plagiarism are completely unacceptable. If I catch you doing either, then I will fail you in this class and I will report you to the Dean. Cheating and plagiarism are punishable by expulsion."

The entire time Dr. Donovan spoke he did not take his eyes off of Charlie's group. It was as if he had designed these rules just for Charlie, T.J., and Bart. Even after finishing the rules and procedures, he stared at them for a moment. Finally, he returned to the syllabus and stopped looking at them. Shifting uncomfortably in their chairs, they felt like the speech was an accusation, not a warning.

During the remainder of the class, Charlie had a difficult time concentrating. He knew Dr. Donovan was trying to intimidate them and was hoping for an easy retreat. Charlie had no intention of withdrawing from the class. He was smart and there was no way he could scare him out of class. Charlie could do the work, and as long as he did the work, there was no justification for Dr. Donovan to give him a bad grade.

Charlie hated being pigeon holed. Sure, there were football players who expected something for free, but there were people like that everywhere. It wasn't fair to judge him solely by the sport he chose to play. He was as smart as anyone in the class and he wasn't backing down to a nasty professor who had a grudge against football players. *His wife probably cheated on him with a football player,* Charlie thought, *or he was picked on when he was young and now it is time for revenge. I don't give a shit. He isn't going to scare me out of here. I am going to do all the work and get A's on all the tests,* Charlie vowed to himself.

The class flew by in a haze while Charlie played mind games with himself, analyzing everything that had been said. He barely remembered anything from the rest of the class. After class, Charlie, T.J., and Bart approached Dr. Donovan with more bashfulness than they liked. They had a sheet which they were supposed to give to each of their professors at the end of the first class. The paper was a concise explanation of when and why they would miss class. It also asked for the teacher's co-operation in allowing the students to make up the work before or after the class that would be missed. It explained that the student athletes were responsible to turn in the make-up work when the professor requested it. It didn't ask for any special favors, only understanding that there would be classes which the football team members would not be able to attend.

As they approached the front, Dr. Donovan packed his papers orderly into his file and didn't acknowledge the three behemoth young men that were coming his way. He continued to ignore them, despite standing less than three feet from them, until Charlie spoke up. "Excuse me, Professor."

Before turning to acknowledge their presence, he said, "Dr. Donovan, please." He then faced them, looking at them with suspicion. "Yes, how may I help you?"

"Well, I'm Charlie Peterson, this is T.J. Perez, and this is Bart Miller. We are on the football team and we just wanted to inform you that there will be a few classes that we will be missing. We have a letter from our coaches that we would like to give you." Charlie extended the paper, but was left holding it in empty space.

Taking a moment to respond, Dr. Donovan's eyes filled with anger. "There is no need for the letter, Mr. Peterson. I know the situation and I think it is completely unacceptable. Are you here to play sports or to get an education?"

Despite the rhetorical nature of the question, Charlie felt compelled to answer. "To be honest, Dr. Donovan, we are here for both. Our chosen sport is helping us to get an education."

"Is that so? Well, you were here today, so you know the rules and procedures. I expect you to adhere to them, just the same as any other student. I'm not going to treat you any differently than any other student. Do you think I owe you something just because you have an athletic scholarship?" He waved his hand as if to dismiss them and shoo them away.

Charlie wasn't letting it go at that. "No, we aren't asking for anything special. All we are asking for is a chance to do the work that we can't be here to do."

"You are choosing not to be here, Mr. Peterson. That means you are choosing to miss some of the work. It is a choice that you are making, nobody is forcing it upon you."

"It is not really a choice. We are receiving a scholarship in exchange for our athletic talent. It is like a job, it is not for free. Missing these classes in order to go to our games is part of our job. Without it, many of us wouldn't be here and couldn't afford to go to college. Besides, you said there were exceptions for family and work emergencies," Charlie shot back defiantly.

"This is not an emergency. A work emergency is something that comes up unexpectedly. You are trying to schedule your education around your work, where the average student schedules his/her work around his/her education. So, that is not going to fly. Anyway, that is enough. I know your situation and you know the rules. If you decide to miss class, you know the consequences. I am finished talking about it." He turned away from them to signal he was not going to budge.

"Well, can we give you these letters?"

"That won't be necessary. Good day." He picked up his file and walked the opposite direction to the side exit.

Despite his refusal to take the letter, Charlie put his on the podium as Dr. Donovan looked back before leaving the room. Their eyes met, and they gave each other a glare. They both knew this battle was far from over.

Charlie, T.J., and Bart plodded back up the stairs of the classroom and out of the main exit. Once out of the class, they breathed a collective sigh of relief. "Man, that guy is a fucking asshole. What the hell is his problem?" Bart moaned.

"Yeah, dude. He was staring at us the whole time. As if we had already cheated. This is going to be one hell of a class," T.J. pitched in.

"Oh, don't worry about it, guys. He is just trying to scare us. He just hopes we will drop out of class and then he won't have to worry about us anymore," Charlie stated optimistically.

"Yeah, well I say we give him what he wants. I am not going to put up with his bull shit. He thinks he is so high and mighty, he isn't any better than the rest of us. That's why I am out of here. I am going to talk to my counselor right now and get a different class."

"Oh, come on, Bart. We can't do that. Then he wins. He thinks that we are all a bunch of dummies. He thinks that if he scares us with warnings of hard tests and a lot of assignments, then we will be out of there. We're not dumb and we are just as capable as any other student. Come on, don't let him be right," Charlie pleaded.

"Fuck that, dude. I have to stay eligible. I don't have much energy to study during the season, and plus I want to finish this spring. If I fail a class then I won't be able to graduate this spring. I'm right on the borderline. I can't risk anything for my eligibility or my graduation. Sorry. What about you T.J.?"

"Uhhhhh, I don't know. I don't like it, but I also don't want this guy to think he can scare us off that easily. I'm going to try and stick it out with Charlie."

"All right, guys. Well, good luck. I will see you at practice." Bart gave them both a bro hug before leaving.

They watched him walk away until he was out of earshot. Charlie turned to T.J. "Thanks for staying with me. It is going to be a lot easier with someone else in there. It isn't going to be that hard. Let's show that old, skinny bastard that we really are student athletes. I'll help you study and we can do all the projects together. When he has to give us an A it will be like shoving all his preconceived notions right in his face. I can't wait."

"Well, I'm not quite as excited as you. But, I'm going to stick it out. Like you said, I don't want that prissy, over tanned prick to think he is right about all the football players. He's not going to be right about these two." T.J. smiled.

They both nodded their heads and laughed. Before departing, they gave each other a bro hug and promised to be in this one together.

Jocks

Remembering the countless times Charlie had been told to pursue his passion as a career by counselors, teachers, parents, relatives, and anyone old enough to have a job, he now understood why. People always complained of having to go to work, wake up early, and put the hours in at the office, continually looking forward to the weekend so they could relax and be free.

This wasn't how Charlie felt about football, at all. He loved it, all aspects of it. He would listen to his teammates complain about practice, film, weightlifting, and meetings. But he couldn't sympathize with them. All of these activities were enjoyable for him. Most of his teammates were no different than the throngs of mainstream workers who only looked forward to the weekends. For the players it was the game against the opponent, as opposed to the weekend, which they anticipated and went through the week's rituals to reach.

Most guys just showed up at practice and put in the required effort and hoped it would all end soon. Charlie liked it, it was the part of the day that he looked forward to the most. He was usually one of the first people at the facilities before practice started and he was always one of the last to leave. He even liked the smell of it. Walking into that smelly, musty, moldy locker room crammed full of dirty nasty shoulder pads, wet cleats, and sweat stained shirts, it was as if Charlie were instantly ready to take to the field.

The smell must have triggered something in his brain because it was one of the things he liked most about getting there early and staying late. He could have a moment alone to himself in the locker room and absorb the aroma of everything. Taking in the smell, he was instantly transported to his own world, his football world. He liked it and didn't come back to reality for many hours. Not until practice was over and he left the locker room and the smell of the game behind him.

Film sessions and meetings were where he learned the science of the game and there was plenty of this to learn. He had been in the system long enough and had listened when the coaches talked so that he understood what many of the positions were expected to do, not just the offensive line. His grasp of the game had grown over the years. He felt knowledgeable and confident about the front eight, but still had plenty to learn about the defensive backfield and offensive skilled positions. Attending film sessions and watching film with players from these positions helped to increase his overall knowledge of the game.

    Watching film of the upcoming opponent helped to make him feel prepared and ready for anything that might come his way during the course of the game. By Friday night he would know what style of play his opponents would be using and all the guys that might match up against him. If he felt unsure about any of this, he would come in at lunch during the week and catch as much film as necessary to feel confident about the game and match ups.

    Film was also a great way to improve one's own game. One can see all of the mistakes and screw ups he makes by watching film of practice or the game. At times a player doesn't really want to watch it because he is reminded of his mistakes. This was especially true when watching in front of the coach or in position meetings. In these meetings, everyone knew the plays. So if anything went wrong the whole group knew immediately who had fucked up. Often times a player will look silly on tape and hope for whatever reason the coach might just fast forward past a certain play during the game. These hopes are usually dashed in an instant when the pause button is hit and a big finger is put to the screen and the coach tells everyone to watch what "not" to do. As a rule, the player will try to act surprised, as if he didn't know what he had done wrong. Some pull this off better than others.

    Watching film is a skill that one has to develop over time. It is not just acquired instantly. Taking in hours upon hours is the only sure way to gain this skill. Otherwise, it can easily just look like a clump of players with no organization going this way and that, with no apparent goal in mind. Charlie had been watching film since he was a sophomore in high school and had watched more than he could possibly remember, or even cared to remember. He could always find himself and know precisely what he had done correctly, or incorrectly.

All of these activities, watching film, working out, meeting with coaches, running, and practicing, Charlie enjoyed. It didn't feel like a job, it was fun. He loved competing and giving his full effort. This was something people seemed to notice and his teammates would even tease him about. They would ask him how he could always be so happy about being at practice, how he always had energy to run and work out. He thought it was just because he loved it and it was where he wanted to be. There was nothing else he could think of that he would rather be doing. Football was his passion and his love. If he was able to continue playing after this year it would be a dream come true.

One of the great things about football is the tremendous amount of strategy involved in the game. Charlie understood this aspect of the game very well. This was one of the reasons the coaches looked to him as a leader. Some of the players playing next to Charlie were inexperienced and he would help them out with what the correct blocking assignment was and sometimes even tell them who to block. The coaches felt comfortable enough with Charlie to put rookie players next to him, knowing that Charlie would make sure they blocked the right guy and help out if possible.

For an offensive lineman one of the most important things is knowing who to block on pass plays. If this isn't done, the quarterback will be hit hard and often, leading to a long night and probably a loss. For pass protection there are usually seven or eight people that the offensive line has to worry about; the three to four down linemen, three to four linebackers, and maybe a safety. Obviously the down linemen are the first people that have to be blocked. Five offensive to four defensive linemen leaves one extra offensive lineman. The blocking assignment depends on the particular team's scheme and who the uncovered lineman is. It can get pretty complex and some players have a hard time with the assignments and knowing who to block.

Fortunately, Charlie had it down pat. The center or one of the guards is usually the extra lineman. This person is responsible to block one of the defensive people who might blitz on that particular play. It can be from the weak side of the formation or the strong side of the formation. Sometimes the blitz will be straight forward and come from the middle of the defense. If this is the case, then the center or guard can easily pick up the blitzer. If it is coming from the outside then it can get a little more complicated. Now the uncovered lineman will have to shuffle out there to pick the man up, or switch with his teammate to pick up the blitzing player.

    The quarterback and running backs also play a vital role in pass protection. Each player, even the quarterback, is assigned a player and if this player blitzes then he is responsible for blocking that man. When the quarterback is responsible for one of the people blitzing, if he doesn't get the ball off quickly enough, then it is his fault, not the offensive line, if he is sacked. If the defense decides to send more people than the offensive can possibly block, then the quarterback must get rid of the ball very fast. This also creates a good opportunity for the offense because then receivers only have one man to beat and they will walk into the end zone. These kind of coaching chess matches occur throughout the game.

    The running backs are also responsible for blocking a defensive person. Sometimes they forget and decide to go out on a route, or just do a terrible job of blocking. Often times the fans, sideline, and media are quick to blame the offensive line when a sack happens. This, of course, is not always the case. Charlie would get frustrated when people were quick to point their fingers at the offensive line when the quarterback goes down. The running backs and quarterbacks are just as often the ones at fault.

Rituals

  The early September air was warm as Charlie looked up at the stars. It was still a little warmer than he liked for football weather. But since kickoff was slated for 7:00 in the evening, he knew the heat of the day would at least be avoided. He had just gotten home from the team meeting and meal. It was the night before the game and he was trying to clear his mind for a moment. He crossed the street to the campus. A few headlights zoomed by as he walked in between two buildings to get to the quad. It was about 11:00 on a Friday night, which meant that most of the town's traffic would be centered around the bars.

  When he got to the big grass clearing, he began walking to his favorite bench. In order to step up security, lights had been installed every 50 feet to make the quad a safer and more secure place. It also meant that at times it looked more like a parking lot, rather than a quiet place for introspection. Charlie's bench was tucked back in the corner, away from any of the lights and under a cluster of big pine trees. The trees created a deep shadow that kept people from seeing someone sitting there unless they passed directly in front of the bench. Charlie walked quietly across the grass, his feet occasionally crunching as he stepped on brown spots that had died during the summer heat. The only other sound was the chirping of the crickets.

  He sat down and looked out across the big wide grass area. A soft glow came from a few of the offices in the buildings surrounding the quad and the student union. He watched the people coming and going from the union building to keep his mind off of football for a while. Most of the students came and went in groups of three or four. The only sounds of their conversations that he could make out from this distance were murmurs. When an especially boisterous group of students would leave, he could hear their laughter. He would try to guess what they were laughing about. But this proved to be a fruitless attempt at covering up what was really on his mind.

  Football kept coming back and dominating his thoughts. Tomorrow was the first game. It was his first game as team captain. He had to start the season strong and he had to lead the team in the right direction. Tomorrow was a big day. He wanted the game to go perfectly. The way a team started the season often times set the tone for what would follow. Charlie wanted to make sure the proper tone for the season would be set.

He watched the students for a few more minutes before doing what he had come here to do. This had been his spot for the last two seasons, since he had been a starter. He came here before every home game and wrote down his goals for the game. He pulled out a small notepad and pen from his pocket and in the dim shadows began writing.

This ritual helped him clear his mind and sleep better. If he knew what he expected of himself and what he wanted to accomplish then he would rest easier. Sleep before a game was sporadic, but this put him in the right frame of mind.

-Play with full intensity each play.
-Be THE team leader.
-Play mistake-free football.
-Support my teammates and help them play to their full ability.
-Make a difference.
-Win!!!

His goals were always positive statements of things he wanted to do during the game.

After diligently filling in his goals and dating the list, Charlie got up and strolled back to his apartment. It was still early, but he wanted to get plenty of rest before the big game. Lying in bed, he visualized over and over again his proper technique. He pictured his assignment for every play and saw himself doing it perfectly in his mind. Lastly, as he was dozing off, he saw the scoreboard as time ran out. It read Puma 28, Cowboys 21.

Long Wait

The next day the game could not come soon enough. When Charlie woke up at 9:00 it seemed like an eternity until 7:00 that night. The day of a game was always a waiting game. Time seemed to drag on, like thick molasses. On these days Charlie felt like he was in elementary school again. It was like being 10 years old and the final bell at 3:30 seemed to take longer the more he looked at the clock. It seemed like time had almost crawled to a stop. This was the only bad thing about having a night game, it meant an even longer wait until kickoff.

It was an exercise in futility trying to keep himself busy with other things. His mind never wandered far from what needed to be accomplished this evening. He didn't like to do homework because then he found himself having to get focused on school. It was hard for Charlie to get focused for a game, he liked to be in football mentality all day long.

Seeing Mary wasn't an option for him. He had tried this a few times as a younger player and found that if he hung out with his girlfriend during the day, when he arrived at the stadium to get ready for the game his mind was on the relationship, not football. Seeing a girl meant the possibility of drama and he didn't want that to occupy his mind on game day. So, he puttered around his apartment, keeping himself isolated from the world. He relaxed, took a shower, watched some other games that had already began, and dozed off a few times. In between a snack and a nap he even took a brief walk around the neighborhood to loosen up his legs and get some fresh air.

Finally, at 2:30, it was time to go to the team pre-game meal. The air outside was still hot. Charlie hoped that it would cool down before the evening kickoff. The sky was a deep blue, with a few clouds on the horizon. Slightly browned leaves in the still-full trees swayed in the slight breeze.

The meal didn't officially start until 3:00, but he had waited long enough to get out of the house. Taking his time, he descended the flight of stairs to his big truck, rolled down all the windows, and cranked the engine. He took the long way to the banquet hall which was located in the Student Union Building.

Although he was fifteen minutes early, he wasn't the first one to arrive. Players were already scattered about the room at different tables. On game day, the players all wore white polo shirts with the team's emblem on the left breast. It was still warm so most of the guys were wearing shorts, but a few of them had on khaki pants or jeans. The coaches all had pants on and wore matching navy blue golf shirts which were a shade darker than the home jerseys.

Charlie joined a table with Anthony. The o-line shared a table at all of the pre-game meals. During the meal, if anything was talked about, it was only football. By sitting together in positions, they could talk about their assignments, or questions about the opponent. The overall mood of the meal was somber. There was very little talking, most guys concentrated and focused on their opponent tonight.

After a moment of silence, the players, one table at a time, began filing through the food line. It was a great spread with fresh fruit, green salad, soup, and sandwiches. At times it was hard not to pig out on all this great food. But, Charlie knew if he ate too much, it would all be coming up on the field in a few hours. His nerves were even more frazzled than usual since it was his first game as captain. So, he took half a sandwich and a few pieces of fruit. It wasn't much of a meal, but at this point Charlie wasn't worried about being full. His stomach was already in knots, he didn't need anything extra stirring around in there.

The meal began and ended with very little noise. Coach Jackson said a few words before they left. It was still only 4:00. Charlie had another hour and a half to kill before he went up to the stadium. He had no desire to go back to his house and be alone. He wanted to go somewhere comfortable and quiet. He went to Johnny's house.

He let himself in and announced his arrival with a knock. Johnny was in the living room watching sports. Charlie pushed over a pile of clothes and sat down on the couch. They chatted about a few meaningless things, the current game on TV, and the results from some earlier games. It was mindless chatter, but it helped Charlie get his mind off of the game for a while.

Charlie began to thumb through his play book, which he had brought in with him. He didn't need to go over it to remember the plays, he knew them all by heart after four years. But, he liked to look over the plays and notice other positions' assignments. He learned a lot about the offense in these spare moments where he was just trying to kill time. He loved knowing the complete picture of each play.

When 5:00 rolled around, Charlie and Johnny left, riding separately up to the stadium. They were full of excitement and about ready to explode. Charlie had been holding this in all day. Two more hours seemed too long, but at least they were finally on their way to the game. Warm ups began about an hour before the game and Charlie had some pre-game rituals he had to attend to before being ready for warm ups.

Jitters

     Blake closed his eyes and tried to clear his mind. He hadn't gotten much sleep last night. He felt like his mind had never gotten off football. He had been thinking about it when he went to sleep, he had dreamed about it, and as soon as he woke up, his mind had been running over all the possibilities that might happen tonight. He was grumpy, tired, and his stomach was in knots.

     Earlier in the afternoon, before going to the team meal, he played with Conner. This was the only thing that seemed to get his mind off of football for a moment. April had not been happy with him. When she tried to talk to him, he couldn't concentrate and she kept having to repeat herself. He finally asked her not to talk to him about anything important because his mind was not able to clearly focus today. This did not go over well and she had left the house in a huff before he went to the team meal.

     He had decided to come home for a moment after the team meal. The house was still empty and he went into the TV room and laid back on his favorite recliner. As he starred up at the ceiling, he drifted off to sleep.

     A few minutes later he jerked awake. In a semi panic he looked at his watch. *Oh, good. I still have some time,* he thought to himself as he took a deep breath. He felt better after his short nap. It had only been about half an hour, but his stomach felt calmer, and he felt refreshed. He got up and went to the kitchen. He searched a few of the cupboards before finding the peanut butter. He got the jelly out of the fridge and made himself a sandwich. This was the first thing he had been able to eat all day long. It felt good to get something into his stomach.

     He continued to shove the sandwich into his mouth as he left his house and got into his car. On the way to the stadium, he stopped at the convenience store to get a cup of coffee. He was still a little groggy and he wanted to be focused and alert for the game. It was a long evening ahead of him and he needed all the energy he could get.

     Blake arrived at the stadium at 5:10. He walked into the football office and got his defensive play call sheet for himself and his staff. He picked up the notebooks for stats that some of his coaches would be using during the game. At halftime, these stats would be helpful in mapping out the opponent's tendencies.

As he walked out of the office, he bumped into Coach Jackson. "Oh, there you are Blake. I was getting a little worried. It's two hours to kick off and my defensive coordinator wasn't here."

"Oh, no, I'm here. Don't worry," Blake responded, nodding his head.

Coach Jackson bit his lower lip and shook his head up and down for a moment. "How are you feeling? Are you nervous?"

"Yeah, I am a nervous wreck. It has already been a long day. I hope everything is ready," Blake acknowledged, as he walked towards the locker room.

"Well, that's okay. You have put in a lot of work and time, you have a lot vested in the outcome. You care a lot, too. It's good to be nervous. I'm sure everything will be fine. I know that you are well prepared."

"That is for sure." Blake opened the door to the locker room, wanting to get away from Coach Jackson. "I'm going to talk to a few of the guys for a minute."

"Okay, see you on the field. Don't be too nervous." Coach Jackson watched him enter the locker room.

Blake spent a few minutes in the locker room talking to his defense leaders, making sure they had the calls down and understood exactly what he wanted from them tonight. He stopped by Junior's locker last. Junior was the team's middle linebacker and defensive team captain. He would be calling the defense in the huddle. Blake wanted to make sure he had his wrist band with the plays on it and knew all of the defensive signals. After assuring himself that everyone was as prepared as they could be, he left the locker room and walked out on the field.

Blake was tired of talking to people, so he walked around the field. He saw some of the other coaches on the Puma sideline, but he avoided them, walking instead around the perimeter of the field starting on the opponent's sideline first.

It was early September and still warm, but with the sun beginning to fall towards the horizon, the air was beginning to cool. The last strength of the sun was glaring on the visitor's sideline and stands, but would be gone soon. The smell of the manicured grass, mixed with the occasional whiff of BBQ from the parking lot, made him feel at home. He smiled and kept his head down as he walked the field.

After making it seem like he was inspecting the field, Blake made his way to his fellow coaches. "Hey Coach Jones," greeted him as he joined them. He asked his assistants if the headsets were all working and they told him they were all checked and ready to go. He nodded and was excited for the game to come. He looked at his watch. Since it was 6:00, some of the guys would be coming out to warm up.

First Game

As the players began making their way onto the field, the energy level began to grow. Everyone was ready for the season to begin. First the specialists came out onto the field; the kickers, long snappers, and returners. They had to have room to practice their craft before the entire teams were out on the field. The other positions began to trickle out; the quarterbacks, receivers, defensive backs, and running backs. The linemen and linebackers were the last ones to come out for warm up. As they made their way onto the field, the energy and excitement intensified.

The team came together for a cheer and then began their warm up. Jim led the team through the warm ups, while the players were jumping around and hollering with excitement. They were like attack dogs just waiting for the command to attack.

As the opposing team came out to do their warm ups, the noise got even louder. It was as if each side were trying to outdo the other side with more noise, motion, and excitement. The fans began to slowly stream into the stadium, adding even more chaos to the spectacle unfolding.

After warm ups and quick drills with each position group, the team came together for a few plays with the offense against the defense. The intensity level continued to grow. The coaches had to remind their players not to hurt each other, this was still warm up. No injuries were needed before the game even started. The popping and the hitting was reaching a climax after a couple of plays. The players started getting overly aggressive towards each other, they could hardly contain themselves anymore.

After one last play, the Puma seemed ready to kill each other so Coach Jackson had to put a stop to it. He called out the point after touchdown/field goal (PAT) unit to kick one PAT for good luck before going back to the locker room. The PAT unit lined up and the ball sailed through the uprights. They all thought this portended good things to come tonight. Before the ball even hit the ground, Coach Jackson was yelling at the guys to take it back into the locker room. It was now 20 minutes until kickoff.

    The locker room was a mad house. Guys were yelling, screaming, snorting, glaring, pacing, and slamming their heads into things. Charlie hurried to the bathroom. There was already a line of guys waiting for the urinals. One of the nervous guys who was starting for the first time was in the stall emptying his guts, the sound of his retching filled the bathroom. Most of the guys laughed at him, some of them told him to get it all out, and others told him to quit being such a pussy. Charlie got up to one of the urinals and forced his bladder to empty itself. A short stream came out, he didn't have to pee much. It was more of a ritual than a necessity at this point.

    Charlie went back out to the locker room and sat quietly in front of his locker. Hard rock music blared. Some of the guys continued to pace, others stayed in a corner and kept bashing each other's shoulders and heads. Charlie liked to conserve his energy. He looked around the locker room, making eye contact with the guys that looked at him, and focused on getting ready for battle.

    Coach Jackson walked into the locker room, followed by the other coaches. As Coach Jackson made his way to the front, a hush fell over the players. By the time he stood in front of the players, the music was off and all the guys were quiet.

    "Everyone take a knee and grab a hand." They all did as they were instructed. "Take a moment of silence to ready yourself." The group was eerily quiet. It was a sudden transition from what the locker room had just been. Charlie kneeled during this time and focused on how he wanted to start the game.

    With conviction, Coach Jackson broke the silence, "We are going to win tonight!" The quiet was quickly broken by the team screaming its agreement to the statement. "We are going to win tonight because of you guys!" Coach Jackson looked out over the locker room. "You guys have put the time in, you guys have put the effort in, and you guys are a team." He paused, as the grunts and shouts of agreement passed through the room. "This is the beginning of a new season. This is the beginning of an adventure. How do you want this adventure to turn out? How you start the adventure has a big impact on how the adventure will finish. Go out there tonight and make a statement. Go out and start this adventure the right way. From the very first play, go out there to dominate. That's how we want this adventure to be, an adventure of domination by the Puma this year."

From the back of the room, one of the coaches told Coach Jackson the captains were needed. "Wait for one second!" Coach Jackson demanded, as Charlie and Junior stood up. "Are we going to win this game!!?"

"YEAH!!!!" A deafening roar answered him back.

"Well, let's go do it. Everyone together," Coach Jackson pushed his way into the middle of the group. "Win on three! One, two, three…"

"WIN!!!," the group yelled together.

"Charlie and Junior, get out there and win the toss, we want the ball first. We want to score the first drive and every drive," Coach Jackson shouted at them, with spittle flying from his mouth, as they left the locker room for the field. "The rest of you guys sit tight, we'll be going out in two minutes. Get a last minute bathroom break or a water." Coach Jackson walked to the back of the room to give each coach a bro hug and wish them luck. The coaches left the room, hurrying to their assignments. Coach Jackson waited by the door to escort the team out.

Charlie and Junior held each other's hands as they walked out to midfield from their sideline. They shook the hands of the other team's captains and listened to the referee's instructions. Charlie could hardly contain himself anymore. He was ready to explode. He made nervous jitters as he waited for the coin flip.

"Tails," called the other captain.

"It's heads," the referee pronounced.

"We will take the ball," Charlie stated.

"Okay, which goal do you want to defend, Cowboys?"

"That way? Okay, turn this way, guys," the referee guided the captains. "Puma wins the toss and will receive the ball at this end. Shake hands gentlemen and good luck."

Charlie stuck out his hand for the other captains to shake and turned back towards his sideline. He and Junior grabbed each other, slapping each other's backs, and saw their team waiting in the end zone.

Just as they started to make their way to their team, the announcer belted out, "Welcome out your 2000 Puma!" The crowd went wild and the Puma roar came from the loudspeakers again and again as the crowd continued to clap, scream, and yell. Charlie and Junior chest bumped the guys in front of the team and gave fives to as many of the players as they could. Guys began to take up their positions on the sideline, completing any last minute warm ups, getting water, or sitting down. They were ready to go.

They had been through practices, full contact drills, and scrimmages. But nothing can compare to a real game where everything changes, anything is justified in order to win. One might forget how exciting and unique an actual game is between the end of one season and the beginning of the next, but it all comes back in a hurry. All the tricks are pulled out and nothing is held back. It is an absolute dog fight. Each player has their own individual battle every down. Before the first play, the butterflies and anxiousness are flowing freely. With the initial hit on the opening play, all of this explodes away.

Charlie was trying to shake any last nerves out of his body. Impatiently jumping up and down on the sideline, waiting for the game to kick off and get out on the field. Fortunately, the Puma would be receiving the kickoff and he wouldn't have to wait long. Grabbing one last sip of water and pouring the rest of it down the back of his shoulder pads onto his neck to cool off a little in the warm evening, he was ready to go.

At last the whistle was blown. The crowd's cheers became even louder for the opening kickoff of the season. All the players on both sidelines were yelling and pumped up with energy and testosterone. With the crowd approaching a deafening roar, the ball was sent sailing into the air. Bodies began flying by at full speed, almost a blur from the sideline. Opposing players crashed into each other, with no thought of their own safety or health. It was a scene reminiscent of

Braveheart. The kick flew through the end zone, seemingly pushed through with the help of the crowd's extra enthusiasm.

Now it was Charlie's turn, time to get it on. With the excitement overflowing, his mind was a blank. He might not have remembered his name if asked. All that mattered was the play and his assignment. He knew them all by heart and had practiced his technique countless times. By now it was second nature, as natural as walking. They called the play in the huddle on the sideline.

"Zoom to flex left, zone 23, on one, on one, ready…break." *Yes,* he thought, *first play and it is coming to my side, just how it should be.* They jogged from the sideline to the line of scrimmage, Charlie jogged a little faster to make sure that he was the first one there. It was a habit he had developed, a kind of mental game against his opponent.

They lined up on the ball. The defense was just what they were expecting, a basic four-three. No need to make any audibles, changes of the play at the line of scrimmage, or any blocking adjustments. His heart was starting to beat even faster, so much build up and excitement, he and the rest of his teammates were ready to explode. Charlie couldn't remember who the guy was across from him, he didn't even remember what number was supposed to be there. At this point, it didn't matter. He was just another person, another opponent, just someone else in his way, trying to make his job more difficult. He almost slipped a grin, in anticipation of winning and of kicking his opponent's ass all night.

Now in their stance, the crowd quieted down a little bit for the home team's offense in anticipation of the first snap. The familiar voice of his quarterback and friend, Johnny, broke the deafening silence. "Green 82…Green 82…Down…Set…Hut."

Charlie exploded with every ounce of energy and power that he had. He fired right into the chest of his opponent, shooting his hands and head into his sternum. His feet followed as quickly as a piston. He was in the exact position that we wanted to be in. He proceeded to drive the guy backwards. With his hands in place, he locked his grip on like a vise, holding anything that might be there; shoulder pads, jersey, skin, whatever it might be. He continued to drive the guy backwards.

Charlie could feel the running back sneaking up behind him and looking for the hole to dart through. The mass of both teams began to converge around him as the ball was right behind him.

The running back snuck past him and the pile began to form as a linebacker corralled the runner. Charlie continued to pump his legs and drive his man even farther back. With the running back beginning to go down, legs, arms, and bodies were all over the ground. Charlie could sense that he could drive his opponent over someone and into the field. He picked up his aggression just a little more and felt his man starting to go down.

There are many ways to fall; softly, trying to avoid objects on the ground, and hard, with all one's force to make sure that whatever might be under you will get the full brunt of the laws of gravity when applied to a large mass. This was a game, a battle, and a war, it wasn't about being nice. He wasn't a dirty player, but he wanted his opponent to think twice about lining up against him again, wear him down a little, and make sure he remembered who he had played against when he woke up tomorrow morning. With his opponent on the ground, and Charlie on the way down, he fell with elbows, forearms, and knees first. Not really sure where they might end up, just knowing it wouldn't feel good.

In a big dog pile of bodies, Charlie's knees were ground into someone's hips, forearms were squeezing someone's neck, and an elbow felt like it was in someone's kidney. The pile moved fast and people were already getting off the ground. When his body was on top, Charlie pushed off of the guy, not the ground, hoping to push a little more air out of whomever it might be and making sure all the force possible was being exerted. He looked toward the sideline and saw that they gained seven yards on first down, right up his hole. Now that was exciting, and he let it be known. Looking back at the opposing team while walking back to the huddle he yelled out to whoever might listen, "Yeah mother fucker, we're coming at ya all night long. You better be ready for a long night, bitch!!!"

This is how the game is in the trenches, absolutely ferocious. In each play, one after another, two people try to kick the other's ass and make sure they feel it the next day. Any means are used, punching, kicking, pinching, grabbing, chop blocking, poking, holding, pushing, pulling, boxing out, spitting, biting. It is not as if it is dirty playing, just what goes on at ground zero. There is always such a cluster of people and bodies that no referee can see it all. One play might bring a hand, fist, or elbow to the throat, the next might see no contact on an attempted knock out block that misses its mark.

On each play, lineman are close enough to see each other's eyes and exchange sweat, spit, and even blood. Although interaction is only for 60 minutes, you could confuse opposing lineman as lifelong enemies. Pushing and jostling for position carries on long after the whistle is blown. One hundred and ten percent has to be given on every play, because if it isn't, it means getting run over and being the person on the bottom of the pile with knees, elbows, and forearms in one's own various body parts. In the case of a good battle, each player will be completely exhausted, struggling to make the journey back to the locker room following the game. It is a feeling of absolute exhaustion and total satisfaction at leaving one's heart and soul on the field. Great players can also shake hands at the end of a game and tell the other person thank you for a good effort and game. It is hard to duplicate and describe, feeling a sense of greatness within one's self.

Second down and three, back in the huddle, the game was off on a good start. On the way back to the huddle, the running back slapped the o-lines' butts saying, "Great job guys, keep it up."

"All right listen up! Pro right 65 slant and go, on one, on one, ready, break!" Sprinting back to the line to do it again, Charlie checked out the defensive lineup to call out the pass protection.

"Solid, solid, we got #35," Charlie yelled out, pointing to #35 before the QB started his cadence. The battle was on and Charlie had gained the upper hand on the first play. More than half of the game was mental. He already knew it was going to be a good night.

The night continued for Charlie and his team like it had begun on that first play. They dominated the Cowboys all night long. Slapping the outpouring of hands and hearing the crowd yell at the top of their lungs trying to voice their approval of a job well done, Charlie let out a big, "Hell, Yeah!!!" at the top of his lungs. Another successful possession, resulting in a touchdown. He and his teammates had been killing their opponent tonight, everything seemed to be going right. It felt great.

    Grabbing a cup of water, he flopped onto the bench to catch his breath and get ready to go out and do it again. With a moment to think and absorb everything that had gone on tonight, he felt on top of the world, he felt high, on cloud nine. Charlie had been absolutely destroying whoever decided to line up across from him tonight. He felt like he was in a zone. He didn't feel any pain, any tiredness, any soreness, only the game and everything around him. At times it didn't even feel like he needed his eyes tonight, he could just feel everything. He could feel the field around him, his teammates, he was able to know where to be and who to block without even thinking. It all felt right and grand. It was a feeling of power. He owned his opponent tonight. It didn't matter what was done, it all came out in Charlie's favor.

    Charlie's motions and technique seemed to be in super speed while the game was unfolding around him in slow motion. His hands and feet were in the right position even before the opponent had a chance to think and defend himself. This was resulting in complete domination.

    Every time Charlie came up to the line, he could see the fear in the guy's eyes across from him. It was the look of someone who knew what was going to happen and any effort to do otherwise was futile. He could feel it in his opponent. Charlie would barely even have to fight and he was able to feel the other man struggle with all his might just to avoid being bulled over once again. This thought made him smile. Football was great. There was no place he would rather be.

    He had noticed the stands and seen that there were a lot of people there tonight, but he hadn't located his parents or any of his friends. He didn't want to look around too much, though. The game hadn't been completely put out of reach. It wasn't time to celebrate yet. He was having a blast. This is what playing sports was all about. Giving one's best effort and seeing it pay off immediately, each participant putting forth all their energy and seeing who will come out on top. It was Charlie tonight and most nights, that is part of why he loved football so much. In these moments, winning and losing didn't seem to matter. All that mattered was that he would soon be out on the field again. He heard the call of his teammates that it was third down. He smiled, knowing that he was going out there again to kick some more ass.

    Laying back on the bench, Charlie let out a big sigh of relief. He could relax now, the game had been decided and for the last offensive series he would just be on the sideline. The backups got to finish the game. This is what it was all about. He smiled and looked around at his teammates and felt amazing. He got up and grabbed his nearest teammate, it turned out to be Anthony. He gave him a high five and a big hug. While embracing his friend and teammate, Charlie said, "Great job man. It was a great night tonight, a super start to the season. Just remember how we did it tonight and try to repeat it every game. I knew you could do it. Hell yeah!!!"

    "Thanks, dude. It was awesome. I couldn't have done it without you."

    "Well, I am glad you are playing next to me. I enjoy going to battle with you. Now it is time to kick back and enjoy the crowd and the scene." With that, Charlie permitted himself to look into the stands for the first time of the night. His attention was first caught by the short skirts of the bobbing cheerleaders. Their long, skinny legs kicking brought him out of the football world and back to reality. After a great effort and a great game, some lovin' sure would be in order for tonight. He heard some people yelling his name and scanned the crowd for the source of the yells. He waved back to his fans and flashed them a big smile.

    He looked up at the clock, 2:00 minutes and counting down. Only a few more plays and the game would be over. Standing there knowing the contest had been decided, Charlie felt incredible.

    With 0:00 approaching rapidly, the crowd began to let the team hear its appreciation of their performance tonight.

Pumping his arms towards the crowd and hugging any teammate he could find, Charlie was beaming from ear to ear. The sound was deafening and seemed to continue building. He hadn't experienced everything in life, but he didn't know of a better feeling anywhere on earth. Knowing that all parts of his game and his team's game had clicked tonight, knowing they had reached their goal, feeling on top of the world. This kind of feeling can't be duplicated outside of sports.

He felt alive, he felt vindicated. All of the hard work seemed to be worth it at this moment. Nothing else mattered, if he died this instant, he would die happy and complete. People who said that football was just a game had never had this feeling, or they would know better than to compare it to a simple game. This win made all the pain, sweat, blood, aches, and future soreness worth the toil. Charlie had never won a championship, but knew what he was feeling now would only be multiplied ten times and feel even that much better if he did. Wow, that was the dream. That is what athletes hung on for. That is why athletes played past their primes. Just for a shot to win a title. Charlie hoped this might come his way someday, this year seemed as good as any to him.

There were plenty of other times in his life that he had felt on top of the world. All of them were great, all of them were slightly different. He had been in love, he had a great family, he had gotten many awards, he had been drunk, he had been high, and he had had sex. But, he still liked this one the best. This feeling at this moment was one of the major reasons he played football and one of the main reasons he loved it with his heart and soul. Charlie felt like this would be a great season. He dreaded any other outcome.

Bonding

Blake came out of the jubilant locker room with a broad smile. The game couldn't have gone much better. They had almost pulled off a shutout in his first game as defensive coordinator. Even though the backups couldn't keep the Cowboys out of the end zone at the end of the game, Blake was glad all the guys had a chance to play. He knew that team morale was as important as stats.

There was a large crowd waiting outside the locker room. Parents and girlfriends were waiting for the players, wives and girlfriends were waiting for the coaches. Blake looked around for April, not knowing where she would be waiting. He was congratulated a few times along the way by parents that recognized him. He graciously shook their hands and told them thank you.

As the crowd began thinning out, he finally spotted April. She was pushing the stroller back and forth saying something to Conner. She didn't notice him approaching. As soon as he got close enough for her to hear him, he called to her, "Hey babe, you look great. It is so good to see you." He gave her a big hug and a kiss. *She really does look good,* he thought to himself. She was wearing jeans that hugged her legs and a team shirt that accentuated her curves. Her hair dangled down to her shoulders and her eyes were full of love.

"Great job on the win tonight, honey. That was a great game. You must be so excited." She returned his embrace and held on tight.

He pulled away, bending down to say hi to Conner, "Thanks, babe. It was a ton of fun. I can't believe how well we did." He picked up Conner, "Hey there, buddy. Did you like the game? I know you did. You're getting so big so fast. Pretty soon you'll be out there playing yourself." Blake talked to the baby excitedly.

Conner's face lit up as his dad talked to him and tickled his belly. His eyes still showed the signs of sleepiness. "He just woke up at the end of the game. He was really good the whole game, he fell asleep at half time and then slept most of the second half. That made it easy for me to watch the game." April was happy to see Blake with Conner. He was a cute dad, when he was around, and April loved seeing them together.

Blake looked at his wife, smiled, and gave her a kiss. "Thanks so much for coming and bringing Conner. It is great to come out of the locker room to you two." He continued touching and playing with Conner, but Conner struggled to keep his eyes open. "He is tired. It looks like he is ready to call it a night." Blake bent down and put him back in the stroller.

"Yeah, I hope he will fall back asleep and stay down for the night. I am a little worried since he had a nap during the game." April reached out and rubbed his arm.

"Well, we're going to go out and get something to eat and some beers," Blake stated.

"Who's we?" April asked, as a hint of sadness overtook her eyes.

"Oh, just the coaches. Coach Jackson likes to take us out after games, you know that from years past."

"Really? Yeah, I know you have done that in the past, but I was thinking that since we now have a baby that you might be coming home with me after games," she said, with a pleading look.

"This is the only time that we have as a staff to unwind and relax around each other. I think it is really important to go. Tomorrow at 9:00 AM we have meetings to start going over game films. Do you want to come out with us for a minute?" Blake answered back, trying to ignore the disappointment in April's eyes.

"It is late, it's almost 11 o'clock. I have to get Conner home and into bed." She paused, acquiescing her hopes to spend some time with Blake tonight. "I was just hoping to hang out with you a little bit tonight. We don't get much time during the week."

"Don't worry, I won't stay out too late. I will try to get back before you go to sleep so that we can spend some time together tonight." Blake gave her a kiss on the cheek, hoping to soothe her dismay. "I'm going to go grab Coach Miller. I am going to give him a ride. I'll be home in a couple of hours, try to stay up." He bent down and gave Conner a kiss, "Good night, big man. Keep growing up big and strong." He gave his wife a bear hug and kissed her now unwelcoming lips. "Thanks so much for being here. I really am glad you came. I love you and I will see you soon."

"Okay, I love you, too. I hope to see you soon," April responded back, dispirited. She watched him weave through the crowd as he headed for the coaches' office.

At 3:12 AM, April jerked awake. She heard keys pawing at the lock of the front door. The correct key was finally found and the door opened. She opened her eyes for a minute, checked the time, and rolled onto her side facing the outside of the bed. She heard Blake try to walk quietly through the house. He turned off the porch light and the living room light which had been left on for him. He walked into the kitchen and got himself some water. He turned off the kitchen night light and began making his way to their bedroom.

April didn't want to talk to him, so she continued to pretend she was asleep. Turning herself away from his side of the bed made sure he wouldn't touch her. He would have to be up and back at the football office in less than six hours and then the whole football week started again. It was only the first game and she was already tired of the football schedule.

Blake fumbled with his clothes, struggling to get them off. After getting down to his underwear, he slid into bed, his efforts to be stealthy and quiet failing miserably. He smelled like a bar, smoke clung to his body, and his breath reeked of alcohol. April could smell him even though she was turned away. He leaned over and kissed her arm. "Good night, honey."

"Mmmmmmmmmmm," was her only reply. She knew that she would again be the only one dealing with a tired baby in about three hours. Blake was already snoring. This made her angrier, he was already asleep and now she was awake again. She adjusted her sleeping posture, making herself comfortable. Despite her frustration, disappointment, and anger, she fell into her sleep cycle again.

Game Two

Charlie was completely exhausted. Tonight had been a battle and it was coming down to the wire, where games are won or lost. He wasn't going to give up. Somehow, somewhere, he would find the energy to give his full effort and play as hard as possible.

Walking back to the huddle after hustling down field, he didn't know how he was going to make it. He felt like he was breathing through mud. Briefly, trying not to let anyone see, he turned his head to the side and threw up the last substance that was in his stomach. At this point, it was only stomach acid. Trying to get it off his face mask, he made his way into the huddle.

"You all right Charlie?" Anthony mumbled.

"Uhh…, not really, but I will make it," Charlie managed to get out.

"Okay, well hang in there, we need you, dude."

"Yeah, yeah."

Trying to focus on what Johnny was saying, instead of the overpowering feeling of wanting to just close his eyes and pass out, Charlie recognized the play and began to think of what his assignment was. It clicked. He knew what to do and what kind of call to expect. He looked at the clock to see how much time was left in the game. He didn't know how much longer he could continue to play tonight. He felt like he had rubber legs and rubber arms, his whole body felt numb. He might have been able to squat over 600 lbs. in the summer, but now he didn't know if he could even do the bar. Benching even 100 lbs. would be a chore at this point.

I might not make it, slipped into his consciousness. He might stay down the next time he fell down and close his eyes, or might not get off the bench the next time he was on the sideline. Right now wasn't any time to think about death and what might happen, it was time to think about the next play and what he could do to help his team. He didn't want to let them down. It was the fourth quarter and the game was still undecided.

He summoned up all his mental toughness and told himself he was fine. *You can make it. It is already the fourth quarter and you are the team leader. If you don't keep fighting, then no one will. Your team needs you at this critical juncture. You have worked too hard to stop now. Your opponent is tired too. You know he is at least as tired as you are. He has even taken more breaks. Just block it out. You are not tired. You are not tired. You are not tired.*

Because he was concentrating so hard on gathering strength, he had missed the call for the huddle to break. Seeing his teammates clap and shout out, "break!" Charlie was brought back. It was time again. He forgot his tiredness and sprinted to the line. Getting in his stance early, he could see his opponent wearing out. His opponent's body language seemed to say, "Oh fuck, he's back already. Look at his energy. He isn't even tired. We have been going at it all night and he is still fresh." When Charlie saw this, he got a sudden burst of energy. *See, I told you. He is the one who is tired. All right, time to take it to him again.* With that, his fatigue seemed to disappear for a moment, at least until the end of this play when he would have time to think again. Hearing the quarterback begin his cadence, Charlie focused solely on his assignment for the next play, and his technique for kicking this guy's ass one more time.

On his way back to the huddle after the play was over, Charlie's fatigue took control of his mind again. He was trying to block it out, but it kept creeping back. He had given all his energy on the last play, and on every play. He wouldn't last much longer. Winning or losing didn't seem to matter at this point, only making it through the next play and not taking a break. If he took a break, he might not be able to get back out there, or move again.

He couldn't even hustle to the huddle. His entire body was soaked with sweat. His shoulder pads felt as if they were holding an additional ten pounds of water, his pants didn't have a dry spot on them to dry his hands, his jersey felt like he had jumped into a pool and didn't have time to dry off, and sweat was sliding down his arm to the elbow and finally leaving his body from the pinky finger. He had been sweating so much that his hands were beginning to prune from the continuous moisture that had been collecting since warm ups. There was no hope of drying any part of himself, so he tried to ignore it and strolled back to the huddle.

His teammates wanted to communicate, yet this was impossible for Charlie at this moment. It had taken all his energy to get off the ground after the last play and make it to the huddle. To the questions and comments thrown his way, Charlie could only offer a lifeless grunt.

The down marker showed 3rd and eight. That seemed to be his only salvation. If they didn't get the first down, then he could have a break on the sideline and perhaps recover enough energy to play the rest of the game. This almost made him feel selfish. It wasn't as if he didn't want his team to get a first down and continue towards the end zone to perhaps a game sealing score, he just needed to rest for a minute and he wasn't going to take himself out of the game. That would be a sign of weakness. He was the leader of the team, he was needed out there, he had enough mental toughness to make it through the game. Third down, one more play, and he might get a rest. He had come this far, he wasn't going to stop now.

The thought ran through his head that he might die. This didn't scare him, it only took his concentration off the task at hand. He felt as if with the next movement he might just fall down. This possibility seemed okay.

If he were to die doing anything, he wanted it to be while playing football. It would almost be like a soldier dying in battle. This was an honorable thing to do, he would be a hero. What could be a better way to die? He would be revered and honored. He would be a legend. The family and friends that would be left behind didn't enter his mind. This was just his duty, he was doing his job, if death came with it, then so be it.

His mind was spinning and his body was numb. His body followed the commands from his head, but seemed to be protesting at even the slightest movement. His only thoughts were to keep from collapsing. It would be glorious to have it end this way, but he wasn't ready to die. His team was depending on him.

With Johnny calling attention in the huddle, Charlie's thoughts left the underworld and focused on the task in front of him. *I hope this isn't a fucking run play,* was the only thing running through his head. With a pass play called, he felt like he could do it, as long as they didn't get the first down and have to stay out on the field.

Stumbling up to the line and getting into his stance, his mind went blank and he concentrated on his first step and where he wanted to fire his hands, letting the fatigue run out of his head, for at least a few seconds.

Giving his complete effort again, he barely kept the defender at bay. It was lucky for him that the defensive lineman was drained, as well. The play didn't net enough yards to gain the first down. Trying not to look obvious, or happy, Charlie looked towards the sideline secretly wishing that the punt team would be there, getting ready to take the field. Charlie's hopes were realized and the offense began leaving the field. He felt like he couldn't even make it to the sideline.

Coaches and players tried to offer fives, compliments, and advice, to which Charlie didn't respond. Finally reaching the bench, he plopped down, panting, trying to catch his breath, sweat dripping from his brow as soon as he removed his helmet, and praying that this fucking game would end.

Resting, with elbows on his knees, he let out the last of what his stomach held. It wasn't much, but couldn't be helped. His teammates next to him gave him a dirty look, like they weren't very happy about being the reluctant neighbor to the involuntary releasing of stomach acid. He didn't give a shit. His coach approached the bench to talk about the last set of downs and what changes might be made. Charlie saw him without looking up and said, "I'm okay," so the coach would continue and not find a replacement for him on the next set of downs. Charlie reached for the water and tried to listen, just hoping his body wouldn't quit on him.

After absently listening to his coach's instructions, Charlie looked at the clock. There were less than five minutes left. He hoped that the defense would give up a couple of first downs before making a stop, so that he would have more time to rest. Charlie normally got up to cheer on the defense, but he couldn't muster the will this time.

Anthony got up and yelled encouragement to the defense. He looked back at Charlie who sat alone on the bench. He was worried for Charlie and for himself. He played next to Charlie and he didn't feel totally comfortable without Charlie playing next to him. Charlie made all of the blocking scheme calls and told him what to do if he forgot. He walked over to the bench and put his hand on Charlie's shoulder pad. "You all right? You don't look too well. Do you want me to get the trainer?"

Charlie finally looked up and said with a cold stare, "Hell, no! I am fine. Just need a rest." Charlie looked at the clock again, hoping that it would go faster. Anthony was still lingering around. "I'll be fine, dude." He knew that if he didn't get up, Anthony wouldn't leave him alone. "Help me up." Charlie stuck out his hand.

Together they walked over to the sideline. The punt team had pinned the Rams back in the shadow of their own goal post. They had marched the ball out to the 35 yard line, but were eating up precious time. The Puma led 28-23. The Rams had to get a touchdown in the last 4:00 or the Puma would win the game. Charlie could barely hold himself upright, so he took a knee while watching the action. Anthony looked down at him suspiciously. Normally, Charlie was full of energy and a vocal support for the team from the sideline. Charlie was not assuaging Anthony's fears.

The Rams picked up another first down, the ball near midfield. The clock was winding down to 3:35. Charlie began to get nervous. If they lost this game after he had expended this much effort, he would be fucking pissed. With as much energy as he could muster, he shouted, "Come on defense, we need a stop!!!"

Anthony seconded Charlie's encouragement, echoing what he had said. It seemed to work. The Puma came up with two stops in a row. It was now 3rd down and 8. The clock was down to 3:12. Charlie stood up, hoping his solidarity towards his teammates would motivate them for a stop. The crowd got loud, knowing this was an important 3rd down. Through the intense noise, Charlie watched as the quarterback's pass flew wide of its mark as he was forced to get rid of the ball with Junior in his face quickly off of a blitz up the middle.

Charlie was glad the defense had stepped up and made a stop. Now the only thing he worried about was having to go back out on the field. The Rams got into punt formation and sent the ball sailing down to the 10 yard line where it took a high bounce. After settling, the ball was downed by the Rams at the 8 yard line. There was 2:42 left in the game.

Charlie and the rest of the offense gathered around Coach Miller to get the call. They all caught their breath and rested as the referee notified them of the TV timeout. *Whew*, Charlie thought, *another few minutes of rest will help out*. He tried to zone out the aches and pains that were screaming at him. Every movement seemed like it required an effort.

After talking on the headset, Coach Miller called them together. "All right guys. This is it. This is what we practice and work for, a chance to ice the game. If we get one more first down, we wrap this game up. If we get one first down, the game ends with the ball in our hands. That is how we want it. I need three perfect plays from everyone. Come on, you guys can do it!!" He looked down at his play sheet one more time and told the guys the play. They broke the huddle together and jogged out to the ball.

Charlie hustled, but he wasn't the first one to the ball. He didn't want to use up all of his energy yet. Both teams knew the next three plays were going to be run plays, so the defense was stacked up against the run. Charlie saw his man begrudgingly get into his stance. *This guy is tired, too. I have kicked his ass all game. I can do it again.*

Charlie heard the cadence and fired out of his stance. He willed and muscled his man backwards a little bit. It was enough that the running back was able to squeeze through the hole. Charlie's man reached out for the tackle, but didn't even make contact with the running back. Charlie was too tired to even fall on his opponent. He gave him a little shove that wasn't even enough to get him to the ground. He didn't want to force his man to the ground because that meant he would be on the ground, too. He didn't know if he had enough energy to get back up.

When the whistle blew, he looked over and saw that they had gained five yards. It was 2nd and 5. *Hell yeah, run it to my side even when I am dead tired and we still get a good play. Fuck yeah!* Charlie sauntered back to the huddle. He could take his time since the other team had called a timeout. They had to use their last timeouts, hoping to get a stop and one more chance to win the game.

Water boys rushed out onto the field. Charlie waved them away. He was dehydrated, but had been throwing up. He felt like if he put anything else in his stomach, it would just come back up. He didn't want any more of that throw up taste in his mouth. He liked these timeouts, this might make it possible for him to get through the game.

The ref blew his whistle and Johnny called the team together for a huddle. This time a run play was called to the right side. Charlie willed himself to the line of scrimmage and focused on doing the play correctly. This was the only way to block out his exhaustion. He burst off the line again with what seemed like the last of his energy. This time he positioned himself well enough to block his man, but couldn't move him backwards. He continued struggling against his man until the whistle blew. He looked up and saw that they had gained minimal yardage. It was 3rd and 4. *That's what happens when they go to that side. They better fucking run this last play to my side.*

Again the whistle blew and Charlie walked, instead of ran, back to the huddle, something he rarely did. He took some deep breaths and looked at Anthony. "They're going to run the ball to our side. You better dig deep and block your ass off, we need a first down." He was saying this as much to himself as he was to Anthony.

"Yeah, I will, don't worry," Anthony replied back nervously. Charlie looked out of sorts.

Charlie refused the water again. The clock was down to 2:22. If they got a first down, it was all over. If they didn't, they would have to punt the ball at about 1:40. This was the Rams' last time out. Johnny called the huddle again. Charlie was right, it was a run play to his side. He gritted his teeth and pushed out all of his tired thoughts. His focus was only on this play. If he did everything right, the game was over and his team would win.

He forced his feet to move faster and hustled to the line of scrimmage. He balled his fists together preparing himself for one last battle. He got into his stance and burst off the line with every ounce of energy left in his body. He surprised himself and his opponent with the amount of force he exerted. His opponent seemed to fly backwards. The running back saw a break in the line and got behind Charlie. Charlie could feel the running back behind him and pushed even harder. He felt the whole defense collapse around him and pushed with the last of his energy.

His opponent fell down in front of him. Charlie did not have enough energy to keep himself from falling. He fell forward, trying to push whoever was in his way back just a little more. His body fell hard to the ground, he didn't have any energy to brace himself. He smelled the grass and the dirt in front of his face on the other side of his helmet. Sweat dripped off of his face onto the ground. He tried to look to see if he was in front of the 1st down marker. Bodies slowly got off the ground around him and he heard the roar of the crowd.

That means we must have got it, hell yeah. Oh, fuck, I have to get up. Charlie rolled over and looked for some help up. Anthony extended his hand and pulled him up. He seemed surprised at how much he had to help Charlie. Charlie looked towards the sideline to make sure the marker read 1, meaning it really was first down.

When Charlie saw the "one" in the box, he was ready to cry. He gave Anthony a hug and nodded his head on the way back to the huddle. The offense high fived each other, the o-line bro hugged each other, and they all congratulated one another for their efforts. Johnny came back to the huddle with a smile. "Good job, guys. Now we just have to down it. I am going to wait until there is one second on the play clock to snap the ball. We will go on first sound, get set with five seconds left. We'll have to do it three times. We don't need to huddle any more. Let's do it. Victory on first sound, first sound, ready…BREAK!"

Charlie yelled break with the rest of the team and walked together with his teammates to the line. It had been a battle tonight, everyone was tired. They got in formation, waited until there were five seconds left on the play clock, and got into their stance. Both sides fired off in pretend determination and after one hard step, stopped. In between snaps the Puma began congratulating each other, giving hugs, and fives, or acknowledging the crowd. After the third snap, Johnny gave the ball to the referee and they shook the hands of the Rams.

Charlie went through the line shaking the other team's hands, just glad the game was over. He was very glad they had won, though. He would have been pissed off if he had put forth this much effort for a loss. After shaking hands, Charlie made his way to the locker room in a haze. He collapsed down in front of his locker and almost passed out. His pain and exhaustion hit him. He didn't need to block it out anymore, and it seemed unbearable.

He sat there until he had enough energy to change and take a shower. He didn't even open his eyes as the guys came by to congratulate him on the victory. A couple of guys even came up and gave him a bro hug as he sat there, slumped over. He kind of mumbled in response. He didn't remember what they said and he didn't remember what he said.

Eventually he stumbled to the shower, looking like he was drunk. As the hot water fell onto his body, Charlie thought to himself, *we are 2-0. That is awesome. That is a great start. I made it and we made it. We are going to be all right.* Charlie had taken so long, nobody was left in the locker room. The equipment manager yelled out, "Come on, man. It is late, everyone else is gone. I want to go home."

"Okay, I'm coming. Give me a second." Charlie showered up and threw on some clothes, too tired to even put on underwear. He wandered out of the stadium and drove himself home. There was no way he was going out tonight. He got home, fell into his bed, and didn't wake up until morning.

Ugliness

Charlie was sitting in an empty stadium on the 50 yard line. He was looking around the field when the dance team started doing their routine. As he looked closer, he realized they were naked. He sat up and began to pay close attention. Their boobs bobbed up and down. Charlie smiled, then he heard a ringing. He looked at the scoreboard and saw a phone with the word "ring" coming out of it. Again the ring came over the whole stadium. *Oh shit,* Charlie thought to himself, *damn it.* The ringing sounded again, the girls were gone, and the stadium faded from his mind as fast as it had appeared.

Charlie opened his eyes and felt a pounding behind his eyes. The ringing didn't help his headache. Reluctantly, he rolled over and grabbed the phone.

"Hello," Charlie said, not even trying to hide that he had just woken up.

"Hey, Charlie. It's Mary. Congrats on the big win last night. I came to the game, but I had to go into work for a little bit. The game was going long and I didn't get to stay for the end, but I know that you won," she said, as cute as she could. "Did I wake you up?"

"Hey, babe, thanks. Yeah, you did, but that is okay."

"Oh, I'm sorry. Do you want me to let you go back to bed?"

"No, no," Charlie lied. "That is okay. How are ya?"

"I'm good. You don't sound so good. Where were ya last night?" Mary asked, and before he had a chance to reply, started again. "I called and left you a message, but I didn't hear from you. I thought you might give me a call sometime."

"Sorry, babe. I literally passed out last night when I got home from the game. I just laid down and this is the first time I have woken up."

"Did you go out and party?" she asked, feeling dejected.

"No, I really just came home from the game and went right to bed. It was a tough game, I was exhausted."

"Wow, you must have been tired to not even go out and drink." She perked up. "Can I come over and see ya."

"Sure, sure. That is fine. I might still be in bed when you come over, though. Just let yourself in."

"That's all right. I want to see you. I miss you and want to hang out with you." She sounded giddy. "I'll be over soon. Is that okay?"

"Yeah, okay. Sounds good. See you soon."

"Okay….I….I….I'm excited to see you." She didn't say what she wanted to say.

"Yeah, me too," Charlie replied, not paying attention. "See you soon. Bye."

"Bye, sweetie," she replied, with an abundance of joy.

Charlie hung up the phone and began to feel the soreness of his whole body. He felt like he had a hangover. *Fuck, I feel like I got wasted last night. What a waste, I feel like this and I didn't even get drunk,* Charlie thought to himself. His entire body ached. He rolled over on his back and felt the soreness in his back. He raised his shoulder to feel the bruise developing where he had fallen hard last night. His knees and ankles had a dull burning sensation. His fingers felt like they had been crushed in a vise grip. He didn't want to get up, but his bladder felt like it would explode if it wasn't emptied soon.

While standing and peeing, Charlie could feel some of his muscles tighten. He knew he was badly dehydrated because his pee was still dark. He wandered to his small kitchen and got some water. On his way back, he found the ibuprofen bottle. He popped five pills before laying down on his bed again. He chugged the rest of his water and his back started to cramp as he laid on his elbow, drinking. He put the cup down and sprawled out trying to get his back muscles to loosen up through clenched teeth. All of his muscles felt on the verge of cramping up. He needed more water, but the overwhelming soreness made him stay put. *I'll just wait for Mary to get here. She will be here soon. I'll ask her to get me more water.* He closed his eyes and waited for Mary.

Just as he was dozing off, he heard a knock on the door.

"Come in!!" he yelled.

He heard the door open. "Hey, sweetie," she greeted with enthusiasm.

"I'm in here," he answered back without opening his eyes.

She walked down the short hallway to his room. When Charlie sensed her in the room, he opened his eyes. "Hey babe. Come on in." He scooted over and made room for her on the side of the bed.

She laid down and gave him a big hug. "Hey there, sexy."

With an effort, he turned his head to give her a kiss. This short movement hurt his neck muscles. "Hey, babe. It's nice to see you. Thanks for coming over." Charlie tried to look and sound welcoming, but he was straining himself, trying to cover his soreness.

"So, what's up?" Mary asked with excitement.

"Not much. Do you mind getting me some more water? I am really thirsty and I am too sore to get up." He pointed to the cup next to his bed.

"Of course." She gave him a kiss as she got the cup and went to fill it up. "I can't believe how tired you were last night. I have never heard of you just coming home from a game like that." She talked to him from the kitchen.

"Yeah, it was a hell of a game. I was totally spent. All I could think of was lying down. Beer didn't even enter my mind. I am still tired and sore today."

"I can tell. You didn't even get up. Usually you get up and say hello. You aren't being a very good host," she chuckled.

"Sorry, babe. Just give me a few minutes and I'll be alright."

"I know, I know. I'm just kidding, take your time." She walked into the room, sat down beside him, and gave him the water.

Charlie downed half the water and laid back down. He could feel his muscles loosening up now that he had some water in him and the ibuprofen was starting to ease the soreness. He smiled at her for the first time and caressed her legs. "I'm glad you came over. It's good to see you."

"Me too. I missed not seeing you last night, in more ways than one." She smiled, trying not to be too forward. Then she realized he still wasn't in the mood, even with her obvious come on. She looked at his sprawled out body and understood he was in no shape for fooling around right now. This shocked her and she couldn't help but comment. "I can't believe how sore you are."

"Me neither. But at least the other guy is worse."

Charlie knew that was the case. He played hard and he didn't beat his opponent every time, but he made sure that his opponent would remember playing against him when he woke up the next day.

For Charlie to play this way, he had to get his anger flowing. To get his anger flowing, Charlie liked to think of each play as a fight against anyone from the other team that he might make contact with. This helped to ensure that Charlie would attack his opponent with every ounce of energy and not let up for even a split second. By playing this way, Charlie could release all of his anger and frustration. Anything that tested his patience or made him upset during his time away from football, Charlie would stockpile for the week. A poor grade on a test, a harsh criticism of the team by the local newspaper, a parking ticket, an argument with his girlfriend, his coach yelling at him, expensive bills, anything that got the adrenaline pumping.

At the end of a week, or at times even a day, Charlie would bring all of these to the surface. Once his hostility was on the surface, he let the events fade from his mind. He didn't want to stay focused on the negative events or he would lose his concentration. Instead, he would focus on the intensity of his feelings. His aggression would almost be spilling out of him. When the whistle blew, all of this raw emotion exploded onto every opponent.

Charlie played this way because he found many years ago that it produced the most success for him personally. He didn't like anyone during the game. His sole focus was on the current play and punishing the player in front of him. He only smiled at the end of the game and only if his team had won. He displayed very few commendable qualities while on the field.

The characteristics he did display were ones that were advantageous for a game as violent as football. A game where collisions, pain, and ferocity were the underlying themes. The person Charlie was on the field isn't somebody a person would like to meet, or even be friends with. When playing this way, one cannot be in a pleasant state of mind. This style of football is not about love and happiness. This was the 'football' Charlie.

When it was game time or practice time, Charlie would flip a switch and he was 'football' Charlie. During this time, Charlie literally hated anyone who might be on the other side of the ball that got in his way of achieving victory. He wanted to kick each person's ass as hard as he could and make that person remember who his opponent was the next day. It wasn't as if he wanted to kill someone. He wanted to obliterate the will in his opponent to line up against him again.

He was mean, he was an asshole, he wasn't going to make any friends with this kind of attitude. Opponents who played against him hated him. His teammates loved him. He would take his opponent to the limit. He would push the other guy as long as he could, through the whistle, not letting up until he absolutely had to. His antics often resulted in little scuffles against his opponent that had to be broken up by the referee or one of his teammates.

Charlie's attitude towards his opponent during the game could be summed up best in two words: "FUCK YOU!!!" This is how he felt and this is how he played. "Fuck" was the word he most often used during a game. At times, it was the only word he would use in a sentence, creatively coming up with different forms of the word in as many ways as possible. "Fucking, fuck, fucked, fucker" helped to keep his fury at full tilt.

The non-football side of Charlie is what most people saw and who people liked. He was a leader on and off the field. He wasn't the smartest person. But he always went to class, participated in class discussions, was respected by his teachers and college peers, and got good grades. It would be hard to find a person that didn't like him outside of football. He was nice to everyone, plus he took time to be thankful and appreciative towards everyone with whom he interacted.

This angry style was by no means the only way to play the game. For Charlie, it was just the way he found to be the most successful for him. There are as many different playing styles as there are players. Some laugh and smile and have a grand old time. Others focus their efforts on looking good and playing towards the crowd. While still others go about it very business-like and show very little emotion towards the game. Each player must find his own style that works for him. Through the years, this had worked best for Charlie. It got results and kept him on the field. This seemed to be the only thing that mattered, at least at this point in his life.

"You know what? I don't think I would want to know you on the football field," Mary stated matter of factly. "After going to the game last night and really trying to watch you, instead of the whole game and the crowd, I don't think you are the nicest person on the field."

He paused. "Well...you are probably right," Charlie didn't know what to say to this. He knew it was true. That is part of what he liked about the game. He was a different person on the field than he was in real life.

"Do you think that is bad?" she asked innocently.

"Mmmm...I am not sure it is good or bad. Just the way I play." He wasn't really ready to evaluate his playing style or judge it. It was how he liked to play and it produced the results that he was seeking.

"Well, why do you play like that? When did you start playing like that? I am not trying to judge your actions on the field, either. I am just curious. I obviously have never played and don't know what it is about." She stroked his hair to try and assure him that no ill feelings were meant or intended. "Do you not want to talk about it?"

"No, it is not that. It has just kind of developed. I just get really intense while I am out there and don't worry about what I might be doing to that other person, as long as it is within the rules. When I get my level of intensity to a certain plane, it is hard to come down. I can't just switch it on and off. Once it is on, it doesn't come off until the end of the game."

He wasn't trying to hide, he just wasn't used to justifying, or evaluating, why he might do things on the field. "I kind of think of my opponent as an asshole. Even though he probably isn't, he is probably not very different from me. For 60 minutes I just think 'Fuck You!' It doesn't really matter who it is. After the game, I can usually shake his hand and realize that he is just a guy trying to do his thing too."

"Wow, really? That is fascinating. How do you get so angry and so hostile towards a person so fast?"

"It is not always as if I am angry at that single person, just that team. He happens to be in my way and a part of that team. So, for 60 minutes, he is in my way of accomplishing my goal of winning. During the game whoever happens to get in my way, is the enemy." Charlie was even learning something about himself. It is not as if he hated his opponent as a person. He just hated him while he was an opponent. "I put all my anger, frustration, and hatred in my mind and take it out on him, whoever that person happens to be in front of me for any particular play. I put all of that in my mind before the game and just let it flow from me during the game."

She was really amazed. It seemed interesting to her that someone could do this and then a few hours later be one of the nicest people she had ever met, be such a complete asshole on the field and then be such a kind person off the field. "Do other people do this too?"

"Well, I am not positive because I have never talked about it to anyone, but I think so. I mean the kind of music some guys like to listen to is all the anger filled music, heavy metal, gangsta rap, fuck this, fuck that, die mutha fucka, you know all that shit."

He began to wonder if he was the only person to use this approach. If he was, so what? It worked for him. He was a captain, a starter, and a reliable player. "It is a nice way to get rid of one's frustration. Some people do it by running, lifting weights, punching the bag, shooting guns, and fighting. I guess for us it is almost like a fight, only legal." He got up, trying to hint to her that he wanted to change the subject. "Let's go and we'll come back to chill for a bit before I have to go to practice."

"I was enjoying this conversation." She followed him with her eyes as he got up and found some clothes to put on.

"Well, we can still talk about it." Charlie tried to walk normally, as if his body didn't feel like he had been run over by a semi-truck. "Maybe it's a guy thing, all the testosterone. You know?"

"Not all guys are like that. Not all guys want to hurt someone like that."

"I don't necessarily want to hurt him. I just want him to worry more about his body aches and me kicking his ass again than he worries about his assignment and what he is supposed to do on the next play," he said, as he quickly put on his clothes. He wanted to get going. In the car, he could at least turn up the music so that he didn't have to answer any more of this interrogation. Once they were in the car with the music playing he hoped the subject would be changed.

He started walking towards the door as soon as his clothes were on. "Let's get going. We can talk about it at breakfast if you want. It is not like we are on a limited time basis, are we?" he shouted back as he opened the door, trying to get her to leave and keep the wolves at bay. He felt like he was talking to his mother or a therapist.

Mary looked at him with a glare, not even wanting to answer the question, knowing that it was just a way to change the subject. Reluctantly, she got up from his bed and followed him outside to his truck. "Okay, fine. We'll talk about it later. Where are you taking me for breakfast?" She smiled at him as he let her out the door and patted her on the bum.

He knew she had wanted sex and he hoped some breakfast would give him the energy to take advantage of her amorosity before practice. He hated turning down her loving.

Commonalities

    Looking in the mirror, Charlie had a sudden realization that made his stomach weak and his knees shake. It is always a difficult moment when a young man realizes that he looks just like his father. He had a tall, wide frame that seemed to be made for a sport like football. With his development of muscles from working out, Charlie now looked like a poster candidate for an offensive lineman. His legs were as big as tree trunks and covered with hair. In fact, most of his body was now hairy. Luckily for him he had been spared the back hair. Big round features dominated his face, with a prominent nose always making its presence known. Charlie's hair wasn't as dark as his father's and had yet to start receding. His eyes were warm and inviting with a vivid shade of green, as opposed to his father's dark brown welcoming eyes.

    Charlie's eating habits had also not yet produced a stomach that gravity had taken a pivotal role in displaying to the rest of the world. Charlie knew that his dad was attractive. It was just that he had grown up seeing him every day and his dad wasn't the picture Charlie had in his head of what a grown, sexy man looked like or the looks Charlie liked to believe he had.

    Trying to sooth himself, Charlie focused on what a great person his dad really was. He had also married a beautiful woman. Those things were enough to keep him going, even if he did look like his dad. Scott and Michelle, Charlie's parents, were very supportive of him, especially in football. They came to most of his games, at times even driving through the night just to catch the game on Saturday afternoon in some small college town a couple of states away.

    Charlie had grown up with one sister, who had inherited her good looks from their mom and drove the boys crazy in high school and college before going overseas to experience the world and find whatever is was she was looking for. He loved his sister a ton and thought she was a great person, but only communicated with her over e-mail now that she was living abroad. With Charlie being the only child close, his parents had been able to give him a lot of attention, in particular this season, Charlie's senior year.

Growing up as the only boy in the family, Charlie's dad had kind of made him his sports friend. Many times it was as if Scott was disappointed in himself for not making the most of his athletic body type and pursuing sports with more determination, so was going to make sure Charlie didn't waste his gift from DNA. Charlie wasn't ever pushed into a sport. Rather it was what he liked and knew. He had grown up watching all major sports; football, basketball, and baseball.

On the weekend, he would wake up and walk into the TV room where he was sure to find his dad watching sports and sit down beside him. If he ever had any questions, his dad was always eager to help him understand.

The women would usually leave them alone and go do their own thing. The guys would pig out on fried snacks and yell and cheer for their favorite teams, cursing and swearing when a mistake was made or the referee made a bad call against their team. When his friends were having sleep-overs on the weekend, Charlie would be up on campus, watching the local college team play football or basketball. He had grown to love and understand sports and the crowds involved in the games, not to mention the uncountable number of hot dogs and sodas consumed at these events. His dad was never stingy about buying snacks while at a game.

This is when Charlie knew that he would play college football someday. The autumn feeling of a football game with the screaming fans that lined the stands was imbedded in his head. The feel in the air of approaching winter made one's skin almost sting every time it was touched. Fresh cut grass and dying leaves filled the air with their smell, letting everyone know what season it was. Hotdogs cooking and alcohol breath on both men and women were all part of the game. He had fallen in love with it as a pre-teen and now it was a part of him, something he cherished. His dad hadn't usually asked if he wanted to go to the games, he usually just said, "Hey we're going to the game. Come on, get ready, let's go." That was okay with Charlie because he had always wanted to go, it was the highlight of his week.

During high school he went through the stage of being too cool to go with his dad and wanted to go with his friends.

Sometimes with his friends, the main goal of going wasn't to watch the game, but to be seen at a social event and to pick up some chicks. Most times this was fine, but there were times when Charlie just wanted to watch the game and he missed going with his dad. His dad would still go to the games with his own friends. Sometimes Charlie and his friends would find his dad and his dad's friends after the game in the parking lot. They would always be in their tailgating spot finishing off the beer and anything left from the grill. They wouldn't let them have any of the beer, but kindly shared the food. Charlie had been coming to this tailgating spot before and after games since he could remember and could find it in his sleep. The smell of fresh cooked meat and beer permeated the area.

    As Charlie was finishing his senior year in high school, his local university, which he and his dad had been loyal fans and supporters of for years, was giving him minimal recruiting attention. They were both holding on to hope that a scholarship offer would be forthcoming. With the approaching scholarship deadline, they began to realize this wasn't going to happen.

    Charlie had offers from smaller schools in the surrounding states that he had never really paid attention to. They weren't bad schools. It did however take some mental adjusting since he had always dreamed of playing for his hometown university. Even though it was a smaller school and not his dream, Charlie had an offer from a division one school that was close enough to home that his family could come watch him play, and he was being offered a full ride scholarship. As things would turn out, it was the right place for Charlie, he couldn't imagine going anywhere else to school.

    Obviously, Charlie and his father's support for their local university waned at this point. They had a new favorite team, the Puma. Charlie's dad still wanted season tickets, but now to a different university. The trek would be longer, but completely worth the time and money. Scott now also had a new partner to go to the games with him, Michelle. They would come to almost every one of Charlie's home games throughout the years of Charlie's college career and most of his road games.

    Charlie examined his belly from the side angle in the mirror, just to make sure it wasn't getting as big as his dad's. His dad wasn't fat, he just had a belly that poked out. Charlie had gained a lot of weight since playing college football, but he still didn't want a belly. He decided that when he was done with football he would jog more and eat less. It didn't seem to matter what he ate right now, he burned more calories than he could take in, even if he forced himself to eat more. Looking at his reflection, he decided that he better lay off the ice cream this week, though. *Only two or three times a week for a while, not every day,* he thought to himself. *I don't want to start getting a belly yet.* And with that he switched off the light and went to finish getting ready for class. He now needed to hurry, or he might be late.

The Zone

This game was turning into a fight. It was halftime and the game was tied. The Puma were visiting the Bears and they were in hostile territory. The crowd for the Bears was always very intense, loud, and a part of the challenge. This year the Bears were expected to win the conference championship and were entering the game undefeated. The winner of this game would emerge as the early frontrunner to win the conference championship. Sitting in the locker room after going over some adjustments, Charlie and the Puma were preparing to go back out for the second half.

Charlie was preparing himself mentally for the second half. He had been beaten a couple of times in the first half. He was not dwelling on his mistakes, he was just focusing on having a better half than the first one. A player has to be able to forget about his own mistakes. Otherwise, it is easy to stay focused on mistakes and never get out of a funk during the game, continuing to second guess himself and think about what he did wrong instead of what he can do right the next play. There are plenty of plays during a game. Athletes have to forget about the last play and come out full force the next play.

This was true for every person that played football. Football is such a team game that each player has to concentrate on his job and make sure he puts forth his best effort. Guys cannot worry about other players, other positions, or what someone in the crowd might be doing. Losing concentration results in the play failing and maybe even an injury for himself or a teammate. Players must give 100% effort each play and concentrate on the task at hand. If one were to worry about what another position might have failed to do, then his energy will be hijacked and the play will be a wasted effort for him. Each person screws up enough that everyone has to be willing to quickly forget. Holding a grudge or getting frustrated at another person during the game only results in wasted energy and divisions among the team.

Charlie had played long enough that he knew all of this. He wasn't replaying any of his mistakes during the first half. He had let those go immediately after they had occurred. Instead, he was trying to focus on what he needed to do in the second half to make sure his team won and that he didn't lose any more personal battles. The defensive lineman that he was going against this game was good and Charlie would need to play a great game to ensure that he did his part to help the team win.

As the Puma walked out onto the field for the second half, the crowd booed at the top of their lungs. As the kickoff for the second half approached, the crowd noise continued to build. There was excitement in the stadium. As the offensive unit was called together for one last discussion of strategy for the second half, Charlie could barely hear his coach. He was yelling just to be heard above the crowd.

The crowd noise inched up with the kick off. The Puma got the ball and the team had to huddle extra tight to hear the quarterback who was only five feet in front of them. The crowd believed they could help the Bears make the big play. They wanted to be a part of the game, as well.

The deafening noise continued throughout the second half. The Puma struggled to hear the quarterback call each play. Charlie and the offensive linemen had to confer with each other on the way to the line of scrimmage about what play had been called. Once they got to the line of scrimmage, the Puma were not able to communicate. The roar of the crowd dominated everything. Some grunts from other players might be heard. Bodies slamming into each other, sweat flying, and body parts flailing are all that the players experienced. Their focus had to be precise, or they could not perform. The roar of the crowd had to fade to the background of each players' consciousness. Once this happened one would not be able to tell if the crowd's intensity had picked up or weakened.

To combat the noise, Charlie had gotten himself into a zone. This process began in the locker room where he had started to focus on exactly what he wanted to accomplish this second half. All of his senses had merged into a focal point directed at the task at hand. The roar of the crowd faded out of his hearing. He heard only the faint sounds of the snap count as it broke through the commotion at regular intervals. It was like a fog of existence where everything but what was directly in his field of vision faded into nothing. Even the shrill of the whistle didn't break through to his consciousness. He only stopped playing when everyone around him began to stop. His vision was sharp and clear, his opponent's uniforms were in vivid contrast to everything else he saw. He was almost able to anticipate what would happen next. He seemed to be in the right place at the right time. His movements were at a quicker pace than the slow motion movements of those around him.

When Charlie was in a zone like this all sense of fatigue, physical limitation, and pain were left behind. It was as if that moment, then and there, was why he had been born. As if everything in his life had led him to that instant. Time was of no factor; it didn't matter if the game lasted hours longer or ended right then. All of existence seemed to be concentrated on that one moment. He could not even understand it was happening when it was happening. Only after the fact, upon reflection, would he realize what had happened. This was possible because no thought is required or used when one is in the zone, everything comes naturally from instinct. There is no chance of failure or loss because everything is perfect. One is almost led to the outcome by one's unconscious powers. These unconscious powers are not able to take a person to any undesired location, they can only help a person.

Charlie played most of the second half this way. It was an incredible feeling, one that Charlie wished he could duplicate on cue. It seemed to happen to him a few times a year, unfortunately not every game. Once Charlie came back to consciousness, being aware of the world around him again, he realized it was the end of the 4th quarter with his team now two touchdowns ahead. The crowd had been silenced. The energy had been drained from the stadium. The only positive vibes were coming from the Puma's sideline. Charlie could even see people leaving the stadium. With a puzzled look, Charlie remembered how dominant he had been in this second half. It was a tie game at half and he had been exhausted already. But, he had dug deep into his reserve well and produced one of his best performances. He smiled because his play had been almost effortless. It would not be until the next day that his body would feel the full effects of his extraordinary performance.

The Puma were now 3-0, on top of the conference, and feeling good. That is all that mattered to Charlie. He felt like his leadership was making a difference. He would continue to put the team on his back and carry them to their highest goals.

American Diner

Charlie ran into Johnny leaving campus after his American history class and talked him into having lunch with him at the corner café. It had been there since the 1960's and still had the same style as when it was originally built. An ugly lime green paint adorned the outside with black wooden paneling outfitting the inside.

Johnny wasn't a hard person to get alone, he was just a hard person to find. If he didn't want to be found or be seen, then nobody was going to find him. Calling his house and leaving a message didn't guarantee that he would return a person's calls, no matter how many messages one might leave. He could be at a party and barely have his presence known if he didn't want to be noticed, with not a person remembering for certain if they had seen him. At other times he was the life of the party.

On campus he would dart from class to class and when he was finished he would zip back home, making sure he spent as little time on campus as necessary. Johnny didn't wander around campus just to make appearances. For that matter, he didn't go anywhere to make appearances. If he went to a party or a bar, it was for a specific purpose, to get drunk, or see a certain group of girls. Sometimes he chose a party or destination based on how few people would be there, not how many. Because of this he was an enigma to many people. He was the starting QB for the Puma, yet he didn't seek out any extra attention.

He had the looks of an all American boy, tall and athletic. The proportioning of his body looked as if it had been given thought. It was the handsome beauty that drove women wild, the kind of looks that countless young ladies would fall in love with at first sight. He carried himself as if none of this mattered. He had an air of rebellion about him that was even more attractive to the college girls than his looks.

Women mattered to him only when he had nothing else to do. He received so much attention from women that he didn't treat it with sincerity. It wasn't that he disliked women. He constantly had his pick of girls and dated a lot, but didn't get very close to any of them. He had his heart broken by someone he thought he still loved.

He couldn't get totally into a girl when his heart was still wrapped up with someone else. She would occasionally make an appearance at a football party and Johnny's feelings would come flooding back. Every time they would see each other, the prospect of getting back together was on their breath. It would take more than a day for Johnny to get back to his normal self after just seeing her, especially if she happened to be with another guy. But, he would get over it once he realized she was just playing him, she was trying to keep him around and prevent him from moving on.

Her name was Vanessa and it didn't take long to see why Johnny had fallen in love with her and still not recovered. She was drop dead gorgeous and had that wild side that most guys longed for in their girlfriend but were afraid to admit. She was nice, but fucked around with Johnny's mind, which was why Charlie didn't like her.

Besides Vanessa, Johnny lived a very carefree life. He put his full effort into football, but he didn't let the outcome affect his demeanor. He played with an air of confidence that bordered on cockiness and made the other team think he was beyond being rattled. Off the field, praise and awards were not things that motivated Johnny. He shied away from these things and preferred to be a solid part of a whole rather than a leader and attract too much attention to himself. He rarely talked about his accomplishments or skills. It always seemed to be others that did the bragging for Johnny.

His ability in school came naturally. He wasn't the smartest guy ever, but he pulled off a 3.0 GPA without much effort. He went to class and showed up on test day, not needing any reading or studying to get a B.

He acted how he wanted to act, he didn't comply with social norms. He didn't care about being somewhere just because it was the cool place to be. If he wanted to go to a party, he would. But he also didn't mind sitting at home drinking beer and watching TV by himself on a Saturday night. Despite his good looks, Johnny's wardrobe was not something to envy. On the rare occasion when Johnny would dress with style, he was a figure that was noticed by everyone. Most of the time his clothes looked like something bought from a second hand store, or if he felt like splurging, perhaps Walmart. It wasn't because he was low on money, it was that fashion didn't make his list of priorities.

Johnny's carefree attitude was on full display at his apartment. It didn't smell, but the level of tidiness, upkeep, and general cleanliness would be appalling to any mother. It looked like it was the sight of the latest natural disaster. He was a nice person who was concerned with himself first. As a result, he was happy most of the time and pleasant to be around. It was easy to be one's self around him because he was honest and genuine.

Finally having a moment alone with Johnny, Charlie remembered some of the questions he wanted to ask him. Sitting down waiting for their orders, in the dark, dank, greasy smelling diner, Charlie was the first to break the silence. "So, how was class?"

"Oh, it was okay. I like the history part, I think all that shit is interesting. It's just that the teacher is fucking boring. He stands up there and lectures the whole time. With his monotone voice, just standing in the middle of the class never moving, expecting us to take it all in and stay awake for the whole fucking boring lecture. Sometimes when I am really tired I doze off in there." Johnny shrugged, indicating there wasn't much he could do about it. "I just want to get a good grade and get done with the shit. You know what I am saying?"

"Yeah, some of these professors sure could use some training. I am not sure how they ever got the idea that they were fit for teaching. Sure they know a lot about the subject, but that doesn't make the class any more interesting."

"That's for sure. Plus, once they have tenure they don't have to do a damn thing besides publish. They could be the worst, most boring damn teacher and still have a job for life," Johnny quipped just as the waitress brought their food.

"Here you go, gentlemen. Two specials, one with pickles, one without," she said, putting down the food. She looked as if she might have been working in the café since its inception. Her scraggly hair was loosely tied into a bun with pieces showing their resistance to being told where to stay put.

Her apron was stained with a year's worth of grease from the endless cheeseburgers she had been serving. Her body didn't seem to have any shape to it. If a person just looked at the body, instead of the face, one would have a hard time guessing if it was a man or a woman. She didn't look anorexic, more like a stick figure come to life. Her face didn't have much makeup and showed that too many years had been spent in this dump of a restaurant. Wrinkles made their presence known at the corner of her eyes and mouth. She was nice, but would never be confused for attractive. As she was leaving the table after serving their meals, she acknowledged that she knew who they were. "Good luck in the game on Saturday."

"Thanks," Johnny and Charlie replied simultaneously, already dressing up their burgers.

"Damn, I am hungry," Charlie blurted out before stuffing his mouth full of a big greasy bite. It wasn't a sandwich that was made for a white table cloth meal. Crunching his way through his first bite, juices began to run down his hands. Red and yellow were the most vivid colors, accompanied by clear, hot grease, and liquids from pickles and tomatoes completed the artistic display. *If it's messy, it must be good. The more grease the better,* he thought. Reaching for a handful of napkins, Charlie brought up the subject which had been on his mind. "So, why are you always so hesitant about talking with reporters after the game and practice? It seems like you don't want the press and that you couldn't care less what people think."

Finishing his mouthful and cracking a smile out of amusement by Charlie's question, Johnny answered evenly and without any doubt. "Well, who does care? Why should I care what people think? Especially the newspaper people. They are only trying to sell more papers and make money. They don't know me and the people reading their stories don't know me either. I don't really care what people think who don't personally know me. The people that know me either like me for who I am or don't, and I don't give a shit. I am not going to try and be some pretty-boy celebrity just to get stories in the paper about me or to gain popularity."

"Well, that's true," Charlie acknowledged, between chews. Pausing for a moment to finish breaking the food down enough to swallow, he answered, "What about all the people who are interested in you? Not everyone will have a chance to meet you or get to know you personally. You have a lot of fans and a lot of people who would like to know more about you. You don't buy into the idea of athletes having an obligation to their fans?"

"Hell, no!!! I don't play the game for them. They might be the ones paying to come and watch me, but that doesn't mean I have any obligations towards them. If I was playing for anyone besides me, then it might matter. I just go out and do the best I can, that's what I like to do. I don't want all the publicity. I play football because I love the game, not because I want to be famous." Johnny gave Charlie a shrug, trying to portray his honesty and grabbed a handful of fries to shove into his mouth. Talking out of the corner of his mouth, he added, "Anyways, I don't like everyone knowing about me. I am a private person and the reporters and fans don't seem to have any concern about that. They don't need to know everything about my life. There is plenty I don't want to tell them. After games, I take my time and try to wait until everyone is gone, or disappear really fast so that I don't get hounded. Sometimes it is nice to be left alone."

"Yeah, those are all good points. It is just funny, the person who is getting the most press is the one who really doesn't want it."

"I know, I love screwing with the guys after a game. They come in and tell me to hurry and get ready and come down for an interview. That is when I take as long as I possibly can. If they really want to interview me, then they can wait. I am not going to be on anyone's schedule, they can be on my schedule. I am fucking tired and want to relax. I don't want to talk to anyone. I don't want anyone evaluating my game and questioning my motives. They act like they know more about football than I do. It just isn't something I am interested in. Sometimes when I am done with football I don't want to talk about it. I love it and it is great, but it isn't my life and there are other things I would like to talk about."

"I can tell. It makes me laugh. The guy keeps coming in and asking you to hurry, acting like the reporter has somewhere to go and that you need to get your act in gear." Charlie shook his head and let out a soft chuckle.

"Seriously." Johnny smiled, acknowledging his behavior. "The more they come in to bug me, the longer I take. Then when I get down there, I give them the simplest answers I can think of. They get this look on their faces like I should be more polite and hurry down when they want to do an interview. Well, maybe they should be more polite and ask when I have time, if they want to interview me so badly. They act like their time is more important than mine. Sometimes they ask me to hurry because they have a deadline. When they pull that shit, I just give them a nod and say 'sure', having no intention of hurrying. That kind of attitude just seems to permeate the press. Almost like I owe them something for putting my name in the paper, for getting me more press. I could care less, dude. They act like I owe my fame and my future to them because unless they keep my name in the paper then people won't know who I am. Well, to tell you the truth, I don't give a shit. They can keep it, I don't play for them, or for anyone else. If they didn't have me to interview then what else would they fill their shitty newspaper with?"

"All right, man. No need to start getting angry with me. I am not a reporter and you don't have to defend yourself to me. I agree with your position. I was just curious about it. Just wanted to get to know what makes you tick and what the hell you are thinking when they keep coming in and bugging you for an interview."

"Yeah, I know, it just gets old. But boy, these burgers sure are good," Johnny said, changing the subject and diving in to his burger again. They finished off their lunches, only occasionally conversing about dull subjects like girls and what was going on in their classes. Upon leaving the restaurant, they noticed that their clothes smelled like the food they had just devoured. This seemed to be a characteristic of restaurants that specialize in greasy foods. It didn't matter much to Johnny and Charlie, having a good lunch was worth a dirty shirt.

They were just glad it was Monday and there would only be a light 'voluntary' workout and film session. Otherwise they might be tasting today's lunch once more and it always tasted better on the way down.

"Get some guys and come over for cards tonight after film," Johnny stated more than questioned.

Charlie was pleasantly surprised. "Okay, cool. See you tonight."

"Not too many. I have to keep my profile low, right?"

They smiled, gave each other a bro hug, said goodbye to each other and went their own ways, Johnny to his house to have some quiet time before having to watch film and being dissected in front of everyone and Charlie back towards campus to see who he might run into and be able to chat with.

Turmoil

Blake pulled into the driveway. The porch light wasn't even left on tonight. This was an indication of how things would go for the night. Conner was asleep, his wife was in bed, and activity in the house was over for the day. It wasn't much fun coming home to a quiet, dark home with nobody to greet him.

He looked through the fridge and pulled out a bowl of some kind of leftovers and a beer. While heating it up, he pulled out some notes on the tendencies of this week's opponent. He sat down to eat while checking his notes against his game plan. Finishing the bowl of leftover casserole and beer in solitude, he realized he had yet to say hello to April or let her know that he was home. This thought passed quickly through his mind.

Blake stopped by Conner's room and gave him a kiss on the cheek. Conner didn't move from the gentle show of affection. These kinds of interactions between father and son were becoming more common as the season passed along. He walked into the master bedroom and found April sitting cross legged on their footstool, sitting less than a foot from the full length mirror studying her face. Her curled up, compact position had a sexy, mysterious feline quality to it.

"Hi, honey," he let out slowly.

"Hi," she replied back, with a hint of disappointment at his late arrival again. It was past time for bed and neither of them had energy to talk about anything of importance. *I might be married to you, but I don't have a relationship with you at this point,* she thought.

Blake was content to let the conversation stay simple. He walked over to the closet to take off his clothes. In the closet he noticed how full the laundry basket was. It was stuffed full of clothes. He had never seen it this full. It had to have been a full week since any wash had been done.

"Why's there so much laundry?" he asked with more sternness than he intended.

"I've been busy lately and really tired the past couple of days." Plucking a stray eyebrow, she made eye contact with him through the mirror.

"How can you be tired? You are home all day," was the first thing to come to his mind and he said it aloud. He knew this was not the right thing to say at this moment and wished he would have kept quiet.

She stopped in mid action and looked back at him to see if he was serious. His back was to her and she tried to stay calm. To keep from erupting, she remained quiet. Her gaze didn't leave Blake. Once he turned around, the gaze became more of a glare. He didn't feel like talking about anything, but couldn't ignore the intense way she was staring at him. 'Wwwwhat?" he shot back defensively.

"You know what! I hope you're not serious." Her eyes grew more glaring and pointed.

"Well…," he scratched his head, knowing this was not going to end well. He wasn't willing to apologize. He said what he felt. "How can you be so tired? You are home all day and don't even have to get dressed or take a shower if you don't want to," he said, trying to hold his ground.

"I can't believe you would say that." She paused, the emotions mixing in her head running from anger to hurt. Her eyes started to well up, but she held back. "I work my ass off here all day and don't get any recognition or praise. The only time you notice anything is when I don't do something, like now."

"You've had all day, every day. I know I don't help much…"

"Much!?"

"Okay, I don't help. But I'm out making money so that we can survive. I work my ass off all day. I do my part. This is a team effort, every person needs to do their part."

"Do you think I don't do my part? Is that what you're saying, Blake?"

"I'm not saying that. It's just that right now…" he cut his sentence short, ending it by pointing to the hamper.

"Oh, that's brave. This home wouldn't even function if it weren't for me. I am up with you every morning and don't go to bed until you are home. In between that time I take care of our child, which requires my full attention every minute. In my spare seconds of the day, I clean, cook, wash the dishes, do the laundry, pay the bills, and try to have a spare moment for myself here and there. It's not easy. I don't have anyone to communicate with all day, it's only baby talk. Then you come home and ninety nine percent of the time don't feel like talking. I don't have time for friends anymore. The only people I talk to on the phone anymore are my parents." She paused, trying to collect her thoughts and keep her emotions under control. Calmly and quietly she went on, "Blake what happened to us? I don't see you or know you at this point. You have no idea what is going on in the family. Conner barely knows you. He is growing up and that doesn't stop for the football season. It will carry on with or without you."

He took a moment before responding, "I know honey. This is not the easiest situation for anybody. It is my dream, though, it is my passion. It is what drives me. It is why I wake up in the morning. It is so great that I get paid to live out my dream and do my hobby. I will have more time for you and Conner in the off season. We seem to go through this each season. It is something we both have to get used to because it isn't going to end anytime soon."

"That's what I am afraid of," she let out under her breath.

"Well, don't be. Always remember that I love you." He gave her a kiss on the forehead and slipped into bed, flashing her the most loving smile he could muster at that moment. "I've got to go to sleep, honey. We'll talk about this some other time. I love you." He flipped off the overhead lights, leaving only the light in front of the mirror on.

No, we won't talk about it, April thought in the now dim light looking into her own eyes. *What does love mean if the people aren't together to share it and express it to each other?* Her feelings of loneliness were reaching an all-time high. They had been growing ever since Blake had taken that first coaching job. She used to think she only needed time to adjust to the schedule of a coach's wife. Now, it had taken another dramatic leap forward. He had gotten a promotion and the money was nice, but he was gone even more. His mind was even more consumed with football. Football seemed to be his life. Plus, this wasn't even the final stop of the coaching ladder. He wanted to be a head coach someday. Being a head coach meant even more commitment to football and even more responsibility. She didn't know where it would end. She questioned if she could live it. She allowed herself, for the first time, to wonder if this was all worth it, if she could be in this kind of a relationship for the rest of her life. She studied herself in the mirror, looking for an answer she wouldn't find.

Chillin'

It was Monday, which meant a night away from football. This weekly reprieve helped to keep football from becoming overwhelming to Charlie. Tonight he had called a couple of the guys and arranged a game of cards at Johnny's place. They were hanging out and just relaxing. They sat around Johnny's table which hadn't been cleaned off for company. If cards were placed in the wrong spot they would stick to the table. When someone wanted to join the game he needed to move the empty beer bottles and dirty dishes out of the way. Limp Bizkit was yelling in the other room and pizza was on the way.

It was Charlie's turn to deal, and after the cards were out he felt like some discussion was needed. So he asked those at the table, "What other country would you guys like to visit?"

Johnny was the first to answer while arranging his hand. "I have always wanted to go to Thailand. I hear it is beautiful, the people are nice, and everything is really cheap. It is just a pain in the ass to get there and the airplane ticket is really expensive. I know someday I'll get there, though."

"Yeah, that is somewhere I want to go, too," Mike chimed in while scanning his cards. "I'll tell you the place, though, Australia. That place is wild. I think we should all go there sometime. Do you ever watch…"

"Whoa, whoa, whoa, hold up there," Brent interrupted, setting his beer down. Brent was the kind of guy who only added to the stereotype about football players being dumb. He was a defensive lineman and if he didn't have an athletic scholarship there was no way he would be in college. He cheated his way through his classes and barely had more smarts than the table where they were sitting. He was incredibly loyal, and a defensive coach's dream weighing in at 305 with 12% body fat and athleticism that few could match. The only problem was he couldn't remember his plays. He could barely read and couldn't do more than simple addition. During the games, he would be told where to line up and if something tricky was to be done, Junior, the defensive team captain, had to tell him what to do. "I know Australia is far away man, but he said other 'country.' Australia is part of America, dummy."

A chorus of "Fuck yous," was accompanied by boisterous laughs and blank looks of astonishment at this comment. *I hope he's kidding,* Charlie thought.

"Dummy, who you calling dummy!? You're a fucking idiot. Australia is not part of America. It's on the other side of the world, its own country, and even its own continent. You are the fucking dummy," Mike said, chuckling, and threw an empty beer can at him.

"I know you don't go to class Brent, but you must have learned about something, anything, at least once during your years of school. That is pretty fucking stupid, dude," Johnny said, shaking his head in bewilderment.

"Well, maybe I did, I just don't remember. My brain stopped working a long time ago," Brent said in his defense, trying to act cool and not seem embarrassed even though his face was bright red. "Why does it matter? It's so fucking far away that I'll never go. Whatever came out of there, anyway? I mean, besides Crocodile Dundee and the Crocodile Hunter?"

"You're still a fucking idiot and maybe you should slow down on the beer. I think it's taking a toll on your brain. We need you this season and even defensive linemen have to think a little," Charlie said sarcastically.

"Yeah, yeah, just hand me another beer asshole."

Very few players are as dumb as Brent. It just seemed like every football team had a guy like Brent. But there were plenty of smart guys. A few of his teammates were in pre-med, pre-law, pharmacy, and engineering. One of the seniors who had just left got his bachelor's and master's degrees in five years. He had worked his butt off academically and athletically.

Charlie wasn't a genius, but he was smart. He got As and Bs in all his classes. It was important to him to not be just another dumb football player. He was different and he wanted to act like it on and off the field. In fact, some of his teachers had even joked with him, asking him if he really was a football player. He liked that. He liked to tear down stereotypes and preconceived notions. Charlie believed he was more than just a football player. He made sure to give other areas in his life focus, as well.

The doorbell rang and Brent's geography faux pas was quickly forgotten as the pizza arrived. They continued to play cards as they stuffed their faces with pizza and talked shit to each other until it was time to go home.

Thriller

Charlie trotted up to the line. It was the end of the 4th quarter and he was one of the few players on the field who was still hustling in and out of the huddle. It had been a battle all game long. The defensive lineman across from him had stayed in the same position almost the entire game. Their skill level was evenly matched, it had been a fight against each other the whole game. Each of them had taken their shots at the other whenever the opportunity presented itself. There weren't any cheap shots, they both had to be alert at all times though, or they would end up on the ground.

It was 4th down and goal from the three yard line. There were only fifteen seconds left in the game. The Puma needed a touchdown to win the game. They were down by five and trying for their fourth win in a row. Knowing that a touchdown would win the game, Charlie summoned every ounce of energy he had left. This was the reason he had put in all those hours of training at the gym, why he had pushed himself a little harder each day, so that here and now in this situation he would be the one in better shape, the one called upon to make the play when it was needed, and the one to emerge victorious.

The play had been called right up Charlie's hole. It was up to him. If he blocked well they would score and win. This vote of confidence by the coaching staff added to his adrenaline. He approached the line with almost a skip in his step and had to hold back a grin of excitement about the upcoming play. He was exhausted, but it all disappeared by the time he reached the line.

Getting into his stance, Charlie caught his opponent's eyes. He locked on to him, mentally telling him that this was it and that it would be decided between them. He didn't care if his opponent knew it, Charlie was going to win this battle. Charlie's look of determination combined with his high energy seemed to take the last bit of steam from his opponent. Charlie knew the play was his, it had already been decided. He tensed up into a solid ball of energy waiting to explode. The crowd noise died down as the home team got ready to snap the ball on the decisive play of the game.

"Down…set…hut!" Johnny barked above the din of the crowd.

Charlie exploded like he was being shot out of a cannon. His feet pumped and his hands were locked onto his opponent's chest. In a split second Charlie had plowed his opponent into the linebacker and had created a pile up of other defensive players following the ball. Not letting up, Charlie continued driving his opponent over the mess of limbs and bodies created by the pile up and into the ground with all his force. Landing on top of him, Charlie could hear the breath being forced out. Hearing the whistle and the crowd roar from his position on and under bodies, Charlie knew the result. They had scored a touchdown and won the game.

Standing up, acknowledging the outcome, Charlie extended a hand to help his opponent up. This was a little bit of a sympathetic gesture. Charlie had won the war tonight by winning the last battle. He felt powerful. He had kicked this guy's ass when it mattered most. They were of equal skill and Charlie had willed himself to victory. Knowing that he had demolished his opponent's will, and reduced him to a bump on the ground, made him feel like the dominant male. The gesture of helping him up seemed like a tacit acknowledgement that this was the case.

With his last bit of energy, Charlie joined the Puma's celebration in the end zone. They had finally put the finishing touches on this victory. Allowing himself a moment of enjoyment and relaxation on the field, Charlie leisurely made his way back to the huddle for the extra point. He stopped to salute the crowd by giving a few fist pumps to whoever might be watching.

After the extra point and a squib kick to run out the clock, the rest of his teammates joined in the celebration that continued into the early hours of the next day.

National Recognition

It was Tuesday, the day the polls hit the newspapers. The Puma had cracked the top 25 for the first time in over four years. Charlie was on cloud nine. He walked around campus with a spring in his step and a permanent grin. It was the look of a man who had just been laid after a six month dry spell. He didn't know what it was, but more people seemed to acknowledge him and more girls seemed to look his way. It was an amazing feeling, one that Charlie knew would only continue with another win this weekend.

Back at practice, their ranking was the talk of the locker room. Outside of the locker room it was barely discussed. The coaches went about their business and the routine stayed the same. It was just another week, expectations hadn't changed.

Without the topic being brought up in meetings or in conversations between players and coaches, the hype seemed to die down. Perhaps this was the goal of Coach Jackson because it had the effect of making the players realize nothing had changed and the same things would be required of them this week as had been required any other week. The players might think they were hot shit, but the coaches didn't treat them any differently.

Whatever the strategy was adopted for, it seemed to work. Practices went off like any other week. Charlie hoped it would lead to another victory.

Shattered

Charlie walked into the football office with an air of happiness. The Puma were on a winning streak, nationally ranked, and he had been THE MAN so far this season. He felt like he was living up to the lofty goals he had set.

This defused instantly when he saw La Dean's face. She was normally so happy to see him and all the staff of the Puma had been outright jolly with the extraordinary start to the season. Her normally sanguine and welcoming face instead had a look of foreboding that scared the shit out of Charlie.

Hoping her solemn face didn't portend anything too severe, Charlie greeted her with as much cheer as he could at that moment, "Hi La Dean." He managed a nervous grin.

She took a moment before replying, almost trying to tell him everything that she was thinking. What came through loud and clear to Charlie was her look of disappointment. This crushed him. La Dean had always liked him and had always been so happy to see him. *Oh fuck, it must be something bad, if I am already getting the third degree from her. I don't know what the hell it could be, though.*

"Hi Charlie. Coach Jackson is expecting you." Her facial expression didn't change as she watched him walk into the office.

Acting casual, Charlie knocked on the half open door to Coach Jackson's office and stepped halfway into the room to get away from La Dean's glare. As Coach Jackson looked up he tried to act as nonchalant as he could. "Hey Coach." He noticed Coach Jones was still in there and had a glimmer of hope that it couldn't be too bad if another coach was in the room. "Is now a good time?"

"Hi Charlie. Yes, now is a good time. Close the door and sit down," he said with more gruff than Charlie had heard from him in a long time. He turned his attention back to Coach Jones. "You can stay. I think you should know about this, too. I'm sure you will have to deal with this kind of stuff when you are a head coach. We will get back to our adjustments in a minute, but I need to talk to Charlie for a few." He looked back at Charlie, motioned for him to sit in the chair directly across the desk in front of him, leaned part way back in his chair, and fixed a scowl on Charlie.

Charlie sat down and was instantly nervous. "Hi Coach Jones," he blurted out quickly, showing his nervousness. Coach Jones just nodded at him, knowing whatever needed to be discussed was serious. Charlie looked back at Coach Jackson and began fidgeting with his hands. "So, what's going on?" Charlie asked, not liking the awkward silence.

Coach Jackson just sat there looking at him for a minute, letting the tension build. After a couple of moments that seemed to last for hours Coach Jackson slammed his fist on the desk. "FUCK!! Charlie. What the FUCK were you thinking?"

Charlie's eyes got big, his mouth dropped open, and his heart was pounding in his chest. He had no idea what was going on. He couldn't imagine what made Coach Jackson so upset. He didn't know what to do. He was flabbergasted. He couldn't take anymore of the piercing eyes, so he said the only thing he could think of. "What do you mean, Coach?"

The scowl lightened a little bit and Coach Jackson took a breath. "I mean this summer out at the lake with Ron. That's what I fucking mean."

Oh no. Charlie's heart dropped. He had no idea how Coach Jackson had found out. He knew this was bad news and with the reaction of his Coach it was worse than he thought. *If something happens because of that, I don't know what I will do.* He felt frozen. He couldn't say anything.

"Well, Charlie. Tell me what in the hell you were thinking. Do you want to be done playing football in college? Do you want it to all be over right here and now? That's what could fucking happen if I can't keep a lid on this." He glared back at Charlie.

Charlie's shoulders slouched unconsciously. He couldn't believe what he was hearing. Tears started to form at the corners of his eyes. He bit his bottom lip, he didn't want to cry, he couldn't cry right here and right now. He looked down at his lap. *This can't be happening. Not after all I have done and how the season is going. This can't be happening.* His heart felt broken. He wanted to melt into the chair and not have to face any of this stress and pressure again. He regained his composure as much as he could, put his hand over his mouth, and looked back up. "I don't know Coach. I didn't know it would be so bad."

Coach Jackson shook his head. "Do you think the NCAA cares about what you know and don't know? If they find out, you are done, Charlie. There is nothing I can do to help you if they find out." He sat up and put his hands on the desk. "I want you to know that I am meeting with Johnny in an hour and I will discuss this with him, too. I wanted to talk to you first, though. You are the team captain and the team leader. You are who I am counting on and who I need. I am really disappointed, Charlie. I really didn't think I would have to go through this with you."

Charlie nodded at him, agreeing that he had screwed up and that he didn't have any excuses. He was still trying to fight back the tears. He was a 22 year old and this was his life, this was all he had.

Coach Jackson broke the silence. "I think I can keep it under control Charlie. This has to stay quiet, though. Nobody else can find out about this. What we talk about here does not leave the room. GOT IT!?!?"

Charlie hoped this reprieve was for real. "Of course Coach. I never even told anyone to begin with. I certainly won't tell anyone about what happened or about this meeting." He looked back at Coach Jackson with as much honesty as he could muster through still watery eyes.

"Okay, good. Now get out of here, enjoy the rest of your day, and be ready for practice in a few hours." Coach Jackson did not let go of his scowl, even though he seemed to be letting Charlie off the hook.

"See you soon, Coach. Coach Jones, see you soon, too." Charlie nodded at both of them as he left the office without loitering. He didn't want to press his luck.

After Charlie left the office, Coach Jones looked over at Coach Jackson. "What was that all about?"

Coach Jackson slowly shook his head. "You'll go through the same shit many times, Blake. He took money from a booster that he shouldn't have taken. They did a little bit of work for Ron Jensen and got paid $1500. Nobody can justify that amount for the work they did."

Coach Jones' eyes lit up. "Wow that is a lot of money. How'd you get them off the hook?"

"You'll learn, Blake. We have a lot of influence in the community. His wife came in and told me about it. She said they weren't supposed to receive that much money, but that with Ron's dementia he had given them part of their emergency money from the safe. But, guess who is another one of our boosters?"

Blake shook his head.

"Dr. Hanson. He is a neurologist. I promised to speak to Dr. Hanson and get Ron and his wife into the office first thing next week for a consultation. Plus, I upgraded their season tickets and it was a done deal. She said it was all an honest mistake and promised to keep it to herself."

Blake nodded his head in approval and awe. "Nice job, coach. I need to learn some more people skills."

"Yeah, it is a multi-faceted job. Just be nice to people because you never know when you will need favors. Stay on everyone's good side without kissing any ass and you will be good." Coach Jackson shrugged his shoulders as if it was all just another day at the office. "Well, let's get back to those adjustments now."

Nice Surprise

Blake walked in the door without hesitation, as if his appearance had been expected. Hearing the door and knowing it could be only one person, April stopped suddenly. She looked at the clock in disbelief. It was a Thursday at 7:00 PM and he was home. An anxious excitement rose through her body beginning in her toes. Forgetting what she was doing, she left Conner in his high chair with a plate of food, the water running, and cupboards left open, and walked into the entrance area to make sure she wasn't going crazy and that the sound wasn't just wishful thinking.

As she turned the corner, she saw Blake hanging his jacket, the evening air was beginning to have an autumn chill to it. Their eyes met as he turned to make his way to the kitchen. With a blank, emotionless face, April stood staring at him in shock. Since the beginning of two-a-days they had spent an average of ten waking hours a week with each other. All of Blake's effort lately had been put towards getting more wins for the Puma. When Blake began to walk towards her with a big grin and a look of sympathy, all of April's negative feelings faded away and she bolted into his arms. They embraced and for a moment all else was forgotten. This is what she wanted. It had not been happening very often lately, but for this moment nothing else mattered. Through their lips each of them could feel the passion they had for one another. April hoped this would never end, but was quickly startled back into reality. She pulled her head back looking into his eyes without the slightest bit of desire to move from this spot and waited until he made the first move.

"Ma, ma, ma," the young little voice seemed to shatter the moment. "Ma, ma, ma," was this time accompanied by a plate and spoon crashing on the floor.

"He's talking?" Blake didn't hide his surprise. "Why didn't you tell me?"

She smiled and replied with candor, "I haven't had a chance. She reached out for his mouth again and kissed him with all her pent up loneliness.

Conner began to rustle again in the kitchen and Blake pulled away, wishing he could just pick her up and take her down the hall to their bedroom. He knew some wild sex would go a long way towards making things better. "Well, it's nice to see you, too. Let's go surprise Conner," he said, walking towards the source of the summons with her hand in his.

Focus

    Leaving the meeting, Charlie tried to escape the crowd. He still felt edgy from his scare with Coach Jackson earlier this week. He needed some alone time to get his emotions in check. The meeting had been more tense than usual. The guys were feeling confident. They were 4-0 and ranked #19 in the country. The coaches walked a fine line of acknowledging the results and great effort, while also trying to keep the team from feeling like they had arrived, like they had already put in all the effort that they needed to for the season. The guys were excited and wanted to show it, but the coaches kept them in check and weren't allowing any celebrations or self-indulgence.

    It had been like this all week. The dichotomy between both sides had been pulling at each other. The meeting had been called to an end, none too soon, as the players needed to express their new found cockiness and the coaches needed to be away from the premature display of a complete team. Charlie was more cautious than the rest of his teammates. Tonight more than ever he wanted to be alone with his thoughts and prepare himself as he always did. He knew that there was a lot of work still to be done this season. Their 4-0 record and national ranking weren't going to win them the next game, only continued effort and execution would do that.

    This would be the last real team meeting before the game tomorrow. There might be a few brief pep talks, or something tomorrow, but this was the last organized coach-led meeting. It now meant that each player had to do his own mental preparations for the game. For Charlie it was important, even now, almost 24 hours before the game, to start concentrating with the hope that if he started early, it would help him maintain his concentration during the game. This was one of the areas where Charlie was in need of improvement. At times during the game, his mind would wander. He might start thinking about a girl, his exams coming up, or family issues. This is when his game and play was sub-par and the likelihood of mistakes increased.

    During a game in middle school he had come off the field for a rest. He looked around the sidelines to see where his family was. He spotted them and caught the eye of his mother. He gave her a quick gesture to acknowledge her and noticed his grandparents sitting with his mom and dad. Quickly he turned his attention back to the game, lest he get caught by the coach not watching the game and get scolded in front of everyone. His eyes back on the field, Charlie could not get his young mind off the thoughts of his grandpa. Less than a week earlier his grandpa had been diagnosed with cancer. It had not been found early and the prognosis was not good. There were few treatment options and his family was still even considering no treatment, so that his grandpa might live out his remaining life with comfort.

This had a big effect on Charlie. He was very close to his grandpa and had spent almost every summer fishing with him since he was old enough not to be bored without TV. He was young and wasn't ready to deal with death. It wasn't really even talked about around his house. The talk around his house was more of just keeping things normal and not worrying about what would happen to his grandpa. All these thoughts were swirling through his head. His mind was anywhere but on the game.

Suddenly, the coach yelled at him to get back on the field. Charlie didn't feel any sense of physical tiredness, he just didn't know what was going on around him. He had been yanked from a daydream and now had to be ready to go to battle on the football field. It was only middle school, but it was a close game and his team needed him. Running to the empty spot in the huddle, Charlie barely made out the call. He recognized the words, but they didn't click. He had no fucking idea what the hell he was supposed to do. There was no time to think, no time to ask any questions. The opposing team was already approaching the line. Charlie had to get in his stance and be ready. His mind wandered back to his grandpa and how much it meant to him that his grandpa would come even when he didn't know how much longer he had to live. He looked back at the ball, trying to focus on moving, when it was snapped.

Before Charlie even realized the play had begun, his man had already fired across the line of scrimmage into him. He was fucked. This was going to be a bad play. Trying to make up for his lateness in moving, Charlie tried to go around his man and prevent himself from being driven back any more. This seemed to stop the damage of the play for a moment, when all of a sudden Charlie was run into from behind. Falling down in a big pile he tried to catch a glimpse of who it was that ran into him. It was one of his teammates, the linebacker who played behind him. Now he realized how bad he had fucked up. A stunt had been called and Charlie was supposed to go to a certain area. He had gone the wrong way, after getting his ass kicked. He could tell this was going to be bad.

Realizing the play was over, the pile he had become a part of started to clear up. He turned to see the other team celebrating a touchdown. His teammate, the one who ran into him, was also coming out of the pile. He slapped Charlie on his helmet hard and asked him what the fuck he was doing. Didn't he know the fucking plays? They went right up his area and had scored because nobody had been there. Entering the huddle again to call a play against the conversion attempt, the team was staring at Charlie. A couple more guys asked him what the hell had happened. He didn't know what to say and just shrugged his shoulders.

Once on the sideline he got more from the coach. Not having any comment, Charlie just took the verbal onslaught with all thoughts of his grandpa now out of his head. His team ended up losing a close game and Charlie got dirty looks from a few of his teammates after the game.

In high school a similar situation had happened, only this time it was worse. It was over a girl. He had a crush on this particular girl for a long time. Her name was Julia and he had always thought she was pretty. She was beginning to pay attention to him during school. Then, prior to a game, he saw her in the training room helping the trainer get ready for the game. Apparently, she was an aide to the trainer and had come to the game this week to help out. She smiled at him and moved toward him to talk. He was now in a rough situation. He needed to stay focused on the game, but he wanted her and this kind of opportunity didn't come around often. Remembering why he was there, he cut their conversation short, telling her that he had to finish getting ready. Walking away, his thoughts were still on her and how she had flirted with him and how he might ask her out.

Throughout warm-ups, his mind would not come back to the task at hand. Finally, after receiving a good, hard hit from his teammate that almost knocked him over, Charlie's focus was back on football. Things were going great, Charlie was having a good game, the kind he needed to help his team pull out this tight ball game. Charlie didn't come off the field very often in high school team as he played offense, defense, and special teams, but the next time he came off for a rest, there she was. She was giving water to the players while they caught their breath. She flashed her cute smile and said hi to him. His mind was immediately off the game. He followed her movements for a moment. Her legs moved gracefully in her jeans. The hat pulled over her head to keep her warm made her look all soft and cuddly. She turned around again to catch him staring, and flashed him a grin and a wink. He was almost getting excited. There was no time for that during a game.

    Walking towards the sideline again to see what was happening, Charlie tried to bring his mind back to football. With fourth down approaching for the other team, he would be out there in a matter of minutes. After the punt, Charlie jogged to the huddle shaking his head, as if that might clear his thoughts. The next three plays were terrible. Charlie's man, who he had been dominating up to that point, made two tackles and looked like an all-star. On fourth down, Charlie caught a glimpse out of the corner of his eye of Julia standing there in a baggy sweatshirt that seemed to cling to her breasts. This wasn't good. He was the long snapper on the next play. The huddle broke and Charlie seemed to be in a dream world.

    He saw the punter flash his hands for the snap and knew he had to snap the ball. It took his muscles a minute to respond to his brain's demand. At last, he snapped the ball to the punter. It sailed high over his head. Trying to act surprised, Charlie set out to block whomever he could get in front of. Luckily, the punter picked up the ball before the opposition and just fell down so that nothing else bad could happen on the play. Now the other team only needed six yards and they were in the end zone.

    Not tired, but knowing he needed to adjust, Charlie once again came off the sideline. His coach asked him if everything was alright. It wasn't like Charlie to lose focus, he didn't normally need this many breaks during a game. He told him everything was fine, that he just needed a couple more plays off. His coach reluctantly let him have his way and hustled down the sideline to keep up with the action.

  This time Charlie avoided looking at anyone. He kept his eyes and focus on the field. He didn't go farther back from the sideline than two yards. After the other team easily scored in two plays, making it a tie game, Charlie knew he needed to come back to the game, for himself and for his teammates. He got upset with himself. Anger started to flow. *How could he let this happen? How could he put his team in this kind of a position?* He wouldn't let that happen anymore. Feeling the anger swelling up, Charlie was ready to get back out there and play his kind of game again.

  His team did go on to win, and he did hook up with that girl for a while, but from these two experiences Charlie learned a lot. After the second time, Charlie promised himself that when he played he would stay focused on the game and block out everything else. He stopped looking into the stands, he stopped smiling at games, and began putting on his serious game face about three hours before a game. From that time on, all he talked about and thought about during the game was football.

  Now on this chilly October evening, Charlie exited the building slowly, allowing everyone else to disperse before making the walk to his car. He didn't want to get caught up in any useless conversations. He didn't want to think about anything else but football. He enjoyed these moments alone. It was a time to go over his personal goals for the game tomorrow. There were plenty of ways to prepare for a game, all of them good, but through experience Charlie had found that this worked best for him.

  Calmly walking out the door, the cold, crisp autumn air hit Charlie's face. His ears and nose instantly turned red. He pulled his hat tightly over his ears. Looking up at the sky, the stars seemed to be illuminated by the first of this year's cold air. He looked towards the parking lot to see cars starting, exhaust spouting out, and lights fading into the night. Hoots, hollers, and laughs also came from the mix of the crowd. Charlie was glad he waited and avoided that scene. He wasn't in any kind of mood for that now. Returning back to his goals for the game, Charlie enjoyed the peacefulness of the silence around him and casually walked to the grassy quad in the middle of campus to find his bench.

Violence

By the end of each game, it is not if a player is hurt, it is how badly one is hurt and how much pain and punishment one can handle. On every play something gets dinged, banged, smashed, hit, crushed, or hurt, from the opening snap to the last play, all accompanied with various degrees of pain. Sometimes a player can tell when he has given some pain back to his opponent. It is not as if he wants to permanently injure someone, just to make sure he gets back everything he has been dishing out and perhaps make the opponent a little hesitant during the next play by being worried about getting hurt. Some plays it is just a nick, and other times it is an actual injury. Being able to tell the difference between the two is something that a good player learns early in his career.

One of the things that makes football such a tough sport is the number of times a player falls down during practice and games. In each play there is at least one person that ends up on the ground. The linemen, especially, are on the ground almost every play. There are a lot of ways this can happen; he might trip, he might be pushed or knocked down, or even purposefully end up on the ground diving for the ball or getting in an extra hit.

Ending up on the ground doesn't always mean that the player will have any more pain or injuries, just that each fall adds up. Falling down jars the body each time it happens, only adding to the punishment the player endures. On top of that, after a fall, he has to get back up. This takes effort and drains more energy from the player every time he has to do it. Falls and injuries can reduce the length of time a body can last, especially at a comfortable and enjoyable level. The amount of pain and punishment a football player puts his body through adds years to a young body, possibly taking off years in later life. Jarring a body with countless tumbles onto an unmoving ground only adds to this unrelenting physicality.

It is a violent game and violence is never kind to one's body. With helmets and pads on, players begin to think they can do anything with their bodies, like throwing them unthinkingly into other bodies, piles, and the ground. These collisions affect different body parts, a player's head being one of the most frequent.

One of the results of many head on collisions is an annoying, but temporary pain. It happens when a player gets a hit right on the jaw, in between the protection of the helmet, face mask, and shoulder pads. This is one of the bangs that hurts the most, if only for a few moments. The jaw gets jarred so hard that it feels like a player is bleeding from his ears. It is a unique feeling. Ears aren't supposed to bleed, so it can be scary for a moment. Trying not to show any pain, the player will wait until he is on the way back to the huddle to stick his finger in his helmet to check for blood. Expecting to see a red stained finger and needing to leave the game, he is relieved to see a clean finger. It is hard for him to fathom, though. He swears that something is flowing freely from his ear and the only thing it could be is blood after sustaining a hit like that. Without visual evidence and not wanting to ask a teammate to check his ear, the player will ignore it and move on when the QB begins to call out the next play. He has no choice. If he isn't focused on what is going on something worse could happen, maybe even a severe injury.

Most players experience minor concussions throughout their career. If it was a major one, he would not be able to stay in the game for very long, or at least not be effective. Many times it will just be a short blackout of the vision or a prolonged sensation of seeing stars. A blackout is usually only momentary. After a vicious hit to the head from another player, or even falling onto the ground, a quick blanket of blackness will envelop the player's vision and head, after which he will regain his eyesight and have to shake off the hit and get ready for the next play. Stars are seen on a regular basis during a game. These can usually be shaken off easily, but an extended period of seeing these heavenly images can force a player to take a play or two off, or at least hope for a break on the sideline in between possessions.

One of Charlie's worst experiences with a concussion happened during practice at two-a-days. He was attempting to get a few extra blocks around the forming pile when a safety flew in out of nowhere to get a big hit on anyone in his way and made contact full steam with the side of Charlie's helmet right above the ear hole. When the whistle blew, Charlie was dazed. His helmet felt loose, so he looked around for missing pieces. He saw that an ear pad had been jarred loose. He bent down to pick it up and made his way back to the huddle for the next play.

This is when it got weird. He knew where he was supposed to be, but he didn't know the people around him. Totally confused, he looked around at his teammates. He didn't recognize any of them. For some reason, all of his teammates had been traded in for other people.

With a deep breath and a shake of his head Charlie began to realize what had happened. He had gone back in time. He was now practicing with his middle school team. It was nice to see these guys again. It had been over six years since he had seen them. He didn't really hear the play but heard the signal for the huddle to break and yelled out, "Break."

That evening, sitting at dinner, Charlie realized he had no idea how he got through the rest of the practice. He actually didn't remember any of it after rejoining his little league team and breaking the huddle. *What the hell had happened?* He looked around and this time recognized the people around him as his college teammates. Feeling more at ease, he dug into his dinner. After a few bites he felt himself fading. With a fork in his mouth and in mid chew, he dozed off. Quickly awakened by his nearest neighbor, who wondered what the hell was going on, Charlie jumped back to reality.

"Are you okay Charlie?"

"I'm not sure," Charlie mumbled back.

"You need to go and get checked, dude," Luke said with a concerned tone.

"Yeah, I will do it first thing in the morning. Right now I have to get to bed." With that Charlie took his tray to the corner and headed off to bed. A little early, only 8:00. He was lucky there were no more meetings that night.

The next morning, the trainer confirmed his suspicions. "Yep, you've got a concussion. You will have to sit out at least three days. After that I will check you again and we will see if you can get back in there. I will let the coaches know. Go get some water and change into some more comfortable clothes. You are just a spectator for a few days."

He was sad to be missing practice, but knew there was no way he could do anything right now. His head was pounding like someone was continuously hitting it with a small hammer on each temple. This continued for two days and on the third day, with the headaches subsiding, he was cleared to return to practice the next day.

Game 5

    With time winding down in their 5th game, the Puma were not much more than the walking wounded. Charlie and his teammates hadn't withstood the pain of football well this evening. With five minutes left in the fourth quarter, the stands were beginning to thin out. The Puma had underestimated their opponent tonight. The Frogs had come ready to play. They had been more physical and were the ones to dish out the pain. The game had already been decided. The Puma were just trying to limit the amount of points scored by the Frogs.

    Charlie sat on the bench, dejected. He could only watch as the Frogs picked up another first down on their way to running out the clock and spoiling the Puma's perfect record. Charlie was disappointed in himself. They had lost their chance to show the country that they deserved to be considered one of the best teams. He had not played his best game, he had not demanded that the guys ignore their high ranking during the week of practice. He had gotten into the hype and talked it up with the guys. He should have been the one telling the guys not to believe the exaggerated claims. It didn't mean much when the coaches said it. It meant more when one of the players said it. Players listened to their peers more than their coaches about not giving in to media's ballyhoo. After a while they zone out their coaches and need to hear it from someone else. As the team captain and the leader, Charlie should have been the one to say it. That was the role he had wanted and the role he had sought out. He stared at nothing with his jaw clenched as these thoughts ran through his head.

    The Frogs picked up another first down and now could take a couple of knees to end the game. After the second knee, Charlie pounded the aluminum bench with a closed fist. The members of the Frogs began to celebrate on the field, jumping up and down and giving each other hugs. Charlie became angrier by the second.

    The teams began to line up along the 50 yard line to shake each other's hands. Charlie couldn't contain himself any longer, he had to leave. *Fuck this, I am getting out of here. I can't stand this any longer,* he thought to himself, and instead of joining his team in a show of sportsmanship by congratulating the other team, Charlie turned and walked towards the locker room.

He walked with his eyes down, not wanting to make eye contact with anyone. He ignored someone who was yelling his name from the crowd. He shoved the locker room door open and swore to the empty room. He dropped his helmet on the ground and plopped down in front of his locker. He began analyzing his performance, trying to pick out things he could have done differently, ways he could have better influenced the outcome. He then began to think about how he needed to be different in practice, how he must be the one to say things, not just the coaches.

He continued to stew over how he could improve the team as his teammates started to trickle into the locker room. He avoided eye contact with everyone that came in. Some of the guys came over to pat him on the pads, or tell him 'Good job,' but he ignored them.

He sat silently for a long time. Finally he changed and left for home. There would be no victory party tonight. He picked up a 12 pack on his way home to drown out the self-defeating thoughts and the constant analysis of his performance that would go on in his head while he sat by himself watching ESPN.

Love?

Mary leaned over and kissed Charlie gently on the forehead and rolled off of him. She pulled the pillow under her head and scrunched next to him. She squeezed him tight with her free arm and gave him a playful kiss on the cheek. He smiled and turned his head to look at her. He rubbed her bare curves and almost got excited again.

Charlie loved spending time with Mary. She was his escape from football. When he was with her his worries about football and his struggles of wondering if he was doing enough disappeared. They had so much fun together and still allowed each other space. Many of the guys' girlfriends were clingy. They had to be with their boyfriends all the time and expected all of their spare attention. Charlie couldn't deal with someone like this. His focus and number one priority was football. Mary was fine with this, her priority was school. She was a straight A student who was intent on getting a good, high paying job right out of college. She allowed him to focus on football and he allowed her to focus on school.

But when they were together, Charlie felt like football might not be that important. He felt free and he felt giddy. Mary felt the same way. Her parents' expectations were sometimes crushing. They were paying for her college and expected her to make the most of it. If she didn't have a good job after graduating, her parents would be very disappointed and they let Mary know this. When she was with Charlie she didn't want to be anywhere else. She had a hard time leaving him when they were together. She had to pull herself away from him in order to get any studying done.

They hesitated to use the word 'love.' This was more out of fear than from a lack of mutual feelings between each other. They knew they felt love for each other, but were afraid of what would happen if they started saying it. Neither of them knew where life would take them after college. They had casually discussed staying together, but both of them had been hesitant to make a full blown commitment. It was as if they could avoid possible future heartbreak by not consciously acknowledging their feelings for each other.

They had been together for over two and a half years and the phrase 'I love you' had slipped out a few times, but was treated like a mistake. They had been dating exclusively and were faithful to each other. They weren't looking to fool around, they both loved their relationship and didn't want the dating game to interfere with their personal goals. They wanted to stay together, but avoided talking about their future. They felt like by ignoring the future they might not have to face it.

It was a Monday night and Mary was staying over at his place. They spent the night at each other's apartments on a regular basis and both felt comfortable at the others' place. Charlie lived alone, so Mary more often spent the night with him. The sex was always better at Charlie's place. They didn't have to be quiet, worrying if Mary's roommate might hear them humping their brains out.

Mary looked at Charlie with adoration in her eyes. "How are you feeling?"

"I'm okay. I just can't get over the loss the other night."

"Are you sore, at all?" she asked with tenderness.

"Yeah, a little bit," he lied. His body was always sore. Without ibuprofen everyday he wouldn't be comfortable.

"You sure do give football your full effort, don't you?"

Charlie took a deep breath, "Yeah, I do. I really do love it. Right now, it is me. It is all I really know. I don't know what else I am this good at, so it is how I define myself. I want to be the best, so I give it my heart and soul."

Mary stroked his head, "Did you always know you were going to be a football player?"

"I don't think so." Charlie thought for a moment. "No, not at all. I didn't even get into football until sixth grade," Charlie chuckled.

Mary smiled, wanting to know more, "What is that all about?"

"Well, I had an interesting introduction to football. To be honest I didn't even know it was coming."

"Oh, really? Tell me about it," Mary implored.

"Okay." Charlie smiled and looked up at the ceiling. "Well, it was way back before my sixth grade year."

Charlie relived the day in his head as he told Mary the

story of his first day of football. It was a late August afternoon. School still hadn't started, so Charlie should have been playing with his friends, enjoying their few last days of freedom from school. Instead, Charlie was on his way to sign up for football tryouts. He was in middle school and would be trying out for the school team. As his dad pulled into the parking lot, Charlie saw scattered groups of kids running into each other at full speed. This sight, coupled with a long line for the sign-ups, made Charlie nervous. His heart started to beat fast and he was beginning to have second thoughts. He was glad his dad was there to make him go through with it.

They pulled to a stop under one of the few shady patches. Charlie got out and tried to act calm, walking with a nervous smile behind his dad towards the group of tables. Once in line, Charlie allowed himself to look around and take in the scene. He couldn't locate any faces that were familiar. None of his friends, up to this point, played football.

It didn't take long for someone to notice two unfamiliar faces and a big body. A friendly gentleman came over and introduced himself to Charlie and his dad. He was the organizer of the middle school teams. His excitement for a new face seemed genuine and he said that he would go and find the coach who would be working with Charlie, so that Charlie and his dad could meet him.

A surge of anxiety swept through Charlie's body again at the thought of meeting his first football coach. His dad seemed more excited than he did. He bumped Charlie and told him to relax, that everything would be fine, that these people were nice and they were excited for him to be there. He told him it was normal to be nervous whenever a person started something for the first time. Charlie tried to relax, but couldn't bring himself to look around for his approaching coach until he was in front of him, stretching out his hand.

Charlie looked up at a behemoth of a man. He wasn't in good physical shape, just a huge man. He was well over six feet tall and had legs that were the size of most people's waist. His stomach was big, but didn't poke out too far, almost looking normal for his size and stature. He was wearing shorts with his tree-trunk calves protruding from the bottom and a golf shirt tucked in to show off his chest and arms. With his natural dark Italian complexion, Charlie thought he almost looked like a hit man from the mob. He could have been a perfect fit for a role in The Godfather.

Betraying Charlie's first image of him, his coach was a very nice man. He warmly welcomed Charlie and his father, making them both feel like they were already part of the team and were as important as anyone. His voice was loud and gruff and sounded as if he were constantly talking through some sort of nasal congestion. His speech was befitting of a mob movie, cuss words were let loose like there was no tomorrow. Charlie wasn't used to this yet. The only time he had heard his parents swear was when they were angry. Looking at Charlie, his eyes were pale green and had a look of intensity.

After introducing himself, Coach Larson excused himself to get back to practice and let Charlie get through the line to get his pads. His final words before parting were to tell Charlie that he expected a full effort all the time and no walking. He pointed around the big complex of grass fields to the dry brown spots. He told Charlie that the dead grass was due to someone's walking when he should have been running. Hustle was mandatory on his team. This seemed okay to Charlie and he felt better about being there already.

Finally getting to the front of the line, Charlie and his dad filled out the few forms and paid the friendly lady who was working the sign-ups today for the uniform. She had a motherly look that would not get her confused as a supermodel. Her smile and friendly manner made up for any lack of good looks. She asked them a barrage of questions and gave them more information about her family than Charlie and his dad had ever wanted to know. Her son was also a football player. He was on the team one year younger than Charlie.

The next thing Charlie would find out was what position he would play. He expected to be an X because he was big for his age, which meant he would be a lineman. He wasn't fat, just a big kid, and wouldn't make the low weight limit the league had for the non-lineman positions. Charlie jumped on the scale, and as expected, he was well over the weight limit for his particular age group. So, the helmet they had found for him was adorned with a big X made from black tape. It was done on both sides just in case somebody couldn't see it from the front.

Once Charlie was all fitted out, he was given one last good luck wish from his dad and pointed where to go by the organizers. It was a small cluster of bodies all the way across the compound. His dad pulled all the straps a little tighter to ensure he was ready to go and gave him a slap across the backside, as if he were a horse and needed some sort of external motivation to get moving.

Jogging across the grass fields in between him and his new team, Charlie had a sense of trepidation. This was what he had been wanting to do for a long time and his dream was being fulfilled. It was also a very difficult thing for him. Here was a group of guys who had been playing together for a couple years in elementary school and had formed their own friendships already. He knew none of the guys and would be trying to break into this group as an outsider. On top of this, he had never played organized football. He had played many times in his front yard and watched countless games in person and on TV, but he didn't know all the rules and didn't know what to do besides just run into people.

By the time he reached the group, Charlie was out of breath. This was already hard and he had only jogged a few hundred yards. With all of this extra equipment on, Charlie felt like he was running in cement. There must have been an extra thirty pounds of stuff he was wearing. It was big, heavy, and uncomfortable.

With all of these thoughts swimming around in his head, Charlie stopped behind the group of players and the two coaches. The practice stopped for a moment and the coaches took time to acknowledge the arrival of their new addition to the team. A few of the players nodded their heads and offered a few short welcomes. Most of them gave him a questioning look and got ready to get back to the drill.

Without any instruction, Charlie jumped right into the drills, trying his best and not getting frustrated when he screwed up. Many times he had to give all his effort just to avoid being killed, but he did well. The first few weeks were more of a lesson from the school of hard knocks. His technique at this point was based more on survival than proper fundamentals. The number of times he was knocked over was higher than he could keep track of. His head pounded almost constantly as he tried to get used to the collisions and the fifteen pound thing strapped to his head. This would prove to be a never ending battle. Each year Charlie and his many teammates complained about the headaches they would get the first week of football as they tried to get used to the helmet and the collisions.

Many of the players were very nice to Charlie. They came up to him and introduced themselves, chatted with him, and asked questions about his life. Some of them seemed to like Charlie and treated him like they were already friends. Much of the practice was new and surprising to him; the violence, the anger, the yelling, and most of all, the swearing. Charlie couldn't believe his ears. It wasn't as if Charlie had never heard cuss words, it was just he felt like he was in the middle of an R rated movie.

There was no holding back. It was as if the official language of football was four letter words, for both players and coaches. When somebody screwed up, he would swear. When somebody fell, he would swear. When somebody forgot the play or the technique, he would swear. When somebody got their ass kicked, he would swear. When somebody kicked another guy's ass, he would swear, this time in triumph. When somebody stopped early, a coach would swear. It seemed to go on and on, an endless string of cursing, from the moment Charlie got there to the moment he left the field. The swearing itself wasn't so shocking, it was more the group of kids who were doing it; a bunch of twelve and thirteen year olds who already had mouths like Rambo, Terminator, and the guy from the Die Hard movies.

During this first year of football, Charlie would often come home covered in bruises. His mother's natural tendencies came out in full force, giving him unlimited sympathy about his nicks and bruises. On the other hand, his dad just told him to tough it out, keep trying hard, and that it was part of being a man and a football player. He also advised Charlie not to show his mother all his injuries just to get some sympathy.

With his constant hustle and natural athletic tendencies, Charlie quickly became a solid player. This, probably more than anything, helped Charlie to make friends with his new teammates. His teammates' acceptance of him and his success on the field left Charlie with a good taste in his mouth for the game of football. When his first season ended, Charlie was excited about the next season with his team and his future prospects of becoming a good player.

As Charlie finished the story, Mary still lay propped up on her arm listening with excitement. She never interrupted him when he talked. It was hard to get him to open up and she lapped up every detail that he would give her of his life.
"That was fun to hear about," she said with complete honesty.
"Oh, it's a fun memory, thanks for listening. I haven't thought about that for a long time." Charlie scooped his hand under her body and rolled her back on top of him. He pulled her face down to his and gave her a passionate kiss. She returned the kiss with energy and they intertwined with each other again. After another pleasurable experience, they fell asleep next to each other.

Tug of War

"What's that look for?" Blake let out with a hint of anger in his voice.

Allowing the silence to grow uncomfortable, April looked at Blake with an intense glower, behind which a flood of frustration was being dammed up and was about to break.

"Well, are you just going to stand there and look at me?" Feeling self-conscious, he shifted his weight and broke away from her gaze. "If we're not going to talk I have things to do," he stated as polite as possible, hoping he could avoid this and get back to his work.

"I'm sure you do. Yes, I want to talk. We are going to talk," April said as calmly as possible, keeping emotion out of her response to avoid crying and to stay strong. "We've barely spoken for days. We haven't had a decent conversation in months. Sex seems to be part of a different past that we don't share anymore. I'm not comfortable living my life like this. I feel like I am just a second thought to you now. Just someone to take care of the house, bills, and our child so you can be left alone to do football. Is this the kind of relationship I should expect between us from here on out?"

With only a moment's hesitation, he shot back, "How am I supposed to answer that? This new job is a big commitment. It is also a step towards my ultimate dream of being a college head coach. This week has been crazy. We are entering the most difficult part of our season. We have three road games in a row and we are trying to avoid having this season go downhill."

"Yeah, I understand all of that. Marriage is also a big commitment. A strong loving relationship used to be our dream. That also takes work." Her voice was louder than she had anticipated.

"We have been working at it every day. It is strong, we have a great relationship. Nothing will change that," Blake asserted.

She was almost pleading. "It was strong. I also need attention and effort from you on a regular basis. Most importantly, I need communication. Without this, our relationship starts to deteriorate and distance grows between us.

We lose touch and begin to drift apart. Our relationship used to be the number one priority for each of us. I need to be one of your top priorities, Blake."

"You are one of my priorities. In order for my football dream to succeed like I want it to, I have to give it all my time and effort right now. I am just beginning and this is my first big chance and break. If I don't make the most of it, I might not get another chance." He paused, summing up his thoughts. "This coach, this system, and this team, have a chance to reach greatness. It takes time, though. It doesn't happen overnight, a lot of effort and sacrifice are necessary. This is the beginning of a long, hard journey. Then, once we get there, it is even harder to maintain greatness than it is to reach it."

"Above all else? What happened to the other areas of your life? Now, all your life is just football."

"Are you trying to give me a guilt trip?" he replied forcefully. "It seems like you're trying to make me feel bad for chasing my dream, for finding my passion and going for it."

"No. I am not trying to do that at all. I don't want you to feel the least bit guilty, that is why I have been supporting you so strongly these past few years. But.....I do expect you, as my husband, to support me as your wife. You aren't giving me anything right now. I need to be your priority. I need time from you every day to connect and share our lives together. All I am asking for is one or two hours a day of your time with me. No football, no TV, no kids, just us."

Blake paused, looking around the room as if weighing his options. "I can't promise anything. A lot of people are depending on me."

"I'm depending on you!"

"There are a lot of things that come up. Meetings, film sessions, game planning, player concerns. When I get to be the big man, I can make my own schedule and make time for other commitments. It's a demanding job."

"It's just a game!"

His eyes narrowed, and contained a sense of hurt. He took a deep breath and slowly brought his gaze back to her eyes. "It's not just a game! I love this thing you call a game. It drives me, it keeps me motivated, it gives me purpose in life. I don't want to sleep because I will miss out on doing more football. The moment I wake up it calls to me. I feel fresh and energized pursuing it all day. It is a part of me, I am a part of it. I am good at it and want to be the best. It's a lot more than just a game. It also happens to be our bread and butter and livelihood."

Not wanting to give in to his assertion, she moved to another topic. "You talk about greatness, what about our marriage?"

"It is great. We have spent many years getting it to the level where it is. Arguments are normal. All relationships have ups and downs. We have to be strong, rely on our love, and know we will get through this hard time."

"It's like you said Blake, it takes more work to stay great. That goes for everything, not just sports."

Shaking his head in disbelief, he asked, "Well, what do you want me to do? Give up football?"

Rolling her eyes and sighing, she replied, "No, I never even mentioned or hinted at anything like that."

"Well, that's what it feels like you're pressuring me to do."

"It's not," she stated, as a matter of fact. "Our relationship is approaching a level I always hoped we would never come close to. We need to do something. I think a good idea would be to get some counseling. We need some help and it is fine to admit it," April said, calmly and collectively, with defeat in her eyes. "I know someone whose wife is a counselor and would be willing to see us later in the evening so that you will be able to come after football. She might even come here, to our house."

April waited for Blake to respond. Moving towards her and running his hand over his face, he said, "Okay, honey, if you think that will help. I will do it. Is that okay?"

"Yes," April whispered back to him as he embraced her. Allowing the moment of reconciliation to last longer than he wanted, Blake smelled the clean scent of her hair and felt the curve of her neck against his cheek.

Growing impatient, Blake broke away from her. "Okay, now I have got to go downstairs and look at today's practice film. This is a big one, honey. We really need it this week. We can't let one loss turn into more." Without waiting for a response, he made for the stairs. He looked back at her still sitting and added, "I love you and always will, babe."

Mustering a half smile, she looked him in the eyes and shot back, "I love you, too."

About four hours later, the pale moonlight peered through the window creating a silhouette of April lying alone in bed. It was 3:00 AM when Blake silently crawled into their bed next to the silhouette.

Special Treatment

Sitting on the chartered plane with an entire row for him and one other teammate, Charlie began to relax for the short plane ride to their game. His mind started to wander. Charlie was in a thinking mood and didn't want to start concentrating on the game yet. *I love being treated like this, but doesn't everyone deserve this kind of treatment? Just because I am a football player doesn't make me cool or special. I am cool, but that is because of who I am, not just because of the sport I play. It would be a lie to say that we aren't treated differently as athletes.*

This wasn't something that he liked to admit to everyone, but he knew it was true. He wondered if this was part of why people wanted to get involved in athletics. Athletes were treated better only because they were good at a sport, no other reason. Some of them weren't nice people and didn't deserve the amount of respect given to them, yet they were still treated as heroes. Maybe it is because their names and pictures are in the newspaper, or maybe because they were living a dream. Charlie couldn't really understand why athletes were so revered in society. He was one and he was just a normal dude, he didn't feel any different. At the same time, when he told people he was a football player, there was an immediate reaction. Either one of awe and respect or one of mistrust because of past interactions with athletes and the preconceived notions that are inevitable with positions of privilege.

He didn't feel any more important than the next person, but people wanted his autograph. This was fine, he didn't mind doing this small thing for someone, it just felt strange that someone might want his name scribbled across a ball, a shirt, a poster, or anything for that matter. These people didn't know the slightest thing about him and they still treated him with deference. The people who mattered and knew him didn't seem to want anything or treat him differently. He liked that. Not that he didn't like being treated as a celebrity, but he would rather have people admire him for who he was, not what he did.

Thinking about his teammates, he began to wonder if the fame and celebrity stature was the reason some of them played.

There sure were plenty who liked to be in the spotlight, who liked the attention, who even did things to attract attention. They wanted interviews, front page newspaper photos, recognition, and more respect. This last one puzzled him the most. When players complained about there being a lack of respect for football players he almost wanted to laugh. What did they deserve extra respect for, playing a game? He liked to believe a person would get respect when he has earned respect. These guys just seemed to have an ego problem. If they weren't the star of the team, then they would complain and nothing was ever their fault. There was always someone else or something else to blame for their mistakes.

    Charlie didn't think he was one of these guys. He didn't want anything that he hadn't earned. He didn't ask for special favors or privileges. He knew that football wouldn't last forever and that he needed to be more than just a football player. He wondered how many of the other guys believed they could just be football players for the rest of their lives. He felt bad for these guys because he knew they would always be stuck in the past. These were the types of guys who never got over their playing glory, guys whose lives were never as good as when they were playing. Life is long and if the peak of one's life was in his early twenties, then he would have a long, unhappy life.

    As these thoughts swirled through Charlie's head, he felt himself dozing off. He spread himself out, as he had plenty of room on the chartered plane, and fell into an uncomfortable sleep.

Down, Set, Hut

Ambivalence

Charlie wasn't a future hall of famer, but he was a good, solid player. He was in physical control of his opponent more often than not. This was one of the many reasons he loved the game. This feeling of domination and control was one that he did not want to acknowledge or explore, yet was underneath his burning desire to play.

It didn't happen every game, every play, or every practice. The feeling was elevated during a game because more was on the line than at practice. The feeling came from completely dominating a player. It occurred often for him in high school. With a more level playing field in college it didn't happen as often.

The feeling came when he would completely crush an opponent play after play. At times it didn't even seem like the other player was giving his full effort. It didn't matter what the other guy did, Charlie would kick his ass. By the end of the game, the other guy's frustration would be evident, his posture would be changed, his demeanor, his confidence would all be gone. It would just be a guy in Charlie's way, trying to keep him from getting to another defender and taking him out, too. Often times scuffles would break out between Charlie and the player whose ass he was kicking because of the other guy's frustration. In practice, the frustration level rose quickly, but after realizing they were teammates, they would only swear or shout at each other instead of ending up in an all-out fight.

The scout team players hated Charlie because he treated every play at practice seriously and never let up on them. It was as if they were the enemy, not teammates working together to accomplish the same goal. The same guys loved him off the field and followed his lead on the field, but they dreaded that time of practice when they were called upon to go against Charlie and the first team offense.

Charlie was having one of those types of games. He was obliterating his opponent tonight. He was kicking his ass so badly that he didn't care if the guy knew the play was a run or a pass, or even the exact play. The guy could know, adjust, prepare, and anticipate, but the result would still be the same. He almost wanted to tell the guy so that he might be able to give Charlie more of a challenge.

On run plays, Charlie was plowing the guy over, and over, and over again. On pass plays he was stopping him dead in his tracks, not even allowing the guy to move side to side, let alone towards the quarterback. In between plays, Charlie would get that feeling of control and dominance over his opponent. He loved it. After driving him into the ground, Charlie would look straight into his eyes. His mouth would begin showing the traces of a smile and his own eyes would be silently letting his opponent know that this is what would happen again the next play and there wasn't anything that could be done to stop it. His eyes gave off an extra radiance full of confidence. His opponent looked back at Charlie with blank eyes. It conveyed a message of helplessness with a plea for leniency on the next play. His opponent knew he could not stop Charlie, he was now full of fear and self-doubt.

Charlie looked away first, he wanted to spare the guy any more humiliation. He knew that he was going to have his way with this guy the rest of the game, clearing running lanes and pass protecting at will. It was a feeling of power over another person, of ultimate domination. He had crushed another person and it felt great. This feeling of power was made even greater by the fact that Charlie had ground him to defeat before the contest was even decided. It was the feeling of reducing a strong, in shape, athletic, tough, young man into nothing more than a bump on the ground. A bump that was in the way of achieving his goal of winning. At this point, his opponent didn't deserve any more thought than one would give to a small obstruction.

Despite feeling in touch with his animal side, he began to show some humanity as the game wore on. As if in recognition of reducing his opponent to a mere bump, Charlie helped him off of the ground after every play instead of leaving him to use any last bit of energy he had left. Charlie offered a hand to the vanquished. It also ensured that the guy would be back the next play ready to receive his ass whipping again.

Charlie was so into his raw emotions of reducing a man to obscurity that he was unaware of what was going on in the game. He was having a great game, but his team was not. They had scored plenty of points behind his great performance, but the other team had scored more points.

As the game came to an end, with a score of 49-42, Charlie didn't feel upset. He still felt high from his feeling of power and conquest. He was not happy with the team result, but it was difficult for him to feel bad because of his personal performance. He even stayed on the field to shake hands. As he passed his opponent for the night, Charlie knew he had won as his opponent lowered his head in submission.

He walked quietly back to the locker room feeling ambivalent. His testosterone was still overflowing after an exhausting three hour game.

Release

Their bus pulled up to a side security gate at the airport. The driver spoke to the guard who then walked back to his little shed and the gate began to open. They pulled out in front of a gigantic air hanger alongside an airplane. They walked off of the bus and directly onto the airplane. The equipment manager and his assistants shuffled the bags from the bus to the luggage storage area of the airplane. This impressed Charlie when he first started traveling with the team his redshirt freshman year, but now it was just part of the routine for away games.

The mood was somber. They had just lost their second game in a row. The players knew that the plane ride home wasn't going to be a party. They knew Coach Jackson's expectations; after a loss it was a long, quiet trip home. Charlie didn't go against the expectations, but he still felt amped up from the game, his feeling of power had not subsided. They didn't have to wait for takeoff. He sat back for the short flight and tried to relax. He would not be able to sleep on the flight home and needed some relief. There was only one way he would satisfy it and that wouldn't come until later tonight, when he got to see Mary.

On the way out of the airplane, the noise level began to pick up. They had been told about practice tomorrow and were dismissed. It had been a day game and was still evening, so there was plenty of time left for partying.

Drinking goes together with football naturally. The tailgating parties that start hours before a game and continue at the halftime break and carry on even after the game, the beer guys walking the stadium peddling their frothy beverage, and the smell of booze oozing out of fanatic fans' yelling mouths.

This drinking tradition carries over, perhaps even stronger, to the players. At times, Saturday night binge drinking seemed as mandatory as end of practice sprints. A big night of drinking helped calm players down after a long week of football. Whether the game was a win or a loss, it helped Charlie clear his mind from a week of yelling, pounding, and physical exhaustion. He did realize that destroying his body with alcohol after a difficult game probably wasn't the best thing to do to himself, but this didn't matter by Saturday night.

Football was hard and there was a lot of stress that came along with the game. Each day at practice there were numerous coaches that would yell at a player or the team as a whole. First, there was the head coach. He had to make sure that every player on the team was heading towards accomplishing his goals and was putting forth enough of an effort, as if he knew when each player wasn't giving his best.

At times, it was hard for a player to be told he wasn't giving his best effort when, to him, he felt like he couldn't give any more. Usually the head coach ended each practice by telling the team what more they still needed to accomplish. This lecture seemed inevitable and when it occurred Charlie would think, *Oh, here it goes again. Never enough, always more to do. I'm not sure why we can't ever get compliments and be told we have worked hard. Maybe he thinks that will make us lazy and complacent. Well, he has turned the program in a positive direction, I guess that is what matters. It is just hard to never be told what a good job one has done on any occasion. Only when we win do we get compliments bestowed on us.*

Next, there was the player's position coach each position had at least one coach. This is who each player spends the most time with. With this coach, a player goes over his technique, assignment, and strategy. One can get yelled at and berated for forgetting or making mistakes on any of these. Charlie felt he was lucky because he had a great position coach. Coach Havili, the offensive line coach, rarely yelled or made the player feel like less of a person. Instead of yelling, he would just look at a player like a parent might, with a look of disappointment and understanding.

From Coach Havili, Charlie learned that failure and risk are not bad. He would tell them that mistakes were okay, that if one makes a mistake, not to worry about it, just forget about it and move on to the next play. One of the things Charlie liked best about this coach was how he acknowledged the players' efforts. He knew that they worked hard and so at times during practice they would just stand around in a group and talk about the plays, strategy, or shoot the shit. The coach would even say,

"I know you work hard and need some rest, so let's just relax and go over a few things." All of the offensive lineman would break out with big grins at this point. They would usually look around the practice field and see the other groups of players still doing drills and being barked at while they got to soak in the scene.

After a hard game or a difficult week of practice, Coach Havili would say something that would shock new players that weren't used to his style. "I appreciate your effort. I know you work hard and try your best, thank you for that. I try to put in the same amount of effort that all of you put into this game." Because of this coach's approach, his players had a fierce loyalty to him and a love towards him, at times wanting to achieve, win, and play for him, their coach, as much as they did for themselves.

Finally, there were all the other position coaches. Some of them were cool and calm, but just as many were ornery, unhappy, spiteful coaches that liked to yell to make themselves feel better about their sad lives. These types yelled at anyone they could, it didn't matter if they were the player's position coach or not. Charlie didn't like these coaches and was glad his position coach wasn't one of them. If a block was missed or an assignment forgotten, these coaches would make sure everyone knew who the guilty party was. Many of the players who were under these types of coaches lost their love for the game, or were the heaviest drinkers on the team.

Charlie remembered a time when his position coach, Coach Havili, defended his players against Coach Empy's constant verbal attacks. Coach Havili was a huge former NFL player. He was a man who didn't use his size to intimidate, though. He was a very fair and honest coach who genuinely cared for his players. His coaching style created loyal players who loved him and would do anything for him. He was normally a calm person, but when his buttons were pushed enough it was a scary sight.

It was a late September afternoon a couple of years ago and the summer heat was making a final appearance, delaying its departure in the northern latitudes for the year. Everyone was a little on edge because they had lost the game the previous week to an opponent they should have beat and now were playing a tough opponent. During a run game drill, Coach Empy, the running backs coach, was on a tirade. He had been yelling at his running backs for the entire drill and now seemed to be shifting his energy to the offensive line. After a few outbursts towards the offensive line, the players began to look towards Coach Havili, hoping for some support. Coach Havili also seemed to be growing weary of the verbal onslaught towards his players.

On the next play, Coach Empy went overboard. It was a routine guard trap, a play they had run a thousand times, but the pulling guard forgot to pull, resulting in the running back getting blasted by an unblocked defensive lineman. After the cheering by the defense died down, everyone looked at Nakeem, the guilty party, knowing he had blown his assignment. This is when Coach Empy went berserk. He walked over to Nakeem and stepped in front of him before he could reach the huddle and began to berate him in front of everyone. "What the fuck was that?! How could you forget to pull on that play?! Your guy just got killed because you forgot your fucking assignment! We do this play at least ten times every day!" With each shout he got closer and closer to Nakeem's face and was eventually touching Nakeem's facemask with his forehead, staring directly into his helmet.

Being too afraid to respond, Nakeem humbly accepted this verbal onslaught, meekly responding, "Yeah, I know. I'm sorry, it won't happen again."

"Well, it better not fucking happen again! I can't believe…"

"Excuse me, Coach Empy!" Coach Havili let out confidently, while stepping towards him and releasing Nakeem from this unwanted verbal assault. "May I speak to you for a moment over here," he bellowed out, nodding his head to an empty patch of grass behind the clump of players waiting to relieve the starters and get their reps. Walking the short distance, Coach Havili turned toward Coach Empy, looking at him intensely, with a sense of confidence.

Coach Empy looked around, confused, wondering if this was something he had to do, or should do. No one would look at him directly in the eyes, and all were secretly glad someone had finally gotten up the courage to speak to him and maybe shut him up for a little bit.

  Silently, with a look of defeat, Coach Empy walked over to the awaiting Coach Havili. The players' full attention was now on the two coaches and they were hoping to witness a full-fledged argument. This hope was quickly dashed when Coach Havili made some sort of signal to the defensive coaches to keep the drill going. Everyone was mesmerized, including the coaches, and it took a moment for anyone to realize that they couldn't just stand there and watch this transpire.

  Trying to act like he hadn't missed a beat and knew how to take charge, the defensive line coach walked over to the offensive huddle and told the quarterback just to call plays and for everyone to stick to their rotations. Finishing his instructions, he blew his whistle and let out a big, "Let's get going boys, daylight is a wastin'."

  With that, the quarterback called the huddle together and called out a play that he wanted to run. They all were trying to keep their attention in two places at once, but trying to listen to the quarterback and the interaction that was going on between the two coaches was a difficult task. Before the huddle broke, Charlie could hear Coach Havili sternly say, "They are my players and I will take care of them, including their discipline. I don't interfere with your players, please don't interfere with mine."

  In between plays, Charlie tried to listen to as much of the exchange as he could. He was unable to pick up very much of what was happening, but after each play their voices were getting louder and their faces more red. The players were going through the drill, but didn't have their whole concentration on the task at hand. Each player seemed interested in the outcome of the interaction. Everyone had a small smirk on his face because Coach Empy was finally getting called out and being told to shut up.

  From across the field with the skill position groups, Coach Jackson noticed what was going on and began to walk across the field to calm things down and restore practice to its normal flow. Trying to betray his sense of urgency, he avoided running to the situation that was clearly beginning to escalate out of control. Picking up his pace from a brisk walk to a jog, he finally arrived and intervened to put a stop to the two coaches' bickering. It didn't seem like they got very much solved during this brief interlude, but for the rest of the day Coach Empy was more quiet than usual and for the rest of Charlie's college career no other coach besides Coach Havili ever yelled at or disciplined the offensive line. They were all grateful for Coach Havili's display of compassion for them and this story was often repeated when they were recounting what a great coach he was.

Stress is built up from a week of practicing and then there is still more added when it is game time. The pressure a player feels about a game is enough in and of itself to drive any man to drinking. The preparations for the game begin on Friday night, the night before a game, when the sole focus in a player's life becomes the impending game. Each player has to be completely physically and mentally prepared while at the same time not getting burned out by using up all of his energy and emotion before the game has even begun. He knows that his performance during the game will be judged by his coaches and the thousands in attendance and perhaps even the millions watching on TV. After the game, his performance will be judged in even greater detail, with every move getting the utmost scrutiny during film sessions.

On top of all this mental stress comes the complete physical exhaustion a player feels by the end of a game on Saturday night. Each day at practice he must give 100% effort, during the game he must give 110% effort, and all of his mental and physical strength has to be relied on to complete and excel during the game. It is enough for a player to want to go home and collapse into bed. This, however, is not what usually happened, especially with Charlie.

Saturday night was the one night to let loose, the one time to not worry about anything, especially football. They always had practice the next day, but that wasn't until two in the afternoon and it wasn't something that required a fully rested body. For Charlie, Saturday was the one night during football season to go out and just be a college kid, not a football player. To go out and get shit faced and have a good time.

These nights inevitably involved too much alcohol, but at his age Charlie didn't think about moderation. Things usually progressed into a contest to see who could drink more and, with the competitive nature of football players, this would send the party into a binge drinking fest where many would end up blacking out before the night was over. Keg stands were a good method to get quickly inebriated. Chugging contests, beer bongs, and shot gunning were other popular methods to achieve this objective.

At the end of the night, guys would be trying to recall how many beers they had consumed. This usually ended up being exaggerated, but most of them could drink enough to kill a small animal. By his senior year in college, Charlie could drink 15 beers and still get himself to bed without any help. It was when he went over the 20 mark that things started to go downhill. He knew this was a lot, but it seemed as much a part of college football as weight training.

Tonight was going to be a good party. Most of the guys wanted to drown their sorrows from a second loss in a row and Charlie needed to tame his testosterone. Charlie got the scoop before getting to his truck and knew that it would be a big one tonight. Justin had three kegs that were waiting at his house. Four other football players lived with Justin, so it was a big house and the parties were always wild. The place was a mess. None of them were big on cleaning and personal property didn't carry much meaning at this house. It seemed like a house where anything and everything was okay.

Most of the team went straight from the football complex to the party. Charlie still wasn't able to loosen up after several hours of drinking. He still carried himself with intensity even as the beer began to take its hold on his senses. It had been a fun party with most of the guys from the team and a lot of pretty girls. He didn't know why, but he was getting hit on more than usual. Maybe it was the powerful way he had been carrying himself. Maybe the young women could sense that he was full of testosterone and was the dominant male tonight.

One girl, Kristen, couldn't keep her hands off of him. Every twenty minutes or so she would find him and approach him again. She would rub his arm as she asked him about the game or his classes. He knew that she wanted him. She was just waiting for him to ask her to leave the party, or even to take a walk down to the park.

Charlie's testosterone was still pumping from the game. His sense of power and domination was still surging. This young hot girl who was basically throwing herself at him was sending him over the top. *Okay, what are we going to do?* Charlie tried to reason with his drunk self. *You can take this girl home and fuck the shit out of her or you need to leave right now because your self-restraint is going fast.* She looked at him from across the room and smiled. He smiled back and she began to walk over to him, as if she were walking in for the kill.

Oh, shit! I don't want to get into this kind of drama. I don't want to do this to Mary. She is an awesome girl, one that I want to still be with after tonight. It's still a long season and I don't need this kind of shit messing with my focus. I love Mary, I don't want to do that to her. Love? I don't know if it is that, I wouldn't say that to her, but I really do like her a lot. I've got to get out of here. She reached out towards him like she was expecting him to leave the party with her. He leaned over to her ear. "Sorry, I have to go. I'll see you around, though." He walked to the stairs without even looking back to see the mortified look on her face.

She followed him up the stairs with her eyes until she could not see him anymore before she realized she was standing in the middle of the room. Her friends looked at her and seemed to grin at her failure. She ran her hand through her hair to hide her disappointment and walked towards the porch and away from her friends.

Charlie got into his truck and pulled away from the party. *I had to get out of there. Two more minutes and I would have been taking her home.* He started driving, not really knowing where he was going, and realizing that he shouldn't be driving after all he had to drink. He still needed a release, though. Home and safety were a short five minute drive across campus, but he had to let out his testosterone. He drove across town to the bar where Mary worked.

He walked into the bar and saw Mary helping a table at the far end. He walked up to the bar and sat down. The bartender recognized him. He often came in to visit Mary.

"Hey, Charlie. Sorry about the game today. We scored enough, but just couldn't keep them out of the end zone," he said, trying to empathize with Charlie.

"Yeah, it sucked, we'll just have to get it next week."

"Want a beer?"

"Sure." Charlie pulled out his wallet as the bartender filled up a tall glass.

The bartender set the beer down in front of Charlie. "Oh, don't worry about that. This one is on the house."

"Thanks, Dillon." Charlie put a one on the counter for a tip as Dillon turned to help someone else at the bar.

Charlie took a long drink and turned to look across the bar for Mary. She was beginning to clean the empty tables, the crowd was thinning out as the night turned into early morning. Her jeans hugged her butt as she bent over to wipe off the tables. Her hair was pulled back in a ponytail and her apron was tied to accentuate her chest. Charlie knew he had to have his way with her that instant.

She finally saw him as she turned to come back to the bar. Her face lit up and was covered with a smile. She walked towards him and put her arm around him, holding back showing him all the affection that she felt for him. She didn't feel comfortable doing that at work. "What are you doing here?"

"I wanted to see you."

"That's a nice surprise. Usually I don't get to see you after road games. Let me clean up a few things and see if Dillon will let me leave early. It is getting quiet here already."

"Okay." He patted her on the butt and let his hand linger longer than he normally did when they were in public. "I'm excited to get out of here with you." His eyes couldn't hide what he wanted to do to her.

She smiled back at him with suspicion. "I'll be back in a few minutes. You are drunk. I hope you didn't drive over here."

"I really wanted to see you. You can drive now, so I am safe." He winked at her as she walked away shaking her head.

By the time Charlie finished his beer, she had snuck up on the side of him and was holding his arm. He turned and had to restrain himself from kissing her. "Let's go before Dillon changes his mind." She held onto his arm as they turned to go.

"Thanks, Dillon." Charlie waved to the bartender.

"No, problem. You two have fun tonight. Be careful and safe." He waved at them as he served the last customer left in the bar.

As soon as they were in Mary's car, Charlie pulled her head towards him and began kissing her. He could not hold back any more. She returned his forwardness with surprise. "Wow, someone is horny," she teased as she pulled away from him and started the car.

"Yeah, can we go over to my place? I need you now." Charlie sighed as if struggling to contain himself.

"Sure, do you have anything for me to drink over there, or is it just you that gets to have fun tonight?" She pulled out onto the street and headed for his apartment.

"I have some of the stuff you left there last week. It should be enough, I hope."

They chit chatted a little during the remaining drive to his place. Charlie almost bounded up the stairs and into his apartment when they arrived. He closed the door quickly and grabbed Mary, kissing her and grinding into her.

She pulled away. "Grab me a drink first, will ya?" she demanded more than asked.

He walked into the kitchen, opened a drink for both of them, and let her take a few swings before attacking her again. This time he knew he couldn't stop. He pulled her clothes off furiously. She undid her bra so that he wouldn't have to fool around. Before his pants were even off he was inside her. He ravaged her like he had never done it before. He couldn't tell if she was moaning in pain or pleasure. He handled her like a rag doll, having his way with her and doing what he wanted to her. He collapsed on top of her from behind as he forcefully climaxed.

He took a deep breath and almost felt relaxed and at ease for the first time since his pregame concentration. He kissed her on the cheek, this time with love, not animal aggression. She turned her head and touched his lips.

"Wow, someone needed it," she let out as she wiped sweat from her forehead. "I've never seen you like that. That was crazy. It was different, but fun."

"Yeah, I couldn't hold back anymore. It has been a long day. Thanks for letting me get it out." He handed her drink to her.

They sat up with their backs against the couch and finished their drinks. After a few more drinks, they finally made it to the bedroom where they were both ready for another round. Before his pleasure came again he made sure to take care of Mary's needs. He then rolled over and passed out. Mary leaned over and gave him a kiss. She listened to his rhythmic breathing for a few moments before losing awareness herself.

Stubborn

On Sunday, before the team meeting, Charlie arrived early to see the trainer. He had been avoiding this as long as he could. He didn't feel like he could run from it anymore. In the fourth quarter of almost every game he had been on the verge of passing out. He kept thinking he was about to die. He had been playing for years and starting for three years in college. He had been tired before, but this was a whole new level. This wasn't normal. He had to get checked out. He was sure it was something small and that he would be back on the field without any worries after being checked out.

The trainer was a tall wiry guy. His skin was tanned and leathered from being out in the sun for too many practices and games. This combined with his thinning hair made him look older than his 55 years. He still carried himself like he was full of life and didn't slow down all season. He was a nice guy and the easiest going among the entire football staff. This was probably due to the fact that he kept his job regardless of who the coach was. His tenure wasn't tied to the current coach's wins or losses.

His training room was always clean and bright, he liked to have a fully lit room. He also seemed to like female trainer trainees, the college girls who were going into sports medicine for their major. There were always plenty of these coeds around. There were a lot more females than males working with the football team and Charlie thought it was because Rod liked to be surrounded by cute young women. Charlie and the other football guys liked it too. They would all much rather have a cute girl bandage them up than some dude.

Charlie nodded to the couple of guys who were on the padded tables getting treatment for their injuries. Rod looked up to see who they were nodding at and seemed surprised to see it was him. "Hey Charlie, what's up?" he asked with concern.

"Can I talk to you for a minute, Rod?" Charlie tried to sound casual.

"Of course. What do you need?" Rod said, without looking up from wrapping an ace bandage.

"Ummmmm. Can we talk in the back, please?" Charlie nodded towards the trainer's small office.

Rod looked up with hard eyes. "Sure, go ahead and take a seat. I'll be back in a sec." He looked back down to finish.

Charlie told him what had been going on. He was hoping for a quick easy solution. He hadn't bargained for what was coming.

"Charlie this is serious. You need to go see a doctor. I can't let you play or go through a padded practice until a doctor checks this out. Today's workout is fine since it is light, but that is the last one until this is checked out by someone with more medical knowledge," Rod said, trying to be sympathetic but firm.

Charlie just sat there with his mouth hanging open. This couldn't be happening. There was no way he was going to miss any part of this season, not even a practice. He kept staring at the wall, wishing he had never come to see Rod.

Rod saw the consternation on Charlie's face. "This could be something with your heart, Charlie. It's not worth messing around." He knew Charlie wasn't going to say anything yet. "Do you want me to call Dr. Nelson and get you an appointment first thing tomorrow? You won't miss anything if he clears you tomorrow. What time are your classes over?"

Charlie sighed. He felt like he suddenly weighed 800 pounds. He couldn't move. He just nodded his head. This didn't seem real. Too much had been going on lately. He was tired. He didn't need anything to upset his plans and mess with what he had worked so hard to achieve. Things couldn't end like this. This wasn't how it was supposed to happen. "I'm done at 11." His shoulders slumped.

"Okay, I'll get you an appointment for 11:30." He turned and wrote down a note.

The rest of the afternoon was fuzzy to Charlie. He couldn't pay attention to anything at the meeting and couldn't remember anything from the short workout. He was trying to wrap his thoughts around what was happening. He kept trying to think of a way out of this.

At the end of the workout, he finally thought of something. He couldn't see Dr. Nelson, the team doctor. He would talk to Rod right away and they would be too cautious. He had to go see his family doctor back home. He had known Dr. White his whole life. Dr. White was easy going and wouldn't overreact to this. He was an old college football player and would be willing to call Rod and clear Charlie to play.

After practice, he stopped by Rod's office and told him he was going to go home to see his family doctor because he had known Charlie his whole life and would be better able to diagnose him. Rod reluctantly agreed and said he would only clear Charlie to practice on Tuesday if Dr. White called him after Charlie had been in for his appointment. Charlie assured him Dr. White would be calling him before noon tomorrow with good news.

He sped home and called his mom. "Hi Mom." He tried to sound quick and not in a talking mood, but had already left too much silence.

"Oh, hey sweetie. How are ya? We were just talking about you. You sure seemed tired on the phone after the game last night. Everything o..."

"Mom, mom. Hang on for a sec." Charlie tried to not sound rude. "I'm fine, everything's good. We can talk about it more tonight. I'm about to leave and come home for the night and the morning."

"Why? What's going on?" She was suddenly worried and he could hear it in her voice.

"Nothing, it's fine, mom. I just need to see Dr. White tomorrow morning. The trainer is a little worried about my extreme fatigue and wants me to get checked out by a doctor." He tried to sound nonchalant.

"That doesn't sound very good. If the trainer is worried it's probably something bad Charlie. Are you sure you're okay?"

"Yes, yes, I am fine. I promise I will be okay. I need to see Dr. White in the morning so that I can get back to town in the afternoon to do some homework and get caught up from missing my classes tomorrow. I have to get it done tomorrow so that I am back for practice on Tuesday. Tomorrow is my only day," he said, trying to end the conversation.

"Why do we have to do it so quickly? We need to make sure you are okay Charlie." She tried to sound firm.

"Oh, mom, they are just being cautious. I'll be fine. If it was something really bad, the trainer wouldn't have let me even go through the workout today. Can you see about getting in touch with Dr. White's office this evening? I'm leaving in 10 minutes. How about dinner too when I get there?"

"Yes, of course we will have dinner when you get here. I will call his office and leave a message. They will get you in tomorrow, we have been patients for ages. I'm concerned, though. I want to go with you tomorrow," she stated, as unyielding as a mother can be to her 22 year old son.

"No, no, mom. That won't be necessary. I need to go by myself because I will have to leave right after the appointment. Plus, I can handle it. I don't need you to go with me. Please, don't persist." He needed to end this now. "I've got to go, mom. I love you. See you in about three hours. Bye, love you."

She let out an unsatisfied huff. "Love you, too. Drive safe."

"Okay, bye." He hung up and grabbed his bag. He threw in a change of clothes for tomorrow. He didn't need anything else, there would be extras of whatever else he might need at his parents' house.

He was about to leave when he realized that he needed to do one more thing, call Mary. She would be expecting him tonight, but he would have to postpone the rendezvous. He would ask to borrow her car, though. Her car was small and fuel efficient, the antithesis of his. The journey would be much quicker with it. He sped over to her house and made the vehicle swap with as little chatting as possible and was quickly off.

He drove to his parent's house faster than usual, with the music as loud as he could handle. He was desperately trying to keep his mind from wandering too far down into hapless thoughts about this being the end of his football career.

Charlie got out of his parents' house the next morning after finally convincing his mom that he could manage by himself. His dad had stayed neutral. He didn't brush off his mom's fears or feed into them. Charlie was hoping for a little more help from his dad, but realized he had to live with his mom and couldn't put himself into a tight spot that would leave him in the doghouse after Charlie had left.

He was in with the doctor by 9:30. Dr. White was a healthy, middle aged man. It looked like he kept himself in shape with regular exercise. He had a calm, wise air about him that made Charlie and his other patients comfortable around him.

Charlie told Dr. White about his symptoms, muting much of the intense description he had given to Rod. Dr. White nodded his head, taking all of the information in. He was quiet for longer than Charlie liked. Charlie was hoping that he would just let him out of the office after his explanation of symptoms and the obligatory vital signs check that had already been done by the nurse.

"Well, Charlie I think we should do an EKG. I need to see what that tells me before I can make any decision. I'll send Marcy back in to run that on you. It shouldn't be too long." He nodded at Charlie, patted him on the knee, and began moving towards the door. He noticed Charlie's look of dread. "Don't worry yet. You need to take off your shirt, though. Okay?"

Charlie took a deep breath, trying to stay calm. "All right." Dr. White looked him in the eyes, trying to reassure him.

After getting some random patches of his chest hair shaved off and having the test run on him Charlie sat anxiously in the chair beside the patient bed. He couldn't lay down anymore and he couldn't sit without a backrest right now, he was too nervous. He kept checking the clock, thinking it had already been hours. At 10:15 Dr. White walked back in with a white print out in his hands. His eyes were studying it more intently than Charlie liked.

Dr. White sat down on the rotating doctor's chair without taking his eyes off of the paper. He rolled the chair next to Charlie and finally looked up. "There's something a little bit quirky here." He pointed to the paper with spindly lines all over it. He looked at Charlie and pointed to one spot on the paper.

"See right here. There's a little bit of a hiccup that isn't quite normal."

He paused, letting Charlie process this information. Charlie just stared at it, not knowing what to say. After an awkward silence he let out, "What does that mean?" He didn't want to ask. He had always liked his grandmother's advice to not ask questions that he didn't want to know the answer to. He didn't want to know what it meant. He just wanted to leave and get back to college life and being a college football player. That was all he cared about. That was all that mattered to him. But this time, he had to ask.

Dr. White nodded. The nod didn't seem like a good reply to Charlie. "Well, because you are so young, I'm not too worried about it. I don't think it will be a problem in the short term. You are in great shape and should be fine. For the long term it isn't good to have any kind of abnormality like this. I do want you to see a cardiologist. I'm going to call Dr. Thompson and see when he can get you in." He whirled around in his chair to the phone in the room.

After what must have been a couple rings, he said, "Hi, this is Dr. White. I need to get an appointment for one of my patients. He has a slight abnormality on his EKG and needs to see Dr. Thompson." He paused to let the receptionist talk. "Is that the earliest you can get him in?" He rolled his eyes, "Okay, let me ask." He turned to Charlie. "How is January 4th at 9:00 AM? He is going on an internship back east for a couple of months. I think this will be soon enough, though."

Charlie's eyes got big. That would be after the season. That was like a breath of fresh air to him. He was suddenly excited again. "Sure, sure. That would be great." He sounded almost too excited.

"Okay, let's get that appointment set." He paused for a second and hung up the phone. He wheeled over to Charlie again. "I think that will be fine. You will be okay until then. I need you to come back and see me if these symptoms get any worse, though. Okay?" He peered at Charlie.

"Sure, I will do that. Of course." Charlie was ready to jump for joy. He didn't have to miss any part of the season. Everything was back on track. Life was whole again. "Can you call my trainer, Rod, and let him know about everything, please?" Charlie pulled out his trainer's business card and reached towards Dr. White.

"Yeah, I will do that. I will let him know that he has to keep an eye on you and that I need to see you if it gets any worse."

Charlie didn't care about anything else now. He could tell him all that he wanted. Deep down Charlie knew the symptoms wouldn't stop. He thought they might even get worse, but he didn't care. He would never be talking to Rod about it again. He would get through the season no matter what. He wasn't going to let a little blip on his EKG stop his season. "Okay, I will make sure to keep Rod in the loop about my health." Charlie smiled right through his lie.

"All right, just stop by the front desk on your way out. Good luck with the rest of the season. Let me know how it went next time you are in." Dr. White gave him a firm handshake and let himself out of the room.

Charlie drove back to town without music this time, letting his mind wander. He would put this all in the back of his mind and will himself through the rest of the season. He smiled and was looking forward to seeing Mary again tonight. His mind drifted back to their last encounter and his blood began to flow below the belt.

Fearless

Charlie lay awake in bed thinking through the scouting report he had been given at today's practice. This week was going to be a much tougher test than he had faced all year. The guy he was going against was an All-American defensive lineman, someone who was sure to be a high pick in the NFL draft. Charlie knew it wouldn't be like last week when he had destroyed his opponent. He didn't want to be on the destroyed end of the equation this week. This guy was bigger, stronger, and better than Charlie. This knowledge was keeping him awake tonight.

He was also trying to keep Dr. White out of his mind. He didn't want a minor heart abnormality to distract him. He had to put this out of his mind and focus on more important matters like how he would be victorious this week.

Charlie had played against bigger, stronger, and better opponents many times. He had never been the biggest, strongest, or best player, but he didn't let this stop him from getting his job done. A big part of the battle in football was mental. Having a positive attitude and giving full effort could make up for many things. Part of this meant playing without any fear. It meant no worries about not being able to compete against whoever might line up in front of him at any given time or play. Charlie discovered the benefits of playing without fear a long time ago. He remembered the last time he had played with fear and how disastrous the results had been.

It was back in his freshman year of high school when Charlie had last felt afraid on the football field. He had made the sophomore team as a freshman. It had taken him a few weeks to feel comfortable with the fact that not many freshmen had made the sophomore team that year. At the beginning he had felt like an outsider, but after two weeks of team conditioning without pads and making it through two-a-days he had proven that he could play with the older classmen. This finally gave him some self-confidence.

One day, feeling the need to teach some humility, the coaches decided that the sophomore offensive line would do some drills against the varsity linemen and linebackers. This wasn't announced before practice so Charlie didn't have time to build up the scene in his mind with extra worry. But on the short jog to the varsity side of the practice field, his heart had plenty of time to quicken its pace.

It was late August and school still hadn't started, so he had yet to see these upper classmen interact in a school environment. To him they seemed larger than life. They drove cars to school every day, talked about their latest attempts of conquest in the locker room, drank beer on the weekends, and had to shave their faces on a regular basis. These guys might have been normal humans, but to Charlie they seemed like giants.

It was a hot day and tempers were quickly rising. These varsity guys grew into an even nastier mood when the group from the sophomore team showed up. To the varsity guys this was insulting. Looking into their helmets, Charlie saw eyes filling with anger, aggression, and meanness. He felt like his coaches were leading this group of young boys to the slaughter. Charlie didn't know if death was possible in football, but if it was, today might be that day.

Charlie had earned a starting spot on the sophomore offensive line, so he had to be in the first group to start the drill. In the huddle, with the coach calling the play to the linemen and running back, Charlie could only think of the fears running through his head. He hoped not to be crushed by these huge, possessed giants. His technique and self-confidence flew away with the gentle breeze rolling over the field.

He stepped to the line, not remembering the play that the coach had called. He would just block the guy in front of him and hope he wasn't doing the wrong assignment. He faintly heard the cadence being yelled out by the coach. He fired out of his stance at the snap of the ball, but seemed to be crushed before even taking his first step. He was two yards in the backfield and thrown to the ground before he even knew what was going on. The next play he and the center were supposed to double team the tackle. The tackle exploded into them so hard they were off balance and before they could compose themselves he had thrown them to the ground and creamed the running back.

The next few plays in a row, Charlie's assignment was to block the linebacker by himself. Each time he was knocked to the ground by a fierce blow to the side of his helmet from a spearing, flying linebacker. By the end of ten plays, his mouth was bleeding, his uniform was dirty, his ribs hurt, and his head was ringing. Charlie didn't know how much more he could take. He was just thinking about surviving the punishment. He hoped it would end soon.

After dragging himself back to the huddle and hearing the play, Charlie just wanted to lay down. His assignment for this play was to go one on one with the tackle again. This guy seemed to be gaining energy, not losing it like Charlie. He seemed to be getting angrier and angrier each play, like he had a demon inside of him. Charlie meekly tried to line up like everything was okay. On the snap of the ball, Charlie was again rammed into as he was getting out of his stance. He was pushed so far back that the running back ran into his back.

The whistle blew and once again the coach called for a huddle. Charlie was silently pleading for it to end. His eyes started to well up with tears at the thought of having to endure any more. He fought back the tears, not wanting to look like a wimp or a crybaby. Charlie was getting his ass kicked, but fortunately so were the rest of his sophomore teammates. His abysmal performance didn't stand out because all of his other teammates were getting their asses kicked. At least he wasn't getting an oral berating to go along with the physical beating. As the coach was getting ready to call another play, a loud whistle blew from far away signaling an end to the current drill and a beginning for the next drill. This seemed like a gift from the football gods for Charlie.

The sophomore offensive line coach took his troops back to their side of the field in a slow jog. Charlie kept his helmet on and stayed away from everyone so that they couldn't see the tears he was holding back from the physical and mental pain he felt from an absolute annihilation.

The coach let them have a long water break and instead of yelling when they came back he just told them it had been a learning experience and showed how much they could improve if they kept working hard. He told them to forget about it and move on to the next drill. Charlie tried to move on, only hoping that the next drill would not involve contact. His head was still ringing with pain and disorientation.

  That night, long ago, lying in bed feeling sorry for himself, Charlie decided that he was never going to play afraid again. It was okay to get his ass kicked from time to time, but he was never going to fear going against someone again. His fear had paralyzed him and had not allowed him to do anything against his opponent. He hadn't been able to give his best effort and he realized it was the fear that had limited his performance. Every opponent was just human and nobody was going to kill him. He told himself he was not going to be afraid of any player he went against, no matter how big, strong, or tough he was. With that, he stopped feeling sorry for himself. What happened that day was a good lesson, one he had to learn from.

  This strategy had paid off for Charlie. From that day, as a timid 14 year old freshman, to the present, Charlie had never gotten his ass kicked that badly again. He never again endured an episode where he played in utter fear of his opponent. There were times here and there when he got beat or where he might have been over matched. But, he never let that decide the next play and was never afraid of what might happen or what did happen. He gave his full effort every time, put faith and confidence in his technique, and let the rest take care of itself. Playing without fear was one of the cornerstones of his playing style from that day forward.

  Now, lying in bed as a confident 22 year old, Charlie knew he had to use the lessons that he had learned as an adolescent. Certainly this guy he would be going against was good and would get the best of Charlie from time to time. He was okay with that. He would continue to give his best effort against this guy and battle him all game long. Charlie knew he had one thing on this guy, he was in better shape. He knew that by the end of the game he would have more energy left than his opponent. If he could survive the first three quarters, Charlie might be able to get the best of him by the end of the game.

  Charlie knew it was a tall order, but that was his game plan. He still had a hard time relaxing and falling asleep as he thought more and more about the game. The Puma had to get out of their slump, and if Charlie didn't have a good game and neutralize his All-American opponent, then his team didn't have much of a chance. As captain and team leader, Charlie welcomed this responsibility. But this was the first time all year that he worried he might not be able to live up to his duty.

    He tossed and turned, agonizing about possibly letting the team down. To gain control of his emotions and allow himself to relax, he decided he would make sure that the tempo in practice this week was ratcheted up a notch and that the team would be prepared. He felt like he could more fully control the practice side of the outcome, rather than the outcome of the game. He might fail at one of them, but he didn't want to fail on two fronts. His team and his coaches were counting on him. At last he drifted off to sleep.

Facade

April was walking down the cereal aisle and was paying more attention to Conner than the items for sale around her. Conner was already a year old now. He was saying a couple of words now, 'dada' was not one of them. She felt bad about that. 'Mama,' and 'ki,' for their kitty were his two words. They were his main companions. She wished he was saying 'dada' instead of 'ki,' that would mean that Blake was at home more often. She wanted Blake around as much as Conner wanted his dad around.

Conner was also starting to walk. She wondered if Blake even knew this. Since the beginning of the season, Blake had usually seen Conner in bed or in his high chair eating dinner. She could recall a couple of times when Blake had been able to play with Conner, but as the season wore on, it seemed that Blake was only home at night after Conner was asleep and left before Conner was awake.

She wasn't angry about this, she felt sad for Blake. He was missing out on a lot. These young days of a child don't come back and she didn't want to have another kid if she was going to be the only one raising the child.

It was mid-morning on a Wednesday and the grocery store was quiet. Not many customers were roaming its aisles. Calming music played overhead. "Hi there Conner. Hey Conner. Oh, you just look so cute." She tickled his pudgy tummy. "Oh yes, you are just the cutest, aren't ya? Look at those beautiful green eyes and those chubby red cheeks." She pinched his cheeks and smiled. He smiled back at her and shook his head in delight.

She hadn't been paying attention and was already at the end of the aisle. She stopped without looking up, knowing that she needed to get something from this aisle. She backed up and found what she was looking for. As she began leaving the aisle again, she saw a familiar face.

"Hi April," Donna said, with what April took as feigned enthusiasm. Donna was Coach Miller's wife. Coach Miller was the Puma's offensive coordinator and was also under immense pressure to produce results this year. Donna was dressed up for the grocery store like she was going to a fancy party. Her hair and makeup were done to perfection and her clothes were overboard for a trip to the grocery store. Her jewelry was picked out to match her outfit and her perfume could be smelled from half way down the aisle. April, on the other hand, was wearing jeans and a t-shirt. She hadn't taken a shower yet. She had pulled back her hair and put on a little foundation before leaving. She wasn't wearing any jewelry and her only perfume was her natural smell.

"Hey Donna." She instantly felt like Donna was scrutinizing her, judging what she was wearing and how she was carrying herself. She already wanted their conversation to end.

After looking her up and down, Donna approached her and gave her an awkward hug. She looked down at Conner in the cart and stroked his soft hair. He looked up at her with a curious smile. "Wow, he is getting big. They grow up so fast. Soon you'll be taking him to preschool. Then before you know it they are in high school."

"Yeah, he sure is growing fast."

"It's almost time for another one, isn't it?" Donna's eyes widened and she shook her head as if the answer was a foregone conclusion.

"Mmmmm, I don't know. This might be it for us. He is a handful and we have plenty to keep us busy." April gave her a polite smile.

Donna was surprised, and after an uncomfortable moment of silence, she changed the subject. "I haven't seen you for a while. You haven't been coming to the wives' functions or the games with us. Is everything okay?"

"Yeah, I have been really busy keeping up with this guy. It is hard being the only one available to take care of him."

"Well, once you have a handle on things, come back out with us. I know it is busy, but you'll get used to it. After a while you will really love your alone time. We sure get a lot of freedom." She nodded again, expecting an affirmation from April.

"I don't know if I want to get used to it. It is hard. Blake and I are away from each other all the time. I hardly get to see him and he barely gets to see his son. I love him and I love being together; that's why I married him," April said, bursting Donna's bubble.

Donna's eyes grew narrow and her voice lost some of its bubbliness. "Oh, honey. Don't think of it that way. We get to have mostly carefree lives. Our husbands get to do the worrying and the hard work. We get to raise the kids, keep a nice house, and look pretty." She had to fight the urge to point to herself as an example, since she thought April was slipping on the looking pretty part of the obligation. "That's part of why we have the wife get-togethers every week. We need time to vent and to let loose. Make sure you start coming when you can. I think it will help you feel better." She patted April on the shoulder.

"Okay, I will try to get to one of them soon," she lied, having no desire to go to their silly gatherings. She had gone to one and she hated it. It was a whine fest with a bunch of spoiled wives who got whatever they wanted because their absent husbands felt guilty for leaving them alone for most of their married lives. "I'm hoping to get back to work, though, too. I loved my job and I really got fulfillment out of being a working woman. I hope to go back when Conner is a little older," April said, trying to stay cheerful.

"No, no, no. You don't need to do that. You just focus on being a good mother and wife. You'll get plenty of fulfillment from that. Life's hard as a coach's wife, I know that. But don't make it harder by forcing yourself to go out and work, too. You have to be the one to raise the kids and take care of the house. You aren't going to have much help, you know that by now. Doing all of that and working would be way too much. Just relax and be okay with your role as a coach's wife, dear. You'll be fine." Donna rubbed April's arm, as if she were consoling her. She smiled and nodded her head as she did this, hoping April wouldn't counter back with any more silly ideas or notions of being a working woman and not enjoying her freedom.

April knew the conversation wasn't going anywhere, so she just shook her head. She didn't want to agree, or disagree, so she just kept silent.

"Well, dear. I am going to finish my shopping. Then I have an appointment to get my nails done. Have a great day and make sure to take care of yourself. Remember, you are all you really have, especially during the season." She reached out again for a hug.

"Bye, bye." They smiled at each other and went opposite ways down the aisle.

April was stewing inside her head. *I hate that woman. I hate all of the coach's wives. They are all like that. I hate this town, too. I left all my friends and family to come here for Blake and now I am on my own. I hate this shit. I'm not going to be like her, I can't be like her. I promise myself that I won't end up like her. I don't just want to be a coach's wife for the rest of my life. I want my own identity, too. This sucks.*

She was brought out of her anger when Conner dropped his toy. She felt better seeing his cute little face begging for her help to get his toy back and smiled genuinely this time. She bent down and picked it up for him. "Here you go, baby." He smiled back at her, thanking her for saving his toy. She bent over and kissed him on the forehead.

Draw

It was the night before the game and Charlie was very nervous. The game plan all week had been based around Charlie keeping the All-American in check. The coaches had built it up and Charlie was feeling the pressure. He knew from experience that he would become overwhelmed and would be an insomniac tonight if he allowed himself to brood over his duties for the game tomorrow. To help prevent this, Charlie fell back on his regular strategy, he didn't want to do anything differently than he had in the past. He had to approach this game just like every other game.

He and Anthony always shared a room on the road. After dinner and the last team meeting of the night, Charlie and Anthony went down to the hotel lobby. They found the gift shop and bought themselves some dessert. He didn't need the extra calories, but knew that they would be burned off tomorrow during the game. He looked around for his favorite, ice cream. When they didn't have any, he had to settle for an oversized chocolate brownie. He didn't even want to look at the amount of calories in this giant treat.

They took their time getting back to their room and turned on the TV to find some mindless program. Before the coach came by to remind them that lights out was in ten minutes, they were already settled into their beds ready to sleep for the night. Sleep was important for Charlie, he didn't do well on less than eight hours. Some guys stayed up and watched TV after lights out, but Charlie was always lying with his eyes closed to ensure he got the rest that he needed.

Once the lights were off, he was in his own quiet world thinking about the game while trying not to let worry take hold of his mind. Instead of focusing on what might go wrong, or negative thoughts, Charlie stayed positive. With his eyes closed, he thought about his technique, picturing perfect execution. Short, powerful, explosive steps, one right after the other. Firing his hands into the All-American's chest, locking on, and overpowering the guy. Now that he was in control, he would picture himself finishing the job, either driving the player into the ground downfield or neutralizing him at the line of scrimmage during a pass play.

After going through his technique many times, Charlie started to think about the All-American himself. What was his technique like? What kind of moves did he use? What style of play did he use? What could he expect tomorrow? These were all things Charlie had picked up during the week while studying film on his opponent.

These positive visualizations soon turned into random neural activity as Charlie fell asleep.

The next day was not a good day for the Puma. Charlie played a good, hard, tough game, but it wasn't enough. The All-American had not had an All-American day, Charlie had made sure of that. Charlie had probably battled his opponent to a draw, an accomplishment by itself. Despite his extraordinary efforts, the Puma had to lick its wounds as they returned home from another disappointing road trip.

Down, Set, Hut

Student Athlete

Charlie couldn't believe that it was already the end of October. There were only four games left in the season. They had already played seven games. This team had been together for almost two and a half months.

During the season time zooms by. Part of that is because a player is so busy the whole damn season. With football and school there isn't much time for anything else. Football is seven days a week and school is five. To stay caught up in school a player has to be responsible and dedicated to setting aside time just for studying. This is not always an easy task. Drinking, girls, and friends all take a dent out of one's time.

Not that most football players are the greatest students. Some of them are flat out dumb. In fact, Charlie wondered how many of them ever stayed eligible, let alone finish school. He swore some of these guys who had come and gone through the program were illiterate. How some of them left town with a college degree was beyond him. One of his former offensive line teammates used to brag, as if it was worth bragging about, that he had never read a book. He would continue this illogical form of bragging by saying that he had no desire to do so.

There were some guys who had their girlfriends do their homework for them. These guys usually had more than one girlfriend, so more than one choice when a big paper was due. Then, of course, there were those people on campus who would do homework for a fee. They were usually freshman in the dorms that didn't have anything else to do and would charge a small fee to write a paper, finish math homework, or do research projects. One of the sad things was that many of these people thought that maybe the football player who requested help would be friends, in exchange for a favor. This usually wasn't the case. The guys offering help would only be treated kindly and approached in a nice way when due dates came near.

Some football players are lazy when it comes to school, trying to get away with as little as possible. After all, most of them are there to play football, school is the secondary priority, no matter how much a coach claims otherwise. As a result, for many of the mandatory general courses, papers, notes, and tests are kept to pass on. This kind of team play can help the next guy avoid having to go to class all the time and not worry about the stress of an upcoming test or paper. Some of the professors are lazy, as well, so the tests will be the same and, not surprisingly, good grades are assured. Sometimes only small adjustments are made to recycled papers and then turned in with a new name. It is kind of funny when the second person turning in the same paper receives a higher score.

Plenty of stories were afloat about the star players who somehow, against seemingly insurmountable odds, manage to stay eligible. Charlie never knew all the details of the stories, so they all might have been hearsay. Nevertheless, on the day grades came out, players who were badly needed for the season always seemed to be eligible.

One of the wildest stories was about the team's leading receiver of the previous year. Charlie didn't have any classes with him, but many of the players did. Apparently, during spring ball, which lasts for six weeks, he didn't attend any of his classes. When asked about this by his friends, the player would just say he was too tired and that he would be eligible, not to worry about it. After all, he needed his energy for practice. He was majoring in PE, so it did seem possible that he hadn't missed too much work.

However, in one of his general classes, Biology, he was only getting a D heading into the final two weeks of classes. According to teammates, he didn't attend class for the last two weeks and didn't even manage to come to class to take the final. However, he managed to eke his way through, ending up with a C average for the term.

As rumors go, there was plenty of talk that the coach had gone and talked to some of the teachers. This may, or may not, have been the case. The only thing people knew for sure was that how he managed to get a C average for the semester and stay eligible for his senior year of football was an unexplained mystery. It turned out that after he was done with football, he couldn't keep a high enough GPA to continue going to school. He was on probation for a semester and again failed to get the required grades, so was forced to give up his scholarship and ended up going home.

These examples might seem like straight up cheating and unethical practices by athletes and coaches. It did, however, manage to save the players time when their lives were very busy during the season. Once games began, the weeks would just fly by.

Monday was supposed to be the day away from football. Although there was no practice, each player was expected to check into the office and watch some film sometime during the day. This was also the day for lifting. Lifting during the season is less demanding, but still takes at least ninety minutes and is no easy task.

Tuesday was the first day of practice to prepare for the new opponent. This was usually the hardest day of practice during the week. Soreness still remains from the game the previous Saturday, but practices get intense with full pads worn and plenty of bang 'em up drills against guys who are your teammates. By the end of the season, it's not uncommon to hate your own teammates while practicing.

Wednesday was another day of hard practice. It was very similar to Tuesday and the rest of the week's game plan was put into place.

Thursday was a lighter day with less contact and perhaps a chance for one's body to recover a little. Half pads were worn and the contact drills were usually kept to a minimum.

Friday is when the fine tuning of the week's game plan was done and everyone was expected to know what their job was for the upcoming game. These were the days full of football, when a lot of time was put in at the football office and on the field.

On Tuesday, Wednesday, and Thursday players would report to the football facility at around 2:00 or 2:30 for meetings and film. Practice started at 4:00. Between meetings there was taping to be done and pads to be put on. Practice usually ended around 6:00 or 6:30, mostly depending on the outcome of the previous week's game. Charlie liked to take his time after practice. Having little energy, he would lounge around, slowly taking off all his pads and clothes and taking a long hot shower.

Even when practice ended early, he was rarely out of there earlier than 7:00. During these days players also are required to lift one more time. Coming to watch film isn't mandatory, but highly suggested. Some position coaches will put more pressure than others to come and watch film, but most good players liked to watch film to know what to expect from their opponent on Saturday and what areas of their game could be improved.

In between all this, a football player had to squeeze in going to class, studying for class, seeing friends, and maybe hanging out with his lady. Already a busy week, there is still more to go.

Friday was when heavy and intense thinking about the game begins. Fridays were better when having a home game. This meant the player would have a little time to relax and even be at home. If it was an away game, this time would be spent traveling to the destination. The day's practice was short and without pads. Only about an hour long with a long stretch and warm up, followed by a run through of all the special teams, it was enough to work up a sweat, but not much more. Then each side of the ball, offense and defense, spent some time going over the game plan for the next day. The team was then dismissed for a few hours until they had to report back for team dinner.

Team dinner was always a highlight because everyone got to fill up on free, good food. Something many guys didn't get when they had to make their own dinners. Roast beef and all the fixings was much better than Ramen noodles and canned peaches. Charlie liked to stock up, knowing that he would burn off any extra calories the next day. After the dinner, there were position meetings for the last time of the week to go over any adjustments that might be expected for the next day, followed by meetings for each side of the ball. A final team meeting was how the night would end. Motivational speeches were given from at least one coach and occasionally players might give a short speech to their teammates. By this point, the excitement for the game was beginning to flow through each player's body.

If it was a road game, the team had to leave on Friday morning. They would get their traveling done, have a short practice, and then a little free time at the hotel. At night they would have a team dinner and then the regular meetings. Finally, at about ten o'clock, they got to go to their rooms and get ready for bed.

Saturday was a day for nervous energy. There would be a team meal and then a last meeting before they had to report for the game. It was a tense day waiting for game time to finally arrive.

Sundays were sore days. In spite of their all-consuming pain, practice still happened the day after the game. Practice was light, it was more of a short run and stretch to get the lactic acid out of their bodies before they got too sore to move. Even Charlie didn't like practicing the day after a game, but he had to admit that he really did feel better after. They also had a team meeting about the mistakes of the previous day and what needed to happen the coming week in order to be successful. The offensive side of the ball and the defensive side of the ball had short meetings to go over the preliminary strategies for the upcoming week. Things might change before the week was over. At five or six o'clock, the team was dismissed to have a few hours of their own time before the school week began again and life kept ticking along.

With so much time being devoted to football, it is hard not to be completely consumed by the sport. It is all a person does from August to November. It is his life. Each player literally eats, drinks, and lives football. It is easy to see how it can be built into something more than a game, into how one defines himself. Winning or losing can become all that a person will use to judge his station in life at that moment. A poor performance in a game can depress a player, while a solid performance can lift one's spirit. A season, a game, a play can become one's identity.

Looking back on the season that was already more than half way over, Charlie didn't feel like he had done all that he could. He felt like the team was not achieving its full potential. Charlie believed that the results of the team reflected the leadership of the team.

He wondered if his leadership had been enough to carry the team to its summit. If they didn't have a successful season, he felt like he bore some responsibility for the failure. He wondered if he had been the right choice for team captain.

Maybe he shouldn't have voted for himself. He rededicated himself to making this season a success. He would continue to strive to be the leader he had wanted to be, he would try even harder, he would sacrifice even more, and he would carry the team towards a successful finish. He had to do it, or he would judge himself and his senior season a failure. He couldn't bear this thought. He would do whatever it took to ensure an ending that he and the rest of the Puma could be proud of.

Faded Dreams

Charlie's exhaustion, nausea, and feelings of being ready to drop dead had continued unabated with each game. This alone had worried Charlie because he had tried to minimize the symptoms when he had seen Dr. White. Dr. White's only instruction was ringing through his head now. "Make sure to come see me if the symptoms get any worse."

Tonight they were worse. He had even thrown up on the sideline a couple of times. At times he didn't know if he would make it through the game. He even pulled himself out for a series during the third quarter. For him to do that, the symptoms were A LOT worse.

He wondered, though, if everything was exacerbated by another loss. He was pissed off and felt like shit. He couldn't fucking believe it, his dream season was slipping away and his heart might give out, too.

He was moping his way off the field, taking much longer than was necessary, when a firm grip grabbed his tricep from behind. With his helmet on, Charlie had to turn his head all the way to the side to see who it was. Unless this was someone important, he felt like slugging them.

Charlie made eye contact and was met with anger. He suddenly became worried. "Hey, Charlie," Rod said in a stern voice, "stop for a minute. We need to talk."

"Hey Rod." Charlie took his helmet off to avoid having to look him in the eyes. "What's going on?"

Rod shook his head and wouldn't stop staring Charlie in the eyes. "You know what's going on. Dr. White asked me to keep an eye on you when we spoke. I watched you tonight, Charlie, and you didn't look good. You looked much worse and he warned me about you getting any worse."

Oh, FUCK, this is the last thing I need. How can I make this seem okay? "Oh, no, no. It was just something I ate," was the first lie Charlie could think of. "I was even feeling it last night before bed. I had diarrhea. You can ask Anthony. He heard me last night and was worried about today. That's really all it was, just a bad stomach. I don't even feel that tired." Charlie wished he hadn't taken off his helmet so quickly. It was harder to avoid Rod's eyes with his helmet off.

Rod seemed to be trying to read Charlie's veracity through his eyes. Maybe Charlie's mad, poor-sport-about-losing glare made him seem more honest. "I don't know if I fully believe you, but I am going to be watching you even closer now. I'm worried about you, but I can't send you to Dr. White if it is just a bad stomach. He won't like me wasting his time." He gave Charlie one more glare. "You need to be careful. I know football is important to you and you have given this season your heart and soul. But it's not worth risking your long term health. Okay, Charlie? I need you to understand that."

Charlie gave a slight nod. "Yeah, I know, Rod. Trust me, I know that. I need to be healthy and ready to live the rest of my life after football. I'll be okay. I will keep you informed," he lied as straight faced as he could.

Rod let him go. "Go get showered up and let's get back home. The plane ride will feel good." He tried to end on an upbeat note.

Charlie continued to saunter along the field, wondering how in the hell he would be able to hide his worsening symptoms for the last few games.

Weighed down by his sweat soaked equipment and uniform, Charlie plopped down in front of the first row of lockers. He didn't want to get undressed yet or talk to anybody. Now that the game was over, and it was his team's fourth loss of the season, Charlie had to come to the painful realization that hopes for a championship were done with. Two losses had been hard because hopes of a national championship had died. But since the last two losses had been against non-conference teams, the lesser hopes of a conference championship had been alive until this game had ended with a loss.

The dream of a championship is underneath the surface of every athlete's competitive desire. It seems to be built into a person's training regimen. It is talked about from the first year of competitive athletics and is given such a priority, that ending a season with anything less seems to be a failure. It's almost as if all the hard work and effort don't amount to anything unless you can end the season as a champion. Growing up, kids see their heroes on TV talk about the burning desire to win a championship and the need to have their career validated by winning a championship. This influences the next generation of athletes into feeling like they also need to follow suit in order to be a great athlete and thinking that their work doesn't mean anything without having a ring to show for it.

Propaganda about the importance of winning and championships is thrown out from every direction. Coaches set the goals for the team at the beginning of the season. Winning a championship is always at the top of the list. Having fun and becoming a better person are never anywhere to be seen. Failing to reach this goal leads to the players getting yelled at and blamed for not trying hard enough. Any effort is deemed insufficient if it falls short of the end goal.

Media also campaigns for this lofty ideal, making championships seem like the crowning moment in an athlete's life. The hype that is given to championship games is amazing. More people pay attention to the Super Bowl than they do the presidential election. Newspapers, magazines, and TV stations are filled with images of 'The Game' for weeks before and after.

To a young person, it seems like the ultimate goal and destination one could hope to achieve. Listening to announcers, one would think they are psychic. They claim that elite athletes still need a championship to fulfill their careers. Speaking for the athletes, they say that the only thing driving an aging player is the pursuit of a championship. When listening to a game and Charlie would hear this he would think, *What the hell does this guy know? How can he speak for everyone? He probably never even played. Maybe the athlete just really likes to play and winning doesn't matter. This guy needs to shut the fuck up.*

It seemed to Charlie, the only people who didn't care about a championship or winning were his family and close friends. After any game, whether won or lost, they would greet him with a warm, loving hug. From them there was no yelling or accusations about a lack of effort. They never thought a championship ring was needed to fulfill his career. They thought he was the best player ever to be seen, in their eyes he was already a champion. That is why Charlie loved having them at his games. Their undying support is what kept him going in times of doubt. At least with his family and friends he knew he had allies and people who would love him unconditionally.

All these thoughts swimming in his head still did not make Charlie any more comfortable with the thought that he might end his football career without a championship. Sure, he didn't want to be done with football yet, but the odds of winning a championship at the next level, whatever that might be, was no small challenge to face. He didn't even know about a possible future beyond this year. This could be his last, which is why this year a championship had seemed so important.

Ignoring his teammates undressing around him, Charlie's mind slipped into thoughts about the past. Through all his years of football in middle school, high school, and now college, he had never won a championship. Many times he had been close. In his senior year in high school his team made it to the semi-finals. In a close game they were barely edged out. This broke his heart and took a long time for him to get over.

The next year, while off at college, Charlie kept close tabs on his alma mater. They were even better than the year before. The road to a championship seemed inevitable. Charlie initially had a surge of excitement on hearing his former team's progression. As the playoffs loomed and a championship season seemed like a forgone conclusion, Charlie began to get jealous. He almost didn't want them to succeed. This would mean that his former team didn't need him to win. This thought, in and of itself, devastated him. He had been the team captain and MVP. How could they carry on without him? It seemed unfair and impossible.

It was almost as if Charlie expected his team to crumble without him. Perhaps this would prompt them to call him up and ask him to come play for them in a crucial game under a fake name with a fake number. This would prove to Charlie that he was needed and that success couldn't come without him. By the time of the championship, Charlie was rooting for his former team again as he realized their success was built upon his earlier struggles.

This didn't take away from the jealousy he felt when he saw their championship rings. His first thought was, *why don't I have one of those? I deserve one of those as much as anyone. I work harder than anyone and I should be the one wearing that. I can't believe they could do it without me. I guess I am not as important as I thought I was.* Charlie, of course, congratulated everyone he saw, but still felt a twinge when thinking about his championship dreams coming so close to reality.

The season had not been kind to the Puma this year. Charlie didn't know what else he could do. This past week of practice had been one of the best this year. He had rallied his teammates the best he knew how. He was stumped. *Maybe I'm not cut out for this leadership stuff,* Charlie thought to himself.

Coach Jackson called the team to attention from the front of the locker room. Charlie didn't even look up, he barely heard a word from the short speech. He continued to stare at the floor. He was in his own world. He felt dejected. He almost wanted to cry. He had given so much to this team, to this season, and to the game again tonight, but everything kept coming up short.

Charlie remained this way until Coach Havili came by and sat down next to him.

"Hey, man, don't worry. You had a great game. Don't take it so hard. We still have three games left and can finish with a great record. We still even have a shot at a postseason game."

Charlie finally took his eyes off the ground and looked at Coach Havili. "Thanks. I know all that, it is just really frustrating to lose after giving it so much effort."

"I know it is, Charlie. But don't be so hard on yourself. You had a great game, again. You have had a great season and everyone knows how much you do for this team. It's time to forget about the game, take a shower, and go home." Coach Havili stood up and waited for Charlie to shake his hand before walking away.

Charlie took a deep breath and felt better. It was nice to hear someone say those things to him. Until now, nobody had even acknowledged his leadership efforts this year. It gave him some hope that this season could still be a success. He decided that he would do what he had done all year in practice again this coming week. It was the only way he knew how to lead and it was the only way he was capable of being. He took a languorous shower and walked out to the bus where the entire team was waiting for its last member before leaving.

Down, Set, Hut

Karma

    Arriving a few minutes early to the football complex, Charlie went to the trainer's room first. Being one of the first guys there he could get his treatment started without having to wait in line. His back had been bothering him for most of the season and a couple of times each week he had been getting electronic stem therapy, hoping to loosen up his lower back muscles that seemed to be in a constant state of contraction.

    It was Monday, which meant they only had weight training and film sessions, so he could get some extra therapy. The room smelled of sterilized cleanliness that was typical of a doctor's office or hospital. Tables with the team-colored cushion tops were neatly arranged throughout the room. Freshly stacked rolls of tape, pre wrap, and various other first aid supplies were next to the tables within reach for easy use. The trainer's assistants were just arriving, still getting everything ready for the approaching rush of players wanting their ailments tended to with some personal care. Most of these assistants were young college girls. The majority of them certainly were interested in being a trainer and working in athletics, but Charlie always wondered how many of them did it just to be around the football team and get to know the guys on the team. There were a couple of the women trainers who knew some of the guys on a very personal basis.

    Charlie had a favorite trainer who always taped his ankles just right. He had tried all of them, some did it too tight, some too loose, but her technique was perfect for Charlie. He still liked to feel his toes after being taped, while wanting some extra support. She saw him and tapped the cushioned table top with some sarcasm for him to jump up and get his treatment started. She wasn't an attractive girl. Her body seemed unevenly proportioned, too much in the middle section. She had a pretty face that always had a smile. Her personality made up for her lack of looks. She had been a trainer since before Charlie was around and seemed to really enjoy her job and helping the guys.

    She gave a courteous greeting to Charlie and started in. Usually they would chat, but she was busy finishing a conversation with another trainer who also just arrived. This didn't bother Charlie, he wasn't in much of a mood to talk. There were a couple of other guys from the team already in the trainer's room at this early hour. Charlie had casually greeted them upon entering, but was trying to avoid a conversation right now. He always made it a point to say hello to everyone and tried not to ignore anyone, even the guys he didn't really like and especially the walk-ons. He knew that for the team to be successful there needed to be a certain amount of camaraderie between all of the players and that every person on the team made a contribution to the outcome of the season.

Rod was busy in his small office. The injury report was due to the media by Monday afternoon. Rod had to have it to Coach Jackson before it went public. Unless it was something new or troublesome he would let his assistants handle it today.

At the far end of the room, next to the trainer's office, was Julius. He looked like he was in plenty of pain and had barely responded to Charlie's greeting. Julius was lying on the table getting treatment on his newly repaired knee. He had torn his ACL a few weeks ago and had already had surgery. He was apparently going through the beginning of his rehab. It had ended his season and, being almost half way through his senior year, probably his career. Injuries were a bad part of the game and unfortunately occurred too often. Looking at Julius going through this painful experience, Charlie's mind kept returning to a conversation he had with Julius in the spring.

It was just a small group of the guys getting together to drink some beer. Spring football had been over for a couple of weeks and finals were the next week. They were going to be out for the summer soon and the real training for the season would begin in earnest with the start of summer. They were just shooting the shit, talking about their goals for the summer and the next season, when Julius after a few beers let out too much information.

"It is going to be my senior year and I am going to pull out all the stops. I have given my all to this program for the last four years and I am tired of limited playing time. I want to be a starter this year. I am going to do what it takes to make this happen, even if that means doing a 'cycle' this summer. I have found a good source and I am going to start it when our summer workouts start. I figure with a little boost I will break over the hump and into the starting lineup. That is my plan," Julius had stated matter of factly, without any emotion and without really looking at anyone in particular.

Johnny, Anthony, and Charlie all glanced at each other with a look of confusion. They didn't really know how to respond to that and none of them wanted to be the first to say something back to Julius about it.

Steroids were a confusing issue in sports but were a presence on every team. Access to the drug was never a problem for someone who wanted them, and they had each known someone on their team that had been using them since high school.

It was just kind of an issue that stayed in the dark, that wasn't talked about. It was rude, and perhaps fight provoking, to accuse someone of using if their numbers suddenly went up. So, it was usually just a fog of rumors about who was using unless one got close enough to know someone was using or, as in this case, heard someone who was drunk enough to admit it to his teammates.

Steroids were viewed negatively by players, coaches, and fans. There was always some effort to keep drugs out of sports, but it was never talked about at length. The only thing ever talked about by the coaches or administration was that if a player was caught using them he would be suspended for a year, losing eligibility for that year. The side effects of the drug were only learned about by outside reading or in health class. The moral issue of cheating was not openly discussed. However, it was a common understanding that using steroids was equal to cheating because they created an unfair advantage for the athlete who used them.

To prevent the use and follow through on the ban of the drug, random tests were administered throughout the year. These tests still allowed for many loopholes. Athletes coming from junior college were never subject to testing at that level. By the time a junior college transfer arrived in the NCAA, the drug would be out of his system and undetectable with a urine test. High school athletes were also not tested.

The tests imposed by the NCAA were not conducted during the summer. This gave athletes a small, but risky, window to complete a cycle before the threat of a test was looming. The tests were done at random times throughout the year, so a particular team might get tested once one year and then four times the next year. Individual selection for the test was also done by chance, so during his four to five years of being on the team, an athlete could possibly not be tested at all, or be tested more than once in a year, maybe up to seven or eight times during his career.

The test itself was very strict, with the test administrator standing uncomfortably close watching the testee pee, ensuring it was coming out of the person being tested and not a tube with clean urine. It could sure give a guy stage fright and some guys had been known to have to stay there for half a day before being able to pee in front of a stranger standing and watching in their own personal space. From Charlie's couple times of being tested, he found the key to be not peeing when waking up, but just holding it and hurrying to the locker room to complete the test. It wasn't fun by any means, but it hadn't been a big deal to Charlie.

With the silence becoming uncomfortable after Julius' statement, Charlie spoke up. "Really, man? Why would you go to that extreme? That is like cheating."

Not moving his eyes, Julius answered back, "I don't really see it that way. Plus, this is my senior year. I am willing to do anything to break into that starting lineup."

"What do you mean, you don't see it as cheating?" Charlie asked forcefully, looking to Johnny and Anthony for support. Without a commitment, they looked at him.

"Well, why is it cheating?" asked Julius. Yeah, I might get a little stronger and faster from it, but it really isn't much different from any other supplement. There are supplements now that we all have taken. We have only taken them because we thought it would help increase our strength, giving an enhancement to our athletic ability. Some of these supplements might even become illegal in the next few years. The trainers even recommend that we stay away from some of them. We have still done it. It seems to me it is just about what the NCAA says we can or cannot take. If steroids were legal and not against the rules, I think there would be a lot of guys doing them. I don't think any of you three could honestly tell me that you wouldn't if it wasn't against the rules. So, I am taking the future of this next season into my own hands. I am not going to let it be limited by my natural ability. This will just give me that little boost over the edge that I need. I just hope that this can stay between us. I didn't want to tell anyone. It just kind of came out tonight."

There was a pause, almost a silent deep breath each of them was taking, trying to absorb everything they were hearing and realizing much of what he was saying might be true. Charlie broke the silence again. "Well, what about getting caught? If you get caught you will be out for the year and your career is done."

"Yeah, I know, but the summer is coming up and there isn't any testing during the summer. I will do a cycle and, if we do have a test and I am picked in the fall, it will be out of my system by then. If it's not, then that is the price I pay. I have given this a lot of thought. I am not willing to stand by and spend my senior year on the bench. It is a risk, but I am willing to take it," Julius said confidently, finally looking Charlie in the eyes.

"All right, well what about the health risks? That isn't a concern to you?" Charlie wasn't going to let this die that easy.

"One cycle of steroids isn't going to do anything to my long term health. If I took it for years I might be worried, but nothing is going to happen from one cycle. For the short term there really aren't any health risks. Plus, it is not like football itself is good for our bodies in the long run. Look at our coaches. Half of them walk around with a permanent limp just because of playing, not from any drugs. Their fingers are crooked. They have scars all over their bodies from too many surgeries to remember. If I was worried about my health, I wouldn't have lasted long playing a sport like football."

Charlie wasn't in much of a state to argue that night and didn't really know what to say to that, so he sat there and let the scene stay quiet for a while. Finally, changing the subject, Johnny spoke up, "So, you guys want to go to that party in a minute? There are supposed to be some ladies there." That was the last time Charlie spoke to Julius about steroids or his decision to use them. He had never even talked to Johnny or Anthony about that night. As far as he knew, they had all just kind of let it slide.

Whether or not Julius now thought the risk was worth it, he had achieved his goal. After spring ball, Julius was a second team strong side linebacker, played a lot of special teams, and was a solid backup. After a summer of working hard and a special boost, Julius was able to gain the starting position from the sophomore in front of him and solidify it as his to lose.

Before the summer, Julius had been a well-built young man. During the summer he put on 25 pounds of lean muscle, increased all his lifts by at least 30 pounds, and decreased his forty time by two tenths of a second. He wasn't really a hard hitter before, but now he was like running into a brick wall. There had been a test early in the season and Julius hadn't been selected. Whether or not he had ever stopped using steroids, it seemed like after the test had come and gone that he had gone back to the drugs, feeling safe in his decision and wanting to keep his starting spot intact.

Charlie felt bad looking at Julius having to go through all the pain of having to get his knee back to regular usage, but didn't feel much pity for Julius losing his starting position. He wondered about karma and if perhaps it had taken back something from Julius that he hadn't really earned.

Laser Focus

"Okay, gentlemen. We have got to right this ship. We have let this season slip away from us. I know that we have redoubled our efforts many times this season but we have to do it again this week. We can't let this losing streak continue." Coach Jackson made this announcement to the coaches with full belief that they made the difference between winning and losing. A coach can't dedicate as much time to a sport as Coach Jackson, and his staff, did without fully believing that coaches, not players, made the difference between winning and losing. He had made this belief clear from the beginning of his tenure and he had preached it to his staff, expecting them to follow his lead.

Blake sipped his coffee and looked at the preliminary scouting reports again. It was Tuesday morning and they had to come up with the week's game plan before the meetings started in the early afternoon. He had already gone through one cup of coffee and was almost done with his second. They usually met at 6:00 AM on Tuesday mornings, but they were already into a meeting at 5:00 AM this morning. Around the large conference table each coach had a large cup of coffee or an energy drink. All of them were suffering from sleep deprivation.

They usually had a two hour break on Tuesdays between the coach's meeting and their meeting with players, but today that seemed unlikely to happen. This made Blake's mind wander. April had made an appointment for counseling at 12:30 and he had told her that he would be there. He couldn't be the one to duck out of the meetings, he was the defensive coordinator. He had to make sure that the game plan for the week was in place and that the scouting report for this week's opponent was complete.

He knew it was going to be a long morning, one that would stretch into the afternoon. He had been spending 12-15 hours a day in the coaches' office or on the field. He didn't have time for exercise or to eat right. He had been living off of takeout and the drive through. The coaches had been taking turns buying food for each other. They needed something to get them through the long mornings, days, and nights. These meal choices hadn't been healthy. This fast food diet, combined with a lack of exercise, had taken a toll on his physique. He had been able to maintain his lean muscular body since his days of college football, but now he was losing muscle mass and gaining belly fat. He could feel the weight slowing him down, but he didn't have time to do anything about it.

He felt a twinge of regret that he would have to disappoint April again, but he put her out of his mind when he realized that he had zoned out and missed some of what Coach Jackson had been saying. If he were to stay focused and fulfill all of his duties as defensive coordinator, he would have to block out his personal troubles and deal with them when the season was over.

"Coach Miller and Coach Jones, I want to see the game plans for this week and the scouting reports at about noon. For this week's scouting report I want in depth information on every starter and every backup. Ummm, Coach Miller, we will meet first at 12:00 and then at 12:30 Coach Jones you and I will meet." He looked at Blake and they nodded at each other. "All of the other coaches I want to meet with you at one o'clock. I want you to have a plan put together about how we can improve moral on the team. We have been in a slump and I want to get out of it. We all know that most of this game is mental. We need the guys to get back to believing in themselves and having fun. I want some ideas for team building." He looked around the room for more nods of confirmation. "Okay, I've got to go get our press release ready about this week's opponent. I'll be in my office if anybody needs me."

Blake knew this meant there was no chance of him even leaving the office before his players reported for their afternoon meetings. His directives were clear and to get it done, it meant more game film and more tactical decisions. He felt stressed. The season was always busy, but this losing streak had put an end to any hope of having a life outside of football. Losing meant that jobs were at stake and when jobs were at stake more time, effort, and responsibility were demanded.

The stress from lack of a life away from football was exacerbated by losing. Nobody liked losing, especially the coaches; losing was an instant evaluation of their work. If they lost, it meant something had gone wrong. The coaches didn't know what had gone wrong, but they felt like the responsibility rested with them and that they must do their job better. They looked for ways to do their job better starting early in the morning and continuing late into the night.

Each loss piled more stress on the coaches' shoulders. After four in a row, the stress had become palpable. It was physically affecting each and every coach on the staff. During the losing streak, time seemed to go slower. It was as if satisfaction and happiness had to be put off until their efforts resulted in a win. The days felt like weeks and the weeks felt like months. It had been less than a month since their last win, but to Blake it felt like half a year.

Blake took a deep breath and focused on doing one thing at a time. He called his defensive staff together. He divvied out the responsibilities to each coach. He assigned a different game film to each coach and wanted a scouting report from each game. He also set up a meeting time with each position coach. He would create the overall game plan and then he would go over each position's specific part of the game plan with that coach. They would collaborate and he would tweak the game plan as necessary.

He would then compile their scouting reports with his and take the completed game plan and scouting report to Coach Jackson at 12:30. This left him with a little less than seven hours. It was a lot of work and he began right away. First he sent the graduate assistant out to get breakfast for the defensive staff. They all needed some type of fuel, even if it was McDonald's grease laden fuel.

At 12:30 Blake walked into Coach Jackson's office. He didn't even think about the counseling appointment that he was missing with April. He wouldn't get her message wondering where he was until after practice that evening. The door was open and he helped himself to a seat as Coach Jackson was finishing up a phone call. He seemed to be trying to reassure a booster that the season had not been lost, that they still could have a successful season.

Coach Jackson hung up the phone and turned his attention to Blake. "Hey Coach Jones. So, let's look at your game plan and the scouting report."

"Yeah, here you are." Blake passed the two packets across the desk to Coach Jackson. "I feel like I have identified the weakness of their offense and the point where we can really attack that will have the biggest impact."

"Okay, great. Let me have a look." Coach Jackson looked through the packets in meticulous detail, discussing what he saw with Blake as he went along. He asked Blake to make a few changes to the game plan. Blake felt like he had to mirror Coach Jackson's style and philosophy. Throughout the season, Coach Jackson had relented a little bit and was becoming more open to Blake's ideas and input, but these compromises were done little by little. Blake still felt like Coach Jackson wouldn't let him have full control over the game plan. This bothered Blake a little bit, but he realized that with success would come more autonomy and more trust. He was still a rookie as coordinator and realized Coach Jackson was acting more like a mentor than a dictator.

After half an hour, Coach Jackson passed the packets back to Blake. "Okay, Blake, just make those few minor changes and have them printed off to hand out to the guys at the two o'clock defensive meeting. You are doing a great job. Keep it up."

Blake was a little shocked at the compliment. Compliments hadn't come easy the past four weeks. Blake wondered if he really meant it, or if he was just tired and it had slipped out. "Okay, sounds good. See you in a bit."

Blake walked out of the room and passed the other assistant coaches waiting to talk to Coach Jackson about team building exercises that could be tried this week. Maybe this was what they had been missing the past few weeks. Maybe some team building would be what they needed to do in order to get the result from their work that they were so desperately seeking. At this point, Blake would welcome anything that might help them get another elusive victory.

He went into his office and made the few changes to the game plan that had been discussed. At 1:30 he emailed the scouting report and the revised game plan to La Dean. He called her to let her know it was done.

"Hey La Dean."

"Hi, Blake," she answered cheerfully.

"Sorry my stuff is so late. I need 60 copies of both packets done in 20 minutes. Is that okay?" he asked, trying to be polite and not demanding.

"Yeah, no problem. I'll call you when they are done." She hung up, knowing that he wanted to get off the phone.

He hung up the phone and closed his eyes.

Nineteen minutes later he was startled awake by the phone. He picked it up before it could ring again. "Hey Blake, your stuff is done. Just pick it up at the copy machine in the conference room."

"Okay, thanks." He tried to hide his groggy voice.

"No, problem, bye, bye."

He yawned and stretched before getting up. He grabbed the packets from the conference room on his way to the defensive meeting. He got there at 1:55. Most of the guys were already there. By 1:58 they had all arrived, they knew not to be late, and he began passing out the packets.

At 8:30 PM the entire coaching staff was sitting around the conference table where they had begun the day. The meetings had gone well and practice was completed with high intensity and good attitudes from the players and coaches. They were discussing any changes that seemed necessary and the team building activity that would take place at the end of practice tomorrow. At 8:43 Coach Jackson dismissed them until tomorrow morning. They could sleep in, the meeting was scheduled for 7:00 AM.

Blake gathered his papers and felt like he could pass out. He didn't know if he had enough energy for the 15 minute drive home. He felt grubby and dirty. Before leaving for home he took a quick shower in the coaches' locker room. The water felt good against his skin. He stood under the stream for a few extra minutes. It rejuvenated him enough that the drive home would be safe.

330

Struggle

Blake walked into the living room and was surprised to find April sitting in the rocking chair. The light on the table next to the chair was on and the rest of the house was quiet and dark. When he entered the room she closed her book and looked up at him. He could tell that she was not happy. She looked like she had been crying. She was wearing her bedtime clothes, but he could tell that she had lost weight. It looked like she had gotten back to her pre pregnancy weight. She looked very attractive and he wished that he had the energy to take advantage of her beautiful body. She seemed to want him to sit across from her on the sofa, but he knew that if he sat down that he would immediately fall asleep, so he stood. "Hey, honey. Sorry I am so late."

"You're more than late. You missed our counseling appointment today. I waited at her office until 1:30, hoping that you would show up. I called and left you a message, but I didn't even hear back from you," she said with a glare.

"I know. I'm sorry. I didn't get your message until after seven o'clock and once we got going at the office I totally forgot about the appointment." He stopped, not knowing what else to say.

"Well, you could at least call me and let me know that you can't make it. Or, you could have called at seven and let me know you were still going to be working."

"Yeah, I know. I will for sure do that next time."

April shook her head. "I'm tired of waiting for the next time. I want you, and I want us.... now. I don't know what to do Blake. This isn't what I wanted."

Blake shot back, "This isn't what you wanted? What...., a beautiful house and a great family? A husband who loves you and has a passion for what he does? You get to be at home and raise our child. What more do you want?"

"I get to stay at home? I never wanted to be a stay at home mom. I want to get back into my career sometime. And what more do I want? I want you. I want a full time husband, not someone that I can't count on to put our relationship and family first. That's what I want!" She shouted this last part, more out of frustration than anger.

"Don't get so loud. You'll wake up Conner."

"Maybe it would be good to wake him up. Then at least you could see him. He hardly knows who you are." She saw the hurt in his eyes at this comment and stopped before saying more.

He closed his eyes and rubbed his forehead. "That was a low blow. I know that I am missing out, but everything in life involves sacrifice."

"You're right, that was not something that needed to be said. I'm sorry," she said, with hard eyes.

"Thank you. I'm trying to be a good husband, dad, and coach. It is hard. I have to sacrifice a lot in order to further my career. You knew what kind of career I wanted coming into this relationship. You said that you would support whatever I wanted to do."

"I know that I did. But, I never knew it would be like this. You were a coach when we were dating and the commitment was never this much. We were able to have a relationship. We don't even have a relationship now. I didn't want it to be like this."

"Well, we all have to make some sacrifices," Blake said, standing his ground.

"I feel like it is more than sacrifice. I feel it is more like selling our souls."

"Selling our souls? That is harsh. What is that supposed to mean?" Blake became defensive.

"In exchange for your dream job, we are giving up a fulfilling relationship and a complete family. Our son is going to grow up hardly knowing his dad. The commitment to football is only going to grow if you become a head coach. That means less time for us and that means less time for you to be a dad. We're selling all of that for your dream."

"Well, isn't that better than selling my dream for mediocrity? If I don't chase my dream then I have more time for us and I will be a better dad. But then I have sold my soul for mediocrity. I'll just be another guy, I'll just be an average guy. Is that what you want? Do you want me to just be a 9-5 regular guy so that we can be together more?"

"No, that is not what I'm saying." She paused, collecting her thoughts. "Isn't there some sort of middle ground? I just want you to be part of my life and part of Conner's life. If things keep going this way, I will be the only one taking part in and seeing Conner's experiences. Can't you be a great coach and be a great husband and father?"

"I feel like I am being all of those. I am giving everything that I can to being a husband and father. Sometimes that just has to come after being a coach."

"That's what's hard, Blake. Your wife and your child come after football. A game is your first priority and what comes first in your life."

Blake looked away from her into the darkness of the house. He didn't know what else to say. He couldn't give up his dream. His dream is what drove him, what gave meaning to his life. Football is who he was. He hadn't known anything else since he had formed his identity as a young adolescent. "Honey, I will try to be better at balancing our life. I will be a better husband and father. I want our family to be my priority. I will do what it takes. I will go to counseling. I have to make this work. My dream is a part of who I am. My family is also a part of who I am. Please, just be patient with me." He looked her in the eyes with sincerity.

Deep in her heart she knew nothing was going to change, but she couldn't admit this to herself. This is who Blake was, he wasn't going to be a different person. He was a full grown adult. She clung to the childish notion that things could be different. "Okay, let's get some counseling and see how we can make this work for both of us."

"Thanks, babe. You are the best. I love you so much. I couldn't do this without you." He walked over to her and kissed her on the forehead.

She was still angry and didn't feel like kissing him on the lips. To her this felt like it would absolve him. "I love you, too."

"I've got to go to sleep. I feel like I am going to fall asleep just standing here." He ran his hand down her arm as he walked away from her and into the darkness towards their bedroom.

Numbers

  Charlie sat at home on a Tuesday evening trying to motivate himself to head off to the library. He knew that if he stayed home to study he would just be distracted by music, TV, or the phone. Finally, getting up the nerve, he ventured outside while first slipping on a jacket. The seasons were changing and fall was beginning to steal the weather with frequent chilly nights.
  It was a night where the dying leaves could be smelled in the air. The autumn sting in the air was felt on one's nose and ears. The time for t-shirts and shorts had passed for this year. Pausing to notice the brilliancy of the night sky as it seemed to be magnified by the cold air, Charlie unlocked his door and hopped into his truck. It wasn't much, but it got him around. Trying to pass the state inspection was always a yearly ritual that involved sacrifices to the gods and prayers to anything that might listen. These usually didn't work and he ended up having to put more money into this clunker just to drive it another year.
  Arriving at the library, he began the arduous task of trying to find a parking space. Being a chilly night, he didn't want to walk for too long, so he staked out the parking areas. This is when he ran into one of those despicable creatures, a parking vulture. Those people made him mad. They were the ones who just sat in their cars with the engine running waiting at a corner for someone to leave and then immediately take the spot. *Didn't these people have anything better to do? They are fucking annoying. Sometimes I just feel like ramming these idiots,* were a few of the thoughts that ran through his head. Seeing far too many parking vultures this evening, Charlie decided he didn't have the patience to wait any longer and parked in the residential area, willing to brave the brisk air and walk further than he would have liked.
  Walking into the heated building, Charlie felt his face flush. Looking for a spot in the lounge area, he saw Jamal sitting alone at a table in the corner. Charlie hadn't seen him since the injury in the game four weeks ago. It had been a bad one, Jamal had broken his fibula and needed surgery. His season was over, and probably his career. Some of the guys had talked about how

depressed Jamal had been since the injury. With his casted leg up on an adjoining chair and a sour look on his face, he did not appear happy tonight. Charlie approached his table, hoping to join him.

"Hey Jamal, mind if I join you?" Charlie asked cheerfully.

Looking up hesitantly, Jamal's face didn't seem to grow any happier at the thought of someone joining him. "Oh, hey Charlie. Yeah, go ahead. Just push some of those books over."

With that, Charlie made a space for himself and sat down across from Jamal. "You don't seem so good, man. Is everything okay? Are you sure you don't want to be left alone?"

"No, it's fine. It is not you, I am just in a crappy mood. I have been since this shit happened. I am actually glad it is you and not someone else. Don't take it personally or anything, dogg, I am just not in a happy time in my life right now. You know what I mean?"

"Oh, don't worry. I just didn't want to be interrupting anything. It looked like you were into your studying. I am sure I would be in a sour mood, too. I can't imagine how hard it is. How is everything going?"

"You are definitely not interrupting anything. I do study a lot more, but that is just because I don't have anything else to do. I have so much free time now, I don't know what to do with myself." Jamal paused, looking at his leg, trying to decide how best to answer the last question. "Oh… it is going as well as it can, I guess. It is such a pain in the ass to get around and I still have to take painkillers on a regular basis. The surgery went all right, I just don't know if I will ever get back to 100 percent again. Right now I just have to focus on rehab. It is hard, you know. I never wanted it to end like this."

"Yeah, I can only imagine," Charlie answered back, trying to be supportive. "Do you miss it already?"

"Hell yeah, I miss it already. Football is almost all I ever think about. I do so much homework now because it is one of the only things that helps take my mind off of it. I just can't believe it is over. I worked so hard and gave so much to the sport and this is the way it ends," Jamal said, fighting off the urge to become emotional in front of Charlie and in the library.

"I always had dreams of finishing up my career on a positive note and possibly getting a chance to play beyond college. Now, that all seems to be an impossible dream. I have to work hard just to walk normally again."

Jamal had been a solid player for the Puma the last three years. He had been a starter since midway through his red shirt freshman year. At the end of his junior year he had been named second team all-conference and had hopes of being first team all-conference this year and even being recognized nationally. He had worked his ass off in the summer and had the work ethic that made his dreams of continuing a football career a legitimate option.

Their defense had missed him immediately, but there were many guys stepping up and looking for their chance to shine. It seemed like within a couple of weeks it was forgotten that he was gone. That is how the game was, one couldn't concentrate on what the team had lost. They had to focus on what they had and on trying to do the best they could during the game.

"How are the coaches and the rest of the team? Is everyone being supportive?" Charlie asked inconspicuously. He hadn't been good about checking in on Jamal and giving him support before their random meeting tonight.

"Well, everyone was cool for a couple weeks. You know, until I had surgery and was good enough to take care of myself. Then all of a sudden, it is like I dropped off the face of the earth. I only hear from my close friends anymore. If I want to see or talk to any of the other players, then I have to go to practice and wait around. I used to be everybody's 'dogg,' now I ain't shit." Jamal paused for added effect and collected his thoughts. "And that's just the players, man. The coaches have been nowhere to be seen. I had a lot of communication when I first had the injury and right after surgery, just to make sure I was okay. Now, I don't hear from them. Even when I am at practice the most I get is a, 'Hey what's up,' you know, that kind of bullshit. As if they don't know. Even Coach Jackson barely talks to me anymore."

"Really, man? That is terrible. I didn't know that Coach Jackson would be like that. I thought he would be cool and still be nice to you even if you were hurt and weren't going to be able to play again. What is he like now?"

"Well, he used to act like he cared about me. He used to go out of his way and say 'hi' to me. I used to be his 'man.' Sometimes he'd pull me aside and tell me I was doing a good job of being a leader for the younger linebackers. He used to tell me that the team needed me, that I was an important part of it, and that he was glad I was there helping the team out." Jamal paused, looking towards the window for a moment, gathering himself. "Now, man, it is like I don't even matter. He gives me the pointless little small chat and then takes off, acting like he needs to be somewhere. It used to be, 'If you ever need anything just ask.' Now it is more like, 'Who are you? I don't owe you anything. I have the next game to get ready for. I can't waste my time on you.' I have only received one phone call from him and that was right after the surgery. It is like I was just a number to him. He sure doesn't seem to care about my future now since it isn't going to help him win anymore. I was just a body and now I have been replaced. You know, man, it is bull shit. I gave everything to this team. I gave my heart, my soul, and now my leg. The least he could do is show a little appreciation. He doesn't care, as long as I helped him win a few more games, so that he can keep his job a few more years and then move on to a bigger school where he gets paid more. His players don't matter, just the wins and the contracts. You know what I am saying man?"

"Uh huh," Charlie nodded, trying to show some compassion towards Jamal.

"I have been thinking about it a lot lately, as you can tell. I guess it is a two way street. He was using me and my body. I was a means to an end. I was helping him get what he wanted, a more successful team. And I was using him to get what I wanted, an education. Only an education isn't really what I thought I wanted. I only came to college to play football. Now, I realize how important it is. I can't count on football anymore. It all just sucks man, you know?"

"Yeah, I hear you. It is a hard situation. I am sorry that I haven't been more supportive and offered more help. I hope everything goes as well as it can," Charlie painfully admitted.

"Oh, don't worry about that. I have come to realize a lot of things. Yeah, we are friends. But that is just because of football. We wouldn't be friends if we had just met each other somewhere else. We liked each other because we are both leaders and hard workers, we just kind of clicked. It is a friendship that began with football and will end with football. I know you mean the best and wish me the best. That is enough for me. Just keep working hard and don't give up on your dream. As I know firsthand, it can be taken from you at any moment."

Jamal stopped for a moment and broke eye contact with Charlie, turning his head to look out the wall of windows beside them. He looked blankly out the window, trying to draw up some kind of courage. When he turned back towards Charlie, his eyes were watering. "This is all just hard man," Jamal let out, trying to hold back his emotions. "I haven't talked about it this much with anyone. Most people are afraid to ask anything. I mean, I used to be the man. I was a stud. Coaches and players used to look at me as someone who mattered. I used to be important, now I am just some dude."

He stopped and let out a big breath. "All my dreams, they just seem to be gone. Who I am and what I do, all of that is gone. Now I am just a person. I am not somebody special." He looked up at the ceiling, trying to hold gravity off from fulfilling its purpose of pulling his welled up tears from his eyes. "I've done a lot of crying and I don't want to do it right here and now."

Not knowing what to say, Charlie sat there in silence, trying to be supportive and a good listener. He knew Jamal a little bit, but didn't feel like good enough friends to go over and offer him a hug. Letting the silence grow to an uncomfortable level, Charlie began to get nervous, feeling like he needed to say something or do something. Fortunately, Jamal finally spoke up again, "But, I also now know that you better damn well get your degree. I know you will. I just worry about a lot of these other guys," Jamal said bluntly. "Enough about this, let's get back to studying. The library closes soon and I need to get some more studying in."

"Sounds good. I just want you to know if there ever is anything I can do for you, don't hesitate to ask or call me. I mean it."

"Thanks man that means a lot. I will." Jamal threw his arm across the table, offering his oversized hand to Charlie. Charlie gave him a high five and smiled at him.

He did feel bad, but at the same time he was glad it hadn't happened to him. Now, Charlie turned his attention to history, opening up his notes and finding where he was in the long, drawn out history of the countless conflicts that always have and always will plague humanity.

After some onerous reading, Charlie took a breather. He leaned back in his chair and took a deep breath. He looked around at the other students in the library, hoping to see a cute girl that he could engage in some harmless flirting with.

He smiled at a cute blond a couple of tables away and then noticed someone odd. An older gentleman walked right by his table. Charlie had a strange feeling in his stomach after seeing this man. He didn't look mean or evil, he even had a warm grandfatherly look about him. Nevertheless, there was something out of place with this man, something almost otherworldly.

He was way too old to be a student and even looked too old to be working here. He had grey hair, he might like to think it was salt and pepper, but the pepper had long since vanished. He was a tall man, almost as tall as Charlie, and looked like he had been some sort of athlete in his younger days. He walked with determination and with no signs of aging as he veered towards the exit.

Charlie couldn't take his eyes off of him. The uncomfortable feeling Charlie got made him study the man with his full attention. Something the man was carrying caught Charlie's eye. Charlie realized this object was the source of his strange feelings, not the gentle senior citizen. The object seemed to glow, even though the library was bright. It looked like a souvenir a person might bring home to a child. Charlie thought it might be a piggy bank in the shape of a big cat. He didn't quite know what it was, but he was certain he had seen something like it before. It was a big white cat with a coin in one of its paws and its other paw extended into the air. The entire object was out of place. He didn't like the aura it exuded. His eyes were glued to it. Finally, he realized he had seen something like this at the entrance to the sushi shop Mary dragged him to occasionally.

    Charlie came back to reality as the elderly man with his bizarre object walked out of the library. He felt like he was in a daze for a moment, almost like he had taken a hard football hit. He shook his head to regain his wits. He looked towards Jamal, wondering if he had seen it. Jamal was still busy reading his book and making notes. Charlie wondered why this short episode impacted him so much.

    He looked at the clock and realized he didn't have time to think about it anymore. He let it go from his thoughts and went back to his studies about the elusive search for truth in the past.

    Returning home that night, with bedtime fast approaching, Charlie began to let his mind wonder. His thoughts returned to his earlier conversation with Jamal. He knew that Jamal's situation sucked, there was no other way to describe it. He also wondered if Jamal was over reacting. Sure, that was no way for the coaches to treat him now that he was done with football and couldn't contribute to winning another game or didn't have anything else to offer to the team. This thought did disturb him, though.

    Remembering some of his other conversations with past players, Charlie realized this was a common theme. Many players felt like the coaches abandoned them and didn't care anymore about them once they were done playing. It is a strange situation, a player goes from being the coaches' 'boy' to just being another guy. The coach puts all his trust and confidence in a player and then, just as soon as the player is done with his eligibility, the coach seems to drop him like a bad habit.

    The coach has other players that he needs to develop and train in the system. The player has other things he needs to do, like finish up school, catch up in school, or just be a regular college student without so many responsibilities. The main thing that changes is the amount of time a player and a coach spend together once an athlete is finished playing. They go from seeing each other every day, for at least three hours a day, to only seeing each other occasionally. Any relationship changes when the parties involved begin to spend less time together.

It is a big change, and changes in life are always hard. The early twenties are a hard time in a young person's life. The transition from life as a football player to life without the game is hard for an athlete. To do this without any help or input from a major role model, such as a coach, makes it even more difficult. There was no doubt in Charlie's mind that a player does grow from the coach's influence on him.

At times, players and coaches can grow very close and the separation can be a challenge for many. He thought back to his time here at school. There were many coaches that came and went, even just in his five years here. Some of the coaches seemed to be happy about moving on, while others had an emotionally draining departure. This was the pure business side of the game. When a coach was offered a better job, he took it. His loyalty didn't lie with his players or the school, just himself.

Charlie was lucky and had the same head coach and position coach for five years. Some of his teammates had gone through a new position coach almost every year. Getting used to a new style of coaching and new techniques was always a challenge. Some of his friends from other universities had had many head coaches. This was a special challenge because the whole team would be completely redone in the new coach's vision. Each player would have to learn an entirely new system.

One of the hard parts about changing coaches, even position coaches, was that some of the players might have made their decisions about going to a certain school based on coaches. When that certain coach left, everything changed. During recruiting, coaches will say almost anything to get a player to commit. But when a player meets his probable position coach, his decision is greatly affected. If he gets along well with the coach and feels like he would enjoy his time working with that coach, then his decision can easily be swung one way or the other. It is similar to having a boss who one would work closely with every day.

When the coach suddenly leaves to take another job, the chemistry, situation, and personal interactions are all at an end.

For some players, it might be a happy time when a coach that they don't get along with leaves.

While for many others, it is a tough time. Some players even feel like they are losing a father figure, almost like they are being abandoned. They feel let down because they gave everything they had to that coach, to his philosophy, to his style. Many times they might even play harder just for that coach. One might feel a love and closeness to a certain coach and if he leaves one can feel deceived, almost feeling like, 'how could he do this? I have given him everything. I thought we were a team. Now he is just going to go and say the same things to another bunch of guys. Where's the loyalty in that?'

All of these thoughts blurred through Charlie's head. He looked at the clock and realized it was already time to go to bed. He had to get up for class tomorrow and he needed to feel good for the rest of the week. They had a big game this week and Charlie needed to be at his best. His team would be counting on him and he was counting on himself.

Power Trip

As Charlie walked to his next class, his already bad mood turned even more sour. The season was quickly going downhill and now he was on his way to Dr. Donovan's class, Health and Society Awareness. Dr. Donovan treated him and Jason badly just because they were football players. This made him begin to ponder the subject of athletes and how they are treated different.

Even teachers and coaches treated a person different if they were an athlete. Charlie recalled some of the interactions he had with various teachers. The majority were supportive towards his situation. He had always approached his teachers on the first day of class and let them know that he was on the football team and that he might miss some classes because of this obligation. They would usually respond in a polite manner and just ask him to keep them informed of when he might be missing classes and they would work things out. This was fine and sure seemed fair, as long as it was applied to everyone. After all, wasn't he in college to study and learn? Why should the teachers care if he was playing sports?

It didn't seem like special concessions should be made just to accommodate a person wanting to pursue something else besides education while attending college. He wondered if these same teachers were as co-operative with people who had other commitments like work, family obligations, and children. His first reaction was that they probably weren't. It seemed like they were more willing to work with athletes, as if sports were more important than class, a job, and even families.

He even had some teachers who were surprised that he was a football player. This would happen when he would get good grades in class, which was the norm for him, and the teacher would wonder if he really was a football player, as if football players didn't have the potential to achieve in the classroom as well.

This happened on numerous occasions, but one particular occurrence stood out in his memory. Charlie's Chemistry teacher was surprised when he did so well in her class. The final for the class was an essay. Charlie was already acing the class and he nailed the last paper with a high mark. At the end of the paper were encouraging remarks including, "Are you sure you are a football player? You did great in the class." This was super nice and Charlie took it as a compliment. It also left him wondering, wasn't everyone capable of this and shouldn't all students be held to the same standard regardless of their sports abilities? He was curious to know if the teacher would put these comments on everyone's paper who scored high or only football players'.

Then there were the teachers who didn't like athletes and carried a grudge, probably from past bad experiences. Charlie knew that football players were treated differently and some of the guys carried this into the classroom, expecting teachers to do the same. Players carrying this kind of attitude would clash with certain teachers. Stories of coaches or athletic directors throwing their weight around and keeping a player eligible surely enraged the faculty and made them prone to future judgment upon athletes.

Dr. Donovan was an extreme case. Charlie had never run into a teacher who had been so unwilling to work with him. Charlie had gotten an A on every assignment and test during the class. He still only had an 88%. Class discussions and participation were part of the class grade and since Charlie had missed a few classes he received a 0 for those assignments. Dr. Donovan would not allow Charlie or Jason to do anything to make up for the days they had missed. As a result, even though Charlie obviously had mastery of the content and had done everything asked of him, he still had a B in the course.

As Charlie thought about this, his blood boiled. He was tired of Dr. Donovan's crap. It had even seemed like Dr. Donovan had purposefully scheduled some of the class discussions on Fridays when he knew the football team would be out of town. Of the four graded class discussion, three of them had been on travel days for the football team. Only one of them had been on a Friday when Charlie and Jason could attend. Charlie had offered to write papers, to meet Dr. Donovan during his office hours, or to write up his own questions and answers for the class discussions to try and make up the assignments he missed when traveling. All of these ideas were met with instant refusal.

Charlie arrived at class without a smile and found Jason in their usual spot, at the back near the left side of the big room. They acknowledged each other and got their notebooks out, readying themselves for the start of class.

A few moments later Dr. Donovan entered the class, dimmed the lights, and began his lecture. He never greeted the class or talked to them about the forthcoming lesson. Instead he always began class as if this 100 level class was beneath him.

Dr. Donovan began lecturing about society's overt obsession with celebrities and how this affects mental health. He talked about the problem of media in our current society and how this only increased the ego of the already famous celebrities. Very quickly the lecture turned into a pointed criticism of athletes.

"Athletes tend to be the worst offenders. They are treated as special by the media and this filters down and they feel like they should be treated as special by everyone. They walk around with their heads held high, like they are some sort of royalty. I have noticed that football, basketball, and baseball players tend have the biggest egos. They seem to need their egos massaged on a regular basis. They make comments and statements just to get in the paper or on the news, and then complain that they don't make enough money, or aren't getting enough attention for their efforts. They want the spotlight on themselves and need to feel superior to the rest of us. This is probably because of the tremendous spotlight that is put on sports, and…"

"Excuse me," Charlie interrupted, as polite as possible. These might have been valid points, but he wanted to stand up for himself and didn't feel like such a judgment was necessary from the professor. He was pissed off because of how the season was going and he was already mad at Dr. Donovan for his complete lack of willingness to compromise. He wasn't going to let him pass judgment about him in front of the entire class.

"Yes," Dr. Donovan smugly replied, as if his insistence on being called Dr. wasn't a need to have his ego massaged.

"Well, I am not sure all football players are like that. My friend here, Jason, is one of the most humble people I know and he doesn't like it when he receives special treatment," Charlie countered back, pointing to his friend sitting next to him, who seemed to have been upset, as well, before he heard Charlie interrupt the teacher. "It seems judgmental and not completely true to just lump one group of people into a category, especially one with a negative label."

"I see your point, but actions seem to justify my grouping and labeling. When I see something different my opinion might change," Dr. Donovan quipped back abruptly.

This got Charlie a little heated and with his next comment he might have gone too far, "So, I guess it would be fair to say that all college professors teach only because they love the sound of their voice so much and don't care to hear what others have to think about a certain topic or subject."

"That seems a little bit of a stretch. Charlie, is it? Thank you for the opposing viewpoint. I am sure we are all enlightened because of it. Now, let's move on. The media seems to...."

With that Charlie zoned out for the rest of the class. *What an asshole,* he thought, *his wife probably made him a cuckold by fucking a football player.*

During the rest of the class that day Charlie daydreamed about his own ideas. He didn't want to listen to someone degrade him. Yet he did realize that coaches and administrators often seemed to treat athletes differently. Sure they had a full load with playing a college sport and going to school, but the standards set by coaches and administrators for eligibility seemed to be the bare minimum. In order to be eligible a player only needed a 2.0 GPA and to pass 24 credit hours a year. That could be done with the slightest bit of effort. Any coach who ever said academics came first was just throwing out a line of bull shit, probably to a player's parents in the hopes that they might be prone to encourage their son to play on his team.

Being treated as special because of an athletic skill and talent seemed strange to Charlie. Sure, not everyone could do it, but there were plenty of other skills he couldn't do. His particular skill could even lead to fame and fortune, no wonder so many people pursued it. All of that for mastering a skill that was part of a game. With all the other skills and talents out there, even though many weren't the amount of importance being placed on sports and athletics seemed out of proportion. Athletes were as well-known as any other people out there and given immediate celebrity status and credibility for their skill.

It made Charlie think of what Charles Barkley once said. "I'm not a role model." Whether or not athletes wanted to be, they were role models that is true enough. However, why should this be the case? They are given this position by society for one reason, because they are able to play a game very well. That didn't seem like enough reason to admire a person. Charlie knew plenty of football players that were assholes that he didn't admire, like, or even respect as people. Yet the kids wanted to be like that athlete when they grew up. Well, he sure hoped that future generations would aim higher than that. It seemed like there was more to life than sports, although what it was he didn't know.

At times it was hard for an athlete not to feel different and like they were special. After all, they were treated differently and better only because they were athletes. They had someone to wash their uniforms and practice clothes for them. Each weekend thousands of people paid money to come and watch them play, yelling and cheering for three hours. Their names and pictures appeared in the newspaper on a regular basis.

When they traveled it was first class, on private, chartered planes with no check in and service any time. For their away games they stayed in nice hotels that they would not have been able to afford on their own dime with a king size bed for each player. Dinners, breakfasts, and lunches were given on a grand scale during the weekend. *All this for just playing a game?* Charlie thought to himself. It seemed like only the strong ones could keep this kind of treatment from going to their heads and acting like they were deserving of special treatment.

Charlie realized that Dr. Donovan had some valid points, but he seemed to be going about it with vengeance. Dr. Donovan seemed to think it was the athletes' fault for being treated differently by society. Charlie knew this wasn't the case. If society didn't worship athletes there would be no reason for them feeling like they were special. Plus, Charlie didn't ask for any special treatment. He wanted to be treated the same as everyone else. He put the same effort into his non athletic pursuits as he did his athletic pursuits.

Dr. Donovan was judging Charlie and his friend Jason based on what group they belonged to, not who they were as people. He was presenting disparaging remarks as facts to Charlie's peers and he was stereotyping a group. *Fuck him,* Charlie almost said out loud as the lecture wrapped up.

Straws That Add Up

It had been another tough game, one where victory was within reach, but slipped away again. At times football is a game of bounces, penalties, timing, and energy. Tonight none of these factors had gone the Puma's way. As usual, Charlie had given his best effort and then some, yet he still felt heartbroken at the end result. This was a team game and there was little to be gained from losing, especially during a now five game skid.

Leaning over with his forearms on his thighs, Charlie sat blank faced and without thought. He didn't want to do anything, he was exhausted. Games took all the energy out of Charlie and any reserve that might have been left was depleted by tonight's final score. He had been a poor loser again tonight. After the game he hadn't even acknowledged his opponents' efforts and determination by shaking any of the guys' hands from the other team. Instead, he had opted for a quick retreat into the locker room where he could begin his sulking.

He almost felt like this reaction proved to himself and everyone else how much he cared about the game and winning. He thought that it proved his devotion to the game if he had to immediately leave the scene of his team's latest tragedy.

Staring at the space before him, he didn't want to be interrupted from his sulking yet. With his mouth open his thoughts turned to a brighter picture. This was a home game and his parents had come to watch the game. This meant that he didn't have to endure any quiet plane rides and that he would have his family around to get his mind off of losing. He needed a diversion. Now with five losses in a row he dreaded letting his mind delve into the team's implosion this season. If he began thinking about that, and his role as team captain in his team's lack of success, this would be a miserable night.

His parents came to most of his games every year. These games were always the best games. Having people around who cared about him as a person made losing bearable and winning even more enjoyable. They were his best supporters, usually complimenting him as if he were the world's greatest football player. Having his family around also kept his mind off of the loss and all the "what ifs" that played through his mind and his looking for a way he might have been able to change the outcome. This process drove him crazy and wasn't easy to let go of when he was alone.

Finding meaning again, Charlie came back to the present in the locker room and decided things would be okay. He had found motivation to move again in the upcoming meeting with his closest and most meaningful fans. Allowing himself to pout for a moment longer and cool down at the same time, he was beginning to relax. His sweaty shirt clung to him like it was spandex. He still had on his pants. They were so sweaty that it felt like he had jumped into a swimming pool. His once clean pants showed signs of the battle tonight with ground in dirt, grass stains, and a few streaks of blood. Although new this season, his cleats looked like they were bought from a recycled shop.

Charlie finally let his mourning dissipate and stripped down. He put all his dirty clothes in a big nasty pile to be taken to the equipment manager and was glad that he didn't have to wash them. Under the rushing shower water he could already feel the emerging sore spots from tonight's game. It had been a dogfight and Charlie knew he would be paying the price tomorrow morning.

Drying off, Charlie looked around the locker room. There were only a couple of guys left, the same guys always seemed to be the last ones out of the locker room. He let out his first words since the end of the game. "So, what's the plan for tonight, Junior?"

"Oh, party at my place. Come over if you want," Junior answered back without even looking while putting on deodorant.

"Thanks, dude. I might. I'm going to hang out with the fam for a while then we'll see. Great game tonight, man."

"Yeah, you too. Well, I'm out. See ya tonight? You better come by, lots of booze and lots of girls. It's the best way to get over a loss," Junior said with a smirk as he gave Charlie a bro hug.

"All, right. I'll come over. See ya later," Charlie answered back with Junior disappearing out of the locker room.

Charlie slipped on his clothes and noticed he was the last one out again. He shrugged, knowing it would be easier to find his awaiting fans since they would be the last ones waiting around. Leaving the locker room, Charlie scanned the small group still milling around the home team's locker room and made eye contact with his parents. Walking towards them, a reluctant smile showed its presence. Stepping into a big warm caring hug Charlie let his guard down and smiled wholeheartedly at the love he could feel being shared between him and his parents. His eyes welled up with a sense of relief. They wouldn't be judging his or the team's performance. It had been a long day, but now everything seemed fine with himself and the world.

    Charlie felt lonely. After a short dinner, his parents had left for their four hour drive home and Charlie had gone over to Junior's for the party. He wouldn't see Mary tonight, she had to work late and again in the morning. As soon as he had left his parents his mind had gone back to the game. He kept replaying the game in his mind trying to find something that he might have done differently to help change the outcome.

    His team had just lost another game that could have gone either way and he was sitting at a lame party with a bunch of drunken assholes and lame chicks. He had a beer, but he was standing by himself in a corner still moping about the game.

    He grabbed a couple of beers and walked outside. He was tired of talking and needed to get some air. Outside dark rain clouds blocked out any light from the stars and moon. The dreary night seemed to accentuate his dour mood. He began walking down the street with no particular destination in mind. As he walked, he knit picked his entire performance in his head, thinking to himself that there were a few plays that he had screwed up. *If I had made those plays the game might have turned out differently,* he told himself and pounded himself in the chest. *Maybe the leadership on the team hasn't been enough to guide us to the top. I could have done more in the off season, I could have done more during fall camp, I could have done more tonight. I don't know what else to do, I have to be better.*

    Charlie crossed the street to the small neighborhood park that he didn't remember was there until he saw it. He found a bench hidden in the shadows of a bare maple tree and sat down.

He looked up at the clouds and crossed his arms. He took a deep breath and slammed his fist into the bench, "Fuck, I have done everything that I can! I can't do anything else!" he yelled into the stoic night sky. "If I had done enough then we would be winning, not losing," he spoke quietly to himself this time.

He took a long swig of the beer and his eyes welled up. He wiped his right eye as the left eye filled up and spilled down his cheek. *I don't know what the fuck to do. I want to be a good leader, but I just can't take it anymore. I don't even know if I care anymore. I can't take this anymore.* The tears flowed freely with these thoughts. He didn't want it to be like this, breaking down in a dark park by himself. He was glad that nobody else would see him like this. He couldn't believe that he was crying like this. *Quit being a baby,* he told himself.

He had even risked his health for all of this shit. He had been throwing up in his mouth during the last few games and then swallowing it so that Rod wouldn't see him and force him to see Dr. White again. Or he would throw up in a cup while acting like he was drinking at the far end of the sideline and putting it in the garbage can himself so that nobody knew what was going on.

The symptoms hadn't gotten better all season. They had either stayed the same or been worse each game. He was tired of this crap. *What the hell am I risking this for? Nobody else is putting this much effort into the games or the team. Maybe going back to Dr. White would be an easy way out of this. No, you can't do that. I've got to get this off of my mind. FUCK!!! This is way too much. I can't take this anymore!!!!!!!!*

On top of everything, the stress of possible NCAA sanctions had been in the back of his mind all season long. Ever since being confronted by Coach Jackson about the extra money for the yard work he felt like he had been walking on eggshells, waiting for the gig to be up. Every time he saw Coach Jackson in the football office he wondered if that was going to be the day he would be told his college career was done. It was too much stress. He didn't know where to turn. *I just want it all to be done!!!!!!*

He sniffed hard and wiped away the tears. *Fuck this, I don't even care anymore. I am just going to do what I want and not worry so much about football. I can't be the only one caring this much. Fuck this team and fuck this season.* As he thought this, his mind twitched a little bit, he was feeling that inevitable tug of cognitive dissonance. Unconsciously he knew that he was lying to himself, but this is all he could do tonight, the pressure had broken him.

I'm tired of being the leader, the one people look to. I don't want that anymore. I'm tired of being the one everyone expects to have the answers. I'm tired of being nice. I'm tired of being perfect. I'm tired of being the one who works the hardest. I'm tired of being the one who cares the most. I'm tired of doing what I am supposed to do. I want to do nothing, I want to do everything. I don't want to always worry about doing what is right and what is best for the team. I'm tired of people looking at me and expecting me to be a role model. I'm just a dude, I'm just a guy. I want to be just a guy, I don't want to be the man anymore!

He knew that none of this was true and that all of it was true. He had to get it out and he couldn't let it out to someone else, he had to be the one who had it all together. He had to be THE BEST. Well, he didn't want to be the best right now. He didn't know if he wanted to be the best anymore. His spirit was broken, he had to do something, something different. He couldn't keep going like this.

He didn't enjoy feeling like this. There were only two options, escaping everything he was and going against it or facing his demons. He wasn't strong enough right now to stand up to his inner battle. He was going to run from it and hope to leave it behind him. He fought against this idea for a moment, but the easy route won.

He felt the anchor of that cognitive dissonance and drained the rest of a beer, hoping that might put his mind at ease. *Fuck this, I really don't care tonight. I don't care what happens tonight, tomorrow, or the rest of the week.* "FUCK IT!!!" He threw his beer can at the stark tree and began walking back to the party.

He threw open the door upon arriving and walked straight to the kitchen. He didn't even acknowledge the people who said hi to him. He looked for a bottle of alcohol and opened the first one that he found. He popped off the top and took a big gulp. It burned all the way down his throat and he had to shake his head in disgust once he got the fire liquid down.

He saw Johnny approaching from the corner of his eye. He was glad it was Johnny, he didn't feel like talking to anyone else. "Hey dude, quit being all depressed about the game. Yeah, we lost, but it is not the end of the world. It doesn't mean you can't have fun and smile." Johnny paused to see if any of this would have an effect on his solemn faced buddy standing next to him.

Charlie, slowly turning his head in Johnny's direction, gave him a look of indifference. "Yeah, I know. I am just sick of losing. I wanted this season to be different. I have always dreamed of a championship and now that is not a possibility."

"Well, this season has been different. We have done better than most people thought we would. Anyways, dwelling on it won't do any good. You are just beating yourself up and ruining any chance of fun for tonight. Get over it and join the party. If you don't then I am going to have to kick your ass." With that, Johnny opened another beer and handed it to Charlie. "I want to see you pound that whole beer and then give me a big smile when you are done. Or, are you a puss?...Huh, motha fucka?" Johnny said, trying to act serious, raising his can in the air. "Here's to us and getting some pussy tonight. See those ladies over there? They have been staring at you since you came back. Let's go see what we can do."

"All, right, here's to two bad asses," Charlie said, finally showing some life. He raised his can and started chugging it. The cold liquid felt good running down his throat. He had plenty of practice drinking beer and didn't have much trouble finishing the whole can. The foam began to outrace his gulps and built up in his mouth. The last gulp didn't quite get all the way down and some of the liquid escaped his mouth cascading on his shirt. Rubbing it in (this would be tonight's cologne) he saw Johnny finishing his beer and leaving a few of his own suds on his shirt. Once they were both done he gave Johnny a big smile and admitted to him, "Thanks, I needed that. Let's go have fun and forget about fucking football for a while. Those chicks do look pretty good."

"Now that is what I am talking about," Johnny let out with enthusiasm, putting his arm around Charlie and escorting him to the next room where the lady situation seemed promising and the music was blasting.

It was a typical after game party. The mood wasn't as good as if they had won, but most people seemed to be drinking their worries away. It was a big house that nobody attending college could afford, but was subsidized by Junior's rich parents. It was always dirty, no matter how many hours were put in to cleaning the house. The only time it would ever be spotless again would be when the football players moved out and professionals came in and took over for an afternoon.

There always seemed to be a smell of beer coming from the basement, no matter how long it had been since the last party. Walls were filled with typical male college posters, flaunting the latest swimsuit models from Sports Illustrated or Playboy and plenty of beer posters displaying the beverage of choice at this house. The basement had one bedroom and a big undecorated room. It had a bathroom with a toilet that looked like it hadn't been cleaned since it had been installed, an ever present keg, whether it was filled or not, a stereo, and couches that seemed like they had been passed down for generations lining the walls. It was the perfect college party house.

As Charlie and Johnny approached the girls, Charlie recognized them. They were at most of the parties and Charlie occasionally saw them around campus. One of them liked to flirt with Charlie. She had tried to hook up with him earlier in the season. As soon as their eyes met Charlie knew that they would be hooking up tonight. The only obstacle that he could sense was that he couldn't remember her name at the moment.

"Hey ladies," Johnny opened up when they were close enough to talk to the girls.

The group of four girls all turned towards Johnny and Charlie and said in unison, "Hey guys."

In a sarcastic tone, one of them piped up, "What took you guys so long? We have been waiting for you to come talk to us all night."

"Oh, we've been busy. We have people to talk to and

things to do. We can't limit ourselves to just one group," Johnny quipped back.

The flirting between this girl and Johnny had already begun. The mates for the night had already been decided. The group of girls made space for the two football players. Charlie moved closer to the girl that he knew would be his tonight. With more forwardness than was appropriate, Charlie put his hand around her waist as they joined the girls' circle. Her eyes showed a sense of welcome surprise.

She had been hitting on him for two years now, but it had always been one sided. Now he was the one going after her. Her eyes lit up with excitement and she returned the gesture, putting her arm around the small of his back and pulling herself close to him. They were close enough to kiss.

Her friends couldn't hide their look of surprise. They knew she wanted Charlie, but they didn't think she had a chance. He had shot her down in the past because he had a girlfriend and they didn't think tonight would be any different. The night seemed to be taking an interesting turn.

"Hey Charlie," she let out, almost embarrassed that they were so close, yet not pulling away. Her eyes told him that he could kiss her now if he wanted to.

"Hey, how are you girls doing tonight?" Charlie replied, finally looking away from her towards the other girls and Johnny. He loosened his grip on the small of her back, but didn't let go of her.

"Good," they replied, with the one next to Charlie beaming with pride at the level of interest Charlie was showing her.

Johnny met Charlie's eyes. His brow was raised and he gave Charlie a surprised look. Charlie gave him a smirk and raised his eyebrow. Johnny could barely contain himself. He didn't really think Charlie would go this far. Charlie always played things safe and had never cheated on Mary.

Everyone at the party knew Charlie and Mary were together. Johnny had always tried to get Charlie to hit on the ladies with him, but Charlie had never taken it to this level. Johnny was glad to see Charlie let it all out. He knew that

Charlie had been stressed about the season and that he needed a release, maybe this would do it.

After an awkward silence, Johnny knew that Charlie wasn't going to introduce him to any of the girls and Johnny had forgotten all of their names, so he did the only thing that could save them both. "I'm Johnny and this is Charlie. What are your names again?" Even though he had already been flirting with one of the girls and Charlie had made his intentions known, he said this totally unabashed.

The one that had been flirting with Johnny started out, "I'm Mikaela. You better remember that. I always talk to you at these parties."

"I know, sorry, it must have been the hits that I took tonight," Johnny defended himself as he touched her shoulder in reassurance.

"I'm Amber," the next girl chimed in.

"I'm Suzzy."

"And I'm Kristin," the girl still being held by Charlie said with a smile.

Charlie was glad that Johnny saved him from any embarrassment of having to ask her name. He noticed that her keg cup was empty. "You want to go get another beer?"

She looked back at her friends and didn't see any protesting looks from them. "Sure, let's go get one."

He turned and grabbed her hand to follow him. He surprised himself at how forward he was acting. They walked down to the keg and Charlie saw Anthony serving beers. "Hey, dude, hook me up with two." Charlie handed him the two cups.

Anthony filled them up and handed them back to Charlie before he noticed that he was holding a girl's hand that wasn't Mary's. He gave him a surprised look. "Here you go, bro." After Charlie passed Kristin her cup, Anthony held his hand out for a five. Charlie grabbed it and gave Anthony a bro hug. "Have fun tonight," Anthony whispered in his ear mischievously.

Charlie grinned back at him and said loud enough for Kristin to hear, "I sure will." He put his arm around her again and led her out of the crowded beer area and back upstairs. When they were in an uncrowded room, Charlie stopped and sat down on a couch. She followed him, but didn't sit as close as they had been walking together.

He held his cup up and she tapped it with hers. They both took a big drink of the cold brew. "So, Kristin, you having fun?"

She gave him a confused look and took another drink before answering. "I sure am, how about you?"

"I'm feeling much better. This beer and a pretty girl sure are helping."

Her face grew warm and she turned away for a moment, smiling at Amber and Suzzy who had started making their own rounds of the party after she had paired up with Charlie and Mikaela had paired up with Johnny. "Well, I'm glad you're feeling better. That was a tough game tonight. You sure played hard. I always watch you when I go to the games. You look sexy in football pants." She rubbed his shoulder.

"Thanks, it was a tough game. Wow, if someone is watching me in my pants I better make sure that I look good."

"Don't worry, I don't think that will be a problem." They both took another drink. She was almost giddy about the attention he was paying her tonight, but she felt a tinge of unease. She was worried that her concern might ruin the moment, but she decided to be bold. "I'm always trying to flirt with you, but you always shoot me down. Are you single now?"

Charlie was shocked at the question, but tried to stay calm. He felt guilty about what he was doing tonight, but he didn't want to be confronted with this uncomfortable truth. "Let's not worry about that anymore tonight, or football, okay?" He smiled at her and again could feel his mind pulling itself in opposite directions. His cognitive dissonance would not leave him alone tonight. *I told myself I don't care about anything tonight,* he repeated in his mind, trying to convince himself.

He did the only thing he could think of to alleviate his hypocrisy. He put his hand on Kristin's neck and leaned towards her. She reached up to meet his lips. Their lips and tongues moved back and forth with each other. She reciprocated with all her lust that she had been feeling for him over the past two years. They were engrossed with each other. They didn't care that the entire room was watching them. Kristin could barely keep herself under control. She moved to straddle him before she remembered they were in a large room at a party with everyone around. She finally stopped and pulled away.

"Wow," she said. "I wasn't expecting that. That was fun." She took the rest of her beer down in a big gulp.

"Let's go get another beer," Charlie said after finishing the rest of his.

They roamed the party for a couple of hours as if they were a couple. Any time they found themselves in a corner or a secluded part of the house their mouths found each other and they exchanged copious amounts of saliva. Each time they got more and more worked up, they both knew what was going to happen tonight.

After an indeterminate number of beers, Charlie pulled her close to him and whispered in her ear, "Let's get out of here."

She didn't need any more nudging or suggestions. She reached for his hand and led him to the door. Once outside, he pointed to his truck and she led the way as if she were in a hurry. He started his truck and was glad that he only had to drive a few blocks to his house. "You wanna go to my place?"

"I sure do, Charlie." Before he could pull away she was kissing him again. Now that they were alone she let her hands wander. Before he got too excited, Charlie pulled his head away and put the truck in drive.

"Well, let's go then." He smiled and drove unsteadily home.

They shared their young lust for each other into the early hours of the morning.

He wasn't someone who cheated on his girlfriend, but last night he had just let the party take him where it would. He had just gone with the flow and this is where it had led him. The sun was now up and making its presence known through the crack in the curtains. The sex had been awesome. She did have a lustful body, he took note as she lay there with a blanket barely covering her nakedness. He contemplated enjoying it again.

This was a good sign, it was bad when beer goggles helped make more of an impression than one might be worth. He wasn't nervous about getting caught. His girlfriend didn't get off until after noon, and it was only ten in the morning. They had planned to meet at his place after practice and she probably wouldn't pull a stop by without calling first. She knew he had practice at two o'clock and that he often went to the library before going to practice on Sunday.

He felt a little bad because he really did like Mary. At times he even thought he loved her. B*ut what she didn't know couldn't hurt her*, he thought. He was shocked at himself for feeling so indifferent. He felt emotionally numb right now. He remembered the scene at the park last night and realized how he had decided to throw all his cares out of the window for the time being.

It was the first time he had cheated on Mary. He didn't feel elation or guilt. The only thing he felt was a little annoyance. He just wanted this young, hot girl to leave. They didn't have anything to talk about. They had both just wanted to get laid and had achieved that goal. Now, it was just an awkward situation. He was even having trouble remembering her name. *Oh shit,* he thought, *how am I supposed to wake her up and tell her I have to leave if I can't even remember her name? Think you idiot,… what is it? Mmmmmmm…oh, yeah, Kristin.*

Thinking up the first lame excuse he could think of, he nudged her naked body. "Mmmmmhhhhh," was the only sound that made it through her alcohol induced stupor. "Hey, I know it is early, but I have to get going. I have to go to the library to get some books before I go to practice. So, you need to get up. Sorry, but I need to get going."

"Okay…just a minute," she replied through her haze of a voice. He got out of bed and found his underwear near the bedroom door. Slipping them on, he went to the bathroom and let out all of last night's poison that his body was still holding.

Coming back into his room he saw Kristin searching for her remaining clothes. She was bent over with her bare ass still showing. *Wow, she is hot. Too bad I got her up so fast. It would have been nice to have some more fun before making her leave,* Charlie thought to himself while staring at her sculpted form. Noticing him checking her out she became a little self-conscious of her complete nudity, but was too hung over to care for more than an instant.

Trying to hide the awkwardness of the situation he smiled and tried to be nice. "So, how are you doing? I am not doing very good. I think we both drank too much last night and stayed up way too late. I had fun, though. I'm glad we ran into each other last night," he said as honestly and politely as possible.

"Yeah, I don't feel very good, either. It was fun last night. You are a stud on and off the field," she blurted out and blushed realizing what she had said. "I guess I probably won't see you very much more, though. I know you have a girlfriend and that the only reason you took me home last night was because she wasn't there."

He hadn't given this girl enough credit. Not really knowing what to say to that kind of directness, he just sat there in silence for a moment. Watching her dress, she finally looked over at him while slipping on the last of her clothes, realizing he felt uncomfortable about her honesty. "Well…," he stammered, "probably not. I feel kind of bad about cheating on her. I think this will be a one time thing."

Without protest or disappointment, she walked over to him and gave him a big kiss on the lips. "Don't worry, I didn't expect anything more. I have had a crush on you since I saw you for the first time over two years ago. I just had to get with you, at least once. I won't tell anyone, it can be our little X-rated secret. After all, it was an X-rated evening. I enjoyed it and it sure seemed like you did." She grabbed his hand, displaying way too much self-confidence for someone who had just been used for a one night stand. "You have to give me a ride. Let's go, I know you are in a hurry."

Driving faster than normal and feeling paranoid as he didn't want to be seen leaving his apartment with a strange girl, he got to her house as fast as possible. Charlie realized his emotions were coming back, he didn't know if he liked it.

The drive to her house wasn't unbearable, just one they both knew would be better if it ended sooner rather than later. The conversation was actually pretty nice. Part of this seemed to be due to the fact that they had both been honest and knew that nothing was going to come of this. They didn't have to try and impress one another.

Arriving at her house, she leaned over and gave him a big, long kiss that didn't lack passion from either person. Letting the moment linger, neither one pulled away. Finally, they were startled back into reality by a passing car and they quickly pulled back from one another. "Well, if you are ever single you know where I live. Consider it an open invitation."

Charlie just looked at her for a moment. He could feel the guilty emotions trying to creep into his conscience. He normally did the right thing. He prided himself on being a good person. He pushed these thoughts back down. *Remember right now you don't care. This might be something I want to continue, or try to pull off again. I kind of like this not caring thing.* "Why don't you leave me your number, then? I like having an open invitation." He gave her a half smile.

She hesitated for a minute, confused at his about face, but not caring because she would love to see him again. "Sure, I am glad to know that some of these feelings are mutual." Charlie just smiled and nodded. She dug through her purse, found a pen, and jotted her number on the back of a receipt that she examined before writing on. "I hope you call me, sooner rather than later." She leaned over the front seat and into his face, she slipped the paper into his short's pocket as if they were already an item. Her hand lingered longer than necessary. She gave him another kiss then abruptly made her way across the front seat and opened the door with confidence. "I hope you call me." She smiled and hopped out of the truck trotting for the door, looking better than she should have with the huge hangover that was raging inside of her.

Charlie started back for his apartment. He didn't have anywhere to be for a while. He didn't need to be at the stadium for practice until 2:00. A shower was in order. He didn't want himself or his apartment to smell like another girl when Mary came over after practice. That would be a bad situation. Before getting in the shower, he changed his sheets and put the old ones in the dirty clothes to get rid of any other evidence that might implicate him. He just hoped Kristin wasn't a blabber mouth. The football guys at the party were the only ones who knew on Charlie's end, but they wouldn't say anything.

With the flow of hot water touching his body, his mind quickly forgot about Kristin and he was brought back to the world of football as he felt soreness over his entire body. Getting drunk and getting laid into the early hours of the morning sure wasn't going to help his healing process. He knew he couldn't do this late night partying much more. He had to be at practice soon. It wasn't going to be a very productive practice for Charlie today and he felt disappointed that he wouldn't be in his best form. But then he thought of his new mantra from last night. *Fuck it, I don't care. If the other guys don't care, why should I? I just don't want to be sick at practice. I just have to make it through, then maybe I will call Kristin again. That sure was fun last night.* He realized he would make it through practice somehow, he always did. He relaxed a little bit. He didn't feel happy.

After a shower Charlie took his sheets and clothes from last night to the Laundromat. He dozed off while getting the smell of last night's escapade washed away. He still felt numb emotionally. He didn't know if it was from his new attitude or from his paralyzing hangover. When he got home he saw that the message light was blinking on his machine. He knew it was Mary and dreaded what was coming.

Charlie pushed play and listened to the message. Her voice was sweet and caring, just like it always was. She never really asked much of him and didn't deserve to be lied to. She had always been nice to him. They still didn't call what they had "love" and avoided talking about their future together. They were both too afraid to tell the other person that they wanted to stay together after college. That meant a long term commitment, something both of them were afraid to think about. They had a great relationship with each other and neither one wanted it to end.

With the end of the message Charlie felt a stab of pain in his chest. He hadn't realized it would be like this and he almost wished he hadn't done it. Not that he had gone to a lot of effort to deceive her, just the fact that she didn't suspect anything and nothing had changed in her mind.

He picked up the cordless phone, walked into his small bedroom, and collapsed spread eagle on his bed with the phone in one hand. Laying down and allowing his body to relax Charlie felt his soreness and tiredness overwhelming him. It had been a tough game last night and he had stayed up too late pursuing extracurricular activities. He could already tell that this was going to be a dilemma that he would prefer not to think about. He didn't want to be bothered with morals.

He decided, for now, to keep it to himself. Holding the phone in his field of vision, he dialed her number without really thinking. It was more just a pattern of where the numbers happen to be arranged on the phone.

"Hey, how's it going?" Charlie asked, forcing himself to act as if everything were fine as he recognized Mary's voice picking up the other line.

"Oh, I'm good. Just doing some studying. Too much work, late night, and then I had to turn around and do it again this morning. But tips were good, so I guess it was all right. How are you doing? I heard it was another close loss last night," she said with sympathy.

"Oh, I'm okay. Yeah, it was a tough loss. I am just hanging out. I might try to take a nap before I have to go to practice."

"Cool, you sure you're all right? You sound a little strange."

"Oh…yeah. I'm just tired. I drank too much last night, too. Plus, I am trying to get motivated to study for a quiz tomorrow. I am not excited about that."

"Yeah, that sucks. I wanted to invite you somewhere tonight. My parents are going to be driving through town and they are going to take me out to dinner. They wanted me to invite you, as well. They said we could wait for you to finish practice and then go out. But, if you are too tired, don't worry about it. There will be plenty of other times."

"Well…" Charlie hesitated, trying to act like he was really contemplating it. He couldn't go out with her and her parents the evening after he had cheated on her. He felt like it would be an even bigger betrayal. He wanted to tell her before facing her family. This was going to make it even more difficult.

He liked her family and they liked him. He knew there was no way he could face her family tonight with any amount of respect. "I would really love to come babe, but I am really tired, practice might be long today, and I want to study a little bit. I really just want to relax a little and try to feel better for Monday and the start of the week. Please tell your parents sorry and I want to come next time."

"Okay, don't worry. I told them you probably wouldn't be able to come anyway. They will be excited to see you any time. Is it okay if I come over for a little bit after dinner? I would like to see you. I didn't get a chance to see you last night or today yet," she asked wholeheartedly and with complete innocence.

Hesitating longer than normal, Charlie blurted out his answer trying to diminish any worries on her part that something might be wrong. "Oh yeah, that is fine. Just come over when you are done. I will see you later tonight."

"Okay, see you soon." Charlie could almost hear her smile and excitement coming through the receiver.

"See you later," Charlie said, pressing the button to end the call. He felt another stab of pain knowing this issue would be pressed to the forefront and that he would have to hurt her. This was the one thing he had always wanted to avoid, being the source of her pain. She would now view him as just another football player, something he had always strived to be more than.

Duplicity

Charlie jerked awake and looked at the clock. 1:40. "Oh, shit," he said out loud. He jumped out of bed and hurried out to his truck. Practice started in twenty minutes. He didn't even have time to brush his teeth. The aching in his head from too much alcohol had been muted by his nap, but he still felt a numbness over his body that was foreign to him.

He got to practice in no mood to do anything and forced himself through the exercises. He didn't talk or make any attempts at being a leader today. He did what he was told, but without emotion and without his full effort. He felt like a fake going through practice like this. But he felt broken, like he couldn't be what he had been before. It had taken too much out of him and it hadn't worked.

At the meeting he listened with one ear. He didn't take notes and barely talked to any of the guys. The entire mood of the team seemed to be somber. The guys looked to him for guidance and when they saw lethargy they followed his lead.

As he was getting ready to leave the meeting room Coach Jackson called out, "Charlie, I need you to stay behind. I need to talk to you in my office."

Charlie's shoulders slumped. His body language was easy to read, he did not want to talk. Instead of standing to wait, Charlie sat down in a chair near the back exit and waited for Coach Jackson.

Coach Jackson gathered up his folders and spoke to some of the coaching staff members. Charlie could overhear him telling the staff to start the meeting and that he would be there after he talked to Charlie.

Coach Jackson looked at Charlie as he walked towards the exit. Seeing his negative body language his face grew stern. "Get up and let's go!" he snapped at Charlie.

This startled Charlie back to reality. He realized that he was moping around like a child. He followed Coach Jackson out of the door and down the hall to the football office. The other coaches were already filing into the conference room while Charlie and Coach Jackson walked into his private office.

"Close the door behind you," he said without looking back. Coach Jackson made his way behind his desk and motioned for Charlie to sit down. He put his hand on his chin and moved his finger up and down. Charlie could see that Coach Jackson wasn't feeling well, either. His eyes were bright red, his stubble was showing itself, and his hair looked like he hadn't taken a shower today.

Coach Jackson looked up from his folder and glared at Charlie. Charlie immediately felt uncomfortable. Coach Jackson let the tension continue. Charlie began to squirm a little bit in his chair. Coach Jackson put both of his hands on the table. "What the hell is your deal?"

Charlie didn't know what to say. He hadn't expected to be called out. He knew what Coach Jackson was talking about, but he didn't want to admit it. "What do you mean?"

Coach Jackson struck back instantly. "Don't give me that shit, Charlie. I made sure your impropriety went away and that there were no NCAA sanctions. You are too mature to act like a child. Plus, we have a good relationship and have gotten along for five years, so don't go there."

Charlie had to look away from his eyes to gather his thoughts. He was hoping he wouldn't have to speak up, but Coach Jackson kept silent waiting for him. "I don't know Coach. I just wasn't feeling it today. I'll be better tomorrow."

Coach Jackson let the air grow tense again. "I sure hope so, Charlie. You might not understand this, but the team is only going to go as far as you take it. I know the losing sucks, but winning will take care of itself. We have two games left and the team needs you now more than ever. Quit feeling sorry for yourself and get back to your old self. If you end the season like this you will regret it for the rest of your life. I have other seasons to coach, I have other teams to coach. Even if we lose these last two games and I get fired I have another shot. This is your team, Charlie. This is your last chance. Do you want it to end like this? Do you want your college football career to end with you giving up and giving in to losing? After all this work and you are willing to go out like this? You're not a quitter, you never have been, don't start now. You'll regret it the rest of your life, Charlie."

It felt like Coach Jackson's eyes were piercing his soul. Charlie shook his head. "I don't either, Charlie. I don't want it to end like that for you. Now, go home and get some sleep. I'm counting on you. Your team is counting on you and you need to count on yourself. Come back tomorrow with your old attitude."

Charlie shook his head in affirmation. Coach Jackson continued to look at him. He didn't know what to say or do. After an awkward moment he got up to leave. "Okay, Coach," Charlie said as he got up and left the office.

Coach Jackson's glare followed him to the door. "I hope so Charlie, for everyone's sake. I hope so, Charlie."

Charlie walked back to his truck with his head down. He felt like a child. He didn't feel like the strong, confident young man he was just a day ago. He felt defeated. He knew that everything Coach Jackson had said to him was true, but that didn't help. He couldn't take the burden and the responsibility right now. It was too much for him. Maybe he would quit, maybe he didn't care if his career ended on a losing note.

He got in his truck and put his hands on the steering wheel. He took a deep breath and put his forehead between his hands. He started to cry. He couldn't face all of this right now. The season was going to be a bust if he didn't change his attitude, and his relationship with Mary was probably over. He didn't want that, he loved her. He liked her. He didn't know which one it was, but he knew that he didn't want her to break up with him. This was too much for him. He felt like he was going to explode. He had to forget about everything. He couldn't handle the stress right now.

He wiped off his cheeks and drove to the convenience store. He picked up a frozen pizza and a case of beer. Alcohol was the only way to get his mind off of everything. He reminded himself of his new attitude, *I DON'T GIVE A FUCK!!!*

He got home and cracked a beer. The first one didn't go down well, his stomach was still upset from the overindulgence of the previous night. After two beers he had a buzz and the alcohol didn't disagree with him anymore.

He ate pizza and drank his mind into a blank.

Obsession

 Blake came home to a dark house again. He was beginning to get tired of coming home to a house with the lights off and no food thoughtfully left for him. It wasn't very welcoming or homey. He barely gave it a second thought. His mind was elsewhere. He was still thinking about the game plan for the upcoming game, trying to run through all the possibilities and probabilities that they might encounter. This was an endless mind game, but not one he could let go of at this moment, not at the most important time of the season. They had to win these last two games to have a winning record. If they didn't have a winning record, the entire staff might be out of a job.

 The pressure on him was immense, it built almost every day, it was burying him, it consumed him, it was the only thing he could think about. Right now it was the only thing he cared about. The upcoming two contests could cement his future or leave it in doubt. He wanted to show his ability by having two great defensive performances to end the season. This would shut the door on any doubts about his permanent position as defensive coordinator with this coaching staff until it was time to move up to a head coaching spot.

 Fumbling through the key ring, he located the one he was looking for. Prodding for the hole, his mind was brought back to his family life. He hadn't been able to give much thought to his family lately. They had taken a back seat to football. He knew this wasn't going to be a one season thing, either. If he was going to stay competitive and continue to improve his prospects for moving up the coaching ladder, the game would become even more demanding. This wasn't how he pictured his family ending up, but he was pursuing his dream, he was doing what he loved. If his family couldn't accept that, then they couldn't accept him.

 He knew this wasn't the life his wife had wanted and dreamed of. They had always wanted to stay close and be each other's priority. Things had changed on his end. He hadn't foreseen this path unfolding before him. He thought football was just a game that could be a way to make money, doing something he loved and getting paid for it. As the opportunities got bigger and the stakes higher, football consumed more and more of his life.

Opening the door there was only one dim light that he could see coming from his bedroom. Suddenly he remembered that he was supposed to be home tonight. April had made another appointment with a counselor and the counselor had even agreed to make a house call. He had promised he would be home at 7:00 and now it was 8:30. It seemed feasible at the time, but the meeting tonight was tense. Everybody knew the stakes of these last two games. They had gone over everything three times before coming to a decision.

The night's meal used to be caringly wrapped for him when he came home late. Now he was lucky to have a sandwich waiting for him. Opening the fridge door, the light sprung out into the dark kitchen which was unusually clean. Perhaps April had done some extra cleaning in anticipation of the counselor's appointment. It looked beautiful.

He now knew that he was in the dog house. If she had gone to this amount of trouble, then it must have been super important to her. To help him brave this difficult situation, he grabbed a beer from the door and immediately downed half of it. The only thing ready to eat was a leftover chicken breast, not the most appetizing meal, being cold and without any sauce, but he could eat anything at this point.

He closed the door and headed off to the only other source of light in the house, not looking forward to this meeting. He knew there would be many too many questions and accusations. This wasn't something he really felt like dealing with tonight. He had other things on his mind. Chewing the cold chicken and taking another big chug of the beer he approached the bedroom with its pale white light streaming freely from the bed lamp. He hoped it would be quick so that he might even have a chance to look at a game tape of this week's opponent that he had brought with him, hoping to gain an insight that might prove effective this week.

Blake broached the corridor of their master bedroom with caution and apprehension. He saw April sitting with her back propped up against the wall reading a book. He used to know what book she was reading. She had probably finished many books since he had even remembered to ask. He briefly thought about the fun chats they used to have about books they were reading. This almost seemed silly to him now with his mind on important matters like winning the game, achieving a goal, not just discussing something that was out of date by the time they had read it.

Pillows were cushioning April's back against the stark white wall behind her. She looked at peace in the soft light coming from the bed side lamp. The light reflected off of one cheek leaving the other in shadow. The shadow being cast accentuated her curves. He noticed how pretty she was. She was still as beautiful as the day they had gotten married. It was a shame he couldn't be around this beautiful woman more often. She would be a catch for any man.

April looked up from her book indifferently, trying to betray the anger and hurt she was feeling. She had been crying for most of the evening, only now being able to clear her mind by becoming lost in her book and trying to forget everything, especially Blake. Without saying a word she stared at him intensely, almost piercing him with her less than friendly gaze. Not wanting to break the silence and let him off the hook she stayed silent, forcing Blake to say the first word.

"Hi honey," he mumbled with a mouth full of chicken. "How are you?" he managed between chews, trying not to show her he could sense her anger and frustration.

A long, uncomfortable silence passed before anything was said. She looked at him, trying to tell him how she was by her demeanor and facial expressions. Finally, after knowing he was completely out of place in the cold silence, she responded, "How am I?...How do you think I am?...I am not very good. I have barely seen you for weeks and you missed the appointment we had for tonight. We really have some things that we need to work on. When we entered into this marriage our first priority was us. Now that is not the case. We can't seem to do it together, so I thought with the help of a third party we might be able to work through some of these things. Now, after a long season, I realize how much time is really going to be given to our relationship. After a long fight with myself I had to accept that things have changed and they aren't going to go back to where they were. I have given a lot to you this season, Blake. I have compromised a lot, made a lot of sacrifices. In a successful relationship there has to be compromises and sacrifices made by both people. I really wanted you to be here tonight. You promised you would."

"I know babe. I just forgot about it. My mind has been really swamped the past few weeks. You know how important these last two games are."

"Your mind has been gone for a long time. I don't think we have had a meaningful conversation for months. When we have a chance to talk, it is just catching up with each other's lives, what is going on with Conner, and financial matters. That isn't much of a partnership."

"I'm sorry, this season has been very busy. This is also the season that is going to put us in a position of security, both career wise and money wise. Plus, this is my dream. I am chasing it and you are helping me get there. I couldn't do it without you." He leaned over and kissed her on the forehead, trying to show that some of this really did have to do with her.

"I know this season has been important and these last two games are especially important. The appointment was also very important. I scheduled it late in the evening and at home with the sole intention that you could be here. I just didn't know how much your priorities had changed," she replied bluntly, fighting back the tears that her heart was trying to push out of her dry tear ducts.

"Well, honey, the season is almost over. Can't it wait for a couple of weeks?"

"We're always waiting. I'm tired of waiting. I wait for the end of recruiting, the end of spring ball, the end of two-a-days, the end of the season. How long can we wait?" she asked with complete honesty.

"I'm giving you everything I can when I am this busy. What more do you want?"

She paused, wondering if he was serious. "….You…."

She continued to look at him as part of the answer to his question. He hadn't been expecting that for an answer. "Okay, just give me some time. When the season is over then we can work on things, we can go to a counselor even once a week if you want to."

"The problems have been piling up, I am not sure how much a counselor is going to help. Then come next August it all starts again. I am not sure if I like having a husband for only seven months out of the year." She looked into his eyes with the pain of a broken heart. It wasn't easy for her to hide. Things had changed and they weren't ever going to go back to how they were before. "I can tell you have other things on your mind. It isn't going to do any good to talk about this if you can't even concentrate," she said, rolling her eyes and looking away from him, almost just trying to silently tell him to get the hell out of there if he wasn't going to give her his full attention and energy.

"See, that is why I love you so much. You are so understanding and unselfish." He gave her a long kiss. There were two pairs of lips touching with only one giving any affection to the other, but he was too busy to notice and wished her a good night on his way to the den to look at the most recent film of this week's opponent.

As his silhouette disappeared into the darkness, April's eyes once again filled with tears. She was exhausted. She had been crying all night and didn't feel like getting into another crying episode right now. With warm, salty drops gently falling down her cheeks she reached to turn off the light and snuggled under the sheets.

Football used to be something that she loved. Now she hated it. She felt like it had taken her husband away from her. Their priority had always been each other, their relationship had come first. Then he took a job at a big university and everything changed. During the season it was like being a widow. The upcoming game was the only thing that seemed to be on his mind. There didn't seem to be anything else that mattered. The few hours that she got to see him each week were such a blur that it didn't even seem like it was long enough to have a conversation. They were lucky to make love more than once a month. He was too busy to give her any attention, even her body. It made her feel like she was becoming unattractive. It was one thing to lose a husband to another prettier, younger woman, but to lose him to a game seemed like an even bigger insult.

Marriages had ups and downs that was something she had expected. The only thing that she had wanted was a partner to share them with. She couldn't talk about the ups and downs with him. He was just too busy, or it had to wait until the season was finished. As if she could turn off her feelings or put them on pause for a few months.

She had turned to her mother so much lately. Blake was once her best friend, who knew everything about her and who she knew everything about. Now he just seemed like a provider who she almost had to beg for some attention. She didn't like how things had ended up, this wasn't where she wanted to be in her life, at any stage.

Even when the season was over it wasn't like he would be all hers again. Soon there would be recruiting. To Blake, these recruits seemed to be more important than his own family. Once recruiting season was over there would be spring ball. This was almost as bad as the season, just not as long. Then a few shorts months and the season started again.

During the season there was no hope for any kind of relationship, save for one based on convenience, when there wasn't anything that needed to be done for the next game. There might be a month's worth of time in there where Blake was all hers. This didn't seem like enough to her. She had married because she wanted a full time partner and lover, not someone who would be there only when it didn't interfere with his precious game.

She needed some time alone. She needed to be away for a while. She wasn't even going to go to the home game this weekend. It wasn't because she wanted to get back at him, she just didn't want to go. To her it didn't matter who won or lost. She just wanted him, she wanted to love him, she wanted to be with him. To her it didn't matter what he achieved or didn't achieve.

She didn't know if she could continue living like this. She also loved herself. She felt like she was a great woman and a great person with a lot to offer. Instead of going to the game she would take Conner to her parents' house for a week and let Blake do his thing. If he wanted to come and see them, then he could. It was the only place where she could go to feel like she got enough attention.

    Blake didn't really enjoy being with her after games. He wanted to go get drunk with the coaches and release some of the stress that he had built up in preparing for the game. To her it just seemed like an endless cycle of lots of stress and lots of booze. It wasn't something she enjoyed, anyway. One of the only times they had a chance to be with each other and then he would just be drunk. It was like he wasn't even there.

Apathy

Mary knocked on the door as she let herself in. "Hey, anyone home? Can I come in?" she called into the apartment with excitement and happiness in her voice.

Charlie had been expecting her at any time. It was past eight and she had told him that she would come over after having dinner with her parents. "Yeah, I'm here. Come on in," Charlie replied back. He finished the last of another beer and put it down next to the growing collection of empties. He was surprised that he had drunk so much.

Mary almost bounded into the small TV room. Charlie turned to see her smiling face. He didn't even get up to greet her. She looked gorgeous. She was still dressed up from dinner. Her make up and nails were done and she smelled nice. He felt the stab of cognitive dissonance again. *Remember you don't give a fuck anymore.* "Hey," he said, without any emotion.

Her expression changed to one of confusion as he continued to lounge back in the plush couch and didn't greet her with his usual warmth. She looked around the room, saw a piece of half eaten pizza and empty beer cans, and knew that something was wrong. Charlie only drank on Saturdays during the season. She had never known him to drink on any other day. He had always told her that he couldn't, otherwise he wasn't his best at practice. He had been devoted to football and had never done anything to jeopardize his performance. Yet, here he was getting drunk by himself on a Sunday night.

Her confusion turned to nervousness. M*aybe something bad happened,* she thought to herself. She sat down next to him on the couch and touched his arm to try and comfort him.

He practically ignored her and opened another beer. He took a long drink from the can and changed the channel on the TV before even looking at her again. He gave her a blank look and returned his gaze to the TV.

She rubbed his shoulder and pulled her long skirt down to cover her leg. She was really uncomfortable. Charlie had never acted like this to her. She didn't even feel welcome. His apartment had almost been a second home for her the past few months. Now she felt like a stranger who had come over uninvited. "What's the matter, Charlie?" she asked as gently as she could. "Don't you have football tomorrow? And I thought you had a quiz tomorrow and that you would be studying tonight."

"Everything is the matter. Yes, I have a quiz, but I really don't care right now. I might not even go to class tomorrow." He took another long drink from his beer.

"You can't miss that class. You know that Dr. Donovan won't let you retake his quizzes. You don't want your grade to drop to a C in that class, then you will have just proved his point for him." She almost sounded like she was giving him a pep talk.

"I just don't care right now," was all that he said.

There was an uncomfortable silence as Charlie flipped through the channels. Mary felt like leaving, but wanted to make sure he was okay. "Charlie you have to talk to me. We have really opened up to each other lately and grown really close. I need you to let me in so we can continue to grow together. I want to help, let me help."

He couldn't take it anymore. They had been together for over two years now and they seemed to be moving towards a relationship after college. She was sitting here pouring her heart out and he didn't care. *I don't care, I don't care.* Again that twinge hit him. He knew he was lying to himself. He had to keep telling himself, *I don't care, I don't care.* He did the only thing that would let him out of this situation. "I cheated on you last night." The words came out without emotion, he couldn't even bring himself to look at her as he said them.

"What?"

There was a long pause. "You heard me. I cheated on you." He leaned up and opened another beer and finally looked at her with blank eyes.

She was crushed. The air seemed to be deflating out of her right in front of him. Her eyes began to water up, but she resisted letting the tears flow. "Why did you do that? We had been getting so close lately. We promised each other that we were seeing each other exclusively. We had even talked about having a future together after college. I thought that maybe we even loved each other." She wiped her eyes to prevent any tears from falling while she was in front of him and sniffed her nose.

"I don't really care about anything right now." He was trying to convince himself of this as much as he was trying to convince Mary. He turned his attention back to the TV to avoid seeing the hurt in her eyes that he had caused.

"Since when did you become such a jerk, Charlie? I loved being with you because you weren't a jerk. I can't believe I trusted you so much. I was just telling my parents tonight how you are such a nice guy. I guess I was lying to them, huh?" she said, letting her voice get loud.

"Don't get so loud. Plus, I don't want to talk about this right now." Charlie shook his head, trying to dismiss her criticism.

She stood up and took a deep breath. She had to look down for a moment to collect herself. She didn't want to cry in front of him. The dam holding back her flood of tears was about to break. She stood there until he looked at her again. "So, this is how it is going to end after two and a half years?"

"I guess so," he replied with indifference.

"Okay, Charlie." She turned and walked briskly to the door. By the time she reached her car her face was wet with streaking tears and her make up was beginning to run.

Mask

As soon as Mary left Charlie felt empty. He thought that he would feel better after he told her. *Remember, you don't care.* The nagging twinge inside him wouldn't stop. He exhaled deeply and got up. He went into his room, found Kristin's number, and brought the cordless phone back to his spot on the couch. The beer wasn't working on numbing the conflict going on within him. He thought maybe some more meaningless sex might.

"Hey, is Kristin there?" he asked, trying to force some cheer into his voice.

"Yeah, just a sec."

"Hello?" a cute voice said into the phone.

"Hey, Kristin, this is Charlie, how are ya?"

"Charlie?" she said loud enough for her roommates to hear. He could hear some chatter begin once they all knew who was calling.

"Yeah, it's Charlie. What's going on?"

"Nothing much. I just didn't expect to hear from you so soon. I'm glad you called. I have been thinking about you."

"Me, too. Can I come over?"

There was a pause at this request. "You want to come over, right now?" She was letting her roommates in on the conversation as much as she was asking him.

"Yeah, if that's okay."

"Sure, that would be awesome. Just give me a few minutes before you leave, okay?"

"Sure, I'll see you in a few."

"Okay, bye," she replied, with enthusiasm. He could hear the chatter of girls in the background increase.

"Bye." He heard her roommates start asking her excited questions as she hung up the phone.

He brushed his teeth and put on some fresh clothes and pulled himself together. Kristin was part of his new life with his "fuck the world" and "fuck responsibility" attitude. Her company would help keep his mind off of the discord in his head.

A few minutes later he pulled up to her place and knocked on the door. She opened the door trying not to portray her enthusiasm. He could tell that she had applied fresh make up and perfume. Her outfit looked like she was ready to go to the club, not just hang out on a Sunday night. She welcomed him with a hug and a kiss on the cheek.

She pulled him inside into the oversized living area. "Hey girls, you remember Charlie, right?" She introduced the girls sitting on the couches and chairs placed around the room. "This is Mikaela, Suzzy, and Amber. You saw them all last night."

"Hey everyone." Charlie looked at them and nodded. They all gave Charlie a questioning look.

"Hi Charlie," they replied.

"I didn't think we would see you over here so soon," Mikaela spouted with sarcasm.

"Yeah, me either. I was thinking about Kristin and wanted to see her again."

Kristin beamed. "Good, I'm glad you called me. Come sit down, we're watching a movie. It is almost over. Finish watching it with us and then I'll show you my room." She led him to the loveseat on the far wall that seemed to have been strategically reserved for the two of them.

They sat down and she cuddled next to him as if they were already a couple. Amber pushed play on the remote and Kristin looked up at his eyes with infatuation. Legally Blonde started again, over half way into the film.

In the dim light with a stupid chick flick playing that he had no interest in seeing, Charlie was alone with his thoughts. His conscience began to gnaw at him again. He felt like he was back in his freshman year of college. He was hanging out with someone who he didn't have anything in common with and who he wasn't really interested in. He just wanted to get some pussy.

He had played that game before as a freshman. When he first came to college he was shocked at all the girls. Not only were there a plethora of beautiful young women, but they were all away from home and were also trying to get laid. It had been so easy to get girls. He had found that the key was to date a girl from each dorm building. That way he wouldn't run into a girl he was dating when he went to visit another girl that he was dating. He had a blast his first year.

But, it was distracting. It took time, effort, and focus away from school and more importantly, football. It was fine his freshman year because he had redshirted. It was okay to be a little distracted when he was basically just a practice dummy for the first team defense.

When he started getting playing time his second year of college he had to lay low a little bit. His days of dating three of four girls at one time were over. He couldn't run around and worry about who might run into whom. That created drama for him and didn't allow him to dedicate himself to football and all the demands that went with getting good grades while playing football.

He had dated a few girls, one at a time, for short periods of time until he had met Mary in the spring of his second year in college. They had been dating ever since. Now in his senior year of football and his fifth year of college he felt like he was backtracking. He felt like he had gone in reverse.

The alcohol was beginning to wear off and he was thinking clearly for the first time all day. He didn't want to be here. He didn't like this new attitude. He realized that he wasn't that cool. Football wasn't that cool. He had always been a nice person who cared about school, friends, and family, more than just football. He realized there was more to life than football, but he had been neglecting everything else. He had always wanted to be more than just a football player and now that is all that he was.

He realized that was what made him cool, that he cared about everything. That he had tried to be the best at everything; school, being a friend, football, being a boyfriend. This desire to be the best was what made him the best. He didn't like this negative non-caring attitude. If he was willing to settle for less than the best, he would only be mediocre. That was not something he wanted in football, school, or in relationships.

Coach Jackson was right, too. He wasn't a quitter. He felt like such a phony being here. He was being one of those guys he had promised himself he would never be. He had never quit on anything before. He had been so proud of all his accomplishments throughout college. If it all ended like this, he would have regrets forever. He couldn't let football or life with his college sweetheart end this way. Those two aspects were a major part of who he was. AND HE WAS NO QUITTER! He had to do something to fix his life. He had to do something now.

Charlie sat up and pulled his arm from behind Kristin's back. She looked up at him to make sure he was okay.

After he freed his arm, he bent down and kissed her on the forehead. "You're a beautiful girl, but I can't be with you. I'm sorry. I didn't mean to hurt you, too. I'm a jerk right now, but I have to go fix my life. I have to go." He could see the hurt in her eyes. He felt like such an asshole. He had broken two girls' hearts in one night. Before she could say anything, he began to show himself out the door.

"What do you mean? Where are you going?" She sat up and her eyes welled up. Tears began to roll down her face.

He stopped at the door and looked back at her. "I'm sorry." He really was. He looked around the room at all of the girls. Their shocked faces were the last thing he saw as he pulled the door closed.

Reconstruction

Charlie contemplated going over to Mary's. He decided instead to go home and call her first. To get back on track and to his old self, he had to rectify things with Mary first. She was a big part of his life and he wanted her to continue to be a part of his life.

He jogged up the stairs to his apartment and found the phone. Ring….Ring….Ring….Ring….Ring….Ring…."Hi, this is Rebekah and Mary, please leave a message."

"Hi Mary," he heaved into the phone still out of breath from running up to his apartment. He took a deep breath, "This is Charlie. I know you probably don't want to talk right now, but please pick up. I really need to talk to you. I made a huge mistake and I want to fix it. Please call me back."

He knew she was home. It was after ten on a Sunday night. They both usually got up at eight for their classes on Monday. He didn't know what to do, so he called again. After six rings the recorder picked up again. "Hey Mary, it's me again. Just hoping that you would pick up."

He didn't know what to do. He was exhausted, but had to do something to fix this situation with Mary. He went into his bedroom and laid down in the dark. The exhaustion of the season, the alcohol that was still in his system, and the drama of the last 24 hours overwhelmed him. He dozed off.

He jerked awake after an indeterminate amount of time and knew he had to do something to get Mary back. He hoped it wasn't too late to do something tonight. He fumbled around in the dark for his bed side lamp. Sitting up in the half light of his room he got a sickening feeling in his stomach. He was disgusted with himself at what he had done to Mary. Mary was great, she allowed him to do his thing and she didn't make demands.

There were some girls to be careful of, ones that dated a guy only because he played football. Mary was not one of these girls. She had known he played football when they started dating, but had only been to one game in all her college years prior to dating him. Now, she took time off of work to come to as many of his games as she could. Sometimes she would even trade shifts with someone so that she could go to his game and then work the late shift after his game.

She was also one of his only links to the world outside of football. All of his friends were on the team. He did have his family, but they were a long drive away. Every day he had to do something or be somewhere for football. Mary was a break from all of this. She didn't really care about football, especially if the Puma won or lost. Mary was one of the few people that Charlie really felt didn't see him as a football player.

When he was with her they talked about anything and everything, but rarely football. Being around her was an escape from everything, all his worries and responsibilities about the sport melted away. When he wanted to talk, she listened with an open heart, allowing him to vent. She listened because she knew how much it meant to Charlie and she wanted to know him. She also wanted to hear about other parts of his life because he was so much more than just a football player to her. She had always been there for him. She was a sweetheart and had given him one of the greatest gifts he had ever received; she let him be himself while supporting him as best she could. He began to wonder if he had been as good to her as she had been to him.

With a sense of urgency he hopped to his feet. He began pacing back and forth, trying to make sense of this situation. He cared a lot about her, she was the best thing he had going outside of football. A sudden realization of what he had risked for a small fleeting sense of reckless abandon sent shock waves through his heart. For the first time, he knew that he loved her. He had wondered about this from time to time, but he had always stopped short of calling it love. He decided that she wasn't going to slip away without a fight.

On the way to find the phone he looked at the clock. It read 12:05. "Oh, shit!" he said out loud. He hadn't meant to fall asleep for that long. *If I'm going to feel rested for school and football tomorrow I need to go to bed now*. He picked up the phone and paused for a moment. *I can't let this go on any longer. Tomorrow is too late. I'll just be tired tomorrow. I will have to have some coffee or an energy drink.* He punched in the familiar numbers.

Ring....ring....ring...*I hope she picks up*....ring....ring. "Hi, this is Rebekah and Mary, please.." Charlie hung up the phone. He didn't want to leave another message. Feeling desperate he clutched the phone in his hand. He began pacing and ended up in front of the fridge. He opened the fridge, just to do something besides pace. Looking through the half stocked fridge, his blood pressure continued to rise. As his patience began to reach its end he knew what he had to do. "Fuck it!" he let out as he slammed the door to the fridge, shaking the entire contents.

He threw on the first sweatshirt he could find and slipped on his shoes. He walked out of the door and started his truck. Speeding through the quiet streets he was at her apartment in about ten minutes.

He ascended the short flight of stairs and hoped that Rebekah wouldn't answer. Through the closed blinds he noticed the kitchen light was on. He knocked quietly on the clean white door. His heart began to pound. *Please answer, please answer, please answer.* Some commotion could be heard on the other side of the door. His nerves almost overwhelmed him as the knob started moving. The door opened in a slow steady pace. Mary's face suddenly appeared. Her red eyes became hard when they met Charlie's.

"What?" she let out with a tone of defiance.

"Who is it?" Rebekah inquired from behind Mary. "It's him, isn't it?" Mary's body language and tone told her everything she wanted to know.

"Can I please come in?"

"I don't know, Charlie. I don't know." Tears began flowing. She stepped back as if she had no choice and no energy to stop him, even if she didn't want him there.

Charlie reached for her shoulder to try and comfort her. She blocked his advance and Charlie backed away. An awkward silence took over the room. All three of them didn't know what to do or say next. Rebekah finally broke the silence. "I wish she hadn't let you in. You don't deserve her and you didn't deserve to be let in tonight. You're lucky she is so nice. Don't take advantage of her kindness again, Charlie." She stared at him fiercely. "I can't look at you anymore. I'm going to bed. Mary, if you need me just yell and I'll be out here in a second, okay?

"Thanks," Mary managed to mumble.

"Good night, Rebekah," Charlie tried to be polite. She replied back with a scowl.

Alone in the living room, Mary moved to the nearest chair and collapsed on it. Charlie sat down on the sofa adjacent to it.

Charlie looked deep into her eyes. Seeing the hurt reflected in her emerald green eyes sent a shudder through him. He was bitterly upset at himself for deceiving someone he cared about so much. He wished there was something he could do to take the pain away, or to redo what had been done.

Charlie took a deep breath before beginning. "I know you don't like me right now and don't want to talk right now. But, I had to see you. I had to tell you how I feel. I had to tell you…"

"How do you feel, Charlie? Am I just a distraction from football for you? Is that all I am?"

"No, no, not at all. I realized how much you mean to me."

He paused and then did what he knew had to be done. He decided to lay out his true feelings. He would be leaving himself vulnerable. If she wanted to hurt him like he had hurt her, she would have the opportunity. But, he knew if she could get over this, then they could get through a lot. He knew that in this moment Mary was the most important thing to him. So he spoke from the heart. "Mary, I love you."

"If you loved me then why did you do this to me?" she asked as more tears spilled down her cheeks. She looked down at the floor, avoiding his eyes and closing her own, hoping that would keep the tears inside.

"Mary, I can give you a thousand excuses. The truth is I was broken. I folded under the pressure. I thought I could handle it all and I couldn't. I snapped and became a different person. My thought process was so blinded that I couldn't think straight. I stepped out of my rational self for a while and let my anger and disappointment take over. Our relationship, us, was always something I could fall back on. It has always been something positive in my life. I have always felt better about everything when I am with you. I was at the breaking point tonight and I lashed out the only way I knew how. I lashed out at what has been the most stable thing in my life the past two and a half years. I wish I could take it back, I wish I could take away the hurt. And I know that is only an excuse. It doesn't make it okay. What I did was wrong. It is something I have never done before and it is something that I will never do again."

"I'm not sure if that is good enough, Charlie. I need some time to think about this." Her eyes were still closed. Her emotions would spill out if she looked at him.

"That is fine Mary. But, I need to say something else. I really do love you, Mary, and I have realized how much you mean to me. I want to be with you. We've shared so much and I want to share even more. I want to make our plans for after university together. I want you to be a part of my life," Charlie said, honestly and hopefully.

"I don't know Charlie, I just don't know," Mary said between sniffles.

Charlie moved across the couch until he was next to her chair. She was allowing him to get closer, so he knew some of her anger had abated. He leaned over the arm of the couch and brought her head to his chest. He hugged her with all of the love and tenderness that were in his frazzled body. The fragrant smell of conditioner that was still in her hair was comforting to him. He felt like he was home.

Mary did believe that he wouldn't do it again. He had been faithful up to this point and she had been a little surprised that he had lasted so long. He was a popular guy around campus and there were always plenty of girls at the parties every weekend. Plus, the guys he hung out with weren't the perfect picture of fidelity. She did love him and she wanted to trust him. The fact that he had come to her about the incident and didn't try to hide what he probably could have gotten away with helped to ease her mind a little bit.

The gentle and warm way in which he held her with his big strong arms made her feel more comfortable. She felt safe and secure in these arms. Despite his mistake, she did not want to give up on this tender hearted man. Life is a long, tough road.

They had stuck by each other this far. She didn't want to give up yet.

Mary remained quiet, not opening her eyes. "Are you still listening?" Charlie asked.

"Yes," she whispered.

"I'm sorry Mary. I realize football is just a game. There is a lot more to life than football. I want to keep people in my life that aren't related to football and you are one of those, a very positive one." Charlie moved to the edge of the sofa and into her personal space. "I want you to be in my life. I want to give you my time and energy." He paused and summoned up the courage, "I love you, Mary. I have loved you for a long time. I'm sorry I haven't ever told you before. I know that doesn't make up for what I did…, but I hope that you will still be in my life."

Charlie looked up and down her body, not knowing what else to do. He stayed in her personal space, hoping for a response. He felt vulnerable. He had put himself out on a limb and had opened himself to being hurt. That was not something he did easily. He was wary of this, but thought it was the only way to get a second chance with Mary. He said the last thing he could think to say. "Shall I go?"

A quiet moment passed. "No, I don't want you to go yet." Charlie grasped her hand, trying to tell her through his touch that he meant what he was staying. Mary opened her eyes, releasing the welled up tears and looked in Charlie's moistening eyes. "I don't want you to go yet."

She pulled her hand back from his, not wanting to be that close yet. She even moved further back in the chair. Looking him in the eyes she said, "I used to think that I loved you too, Charlie. I really did. I thought we might even have a future together. Now, I don't know what to think." She shook her head.

"I know that we will get back to the way things were, if you give me a chance. You have been great to me. I don't think I have been as good to you. I will be a better person to you if you give me another chance." He was almost pleading.

"Right now I don't know what to do, Charlie. I don't feel like saying we are totally finished. I also don't want you over here tonight. I need some time, Charlie."

He was relieved. He felt like he could win her over again even with a slight chance. "Okay, I understand. I'll give you your space. Will you still meet me after the game this Saturday? My parents will be here and it is senior night. I would love it if you would still do that for me. My parents love you and we can spend some time together that night and see if it can work out. Is that okay?"

She looked at him as if he were asking a lot. "Okay, Charlie. I will do that. I don't want to see you or talk to you until then."

He was a little defeated. Waiting until Saturday night to see if they could make it work seemed like a long time for him, but he knew he shouldn't press his luck. "Okay. I'm excited for Saturday after the game, already." He got up to leave hoping that she would walk him to the door. When she didn't make a move to get up with him he walked to the door himself. Before walking out, he looked back at her. "I meant what I said earlier. I love you, Mary."

Section III

"Few things will match the feelings that come from the pursuit of excellence with people who care for each other because of their shared legacy, history, and love for each other."
-Coach Chris "Keeko" Georgelas

"He may get the best of me,
but he won't get all of me."
-Art Shell

End of Season
November 2000

Determination

 Charlie arrived early for the special meeting called this Monday night. The Puma usually only had a short weightlifting session and conditioning on Mondays. But at their workout the players had been notified of the special meeting tonight. Charlie got there even before the doors to the meeting room were unlocked. He leaned against the wall, next to the doors, waiting.

 He was drinking a protein shake loaded with calories. He had had a tough time keeping his weight on this season. He had been eating everything and anything that he wanted. Combined with his profuse intake of beer on the weekends, this should have been enough to keep his weight up. Yet he had dropped almost 10 pounds this season. He was now down to about 275. Jim, the conditioning coach, was concerned about his weight loss and had implemented a protein shake diet for Charlie every evening. They hoped the extra protein and calories would mitigate further weight loss.

 He was feeling much better today, despite a lack of sleep. He had mended things with Mary, as well as he could for the time being, and he had re-adopted his normal attitude. He felt lighter and the dissonance in his head had subsided. He wore a smile and greeted the other players as they began arriving.

 He was chit chatting with a few of the guys when Johnny approached him from the side. He put his arm around Charlie and pulled him away from the group. "Hey, man. I haven't talked to you since you took off from the party on Saturday night. I saw you for a minute at yesterday's meeting, but didn't get to talk to you because Coach Jackson called you into his office at the end of the meeting. You look better, less stressed at least. How are ya?" Johnny asked with a mischievous grin.

 "I'm good man." They kept walking away from the growing group of football players. Charlie knew where this conversation was going and didn't want it to take place where everyone could hear. As soon as they were out of earshot, Charlie stopped and Johnny took his arm from around his shoulder before sitting on the retaining wall of the small garden next to the outdoor entrance.

"You look good man. So, did that new pussy do it for ya? She was hot for you. I'm sure you had fun." Johnny gave him a nod of approval.

Charlie chuckled and shook his head. "Well, it is kind of a long story. I certainly did have a fun time on Saturday night, but it also helped to wake me up."

Johnny gave him a look of surprise. "What the hell does that mean?"

Charlie took a deep breath. "I realized that I didn't want that kind of life again. I already did all of that four years ago. I want to refocus on football and school and I want to try and make it work with Mary."

"You didn't get caught, did you?" Johnny interrupted with shock.

"No, no, no. I could have gotten away with it and maybe even played the game for a while. I actually came clean to Mary and I hope she forgives me. I feel much better when she is around and I am able to concentrate more, too. I don't need all of that new pussy distracting me again. It makes life difficult and filled with drama. I am too old for that."

"Wow, I am surprised. Okay, that's cool man. Whatever works for you. You did it and realized it isn't for you anymore." Johnny looked at him as if he were naive. "At least tell me you had some good sex with that chick. She has been all over you for years."

"Yeah, yeah, yeah. She has been coming after me for a long time. Like I said, it was a lot of fun. We both had an enjoyable night."

"That's what you hope, anyway, right? I don't know if I believe you. If you need any tips let me know. I am always here to help you." Johnny smiled at him and shook his head.

"I'll keep that in mind," Charlie replied through a chuckle.

Then, right at 6:00, the doors to the meeting room opened from the inside. Johnny got up and without a word they walked into the meeting room. Charlie continued to walk towards the front of the room. He was back to his normal self.

He always felt like winners and people that care the most sit in the front. He looked back to see if Johnny was still following. Johnny was more of the belief that the back was better. He could sneak out of the meeting quicker and was less likely to be scrutinized when sitting at the back. He nodded to Johnny to follow him. Reluctantly, Johnny followed him to the front row.

Coach Jackson was already sitting next to the podium waiting for everyone to file in and sit down. The room was tense. Everyone knew what the meeting was about. The Puma were now 4-5. The newspaper had run a scathing article this morning about the slide the team had experienced this season and the need for a different direction. To the newspaper this direction meant a new head coach. They were saying that this was the last straw. They had endured two losing seasons in a row and now this season looked like it would be a third with two tough games remaining. Plus, he hadn't won the conference and been to a postseason game in three years. This season would be the fourth. The paper was calling vehemently for his job.

As soon as the last of the guys took their seats, Coach Jackson stood up and made his way behind the podium. The small talk ceased. He stood with a blank, stoic look on his face waiting for the room to be quiet. After the room was silent, he waited for what seemed like five minutes. This uncomfortable silence set the tone for the meeting.

"Good evening gentlemen," Coach Jackson nodded towards the team in acknowledgement. "This will be a quick meeting. I want you to be able to get back to your studies ASAP. We have all heard or seen the rumors going on in the media and I wanted to address them so that you could hear it straight from the horse's mouth before things got out of control. Plus, I don't want there to be any misunderstanding." He paused and looked around the group of young men. "Our season is not done yet and I am not about to be fired. I have been given full support by the athletic director and the school president. They assure me that no decision will be made until the team's progress is evaluated at the end of the season. I don't want you to think that means anything more than it does. We have two games left, that is all that I am concerned about. That is all that I want you to be concerned about. Your job is to play football, my job is to coach football. I only want you to worry about your job. If we all take care of our own job, then everything will work out. I'm proud of you guys. You are a special group. I love each and every one of you. We have accomplished a lot. We have exceeded many expectations this year. But, we are not done. We have two more games and I expect to win those two games. So, I don't want you to worry about the media or my future. Concentrate on playing football and doing what is asked of you and the future will take care of itself."

He looked around at the guys with confidence that the season would end on a high note. "That's all guys. I wanted you to hear it from me first. I didn't want your only source about what is going on to be the newspaper. Is there anything that anyone else needs to add?" He looked around the room, expecting to just dismiss the guys.

Charlie realized this was his moment. He now had the chance to step up and be the leader he had always wanted to be. He knew that to end the season the right way, the leadership really must come from the team, not the coaches. He also remembered his last conversation that he had with Coach Jackson. He didn't want to end his career with any regrets. He raised his hand before Coach Jackson was about to dismiss the team.

Coach Jackson's eyes lit up. "Yes, Charlie, what is it?"

Charlie stood up and faced the team. "I would like everyone to stay here for 10 minutes. There are some things that we need to talk about as a team. Some things that just the players need to talk about." He sat back down and looked Coach Jackson in the eyes.

Coach Jackson paused with a look of surprise in his eyes. "Okay, everyone stay here for a few minutes. The coaches and I will get back to our work. We will see you tomorrow at 2:00 for your position meetings." He looked Charlie in the eyes as he walked off the stage. He nodded his head in gratitude and seemed to convey to Charlie that this was exactly what he had talked to him about, exactly what he wanted and needed Charlie to do. He gave Charlie a little thumbs up as he and the other coaches exited out the back door to the halls of the football complex.

Charlie didn't know what to do. He now felt nervous and unsure of himself. He took a deep breath and walked up on the stage in front of the podium. He didn't feel important enough to stand behind the podium.

The team was still silent. All eyes were on Charlie. It was almost as if they were looking to him for guidance. To his astonishment, they seemed to be more attentive now than when Coach Jackson was addressing them. He felt his heart rate increase. He realized that if he didn't start talking now he would lose his courage and would freeze up. So, he just started talking about the first thing on his mind.

"Guys, this has been a long five weeks. It has felt more like 10 weeks. It has been hell on everyone. There are so many reasons for this losing streak. The only thing we know about this losing streak is that it isn't the coaches' fault. Sometimes things just don't go how they are supposed to go. Plus, we didn't always practice or play as hard as we could."

He paused and looked around the room. They were still listening to him. "Guys, we have to play and practice these next two weeks for more than ourselves. The future of the coaching staff is at stake. These last two games are a lot more important than just me, than just you, or than all of us. I came to the Puma because of Coach Jackson and Coach Havili. I fell in love with them and their system five years ago on my recruiting trip. I still love their system and believe in what they do. They have given us everything they can. They have sacrificed a lot to be the coaches that they are. I still would choose the Puma and I am proud to be a Puma."

Heads around the room were nodding in agreement. "Plus, these are my last two games with the Puma. I can't believe it is already that time. This week is the senior game. I am not going to end my career on a sour note. We have two games left and if we win these last two games we end the year with a winning record. That is something to be proud of and something that will keep this coaching staff around. I am pledging to you guys that I will play and practice these last two weeks harder than I ever have and that I will play and practice for more than just myself. I will play and practice for the rest of you and for our coaches. I promise this to all of you guys."

Charlie's confidence was growing. The team seemed to really be soaking up what he was saying. They liked his spur of the moment speech. He decided to take it one step further. "As the offensive team captain, I am going to pledge to the rest of the team that the offense will have its best two weeks of the season and that we will play not only for ourselves, we will play for the rest of the team and the coaches." He looked around at the other offensive players. "Are you guys with me on that?" Heads nodded in agreement and a few of the guys blurted out, 'Hell yeah,' 'For sure,' or 'We got your back, Charlie.'

He found Junior in the crowd. "I know our other captain will make sure that the defense does the same thing, right Junior?"

Junior was inspired, for the first time he felt like a team captain. It was strange that it took his fellow captain taking the lead and calling him out to feel like this. He stood up and looked around the room. "You sure can count on me and the rest of the defense. We are going to hit harder and run faster than we ever have these next two weeks. You guys better watch it because I am going to take some fools out at practice tomorrow. Right, defense? Let's start our ass kicking tomorrow by dominating practice. You guys with me?" His taunts and encouragement were met with hoots and hollers.

The energy in the room was incredible. They all felt ready to play a game again. There was a confidence and swagger that had been absent for the past month. They felt like a team again. They felt like they belonged to something bigger. Charlie knew he had accomplished what he had needed to do. The team, for the first time all season, felt like it was being led by the players, not the coaches.

Charlie knew that he needed to call an end to the meeting. He didn't want the thoughts of this meeting to be about anything else besides the energy being felt right now. "All right, all right, one last thing guys." Charlie tried to make himself heard above the now noisy meeting room. "Everybody up to the front for a team cheer. Then we will see you at practice tomorrow where the offense is going to kick the defense's ass." This was met with a combination of cheers and boos. He hopped off the stage and beckoned the players to gather around him. The surging mass of hyped up football players squeezed him even tighter in the small space between the front row of chairs and the stage. He yelled above the rising din of excitement, "Puma pride on three…one…two…three."

"PUMA PRIDE!!!" exploded through the small room. It was proudly heard down the hall in the coaches' office and strained Charlie's ear drums. The team began filing out of the meeting room giving each other bro hugs, talking shit to each other, and getting an early start on the pushing that would ensue again once practice began the next day.

The energy level and enthusiasm at practice even exceeded the hopes of the coaching staff. It was as if the season had just begun and the players were hungry for competition. There were fights that broke out because the competition was so intense. The hits were delivered like it was a game. They practiced like they were inspired. They practiced for more than just themselves, they practiced for each other and their coaches.

Second Guessing

April didn't know if she was in love anymore. She had always had this idyllic image of what love was, a childlike view of love as perfect. But she knew that view of love wasn't true anymore.

She still had strong intense feelings for Blake, but a lot had happened. A lot of unplanned things. Fights, financial hardships, and just learning to live with another person had been more difficult than she had imagined.

She thought getting married would change things. But it hadn't. She thought having a baby would change things. But it hadn't. Life was still the same. Her relationship was still the same. For some reason she thought these things would make Blake more of the person that she wanted, more of her idyllic version of what a husband and father should be. She never imagined that he would continue to pursue his dream at the expense of all else.

Things weren't so bad for her. Family life just wasn't the fairy tale she had always dreamed of. Maybe she had to be happy with what she had and she needed to quit reaching for that elusive pot of gold, which didn't exist anyway. Chasing a vision of what she thought love and marriage should be wasn't going to make reality any better or any more enjoyable.

She had to decide if this life, the life she had right now, was the life that she wanted. Things weren't going to change. She pushed this thought out of her conscious. She just wanted to relax. She was really enjoying this time at her parents' house. She didn't want her doubts to consume her anymore. She just wanted to take life day by day, as she had been doing lately. These days at her parents' had been more enjoyable than most days at home. She wondered if this was a sign that her life wasn't what she wanted. Again she pushed these thoughts away.

She believed that her feelings for Blake hadn't changed and for right now that was enough. These breaks away from home could rejuvenate her. She could take these breaks when she needed to feel good about life again. This thought alarmed her and once more she tried to ignore the realization.

At night at her parents' house she was alone with her thoughts a lot. She didn't have all the responsibility here and she wasn't as exhausted. This allowed her more time to think. She didn't like some of the thoughts that kept coming up, though.

She closed her eyes and daydreamed about the end of the football season.

Senior Night

Charlie stood fifth in line. His heart was pounding, not from nerves, but from nostalgia. It was senior night at Puma Stadium. The lights were off at the stadium. The rest of the team made a passageway for the seniors to run onto the field to greet their parents. There was a spotlight focused on mid field where Coach Jackson would meet the senior player, give him a hug, bestow him with a commemorative plaque recognizing his accomplishment, and present him to his parents. Each player was also carrying a rose to give to his mother.

The seniors were milling about, loosely staying in line, and congratulating each other. Charlie was filled with emotion. He could not believe this day was here. His whole world had been football and now this world was about to end. The end of his career never seemed tangible until now. He hoped that he wasn't done playing football forever, but now the reality that his college career was almost over was staring him in the face. He had to consciously acknowledge this for the first time. He was proud of all that he had done and he didn't have any regrets, but he didn't know if he was ready for this to be over.

As the seniors were waiting, they all came up to Charlie, congratulated him, and gave him a hug. Real hugs could be substituted for bro hugs on days like today, even for football players. Charlie's emotions were ready to spill out, so he avoided saying more than one or two words to the guys. If he said more than that he wasn't sure if he would be able to keep his emotions bottled up anymore.

The announcer called the fans to order and let them know the seniors were about to be introduced. Charlie hopped around, trying to calm himself, as the first guys were called out. During their run to mid field a short bio was read and the parents were also introduced as the spotlight followed the player during his jaunt. Once the player in front of him, Adam McManus, reached mid field, Charlie heard the announcer. "Next is one of this year's team captains, Charlie Peterson!!!" The crowd began to cheer again and he started to jog down the column of players before the tears building in his eyes spilled out. He slapped as many hands as he could as he made his way to mid field. He strained his ears to hear the PA announcer, but he was unable to hear his bio being read.

The spotlight followed him to midfield and he saw Coach Jackson. He swallowed hard and fought back the tears. Coach Jackson grabbed him and embraced him tightly. "Charlie, I am so proud of you. You have done such a great job. You've done more than I could have hoped for. You are a great football player, a great leader, and a great young man. I am proud to have been your college football coach."

"Thanks, coach," Charlie replied as the tears began to flow.

Coach Jackson handed him his plaque and ushered him towards his parents. Even before he could present his mom with the rose, his parents had corralled him into a bear hug. He heard them both sniffling and knew that they were also crying. They lingered in the emotional hug until they realized the parents of the next player were making their way to mid field to greet their son. They moved towards the sideline where they joined the other players and parents to form a line that would be acknowledged one more time before the festivities wrapped up.

Once they had reached their position in line, Charlie gave his mom her rose and with it a big hug. Her tears were still pouring down her face. Charlie moved to his dad and gave him a big hug. His dad's eyes were still wet.

His mom was still unable to talk, so his dad took over. "Charlie, we are so proud of you. You have done an incredible job. The things you have already accomplished as a young man are extraordinary. Congrats, buddy!" They hugged again and turned to watch the rest of the ceremony. His dad stood with his arm around Charlie's shoulders and his mom flanked him with her arm around Charlie's arm pulling herself close to him.

As the last senior with his parents finished the line, the announcer called on the crowd to give the seniors and their parents one more standing ovation as the spotlight moved down the line. Charlie gave his parents one more hug. "Good luck, buddy. I love you," his dad said into his ear. "I love you, Charlie," his mom managed through her tears. "I love you, too." Charlie smiled and then turned to join the team.

The team was gathering at mid-field. The non-seniors had circled around Coach Jackson at the end of the ceremony and now the seniors were joining the group. As the crowd noise lessened, Coach Jackson reminded them of the energy needed to get a win tonight. The energy already seemed to be more than what he was asking for. He strained his voice to be heard above the enthusiastic crowd. He put his hand in the air and the players closed in around him. "Win on three…one…two…three."

"WIN!!!" the team responded with unmatched enthusiasm. They made their way to the sideline and got ready for the kickoff.

The effort and energy that had been present during the week of practice carried over into the game. The Puma played like they did at the beginning of the season. Despite playing a team with an identical record, the Puma played like the dominant team.

For the last offensive series Charlie was able to be substituted to enjoy the end of the game from the sideline. As he jogged off the Puma field for the last time he waved to the crowd and basked in his moment of glory. He walked the last five yards to the sideline, not wanting to leave. He scanned the crowd hoping to find his family or friends. He knew they were watching, but he couldn't find them. He was finally hurried to the sideline by his coaches and teammates as the offense was getting ready to snap the ball for the next play.

Coach Havili grabbed him, yanking him to the sideline and into a hug. "Great job, man. You had a great game. I'm glad you were able to finish your career here with a victory at Puma Stadium. You have been awesome too coach. Go get a water and enjoy." He pushed him towards his waiting teammates who mobbed him.

Support

April had been watching the game and, despite her current loathing of the sport, she was glad the Puma had won. She knew so many of the kids, they were all so young and cute, and they all put in so much effort. It was as if they were willing to give their lives for the game, or the team. Plus, she knew how much it meant to Blake and she completely understood how much effort he put into the God damn game.

April thought back to her chance encounter at the bank yesterday. She had snuck out of her parents' house while Conner was taking a nap to run some errands. She was standing in line at the bank trying not to let the wait get her upset, she told her parents she would be back before Conner woke up. She was trying a little too hard to hear what the geriatric customer at the front of the line was requesting she noticed a sharply dressed young man coming her way from behind the secure bank area. She averted her eyes, hoping her dour look wasn't attracting his attention. She kept looking away from him until he was standing next to her and she couldn't casually ignore him anymore.

As she turned a well groomed young man who looked too athletic to be working in a bank extended his hand. "Hi, I'm Lavon Palmer. Sorry to bother you, but are you, Mrs. Jones, Coach Jones' wife?"

She was pleased he wasn't trying to give her the football player death grip with his hand shake. As polite and natural as possible she responded, "Yes, I sure am. I don't think I know you, though."

"I played for the Puma a couple of years ago. I know you meet a lot of football guys, we met a couple of times at team functions for the Puma. Plus, I always saw you around with Coach Jones. But, anyway, I apologize for the wait today, can I take you back to my personal desk to help you with your needs? I don't want you waiting in line any longer, Mrs. Jones." He held out his arm reassuringly and led her to his office in the back where she could see his name plate with the title, "Bank Manager," below his name. *He sure is young to be in this type of position already,* she thought to herself as she sat down in the plush chair.

"I know you're here for banking, but I have to say it is fun to see a member of the Puma family. As soon as I saw you I smiled. What are you doing over in this neck of the woods?" he asked as he logged on to his computer.

As he finished typing and looked back at April she told him, "I'm just visiting my parents for a few days while Blake, I mean Coach Jones, finishes up the season. You know how busy it gets."

"Oh, okay. I hope they can pull things together these last couple of weeks. I've been on pins and needles for a while this season. I sure want those coaches with our team for a long time. I wouldn't be the man I am today without them, especially your husband. He is the reason I finished college and got this good job at such a young age. He believed in me. He convinced me I could to whatever I wanted if I just worked hard. I haven't had a lot of good role models in my life and he filled that void for me. I leaned on him a lot to get through a tough couple of years in my young life. I really don't know where I would be if it weren't for him," Lavon told her as his steely eyes got a little glassy. "When I saw you I was hoping I could be the one to help you today and tell you how much your husband meant to me and how much he means to a lot of other young men."

"Thanks for telling me, Lavon. It means a lot to hear that from you. Coaches don't get a lot of extra recognition, unless they win championships."

April nodded her head to herself while thinking about this and felt more content than she had in a while. Even though they might not share the same goals anymore, that didn't mean she didn't love him and want the best for him, no matter what happened. She knew now more than ever that she loved him. Being away at her parents' house helped cement the fact. She also had to face the fact that she might not want to live the life that Blake had in mind. Things had been great for the first few years, but their goals and priorities in life had shifted.

Sitting in the quiet comfort of a house she had known so long, she listened to the silence for a moment, hoping it might tell her what to do. Her senses seemed magnified for a moment by the complete lack of noise since turning the radio off after the game. Her parents were long since asleep and Conner was passed out in the portable crib next to the king size bed in the guest room down the hall.

In this meditative state she looked around the house and let her mind wonder to all the great memories there had been here over the years. The slumber parties with her noisy grade school friends where her parents acted so excited for her friends to be there. Now she realized how much they had disliked every minute of those parties.

The first boy she had dared bring home and how nervous she was of what her dad might do or ask. He had turned out to be a loser, but her parents were again very supportive and friendly to him, whether they liked him or not. She knew how nice, loving, and supportive of her they were to open their home up to whomever she might bring home.

She thought of the time when she had stumbled home drunk and her mom had been up waiting for her. There wasn't any use in trying to hide it. She smelled terrible and could barely walk. Her mother held her hair out of the way while she puked her guts up in the toilet. Her mother wasn't mad or angry, just glad that April hadn't been driving. In the morning, her mother woke her up early and asked her to clean the toilet, telling her it was the least she could do after all the worry she had put her through the night before.

One of the best memories was the time she and Blake came over to announce their engagement. Her parents had always liked Blake. He had won over her mother immediately with his gentlemanly manners and could talk to her dad for hours about any subject, especially sports. They, of course, had already known because Blake had asked for permission. Her parents were so excited for both of them. That night they made dinner together and stayed up late talking.

Recalling all these memories, April began to think those were the good old days. Her mind was brought back to the present and all the problems and troubles she was having right now. Her relationship with her husband was not what she wanted, or felt she deserved. She was a great person and deserved the best. She didn't want to feel like she was taking a backseat to anything, particularly football. Driving herself crazy by thinking up every possible scenario, she took a deep breath and closed her eyes.

Lying under the dim yellow light of the desk light, she wondered if she should call Blake and tell him congrats on the big game. She knew it would be a nice thing to do. She knew it was what he would want her to do, what he thought she would do. It was what she thought she would do, but now she didn't know. Her heart began to race at the thought of having to make a decision. She was tired of doing what Blake wanted and what Blake thought was best. She hadn't been consulted on any of his decisions lately, many of which affected the whole family, not just him.

Out of nervousness and realizing this could be a big decision, she could just hear the other coaches' wives being little trouble starters. "Oh, how insensitive. She didn't even come to the game?" "Didn't she know how important it was to the whole season?" "What, she didn't even call after the game to say 'Congrats'?" "Wow that is not very supportive." She tried to rub the sweat from her palms and take deep breaths to slow her heart. Closing her eyes to relax and come to her own comfortable decision, she knew the decision had already been made. She didn't need to call now. He wouldn't even be home yet.

Allowing herself to relax for a moment, she felt the exhaustion grab her body and mind like a vise. It consumed her and took control. In the soft pale light and the comfortable night silence she drifted off to sleep in the oversized love seat.

Amorous

Charlie was energized after the game. He had won his senior game, he was exhilarated. The locker room was a loud raucous scene. It seemed as if someone had already served alcohol. Charlie and his teammates were all smiles and hugs. Charlie didn't even doddle. He took a shower and was making his way out of the locker room while several of the guys were still around.

Charlie handed his game gear to Jim as he was making his way toward the exit. "Here you go, Jim. Thanks."

Jim took the dirty load without any hesitation. "You okay, Charlie?"

"Yeah, I'm awesome. Why?"

"Look around." Jim motioned towards the locker room with a smile. "You're not the last one out. Are you sure you don't want to stick around for a while?"

Charlie chuckled. "Yeah, it is weird being out of here so fast. I think I'll be on my way, though. See you tomorrow, Jim!"

"All right, Charlie. See you later. Be safe tonight."

Charlie flashed him a grin as he left the room. Charlie was buoyed by the victory tonight. It had lifted his spirits and given him more energy. Truthfully, he was also anxious. He hadn't seen Mary since they had talked. She didn't want to see him all week. But, she had promised to come to the game and he thought that she would be waiting for him with his parents.

Charlie made his way through the sea of awaiting parents, family members, and friends chatting with their football player or waiting for their football player. His parents were usually waiting at the back of the crowd. His dad did not like being surrounded by people he didn't know.

He picked up his pace when he saw Mary standing with his parents. It was mid-November and chilly. The first snow had been holding off this fall, but the coming winter could be felt in the air. They were all wearing coats. Mary had on a Puma football sweatshirt over her coat. It was one of Charlie's old warm ups that he had given to her. It fit over her coat and helped keep her warm during the fall games. The ladies had on hats and gloves. His dad was only wearing gloves and they all had their coats zipped all the way up.

Charlie made eye contact with all three of them and his smile grew. He could not take his eyes off of Mary. She looked gorgeous. Her hair was covering her ears and her blue eyes seemed to sparkle in the stadium lights that were still on. Her makeup looked freshly done and the pale fluorescent stadium lights accentuated her facial features. His heart skipped a beat. He was in love again and from the look in Mary's eyes, she was too.

As he got to his parents he looked away from her and embraced his mom.

"Hey mom," he said, muffled through her coat sleeve.

"I'm so proud of you, Charlie. You had such a great game and a great career. You are awesome."

After allowing his wife her time with Charlie, his dad pulled him away to give him his own big warm hug.

"Hey dad." Charlie tried holding back his emotions.

"I'm proud of you, too, Charlie. It has been so much fun watching you play and grow these past five years. You really are a great young man." His dad let him go.

His eyes were welling up and before the situation could get awkward Mary stepped forward and wrapped her arms around him. "Good game tonight, Charlie. It was fun to watch you again. It had been too long. I'm glad I came."

Tears were rolling down his cheeks now. Mary moved to pull away, but he held her for a minute. He didn't want everyone seeing him crying. "Thanks for coming Mary. It means a lot." He paused for a moment and decided to let it out. He whispered into her ear, "I love you, Mary."

They separated and she had to hold back her own emotions. She wasn't ready to say that yet, even though she felt it. She gave him a genuine smile. "I know." They looked at each other as lovers do, before his dad broke in.

"Well, why doesn't everyone hop into my car? We got here early and got a really good spot. It is only a five minute walk. We want to treat you two to dinner and then I will drive you back here so you can pick up your cars. How does that sound?"

Charlie looked at Mary. She shook her head in agreement. "Sounds good, dad. You lead the way." Charlie put his arm around his dad's shoulders and they began walking out of the stadium. Mary and his mother followed behind. They were chatting like old friends.

Charlie's parents took them out to one of the fancy places in town. Charlie ate better than he normally ate. He took advantage of this rare treat. They ordered appetizers, drinks, and even dessert. Charlie was so full from his huge piece of prime rib and baked potato that he could barely eat the dessert.

His parents, like always, got along great with Mary. He knew they would be happy if he and Mary continued to see each other after college. His mom sometimes even dropped hints on him that she would like to see her as a daughter in law. His dad treated her like he treated everyone, with open arms and full acceptance, no questions asked.

After dinner his parents knew that Charlie and Mary had places to be, so they didn't pressure them to spend any more time with them. Charlie's dad drove straight to the stadium after dinner, taking them back to their vehicles without even asking. His dad knew that they would want to be alone and that dinner was enough to ask of them.

Mary told them where her car was parked in the stadium parking lot. As they slowed down Charlie spoke up. "I'm just going to get out here with Mary." He looked at her to make sure that was okay. She gave him an approving smile and grabbed his hand tight.

Bright Future

The car stopped and they all got out to give hugs to each other. Charlie received more praise and compliments from his parents and thanked them profusely. They warmly said good bye to Mary who also offered her gratitude many times. They got back in the car and left Charlie and Mary alone in the now almost deserted parking lot.

Charlie grabbed Mary with all of his affection. Despite her best efforts Mary couldn't hold back her feelings any more. She returned his affection and they started kissing passionately. Mary was the one who broke away. She had to restrain herself and nudge Charlie away from her.

"Charlie, I don't know if I can do this right now." She looked at him with confusion.

"Okay." He paused, not knowing what to say. He knew that he wanted to be with her and he was willing to do it her way. "Let's go for a drive."

She unlocked the doors and Charlie let her in before getting in the passenger's side. He was having a hard time hiding his enthusiasm. He had just won his senior game, he was still stuffed from an incredible meal, and was in love all over again with his college girlfriend.

"Will you come to the party with me tonight?" He felt like showing her off. She was beautiful and he didn't want to leave her side right now.

She began pulling out of the stadium parking lot, not knowing where she was going. She took a deep breath, she couldn't let herself get talked into this tonight. She was still embarrassed. She knew that all the football guys knew about Charlie cheating on her and that meant most of the girls at the party would know. The girl that he cheated with might even be there. She didn't want to go through all of that tonight. She was not ready or willing to deal with that yet.

"No, Charlie. I'm not going to go with you tonight. But, I want you to go. I will even drop you off, that way you aren't tempted to drive home. Plus, I have to work pretty early in the morning. I had to exchange my shift tonight for one in the morning to be able to go to the game tonight." She looked over at him, trying to stay firm. She was glad that she was driving and didn't have to look him in the eyes.

Charlie was disappointed, but knew he had to give her space. He believed that they would be together again and he also knew that he couldn't smother her at this point in time. In resignation he replied, "Okay, that's okay. I don't want to go to the party yet, though. I want to talk for a little bit. Can we drive around for a while?" He hoped for a better response this time.

"Yeah, that's cool. I would like to talk more, too," she replied immediately.

For a few minutes they caught up with each other. They hadn't seen or spoken to each other for almost a week, which was a long time for them. As the conversation was beginning to lull, they passed a park on the edge of town. "Hey, do you want to pull in there so that we can talk a little more seriously?" Charlie asked.

Mary looked, wondering if there was anyone around, and began turning into the parking lot of the park. "Sure, that sounds good. I want to stay in here, though. It is cold out there and I didn't really bring enough clothes to hang out outside for a long time."

"Yeah, that is fine. I just want to get some things off of my chest and talk about us."

"Cool, me too."

Mary pulled to a stop and turned the car off. She undid her seat belt and pushed back her seat so that she had room to turn and face Charlie. She was feeling brave and knew that she had to start the conversation so that she could say what she had to say before her emotions or the situation took control of her.

Before Charlie had a chance to speak, she let it out. "I love you, Charlie. I know that now. That is why this whole thing hurt so badly. That also doesn't mean that you are forgiven yet, or that we are a couple again. It means that we could be again, though. But, if this is just a college thing, let's be done before I get attached again and my heart broken again." Her emotions were already taking over and she had to get these last words out through quivering lips. She pursed her lips and tried to keep the tears from welling up and spilling down her cheeks.

Charlie fought the urge to lean across the seat and hug her. It didn't seem like the right time yet. "Oh, Mary." He paused and looked away, feeling uncomfortable. He wasn't used to being the person who screwed up. He wasn't used to being the asshole. "I can't say how sorry I am. Nothing will ever totally make up for what I did. Just know that that wasn't me. I broke, I became a person I don't want to be. A person who I am not. I am back to myself and nothing like that will ever happen again."

Mary looked at him through eyes that were misting up and nodded her head. She had seen it happen to Charlie and she had also seen him come back to the person that she knew and loved. "I believe you, Charlie. I really do. But, like I said, if there is no future between us after college I don't want to let myself fall in love again. We're young, we can both go our own ways and find other people."

"I know Mary. I agree. I don't know what the future is going to bring, but I want the future to be with you. I want us to be together. Let's move away together and start our life together somewhere new."

Tears began spilling down her face. "Really? Do you really mean that?" She looked at him with hope, fear, confusion, and most of all, vulnerability.

"Yes, I do. Let's do this. Why not? I love you and I have for a long time. I have been afraid to say it because I didn't know what would happen if I did. I'm ready to give you a commitment that I want to be with you for a long time. I'm ready to start a life together with you." He said this honestly. He felt good, this felt right. This felt like the path that he should be taking. Saying this and picturing his life with Mary made him feel content. He felt safe and secure in going down this road.

Mary smiled and looked away to wipe her eyes. This was what she wanted, this is more than she dared to hope for. This broke through all of her anger and gave her a sense of peace. She looked back at him with eyes he had fallen in love with three years ago and ones he would fall in love with over and over again. "Okay, Charlie. Let's do it then. Let's get back together and see if we can make this thing work. Let's go for it." Mary also felt excitement. Even with the anger gone she still hadn't forgiven him, but she was ready to move on and it felt good to her to be going down this road, as well.

He leaned towards her and embraced her. They started kissing again. Charlie started moving closer to her, hoping for more. Mary inched towards him and he put his hand up her shirt. She let it linger for a moment before pulling away. "I'm not ready for that tonight, though. I still need to stop hurting before we can go there again."

Charlie just smiled, he could wait. He had his girl back and that was what he really wanted. "That's fine. I would never push you into anything. When you are ready it will be a great night."

She grinned at him, almost wanting to give into the urge building between her legs. "I think I'll take you to the party now. I want to go home and get some sleep before I have to get up for work tomorrow morning."

Celebration

Charlie celebrated with his teammates. They drank themselves into oblivion. It was a great night for Charlie and the entire Puma team. Charlie innocently flirted with some of the cute girls, but his mind didn't wander far from Mary. He was very glad that they had patched things up.

He even saw Kristin. She acknowledged him momentarily. He didn't blame her for not wanting to talk to him. Charlie wandered around the party, living it up, feeling like life was good.

By the end of the night, Charlie was way too drunk. He decided to leave when he realized he was no longer walking straight. He walked outside to get some fresh air. He contemplated walking home, but decided against this when his mind wouldn't let Mary go.

He wanted to go over to her house to see her. Walking there was too far and fortunately, he didn't have his truck. As he was getting frustrated about what to do, he saw Anthony leaving the party, heading towards his car with a couple of other guys.

He stumbled towards Anthony. "Hhheeeeey maaaannn."

Anthony turned to see where the drunk slurring was coming from. He recognized Charlie and they gave each other an awkward bro hug. "What's up dude, you leaving? You need a ride?" He guessed what was on Charlie's mind.

As Charlie was saying hi to the other guys, almost falling into them while trying to give bro hugs to Tyler and Andrew, some of his other teammates, he mumbled back, "Yeeeahhh that would be ahhhsome. I'm going ova to Mary's dou."

"No problem, man. We are heading to a party just down the street from where she lives." They all made their way to Anthony's car. Tyler and Andrew let Charlie have the front seat. They weren't sure he would be able to get in and out of the back seat.

A few minutes later Anthony poked Charlie. "Hey dude, we're here."

Charlie looked around, wondering how they got there so fast. He leaned over to give Anthony a half bro hug. "Sssanks man."

"Yep, be careful, dude." Anthony shook his head at Charlie as he slunk his way out of the car. He waited until Charlie was at the door before pulling away.

Charlie steadied himself when he got to the front door. He stood up straight and shook his head, hoping to gain some of his wits. He looked at the door wondering if he should knock or ring the doorbell. He had no clue what time it was. He knew a quiet knock might not wake up Mary, so he rang the doorbell before giving it more thought.

The ding jolted Mary out of her sleep. Despite just waking up, she instantly knew it would be Charlie. Not wanting Michelle to answer the door, she got up quickly and got to the door without even putting shorts on over her skimpy underwear. Through a sleepy haze she let him in.

"Heeeeyyy babe." He smiled and wrapped his arms around her.

She smiled back and put her finger up to her lips to let him know he was louder than he thought. "Hey Charlie," her eyebrows furled a little. "I didn't expect to see you again tonight." She was already leading him back to her bedroom, she knew what he wanted.

As he was being led to her room he tried to whisper. "Yeahhh, bu I had to see yu again. I lub you."

"I love you too, Charlie," she said, as she slipped off his shoes and helped him into bed. "But, if you are going to stay here tonight, we are going straight to bed. It is already two o'clock and I need to get some sleep before waking up for work."

He smiled at her while she put the covers over his still clothed body. "No probmm, babe." He reached up hoping for a hug and kiss.

She leaned over and gave him a big smooch. Before she even pulled away he had passed out. She walked over to her side of the bed, snuggled up to him, and fell fast asleep.

Distance Makes the Heart Grow Fonder

"Ring….Ring….Ring," shocked April awake. She began to search for the phone in the dark. She needed to answer it before it woke up the whole house. She knew it was Blake and she hoped that her parents would know that as well, and not try to answer the phone. "Ring.." She picked it up in the middle of the fourth ring. She looked at the clock and saw that it was 2:08 AM.

"Hello." She didn't try to hide her drowsiness.

"Hey, honey, did I wake you?" he said, slurring his words only slightly.

She could already tell that he was drunk, but had been expecting that. He didn't get to stay out as late as he liked with the coaches after the game when she was home. Now that she wasn't home he had stayed out as long as he had liked. "Yeah, but that's okay." She tried to sound sweet and not annoyed.

"Sorry, I just wanted to call you and let you know that we won."

"Yeah, I know. I watched the game. Good job, honey. It was a great game. Did you have fun with the coaches tonight?"

"Yeah, I sure did. It was great to go out with everyone tonight. We were finally able to let loose. We finally got back on the winning side of things. It had been a long five weeks. You know how that goes."

Her eyes closed again, she fought against sleep. "That's great. I'm glad everyone feels better. I know how hard it has been on you. I'm sure that it has been hard on everyone else."

"Thanks. So, how are you and Conner?"

She was surprised that he even asked. "We are both really good. We are enjoying some peace and quiet. It has been a nice week. I think we'll stay up here for another week. We'll come back next Sunday. If that's okay with you."

"Yeah, that is fine. It'll be another busy week. I'm glad to hear that everything is fine with you and Conner. Do you want me to let you get back to sleep?"

"Sure, I'm really tired. Everything is fine here. Give me a call tomorrow, will ya?"

"Sounds good, babe. I love you. Good night."

"Good night, Blake. Love you, too."

He hung up and went to the fridge for one more beer. He didn't need it, but with one more he would fall asleep as soon as his head hit the pillow. He was glad that she was having a good time at her parents' house. He was enjoying his time alone. He felt like this was a good thing for both of them. She got to spend some time with her family and he got to focus on his coaching. For him, this felt like how life should be right now. They were both getting what they wanted. As he guzzled down his last beer he assumed that she felt the same way.

Down, Set, Hut

Team

It was the last Friday night team meeting and Charlie was in the front row again. It had been a tense week of practice. The whole team suddenly had a sense of urgency, from the coaches to the players, even the team managers. They had gotten out of their slump and needed this last game to have a winning season and possibly save their coaches' jobs. This was not going to be an easy task. They were finishing up their season with a team from a higher ranked conference. The Aggies had already clinched a postseason berth. They were guaranteed at least a tie for first place in their conference, were ranked number 12 in the nation, and were a 28 point favorite.

Throughout the season, the coaches had treated each game and each week the same. They approached each game like the opponent was an achievable victory. This week had been different. Each day there had been extra time after practice for positive visualization meetings. It had been drilled into their heads that they were champions. Winning attitudes had been ingrained into their psyche all week long. The coaches were feeling the pressure to produce, their jobs were on the line and they were pulling out all the stops. They had even done more team building exercises to bring the team closer together, which seemed strange since the season was almost over. But, if it produced a victory, Coach Jackson would be considered a genius, and the coaches all would have jobs come Monday.

Charlie and his teammates knew something out of the ordinary would happen at the meeting tonight. Upon walking into the meeting room, Charlie saw what tonight's something special would be, Dan Germain. Everyone who played for the Puma knew who Dan Germain was. He was an All-American who had been the star of the team during the national championship back in 1988. He was a defensive lineman who tore through the offensive line in his day. He was drafted in the first round and had a successful NFL career for 10 years before repeated injuries forced him into early retirement.

His pictures were in the football office and in every trophy case. His number and name were one of the few honored by being up in the stadium. Each year the defensive MVP received the Dan Germain award. It had been years since he had played for the Puma, but there were still plenty of rumors around about how tough, mean, and nasty he had been as a player. When Charlie walked in, there was a small group of coaches gathered around him, addressing him with more respect and politeness than Charlie had ever seen most of them use.

Coach Jackson called the meeting to a start. He went over the brief, seemingly mandatory, introduction to every pregame speech. Then, with more facts than needed, he called Dan to the front. Warmly, they embraced each other. Coach Jackson seemed to prolong it longer than necessary.

Dan Germain was in his mid-thirties and had been retired for two years, yet still looked like he was in his physical peak. His sculpted body could match up to anyone's in the room. He didn't carry himself as if injuries had forced him from the game. His broad shoulders and tree trunk legs were an ideal frame many football players wished for. He could stand next to a fully padded player and still look big. His natural strength came from working on his dad's farm since he was old enough to walk. Combined with his work ethic in the weight room, he was still the strongest person to ever play for the Puma.

Despite his intimidating presence, he was one of the nicest and well-spoken people associated with the Puma. His eyes were a pale blue, as clear as a cloudless sky, and held a person's attention with a look of sincerity and passion. Sandy blonde hair clung tightly to his head, not long enough to comb. He carried himself with the confidence that he was aware and comfortable of every movement and action that he made. Before he began to speak, the entire room was completely mesmerized by this man. A half grin on his face gave him an air of approachability and gentleness that few men his size had.

"Hello gentlemen. Thank you Coach Jackson for the kind words. I think that maybe you went a little overboard." He turned to Coach Jackson and smiled. His voice was not loud, but it boomed through the meeting room. It was steady and clear, only pausing on words when he wanted to emphasize them. "I know you have plenty of meetings and the last thing you want is to sit through another boring motivational speech. So, I will try to talk to you about something that is useful. Something that will help you end the season the way you want it to end."

He walked around like he owned the whole room, like the team was his guest. He looked out at the audience, taking the time to make eye contact with each and every individual. "I have been on many good teams….only a few great teams. There are plenty of things that can add up to a winning season. But when you look at the great teams, the teams that are successful year in and year out, there is one thing that sticks out. What stands out is….the togetherness of a team….when a team comes together nothing can break it. It starts with the eleven guys on the field. But for the team to be great it needs to spread to the entire team, especially the scout team and the walk-ons. Only eleven guys play at one time, but each person plays a part and adds a piece to the completeness of the team.

"I want you to try and remember something. Try to remember it and think back on it while you are lying in bed tonight. Nothing can take the place of good people coming together in the common pursuit of excellence. I'm going to say that once more. Nothing can take the place of good people coming together in the common pursuit of excellence.

"Now….this can take the shape of many things in life. It can be in a family, it can be in a marriage, it can be in a business, it can be in a school, it can be in a community. But, in your case, it is this team and the finishing off of a winning season. If you all come together, the result will be amazing.

"It is common knowledge that football is a team sport. In my mind it is the greatest team sport in the world. However, at the same time, it is also the ultimate individual sport….I know this might not make sense, but give me a chance to explain. There are eleven players on the field, and for each and every play to succeed, each player must do his assignment. Without each man doing his individual assignment, the play is bound to fail. All of you have to count on each other to fulfill your own responsibility. A good team effort is accomplished by each individual doing his job. When a person tries to do another's job, he doesn't do his job, and the whole thing crumbles. There has to be a great deal of trust towards one another. At times this does need to be earned. The way you do this is through hard work and time spent playing together. At this stage of the season you should already be to this point, but it is never too late.

"A team full of individuals doing their best is a team that can't be stopped. When each player is doing his assignment to the best of his ability things click. It is like a locomotive rolling along. If each person does his job then nobody has to worry about anything but his own assignment. This sets each person up for success and in return the team will be successful. It is about each person giving his best effort. No extra human effort is required. If each person is focused on his job, giving his best effort, and not worrying about anything else, including stats, what his teammate is doing, how he looks, success will be a byproduct. It is no secret, it is not magic, it is plain and simple; take care of your own assignment, give your best effort, and believe in yourself and your team. This is a recipe for success.

"Football is a team sport, but don't underestimate the importance and impact of each and every individual contribution. It is a team sport, but....great teams are made up of individuals giving their best effort. Each person making a commitment to coming together in the common pursuit of excellence.

"Like I said before, there is nothing that can compare with the feelings that come with accomplishing something great with a group of people that you love and care for. Some of you only have a short history together, maybe only a season. Some of you care for each other more than others. But when this bond is created there is no stopping the group of people who came together to accomplish their goal. There are plenty of ways to do this throughout one's life. One way a person can reach for this is through the pursuit of a great relationship with another person, whether it is a marriage or a life partnership, the goal is the same. It can be a business partnership, a family coming together to get through hard times, or even a school bonding to educate its students. Right here and now for all of you it is a football team and the salvaging of a great season.

"When people come together like this, their love for each other grows and knows no boundaries. I know you have heard it said before, but it is true. On the football field a person's race, religion, or background don't matter. Everything fades away. It is a group of people striving for the same goal. Their differences don't matter anymore. The love and caring they feel towards each other can even add to their motivation at times. Everyone is going to get tired, there is no doubt about that. In these moments of fatigue that is where your bond will be tested. Will you be able to count on each other? Will you be able to lean on each other? Will you be able to support each other? In these moments of doubt, when the game is on the line, can you look into each other's eyes and find that extra motivation needed to dig deep and finish strong?

"When a team has a bond with each other, they see this and feel this. In the huddle they can look in each other's eyes and see the same look of determination coming back at them. One might be down and struggling to find that last burst of energy. When he looks at his teammates he will find it. We all play the game for ourselves, but there are times when one fights a little harder and digs a little deeper because he sees all the guys around him giving their full effort, their best performance, and he wants to make the same contribution. He doesn't want to be the weak link. He knows how hard he has worked and how hard the rest of his teammates have worked. He isn't going to let anyone down, least of all himself, because he and his teammates have put too much blood, sweat, and tears into their common goal.

"However, it can't be accomplished without each and every person giving his best, being his best, and achieving his best. It is a team sport, yet the ultimate individual sport. Each play is designed to produce success for the team. If each player does his job and only his job then the play will succeed. If even one person doesn't do his job then the play will not be successful. You don't have to rely on anyone else but yourself during the play. When you start to worry about other people's assignments, that is when you yourself will be the one making a mistake.

"You have to have faith and trust in your teammates that they will do their best. In return, your teammates will expect your best. For your team to be successful, you only have to do your job and do it to the best of your abilities. That is not asking for a superhuman effort, just everything that you are capable of doing. Imagine a team where each player gives his best effort on every play, only doing his assignment, and trusting every other player to do his own job. Combine this with love for each other and it is almost a spiritual experience. Not many people get to experience this, even for one game. I was lucky enough to be able to experience it for a whole undefeated season that led to a national championship.

"You still have an opportunity to do this for one more game. It will change your season and maybe your life, just by seeing what can be accomplished when a group of people come together being their best. You can let it slide and say it doesn't really matter. Maybe in the big scheme of things it doesn't. But football doesn't last forever. Enjoy every minute of it that you have, every play. Very few people get a chance to play football, you guys are the lucky few. Even fewer people have the chance to come together with a group of people who love each other and pursue their goal together through their own personal excellence.

"Some of you under classmen might have more chances, but things change each year. You might not be in a situation like this again. You seniors, this is your last chance. There might be a few who get to continue on, but it will never again be like it is now. What are you going to do? I challenge you to do your best on every play, take care of your assignment and only your assignment each play, and allow your teammates to put their faith in you. This group of people is capable of more than you can even imagine. Go out and give your personal best. Play for yourself and you will help your team the most… you will win!!!" The players started to cheer. He nodded and motioned to them to quiet down, that his speech wasn't done. A hush instantly fell back over the room. They were mesmerized.

Dan looked around the room, letting the silence intensify the situation. "You also need to keep something in mind. Certainly football is just a game. But, you guys are doing something amazing. Sports are transcendent. They bring people together. People of all backgrounds, persuasions, beliefs, and lifestyles come together for sports. They inspire people, they make us want to be better people. They have been a part of civilization since the dawn of humanity. And now you guys are a part of that." He paused for effect.

"Tens of thousands of people come to watch each and every one of your games. People don't do that for anything else. It doesn't matter if it is deserved or not, but people look up to you because of your physical talents. They want to be transported when they come to watch sports.

"It is almost an otherworldly experience. It is during sports where one is truly in the moment, or he will not succeed. Playing sports is really being in the now, there is nothing else. It is a chance to live life how it is meant to be lived. It is something that is hard to replicate, once you are done with sports. It is something that becomes a part of your soul. It also develops your soul. You will either be a better, stronger person after sports, or you will be a broken man. Which one will you be?

"It is such a short time in your life. You don't get to be an athlete for a very long time. You have to take advantage of every opportunity that comes your way. Don't let anything slip away. Enjoy your youth and enjoy the small chance in life that you have to play sports and to be a hero to people.

"You will never forget your time as an athlete. How will you remember it? Will you remember it as a time in life when you gave your best effort and were the best you could be? You seniors, you will remember the game tomorrow for the rest of your life. You underclassmen, you will remember it for the entire off season. How will it be remembered?

"If you play like I talked about earlier, giving your best and believing in each other while realizing this is a limited opportunity, it will be a good memory. Go out and do it. Go out and represent the Puma…. Puma Pride!!!" he shouted, signaling the end of his speech.

The players responded with a deafening, "PUMA PRIDE!!!"

Dan walked off the stage to a standing ovation. Charlie and his teammates were ready to play, even the coaches were inspired. It was too bad they had to wait until the following afternoon.

One More Chance

    Lying in the hotel bed, trying to sleep, Charlie drifted back to Dan's speech. He realized how truthful Dan's words had been. When a player has teammates and coaches who believe in each other combined with a sense of self belief, it is amazing. When each player on the field has this, even for one play, it is mesmerizing to watch, feel, and be a part of. It seems as if everything clicks and the goal is achieved without effort. Things just fall into place. It is indescribable, it takes one away from the world and all the worries that come with life. Even winning, scoring, and kicking ass don't matter. All that is important at a time like this is that one particular moment/play. A person feels as if he is lifted off the ground and on a higher plateau with his body moving through space without any effort. It is a place where eleven people click and are ONE, if only for a moment. This is the reason Charlie thought football was the greatest game, EVER. Charlie's body might pay the price later on in life for enduring the hell that goes along with football, but he couldn't ever be asked to trade any of it in, especially because he would have to give up times like this, when he felt lifted up, away from the normal world.

    The Puma had shared a season of dreams, hopes, blood, sweat, and tears. The team had come together over the course of a few months. Charlie loved them and felt the love coming back to him from his teammates. Sitting there holding hands with surrounding players during the moment of silence before going out for the game, Charlie could sense the energy. It was almost as if electricity was flowing through the room, each player passing along their positive energy to the next and sharing it with the entire team. It is a moment that can draw teams close, or push them apart, depending on the energy each player chooses to share. Tonight had a special feeling. Charlie could tell it would be a great night. His eyes started to tear up with the positive energy overflowing in him. He loved these guys and didn't want the season to ever end. He certainly didn't want college football to end. Taking a deep breath, Charlie let the energy bathe over him once more and opened his eyes to take in the locker room before the coach began speaking again.

The game was a ferocious battle. Neither side wanted to give in. The Aggies were more physically gifted and at times were overpowering the Puma. But, on this night, the Puma were playing above their abilities. They played as a team, like never before. They played with energy and with a belief in themselves. They had leveled the playing field with their attitude and passion.

It was a physical challenge that was not going to be settled until the end. Even Charlie was being challenged like he never had been before. It would come down to the Puma's will against the Aggies' strength and power.

Charlie knew his will was stronger. He was trying to pass this determination onto his teammates. So far, it had been working.

The intensity on the field seeped into the stadium. It was pandemonium. Charlie could barely hear himself think. Johnny was yelling as loud as he could in the huddle just so the play could be heard. A couple of times Charlie allowed himself to look around the stadium to absorb the exuberant atmosphere. He was utterly exhausted by the second quarter, but he wasn't going to let down. This was his last game as a college football player. He would make sure he gave his total effort this night and he would pull his teammates along with him.

At halftime the score was even. The Puma could feel their will wearing on the Aggies. Charlie felt it, too. He knew it was possible, it seemed like destiny. They had to win, he had to win. There was no other way for it all to end.

In the locker room at halftime, Charlie felt a burst of energy coming from his teammates whose attitudes were brimming with confidence. He let it be known. As they were waiting for the compulsory speech from Coach Jackson, Charlie bellowed out, "We are going to win this game!"

A few, "yeahs," came back.

He said it louder, "We are going to win this game!!"

More, "yeahs," echoed back.

He yelled it, "WE ARE GOING TO WIN THIS GAME!"

"HELL YEAH!" sounded back from everyone in the room. It began to get rowdy and loud with people shouting their encouragement and belief in the outcome.

Charlie smiled and sat back down to get some rest before the beginning of the second half.

It came down to this, fourth down and six, ball on the thirty yard line, five seconds left in the game. All day it had been a battle and this kick was going to decide the game. The Puma were down by one and right where they wanted to be, with the ball in their hands and a chance to decide the game.

Charlie wasn't nervous, all he had to do was block. As he trotted up to the line, he wasn't getting in his stance yet. He was waiting for the inevitable; the opposing team to call their last time out in an effort to prolong the tension and possibly get the kicker even more nervous. With the Puma approaching their positions and almost looking ready, the referee blew his whistle for the anticipated last time out.

Now, there was a moment to think. He was glad that he wasn't a kicker. This kind of pressure would probably get to him. He thought back to high school and the times he would get nervous just for long snapping. Nervousness would lead to too much thinking and instead of concentrating on his technique and where he wanted the ball to go, his mind would run circles. As a result, the ball would usually sail over the punter, or the holder's head, leaving his team in a bad spot. This sort of worrying is what had kept him from trying out for any of those positions in college. He didn't want to feel any more pressure to perform than he already did.

Shaking his head to clear these thoughts, Charlie was brought back to the chilly, muddy, November evening. He needed to concentrate on his blocking assignment on this play and this play only. This was the game, the season, and his college career. Standing in the huddle, anticipating the next play and its implications, each team emitted an excitement from their huddle, waiting for the whistle to resume play. Because of the autumn chill in the air, each player seemed to be breathing smoke. With eleven people crowded close together the effect was surreal. It looked like a small fire was started each time the teams entered into the huddle.

Charlie began to get a sense of urgency. Earlier in the game, a field goal had been blocked and the player had broken through the gap between him and the lineman to his left, Justin. He now turned to Justin to offer some reassurances. Justin seemed more nervous than the kicker, he knew he had blown his assignment earlier in the game.

"Hey, don't worry about it. Only think about this play and what you are going to do correctly." Charlie said, trying to ease his worries.

"All right man, I got it," Justin responded meekly.

Charlie grabbed his arm and pulled him out of the huddle a half yard, in order to talk to him away from everyone. He put both of his hands on Justin's helmet, leaned forward enough to be touching Justin's face mask, and looked straight into his eyes. "Everything is going to be fine. You know your technique and assignment. Just put all your effort into this one play. One more play and the season will be over. If you get hurt a little bit you have all off season to recover. Do whatever it takes not to let anyone through. I'll be here with you to help. I believe in you. I know you are going to do it and that we will make this field goal. Okay!!!???"

"Yeah, we are going to make this and win the game. I feel good, I'm ready."

"Good." Charlie gave him a big hug and received a big embrace back. The crowd's noise started to grow. They were hoping to add to the kicker's nervousness and help their team to victory. Back in the huddle everyone was positive and upbeat. A palpable energy was flowing through the huddle. Charlie could feel that they were going to win and displayed a big grin at his knowledge of this fact. The holder called the huddle together. "All right guys, listen up," was barely audible above the growing noise of the crowd. "You all know what to do. No one gets through." The referee's whistle pierced the crowd and Johnny's voice. Charlie's heart rate suddenly quickened.

Feeling like taking the leadership role and giving everyone one last bit of confidence, Charlie spoke up. "Okay, everyone bring it in. Enough of the normal huddle bullshit." He called them together, forming a circle with him at the center. "Everyone give all your energy one more time and we are going to win this. Do whatever it takes. It's just one more play. Win on three, 1, 2, 3!!!"

"WIN!!!" The circle broke and they sprinted to the line. Charlie didn't feel any cold, any tiredness, or any nervousness. All he knew is that nobody was getting through his hole. Getting in his stance he thought, *I'm giving it all one more time. I don't give a shit if I break my fucking neck. This is the time, here and now. Leave it all here buddy. One last play to summarize the game, the season, and your career.*

Choices

April sat under the soft glow of the floor lamp. The house was now quiet, except for the radio announcers calling the game. Tonight she felt like listening to the calmer radio broadcast, rather than watching the game on TV. It wasn't a late game, but in the fall evening it was already getting dark. She had put Conner down early and her parents were out with some of their friends. She tried to concentrate on the game, but her mind kept coming back to the state of her relationship. As soon as she pushed her worries away and visualized the game in her head with the help of the announcers, her mind began analyzing her options. It was like a game of tug of war, one that was driving her crazy and one that had been giving her anxiety over the past couple of months.

She knew that now was the moment she had to make a choice. The doubt inside her was beginning to take root. The seeds had long ago been planted and germinated. If she continued to allow it to grow, it would soon take over. She knew in her heart that this choice led to only one outcome. If she cut the doubt now, took it out by the roots, there was still hope.

She knew she was at a crossroads that would set the tone for the direction of her life. The strange thing about it was that it was just another mundane moment. It didn't come with any fanfare or attention. Here she was in the dark, alone on a typical Saturday evening, pondering her fate. She had always pictured a life changing decision accompanied with some drama or even a sudden flash of insight. But, this had crept up on her. She had known it was there for some time and slowly it made its way to the surface. The time had come to choose. She could choose to accept this life with all its contradictions or look for a new life that would have its own incongruence.

She had a conscious decision to make. She might not ever tell another person, but this would be her choice. In the future she might claim that the consequences weren't a result of her actions, but she knew deep down that this decision would set things in motion that would determine the future outcome.

She had to decide if this was the life she wanted to live. It wasn't what she had expected or what she had pictured happening. That didn't mean it was bad, though. Blake loved her, she knew that. She loved Blake. She didn't know if life was as simple as love. There had been moments, even this season, when she felt that unequivocal bond between them, that feeling that was more than just a simple emotion. However, those moments had been overshadowed by the growing branches of doubt.

She didn't like being away from Blake so often during the season. She didn't like feeling second best to a sport. He gave her so much when he wasn't consumed with football. Was that enough to sustain her? She knew it was his passion, his reason for waking up in the morning. It brought joy to his heart and stars to his eyes. She knew all that. It came down to whether or not she could adjust and feel fulfilled as a coach's wife. Most importantly, she had given her heart and soul to him and he had given his in return. They had been through so much together, they had weathered life's storms thus far. They had shared each other's pain, fear, and insecurities. Life isn't as simple as love and what they shared was something more than love. What they had wasn't something to give up easily. It wasn't something that was easily found.

She still felt like they were selling a piece of their souls. Sure his dream was coming true, but at what cost? Their relationship was going to be put on cruise control for four months every year. He didn't have time to raise Conner and he wouldn't have time to see Conner's extracurricular activities when he was older. He was giving up all of these areas of his life for his football life. Was it worth it? Not to her, but that didn't matter. It only mattered if she was willing to pick up his slack for the rest of her adult life. What kind of sacrifice was she willing to make?

She knew there was only one thing to do. She closed her eyes, felt a lone tear trickle down her cheek, and let her mind stop racing. When all was said and done, the decision had been there all along. With the gentle rhythm from the swaying of the chair she felt at peace. Her mind felt free and her world clearer. As she gently rocked back and forth, her body seemed to become part of the soft plush chair. In the next moment she dozed off.

Through the darkness, outside the circle of light created by the lamp, April heard the crackle of the radio. She wondered how long she had been asleep. It was the soundest sleep she'd had in weeks. As her mind came out of its fog, she realized she had slept through most of the game, it was almost over. Realizing this, she sat up straight and her ears perked up to hear the situation being relayed across the airwaves.

"The fourth quarter here folks. Puma down by one with five seconds left. If they make this kick they win the game and finish the year with a winning record. If they miss it they lose and send the Aggies into the postseason with momentum and confidence. It has been a hard fought game all evening long. It is getting colder by the minute in this late November weather. I can see the breath of each guy spouting out from under his helmet. This is a BIG one!" the announcer belted out with enthusiasm and without skipping a beat, sounding like this was his natural speed and tone of speaking.

"The Puma break the huddle and sprint to the line. Don't get too excited yet. The Aggies will call their final time out to try and ice the kicker one last time. The players know this and aren't in a hurry to get into their stances. They're lining up, the center is grabbing the ball, and there it is. The last time out. We all knew it was coming, but the suspense always adds some excitement."

April sat up in her chair. Despite not wanting to get excited or nervous, she could feel her pulse quicken. She knew how much this meant to Blake and all the players. They all worked so hard. It was their life, it meant everything to them.

Inside her mind a conflict of desires was raging. If they made this kick, their season would be a success, all of the work and effort judged to be worthwhile. The happiness and perhaps even well-being of Blake and many of the others on the staff and team hung in the balance. It also meant that Coach Jackson would be around for a few more years. He would keep his staff and the expectations of the team would continue to rise. She knew that with higher goals more time would be required and more stress would be added.

Trying to remain indifferent, the silence of the quiet house seemed to be magnified by the announcer's voice crackling through the speakers and the dim roar of the crowd rising in the far away stadium. April was suddenly aware of only the sound waves coming towards her.

"Well folks, it's down to this. The referee blows his whistle and it's show time." The announcer struggled to contain his excitement. He was partial to the Puma, he was the announcer for the school's radio station. His voice seemed to be growing horse trying to be heard above the intense crowd. "The players tighten their huddles one last time and receive their last instructions, or maybe some words of encouragement. The Aggies break their huddle first. They scatter out on the line of scrimmage taking up their ground. The kicker, Antonio, waits outside the Puma huddle keeping his concentration, not wanting to talk to anyone or get anymore advice.

"The Puma break their huddle and trot to the line with an air of confidence, like this is their game to lose. They weren't even supposed to challenge the Aggies, but boy folks have they shown a lot of heart and really taken it to the supposedly better team tonight. The crowd is on their feet and approaching a frenzy. It is darn cold out here tonight, but these fans don't seem to mind, at least for the moment. It is getting so loud in this stadium I can't even hear myself talking.

"The center, Thomas, waddles into position, widening his legs and getting ready to snap the ball back. The Aggies are tensing up, getting ready to try and break through the line for a possible block and come out of here with a victory. They are loading up on the left side of the line. Remember folks, this is where they snuck through earlier in the game and blocked one. They seem to think they can do it again.

"The kicker lines up, showing the holder where he wants the ball to be placed. He takes his three steps back and two steps to the side. The ball will be kicked from the 32, making it a 42 yard field goal, well inside his range. The players are all in their stances gathering up their strength for this one last play.

"The holder flashes his hand and the ball soars back to him. It's a good snap. He puts it down. A good hold and the kick is off....

"It clears the line....

"It is heading for the uprights....

"It sails through just inside the left upright with plenty of distance to spare. The Puma win! The Puma win! They pull off the big upset and deserve to win today. They are all gathering around the triumphant kicker, Antonio, jumping up and down and into each other. The Puma sideline clears and joins the melee on the field. The stadium has turned silent except for a loyal corner of Puma fans that made the journey and braved the hostile crowd and elements. They are trying to make their presence known and heard. The Aggies are already heading back to the locker rooms with their heads down. The stadium is starting to empty already.

"Wow folks! What a game. The Puma pull off the upset with lots of heart and determination. They end the season with a winning record. The first winning season in four years. They finish with a 6-5 record, a great season for the Puma. I'm sure the calls for Coach Jackson's job will be silenced for another season. Wow, what a sport!!!"

Sacrifice

The Puma locker room was a raucous scene. The players were shouting, celebrating, and hugging. Charlie had a huge grin plastered on his face. He was going around congratulating all of the players. He was fulfilling what he thought of as his last captain duty. He had been the leader all year and in the last official team setting he was going to finish it as he had always done it. He would be THE BEST one more time.

He went around the room giving most of the guys bro hugs and celebrating for a moment. Some of his closer friends he bear hugged and lingered in celebratory chatter.

When he got to Johnny, he couldn't hold it in any longer. Johnny was his best friend, they had been through a lot over the last few years. He grabbed Johnny and Johnny grabbed him back even harder. "You did it Charlie. You led this team to a victory tonight. You led the team all year, to its first winning season in four years. You did it, man."

Charlie started to tear up. Nobody on the team had ever acknowledged all his efforts. He often wondered if anybody even noticed. He knew he had been THE BEST and that he had done everything possible in his power to lead the team, but he had always hoped that someone else thought he had been THE BEST, too.

He had broken but then become himself again. This season had taken everything out of him. If others had recognized his effort then it was all worth it, especially if it was his peers. He knew that if the quarterback had noticed then the whole team had noticed. Charlie tried to keep his emotions in, tried to keep the dam from breaking. A few tears spilled out and he looked at Johnny. "We did it, man. We all did it. I'm so fucking glad we won!"

"I know we did it Charlie, but you pulled us all along. You deserve some credit, buddy. You gave this team your heart and soul," Johnny shot back at him, patting the back of his head as if to tell Charlie not to argue about it anymore.

Charlie was crying now. It meant so much to him that Johnny was the one to tell him this. Not only was Johnny his friend, he admired him as a person. He didn't want to ball right in front of Johnny's face, so he pulled him close again. "Thanks so much, man. It means a lot for you to say that." Charlie paused and started to compose himself. He sniffled back any more tears, and before they pulled away from each other he said what had been on his mind for a while. He knew this was the only moment he could tell him. "I love ya, man. You're a great friend. I couldn't have gotten through all of this without you."

Johnny playfully slapped him on the butt. "I love you, too, dude. It's been fun. You're a great friend, too. Now, let's get back to celebrating." They smiled at each other and rejoined the makeshift party.

The festive scene began to die down a little bit and Charlie made his way to the locker he had chosen for the day. He sat down and began his slow process of getting undressed. He took off his shoulder pads and was untying his cleats when he noticed someone standing in front of him. He looked up. "Hey, Coach Jackson."

"Hey Charlie." He reached out his hand and pulled Charlie up. He hugged Charlie tight and told him loud enough for others to hear, "Great job tonight, Charlie. Great job all year. You did an amazing job. You were the team leader all year and did more than I could have hoped for. I'm proud of you."

Charlie didn't think his smile could get any bigger, but his cheeks seemed to stretch in response to his coach's words. "Thanks coach. It was a great year. Thanks for the opportunities you gave me and for all your hard work."

"You don't need to thank me, you made your own opportunities. You are the type of player we all dream of coaching. Now get showered and changed so we can get home and really party." He patted him on the back and began making his way around the room.

Charlie sat down and stared blankly at his cleats. He nodded his head to himself. With what Johnny had said and now Coach Jackson, he felt validated. It was strange how he wasn't able to feel this sense of accomplishment without external recognition. He had to know that it wasn't all in vain. He now knew that he had been THE team leader. He knew that he had done it. For the first time he felt a sense of pride in all that he had done this year. He was elated. He had accomplished his goal and fulfilled his dream.

No Rest for the Weary

As the last of the players were leaving the locker room, Coach Jackson spotted Blake at the exit and walked towards him, wanting to catch him before he went out into the now chilly evening.

Coach Jackson draped his arm around Blake. This was the friendliest Coach Jackson had ever been towards him. He smiled and Blake noticed how relieved he looked. The stress and anxiety seemed to have left his eyes. He had a look of happiness, something Blake hadn't seen in his face for most of the season. "You did a great job, Blake. I know I challenged you this year and that I demanded a lot from you. But, you really responded. You are a great coach and with this win I know I'll keep my job. So, if you're up for it, I want you back as defensive coordinator." Coach Jackson turned to face him and extended his arm for a handshake, as if to make it official.

"Of course, Coach." Blake tried not to show his excitement. He had sacrificed a lot, knew he deserved to keep his job, and didn't want anything more at this point in his life. He had a wonderful family and was on track to keep climbing the coaching ladder to his ultimate dream of being a head college coach. "I appreciate your trust in me and your willingness to take a chance on me. I'm excited to continue building the Puma program. I'll be an even better coach next year."

"Good, good. I'm glad you'll be back." He nodded his head as if this was the answer that he had been expecting from Blake. "We'll all probably have to work harder. This winning season bought me another year or two of job security, but if we don't win a championship and get to the postseason soon they'll be calling for my head. We have a lot to do and we have to get going soon."

"I know. I'll be ready to give it my all again and dedicate myself to the program." Blake gave him a reassuring look.

Coach Jackson began to direct him outside the locker room as the last of the guys filed out. In the late fall air they walked the short distance to the bus and Coach Jackson reminded him that his duties weren't done for long. "Take a couple of days off. We have a meeting Tuesday morning to get our recruiting strategy in order and then we all need to be off on the recruiting trail by Thursday or Friday at the latest. The next journey begins soon."

Coach Jackson looked around to make sure there were no lingering coaches or players and followed Blake onto the bus.

Relief

Charlie didn't know what his future held for him. He only knew that he was proud of what he and his teammates had accomplished, regardless of their final record. For the first time in almost seven months he felt free. He felt like a new man, like he had achieved what he set out for and that a weight had been lifted from his shoulders. He was genuinely proud of himself, something he hadn't allowed himself to feel until tonight. He had done what he needed to do, but he felt a sense of relief that it was over. On the bus ride home, in between hugs and sips from flasks that had been snuck on the bus, unbeknownst to Charlie his world had all the unknown and limitless possibilities that life has to offer and likes to surprise people with.

Epiphany

After listening to some of the post-game show on the radio, April reached out of the light created by the lamp and clicked the radio off. She got up slowly and stood motionless for a moment in the quiet darkness. She was glad Conner was asleep and that her parents weren't home yet. She didn't want to have to talk to anyone. The darkness and solitude made it easier to hide the tears welling up in her eyes. Without consciously thinking, she walked to her room. Before going into the room and falling asleep she turned back towards the living room and saw that she had left the lamp on. This made her smile. She understood. She felt comfortable. She slept.

Author's Note: Fall 2014

April leaves work with a pile of papers from her most important account stacked neatly on the corner of her desk. She can get back to them tomorrow. She has to go see her three kids. They are all in school now. She stayed home until their youngest was in kindergarten. She has been back in her accounting field for almost five years now.

She will pick up her youngest two from elementary school and they will meet Conner at home. He walks the short distance from high school to their home. It's Friday. They will do their end of the week ritual, order in food for the night.

Tomorrow she will take them to Blake's game. His dream came true. He is now the head coach for the Puma. It is a home game this week which means it will be a family event. They all love cheering annoyingly loud for the Puma. April's parents usually come, too. Conner especially loves it. Now that he's old enough, he gets to tag along as the unofficial team brother. April still doesn't spend much time with the coaches' wives. But, she loves her career, family, and life.

Mary is trying to pick up the pieces and adjust to their new family life since Charlie had his major heart attack. After collapsing at their oldest son's baseball game last spring Charlie has not been able to do any physical activity. He had to have major heart surgery just to stay alive. His doctor expects a full recovery to take about a year. Mary really misses watching Charlie playing ball with their two sons, now seven and five. She hopes he will be back to normal soon.

The cardiologist said Charlie was lucky to come out alive. He also said that if he had come in for a check-up before the heart attack he would have had minor heart surgery to repair a small abnormality and been back to his normal self within a week or two. Charlie knew it all stemmed from the heart irregularity that had been discovered 14 years ago during his senior season of college football, but at the time, he was too scared to face the possibility that the blip might have meant a serious heart condition. He never went to his appointment with Dr. Thompson, the cardiologist, at the end of his senior season. He won't ever acknowledge this to anyone, though. He and Mary are together with their young family and he will always have his memories to fall back on when life gets tough. Memories that he will always cherish. No matter how much they cost him.

THE END

Acknowledgements

Without two people my football experience would have never happened and I would not have had the support that I unequivocally had throughout my playing days. Thank you mom, Pam Witzel, and dad, Bill Nighswonger, for everything you did for me. My football days are full of great memories with your undying support, you always cheering me on, and making me believe I was the best player out there. Dad, my playing days with you driving through the night, at times, to be there and always taking pictures were some great years that I cherish. I learned to love football from all the games that we watched and attended. Mom, I know all the games kept you on the edge of your seat, more concerned about my safety than the outcome, but I always knew you would be there because you cared. I love you, mom and dad.

Next I have to thank the people who helped make this book happen. Again my mom, Pam Witzel and one of my best friends, Jeff Hobbs. My mom served as my editor. Her guidance and perspective were invaluable in the writing process of this book. She has been instrumental in serving as a guide in my growth as a writer. Jeff Hobbs was the other person who helped me get this book done. He gave me great suggestions and helped me realize that I could write a book of my own. He made me believe that I really am an author.

My fantastic experience of playing football is one of the main reasons I wanted to write a book about football. This experience would not have been as fulfilling without the great coaches I had throughout my career. I need to thank some of them by name, Coach Canoso, my first football coach. Coach Ha'o, whose words still echo in my head, "What's on my mind?" Coach Thomas, Coach Kafusi, and Coach Bellini who made my senior year at East such a special season. Coach Salanoa and Coach Borich who I got to be with at Snow and Idaho State. Coach Lewis who came to visit my dad and I in our living room and who really made the players at Idaho State feel like we were important. Coach Uperesa who made my four years in college amazing, I hope to one day inspire my players like you did yours. Coach Keeko who turned around the program at East High and made us believe we could win, your guidance and life lessons are still invaluable. These are all great men who helped me become a better football player and a better person.

    The people I played with made my experience even more satisfying. There are so many great men that I played with I can't possibly thank them all. There are some I have to acknowledge because without them I would not have made the personal connections that I did with the sport and my enjoyment would not have been as memorable, thank you, Francis Hurd, my first football friend. Steve Agbor, my first football friend at East and still one of my best friends, even at 36. Max Burton who made me realize how much football brings people together. Jeff Nighswonger, my brother and one of my best friends, who unknowingly pushed me to be better and who I feel so lucky to have played next to at East and Snow, those were awesome years. I love you, buddy. Tyler Hughes, who taught me about the love of the strategy of the game and who made me realize I would one day be a coach. Mike Watts, who showed me how important heart is when you play football. Luke Rasmussen, who helped me fit in at Snow. Dave Matagi, who showed me what training is all about. Donovan Arp, my buddy at Snow who helped me get in and stay in great shape. Kevin McCarthy, who was a true friend from the beginning of my time at Idaho State. Jason Meador, who was a great workout partner and who stretched me even when I was sweaty. Dustin Fitzpatrick, who was my left side offensive line buddy. Brandon Tuia, who pushed me every day in practice. Robert Poleki, who brought some needed fun and character to the offensive line. Donnell McNeal, who taught me a lot about what a football player and leader really is. Nick Whitworth, who made me want to block harder. And Gene Zuniga, who was a great friend throughout my time at Idaho State.

    I need to thank my two L's. Laurie and Lance. My wife and my son, I love you two so much. You two are my laughter and love. You are great, you both bring so much to my life. I wouldn't be the person I am today without either of you. Laurie, you are a great mother and wife. I'm glad we decided to get married back on a chilly January evening in Japan, even though you had bad nails. Lance, you're a stud. I hope I'll be everything you deserve in a dad. Thanks Laurie for your suggestions and tips for the book. You added a great perspective. Thanks for believing in me, too. If everyone thought my book is as awesome as you do it will be a bestseller. I love my family.

    I have to acknowledge my last family member, my sister. I don't want to leave you out. I love you Lindsey Sherman, thanks for always thinking I'm funny and cool.

    Lastly, I want to thank you, the reader, for taking the time to read this book. It has taken me thirteen years to write this book. It has been a labor of love, helping me to reminisce about my days as a football player and it has been cathartic for me. If you liked the book please share it with a friend.

Matthew William Nighswonger

About the Author

Matthew is a teacher and coach in Las Vegas, Nevada. He has been writing since his college days. *Down, Set, Hut* is his first published book. Matthew is originally from Salt Lake City, Utah. He has a Master's Degree and teaches college level, AP classes in Las Vegas. He played college football at Snow College in Ephraim, Utah and at Idaho State University in Pocatello, Idaho. He was team captain and team MVP for both schools. After graduating from Idaho State he taught in Japan for three years and for nine months in Canada. He has coached various sports for twelve years now. He is married to his wonderful wife, Laurie and he has an awesome son named, Lance.

Printed by Libri Plureos GmbH in Hamburg, Germany